She watched the light slide over the uneven curves of the crystal, watched it go round and round a while, then spill over, dropping down around her. A waterfall of light, a pool of light—she floated in light. She could feel it rippling and lifting her.

Mole's hands held her. He wouldn't let her drown. He spoke. She was inside the words. At first she couldn't understand them; then she did.

"You are inside the flow, Cymel. Experience it. Learn it. Use your senses, not your mind. Shape is in the hands, not the head."

She scooped up a handful of light, poured it from hand to hand. For the first time, she caught a glimmer of what Mole was trying to teach her. She dipped her hand into the swirling light and shaped what she took into a crude representation of a bird, only as long as her pointing finger. She perched it on a finger and watched, amazed, as the creature took on detail, eyes and feathers and delicate pink legs. A moment later, it flapped its wings and flew away.

Tor Books by Jo Clayton

THE DRUMS OF CHAOS
Drum Warning
Drum Calls

DRUM CALLS

JO CLAYTON

TOR®
fantasy

A TOM DOHERTY ASSOCIATES BOOK
New York

DRUM CALLS

A Tor Book
Published by Tom Doherty Associates, Inc.
175 Fifth Avenue
New York, NY 10010

Tor Books on the World Wide Web:
http://www.tor.com

Tor® is a registered trademark of Tom Doherty Associates, Inc.

ISBN: 0-812-55123-0
Library of Congress Card Catalog Number: 97-14502

First edition: October 1997
First mass market edition: July 1998

Printed in the United States of America

0 9 8 7 6 5 4 3 2 1

Acknowledgments

I have many to thank here. Being very close to death can do extraordinary things to your circle of friends.

To Mary Rosenblum who walked in and saved my life.

To Mark and Elizabeth Bourne who acted as my medical advocates and much more, going far beyond what was necessary.

To Javanne who helped me talk back to you folk on GEnie when I couldn't use the laptop or do any of that myself—another friend who gave generously of her time and energy.

To Deborah Wheeler, Marty Grabien, and dozens of GEnie folk who got worried about me and did something about it.

To James Fiscus who battled his own demons and found ways to help me with mine, who carried me to help one day.

To Rory who also helped that carry and did much more than was necessary.

To all the GEnie folk who whirled their furry prayer wheels and sent their good vibes and made me feel wanted and filled with joy that so many should respond to my need with stories that made me laugh so hard that was healing in itself. And to the GEnie folk who sent me furry friends to take the places of those I couldn't have. And those who sent flowers and M&M's and cards and other small delights. And a dream-catcher to round up my hallucinations.

To my visitors, the people who were close enough to come by when they could.

To the splendid, caring nurses of the Cancer Unit at Good Samaritan (who had to put up with those hallucinations and my loud panics).

To my doctors who explained everything they did so I knew what was happening and where the treatment was going.

To the music therapist and the physical therapists and the relaxation therapist who kept me sane and got my mind restarted.

To Debbie Notkin and the folks at Tor Books who have responded generously and have been endlessly patient about a long overdue book.

To the folks in my own family who were there with support and prayers.

In other words, my deepest THANKS to all of you in my several Families of Choice. You are wonderful and it is only because of you that this book is finally finished.

North

NYDDYS

Vale of Carlion
Carlion
Prenpool

Ellar's Farm
Cybareth
Carralon
Lyst

The Halcionet Sea

Sylvestia
FAISCAR

TILKOS

KALE

Mage's Tower

Lim Ashir
the Eingirsade
Aile
Kuvret

Yosun

The Continent of
NORDOMON

C Mitchell '96

GLANDAIR

Jinger
Lakes
Kingakun University
Lake
Mizukor
Banyakor
Idainamin
NIKAWAID
Higamin
Nishamin
CHUSINKAYAN
SEMMERTA
ISLANDS

Mionach

DOMAIN
EOLAIS

the
Comcon

Faranlar River

DOMAIN
PLANDA

DOMAIN
MIONMIOL

Fasalla

Teyas Brota

The Continent of
SAFFROA

C.Mitchell '96

Breith's Troubles

By the calendar of the Domains of Iomard, events dating from the 3rd day of Ardidan, the first month in the Iomardi year 6535, the 722nd year since the last Corruption.

[1]

The wyllan tree that grew beside the wall between the family wyeing and that of the housekin was older than Breith by half a century and almost as tall as the flag tower. Its massive gray branches with their tufts of twigs were softened by a mist of pale green as the new crop of leaves unfolded from the bright red buds and the old leaves left from last year were gradually stiffening from the limp rags of the winter drain.

Breith was perched in the wyllan, straddling a limb up near the middle where a winter windstorm had cracked off one of the limbs and left a gap, a place where he could see into the housekin wyeing without being seen. He was watching girls take linens off the drying lines, laughing and teasing each other, but working fast because the sky was turning black and rain threatened to come down any moment. Their skirts were kilted up so they could run about more easily; their sleeves were rolled up and the wind plastered their blouses tight against their breasts.

The day was one of those in between winter and spring, a strong wind blowing chill and damp, but the bone cold of winter was gone, along with the really murky days when clouds hung so thick and low over Valla Murloch that the sole change between dark and daylight lay in the different ranges of gray. Breith wasn't feeling the cold at all; he was all over hot, his eyes blurring from the sweat that dripped into them. He was watching all the girls, he wanted to grab them, rub himself against them all, he wanted . . . he didn't know what except he was sure it would get him in big trouble.

Then there was Caithin. Whenever she moved from between the flying sheets so he could see her, he stopped breathing and his head felt like it was going to burst. He shifted position on the limb, trying to find a more comfortable way to ride it, then slapped his hand over his mouth to muffle the giggles that exploded through him as the wind caught hold of little plump Sassa's skirt, tore it loose from the kilting and sent it fluttering up over her head. She wasn't wearing her privacy cloth, but she wriggled about so much he almost couldn't see anything but flashes of leg.

Caithin and Flon ran laughing to help her pull the skirt back down and get it tucked up properly.

Breith watched, shivering, but not from cold. Tentatively he dipped into the Pneuma Flow, used it to twitch the wind round Caithin's legs and along her body, pulling her clothing loose, feeling her against the palms of his hands through the touch of the wind.

Caithin whirled and came charging toward the wall and the tree. "You come out of that, Breith! You hear me. I'm going to tell your Mam what you did."

His excitement blown out of him by the wind of her anger, Breith wriggled rapidly back to the trunk. Scane! I forgot she had that much Sight. I'm in trouble now. He edged round to the far side of the tree, caught hold of one of the branches and swung down. He dropped, slowing his fall by catching hold of the branches on the way down, fell the last ten feet and collapsed into a tottery squat. As soon as he caught his balance, he took off running.

Behind him Caithin was still screeching, "You heard me, you little fiend. I meant it."

When he reached his rooms he slapped at the latch, kicked the door open and stumped inside. Mum was going to look so disappointed and long-suffering about that, he'd want to go out and hang himself. Grumbling under his breath, he changed his clothes, caught up a blanket from the bed, then went to find a corner where he could have some privacy and no stupid housegirls to make him feel like fresh steamy dog turds.

The rain hissed down in slanting gray sheets, turning the flower beds to watery muck even under the protecting layers of the winter mulch that the gardeners hadn't yet raked away. As Breith trotted along the gravel path that led to the gate tower, mud and water bounced up under the Pneuma pocket he'd pulled around himself. The wind crept in too, swirling round the cone of protection, chilling him. He pulled the blanket tighter around him and cursed the cold, but he couldn't move faster or he'd lose control of the shield and even with the blanket over him about two breaths later he'd be soaked to the skin.

If he hadn't made such a fool of himself with Caithin, he could be warm and dry in his room, putting the last touches on the model of the riverboat before he got ready to paint it. But he couldn't stand it there now. While he was changing his clothes, he kept hearing housegirls moving past outside, giggling and whispering; he could feel their expectation and their smug self-satisfaction. They knew Mam would hang him out to dry. The *least* she'd do would be to make him apologize to Caithin.

He shied away from the thought as the Pneuma started to shred out of control.

Though it was still only mid-afternoon there were yellow lines of lamplight coming through the cracks in the shutters of the gatehouse. Neech and Young Neech were in there, cozy and warm, no axe in their future. No day coming for them when someone takes them to the gate, points to the street outside and says that's your home now; nothing inside these walls belongs to you, not anymore. Young Neech would be gate-guard when Old Neech was too decrepit to do the job. And Young Neech's boy would take *his* place when the time came. Ordinary folk knew how to treat their kin. At least they had that.

Breith moved into the doorway and let the Pneuma shield collapse so he could push the door open and get inside the tower. Ten more years and that's it for me, he thought. Mam and Mum never really thought I could be Seyled. He looked at the bar, shook his head. Better not. It wouldn't stop Mam and she'd just get madder.

He started up the stairs, the darkness inside the tower so thick he could barely see the slightly paler window slits and certainly not the steps. But he didn't really need to see them; he'd been up this squared spiral so often he could have climbed it in his sleep. He walked carefully, though, because the stone was slippery with damp and a winter's crop of moss.

His hands were shaking with cold by the time he reached the room just below the roof and his jaws ached from the pressure he put on them to keep his teeth from chattering. He pulled his boots off, shook the blanket out, wrapped it more closely about his shoulders and padded to one of the windows that looked out over the street that ran past House Urfa's main gate.

"Scande!" He was looking into strangeness. The veils of rain were gone and a sunlit valley floated before him, jagged snowcrowned peaks on the far side and two armies drawn up facing each other on the valley floor, bright flags whipping in a wind that touched nothing else, sunlight glinting off spear tips and armor, horses sidling nervously, their padded covers rippling about their knees, a black figure radiating power poised above one of the armies, other black figures dancing an absurd jig around him, opposing him in the second army. All of this was translucent as a mirage, yet he knew it was real somewhere.

"That's what Corysiam and Da were talking about. If I ran

fast enough, maybe I could cross over even if I can't Walk."
For a moment he was tempted to try it, then he sighed and
shook his head. Mam and Mum and Da would just send the
Scribe to fetch him back and he'd be in worse trouble.

A breath later and the image was gone. In its place he saw
a dark blob on the loading platform across the street. One of
Mirrialta's spies, huddling in the meager shelter of the hoist
shed while he kept an eye on the gate.

Breith *looked* at him.

The spy was an overage arrth who'd lost too many challenge battles in the Domains, found no place that would have
him as a rido and ended up on the waterfront of Valla Murloch. The refuse basket of Saffroa where you surely will end
up if you slack off like you're doing, young Breith—what
Brother Bullan used to say when he thought Breith was being
lazy. Mirrialta and her lot dipped into that refuse basket and
found an endless supply of desperate men who'd do anything
to earn lodging and meals.

Breith shuddered and moved away from the window. He
loathed them, all of them, those men—not so much because
they kept him shut up here inside Urfa House, but because
they reminded him too painfully of what might happen to him
when he got beyond House age. Yet somehow it did make
him feel a little better to see how miserable they had to be, to
think how much they had to be cursing him for making them
stay out there in the rain and cold.

He sat down with his back against the wall, tucked the ends
of the blanket under his feet and used a pinch of Pneuma to
heat up the air around him and the planks below him until he
was warm and comfortable. Then he got himself together and
thought about Glandair. He needed to talk to Cymel.

She argued with him and made him furious sometimes. She
was stubborn and prickly and didn't understand anything. But
she treated him like an equal. Like somebody with a right to
be listened to.

Not like the housegirls. And they were just ordinary housekin. They worked for him, but they treated him like some

no-account beggar just because he was male. He sighed. That wasn't really true, they didn't work for him, but for Mam and his baby sister Bauli. But Cymel wasn't like that. She didn't care. They were friends, him and her.

When his shivering had stopped and he was almost sleepy, he pulled a shield between him and the rest of the House so Mum, Mam and Da wouldn't feel him playing with the Pneuma Flow, doing something big like the Window, not just twiddling at it. He wasn't supposed to do that when he was by himself, but he was in so much hot water already, he figured it didn't really matter if he heated it up some more.

When he opened the Window, he felt an odd shift as if he were standing on ice and his feet sliding from under him. This had never happened before and disturbed him; he was even more disturbed when he didn't see Cymel, just a shadowy room with moonlight coming through an ordinary house window, printing images of lace curtains on the floor. What was going on? Was Mirrialta or someone like her trying something weird again? Should he back off and try some other time?

Then he heard voices coming through the opening, one of them Cymel's, the other deeper with an ambiguous quality about it he found disturbing. He tried to shift the viewpoint over there so he could see who she was talking to, but he couldn't.

He scowled. A mallach on Cymel. She'd jumped ahead of him again.

Footsteps moved away and the tree outside the window creaked. A moment later Cymel crawled in through the window. She straightened, glanced toward him. " 'Lo, Breith,'' she said. "Give me a minute till I light a lamp.''

He stared as she turned up the woven wick and flicked it with her fingers, then adjusted it so it burned without smoke and fitted the glass chimney over the flame. The casual ease with which she called fire startled him. She was just showing off, but still . . . And what she had on! And her hair! And her face!

Cymel wore a long wide skirt of some sort of soft black

material that clung to her legs when she walked; a strip of black fringe as long as his hand was sewn in a spiral around that skirt to meet and merge with the fringe round the bottom of a vest she laced tight under her small breasts, pushing them up and out against the shining white of the blouse she wore under the vest. Her long black hair had been plaited into a dozen braids along with some sort of stiffening that looked like silver wire; these braids were shaped into loops and spirals precariously pinned on the top of her head. She had a black spiral painted on her left cheek and a bright silver dot on her right and her lips were the color of fresh blood.

The fringes fluttering like frainse leaves in a spring blow, Cymel took herself to the bed. She plopped down on the lumpy quilt that covered it, pulled her legs up and sat cross-legged with the skirt bunched in lumps about her. "So. How come you're visiting after staying away so long?"

"They let you go out looking like that?"

"What'd you know about looks? Hunh. And if you're just going to criticize you might as well go away."

"Does that oig you were talking to know you're only a kid?"

"That oig knows what there's need to know. Saaa, you're in a mood. You got yourself in more trouble?"

He just grunted. The thought of explaining what he'd done made him cringe; there was no way he was even going to bring it up. "I'm just sick of being stuck inside the walls."

"Still?" She sounded bored as she reached up and began taking down the braided loops, slipping the twisted silver wires free of the black strands, dropping the wires on the bed beside her.

"Well, you wouldn't know, would you. You look like you're having a great time."

She shrugged, the fringe dancing with the movement. "There are different kinds of walls. I manage to jump over mine when the smother gets too thick in here."

"You sneaked out?"

Cymel grinned suddenly, the silver circle on her cheek

dancing in the lamplight. "Housemum would have twenty fits if she knew I went out the window and where I was and who I was with."

"You go down that tree a lot, then."

The smile went away. "No." She looked down at the wire in her hands, then set it with the others. It was the last. She ran her fingers through the braids, then shook her head so the long crimped strands fluffed out about her face. "I have to choose my times," she said. "When there's something going on in one of the cellars or I just can't stand it anymore. Being the wonderfully terribly gifted Poet's daughter, I mean. The Watcher's daughter with the wild talent. Not quite the thing, though, a little mongrel. Mixed blood, you know. I get that mostly from those who aren't Scholars. Wives and Broon's daughters here for the extra polish high-schooling gives them. They're so very nice about it most of the time that I start feeling like a trained bear dancing jigs. He doesn't do it well, the wonder is he does it at all. So I go do something stupid which they'll forgive if they catch me at it because after all you can't expect real strength of character from a mongrel. And if you say a single word about this to Aunt Cory, I'll make you sorry."

"Oh," he said and couldn't think of anything else to say.

She got off the bed. "I have to get out of these clothes, get them tucked away so Amys Tyrfaswyf doesn't find them. She snoops all the time. I hate that, but I can't do anything about it. So . . ."

The Window went suddenly dark as if she'd drawn a shade across it. He could still hear her moving about, but he couldn't see a thing. I have to get Da to teach me more and Mum and Mam too. The thought of his mothers put knots in his stomach, so he concentrated on trying to unravel the spell she'd put on the Window.

Before he managed to trace more than a couple of the threads, the Window cleared. Cymel sat cross-legged on the bed again, peeling at the spiral on her cheek. The silver dot was already gone and the red paint was washed off her mouth.

With her hair tumbling in a black waterfall over her shoulders and the roomy white sleeping shirt tucked round her, she looked a good deal more like her right age and the friend he remembered.

He sighed and relaxed. "So what was it this time, something special?"

Cymel inspected the coiling strip of black film that clung to her fingers, then wiped it off onto the quilt. "Sorta." She wrinkled her face in thought, reached out to the bed table and groped around till she found a small ceramic pot with a lid. "I went to see a drama."

"What's a drama? I don't know that word."

"Hm. You've got poems over there, the kind that tell stories?"

"There's a lot of religious stuff we have to learn. Sayings of the Prophet and stories from her life. Then there's sailors' songs, but they're not very nice. Most things written down are dull stuff like trade records and House histories."

"Tell me a Prophet story and I'll show you what a drama is."

"Why should I bother with that boring stuff?"

"It's complicated, Bré. So if you really want to hear this, I should start with something you know."

"Oh." He thought about that for a moment, then knew it was something to talk about that wouldn't get under the skin of either of them and he could look at her and feel her there, and not be alone, with nobody on his own level he could talk to. And after a moment, the story came to him, the one that presented his own problem without him having to whine about it. "I think I know one I could tell to you. I have to translate, so you won't know the whole of it or hear the song in the words, but you'll get the nut of the story."

This is the story called the Prophet and the Braysha Boy.

In the long ago before the Domains were Set, in the days before Great Chadliam wrote the Rule of the Scribes, the Prophet came to a wide field of pole beans where a Braysha

Boy was tormenting field mice when he should have been pulling weeds. And this was the way he did the torment: He snatched a mouse from a nest inside a pole cone and flung it onto the dirt between the rows. When it tried to run, he reached with Power and snatched it up by the ears or by the tail and flung it down again. Finally he let it run, but before it, he set a wall of Power so that it smashed its head against that wall and died.

The Prophet came quietly as was Her wont and stood watching him for long and long before She spoke and made Her presence known to him. She was in the guise of a wandering seeker, Her hair was gray, Her robes were gray and She wore the seeker shell on a thong about Her neck. This was the time when She was yet new to her calling and unknown to most.

"O Braysha Boy, why do you torment these small creatures?" the Prophet said.

The Braysha Boy turned to her and answered with a voice hard as the walls he made. "Because I wish to, O Seeker. Because I can. What I wish to do and what I can do, I will do."

"You do yourself harm by doing so, O Braysha Boy. You make yourself less than the worm that eats the dead."

"Who are you to speak to me of less, O Seeker without lyn or kin to stand behind you? You are less than the mice and I will do with you what I have done with them." And he seized Her then, raised Her into the air and cast Her down to earth. When She tried to stand, bleeding as She was from mouth and hand, he lifted Her again, high this time, and flung Her down once more. But when he went to trample on Her broken body, She was not there.

A hand touched his shoulder and he turned to see Her standing behind him.

"O Braysha Boy, there is no kindness or couth in you."

He curled his lip and sought the Power that he might smash her, but there was nothing that he could touch, nor could he move arms or legs, nor could he speak.

"You are not the first such to come before Me. But you

shall be the last. Where there is no couth or kindness, neither shall there be Power. I mark you, Braysha Boy, as I will mark all others.'' She touched one eye. "Green eye, brown eye, the mark of Sight in men. I grant you your childhood untroubled, but when your manhood comes on you, your eyes will tell all who look, what you are.''

She touched the tip of Her finger to his right temple and then his left. "No more Sight for you, Braysha Boy. No more Power. Learn humility before God and Man. As I have said, thus shall it be.''

Breith wiped his hand across his face. He was sweating and hot. The simple words were the heart of the ache in him and the anger even when they lost half their force by being translated into Nyd-Ifor. He cleared his throat, ran his tongue across dry lips. "That the sort of thing you want, Mela?''

"Yeah, that's good enough to make a drama with.'' She scratched at her nose and drew her brows together. "My head's tired, Bré. So if you get bored, blame that. Anyway, here's how it goes. Some folks come to Cyfareth University to study the Pneuma, others medicine and history and how numbers work, and some come to study to be Servants of Dyf Tanew; they call it Dyftology. And there are Craft schools for painting and carving and music and things like that. And Broon daughters come for polishing like I said. How to laugh with elegance, blink their eyes in a fetching way and say witty things. Not too witty, of course. Saaa. A couple of them aren't too bad but the rest, ack. Anyway, a long time ago, the Dyftology school started writing little stories so they could go out and teach it to folk who couldn't care less about reading scholar's tomes. Like your Braysha Boy story. But they didn't just make poems and chant them, they had reciters who dressed up in costumes and said the lines to each other as if they were the people who said the words the very first time. Morality Dramas they call these presentations.

"If they were going to do your story, it'd go like this—a woman would present the Prophet. She'd dress like folks think the Prophet dressed. A man would present the Braysha Boy and he would dress like such a boy. And there would be a picture of the bean field painted on a curtain. And there would be little mice moved about on fine black threads with someone out of sight making their squeaks and squeals. And the woman would be wearing a harness with a black rope clipped to it so the Boy could throw her about as if he were using Pneuma to do it. And those watching would feel as if they were back in the time before time, listening and watching the Prophet as she gave her message.''

''Scane! If someone did that on Iomard, they'd be boiled and skinned so fast they wouldn't know they were dead. It would be blasphemy of the worst kind.''

''But you do see what a drama is?''

''So you went to see a Dyftology tale?''

''Uh-uh. Lots more fun than that. More lecture. Some students in the Music School got together with painters and poets and they started making up dramas from the old poems and history pieces. There was a big hoohaw of some kind and the dramas stopped for a while, but then they came back as sorta half-secret things that students get up to round the edges of their studies. Usually in cellars. Lots of cellars in the buildings round here, big places. No one knows why they built 'em, but there it is, all that space.

''What happens is, word gets around that there's gonna be a drama and a do in this cellar or that, then people show up, vendors come in from town to sell stuff to drink, hot pies or whatever seems handy. Music students play some stuff, some of the poets do their poems, then comes the drama and then there's dancing for a while, then folks go home and whoever's putting on the drama sees that the cellar's cleaned up. And that's where I was.''

''Who was that you were talking to?''

''My business, not yours. Aunt Cory still visiting you all the time?''

''I wouldn't tell.''

''With Aunt Cory and your Mum and your Mam and your

Pa leaning on you? Maybe not, but anyway it's still none of your business.''

"Was it that Lyanz? He come back to hang round you?"

"Laz? You're weird, Bré.''

"I'm weird? Did you look in a mirror before you went out?''

"Much you know. Mole—um—everyone told me I looked really casta and it doesn't get better than that.''

"Mole? Sounds like a winner for sure.''

"Least Mole doesn't sit round whining like someone who's scared spitless at the thought of sticking his nose outta his house.''

That was so unfair fury shook him; he went blind with it and it seemed that everything that had happened today just fueled the rage. With his concentration gone the Window wavered and threatened to go out of control. He tried to check the lava flow of that rage, but it had seized him and it burned away his feeble attempts at thinking. Fire danced along his arms and legs, his hair stood out from his head, he was hot so hot. . . .

Then he was bent over, gasping for breath as something like a huge snuffer came down over him. He coughed, struggled feebly for a few more breaths, then . . . nothing. . . .

A breath of Pneuma passed over him, burning him awake; he was laid out flat on the planks of the tower room, his skin hot and tender as if he'd been singed over every inch of his body and his clothes were mostly ash. His lungs burned, even his hair hurt, and when he tried to lift an arm, he almost couldn't he was so weak. He heard a step, turned his head.

His father had been over by the window, looking out at the rain and the watcher at the gate; now he came to look down at Breith. "Do you understand what almost happened?''

Breith touched his tongue to his lips, winced at the pain that simple gesture brought. His mouth was so dry he couldn't speak, so he moved his head from side to side.

"I didn't think so. Listen to me, Breith. This time, you

really listen. You don't go off in fog like you did the last time. You hear what I'm saying?''

Breith nodded.

''If that much Pneuma had formed the vortex it was building toward, you might have destroyed this House and killed everyone in it, perhaps including yourself, perhaps not.''

Breith shut his eyes so he couldn't see his father's lined face. But he couldn't shut out the words. The slow soft words that came from a soul grown weary of complicated answers that were never the end of anything.

''I shouldn't have Seyled. It was a mistake. You shouldn't have been born. Yasayl and I . . . it was a bad mix . . . two sports that should have been sterile but weren't.''

Malart reached out and took his hand, held it very gently. Breith didn't pull away though the touch hurt him.

''You're a good lad, Breith, and we love you. You're our son. But you're almost too strong for me now. Fori has to be out minding the business and tending the links with the other Houses. And your Mum's gifts are too strange to let her help you manage. I do know what you're going through. When it happened to me, though, I was living rough out in the wild so it was easier to deal with.'' He chuckled, bent over and tapped Breith's shoulder. ''No housegirls.'' He sobered. ''Everybody I saw was looking to kill me, so I didn't have big choices to make either. It was still hard because there was no one to teach me and I never knew whether the next thing I did would fry me inside my skin.''

He set the hand he was holding on Breith's chest and got to his feet. ''Still raining.'' He looked over his shoulder. ''You're going to be weak as overcooked noodles for a while yet, Bré. That's another reason not to let a vortex start forming. It drains the strength right out of you, and if there's an enemy about, you've just handed yourself over like a tribuf calf to the butcher's knife. Think about it. If you were alone here and that spy outside, and he decided to come in here and toss you over his shoulder and walk out with you, what could you do, wasted like that?''

But I didn't know, Breith thought. How could I know? You never told me any of this.

He was feeling very peculiar; a good sort of warm round his belly and a scratchy, angry hot up round his ribs. His father was right about the weakness, though. He shivered as he thought about the rest of it, how he could have killed everyone just because things inside him got too hot and roily.

"Cold? I imagine you would be. This wet chill can crawl into your bones. Your Mum is sending one of the gardeners over with clothes for you."

Breith closed his eyes, unable to look at his father just then. There was too much anger and envy in him. He was shut outside the warm circle where his father lived. He'd never have a chance to make that bond, which made Mum, Mam and Da so much like pieces of each other that sometimes it was scary to see. He wasn't going to Seyl. Who would have him, a freak like him? Where was there anyone else like Mam with the strength and courage to do what she wanted and let the world go hang?

The only one who came close was Cymel and she was on Glandair and wasn't about to leave. All he'd ever be able to do was talk with her through the Window. If I could just Walk, he thought, I'd go there. He shivered again; the idea of leaving everything he knew for a strange world was at the same time terrifying and very seductive. But Cymel and he always argued; it was like they were flint and steel, striking sparks as soon as they came together. And there was that Mole. She liked Mole, Breith could tell that from the way her face changed when she talked about him. She said it wasn't his business. But it was. It was. It was.

"Seyl Malart." The voice came up to the tower room, thin and reedy. Garra's boy Fayl. "We have the clothes and things. Cay Yasayl says bring the boy to her rooms."

Malart lifted the trap and went down the stairs.

Breith lay on the hard planks, trying to find ease from all the things troubling him, knowing there was no ease anywhere for him. Not anymore. He bit his lip and tried not to think of

what Mum Yasa was going to say to him, tried not to antici-
pate the sorrow and shame in her blind face, in her soft voice.
I want to be somewhere else, he thought. But there was nowhere else. Nowhere.

2

The Wedding

By the calendar of the Domains of Iomard, the 29th day of Antram, the third month in the Iomardi year 6535, the 722nd year since the last Corruption.

{ 1 }

In a ring that encompassed the full round of the sky, wingtip to wingtip, hands palmed before their pure white breasts, the Prophet's Messengers sang their enigmatic wordless song, great resonant chords that shook the body and seized the heart.

And then they were gone.

Radayam lay facedown on the roof of the Flagtower, her arms stretched out straight from her shoulders, her eyes closed. The smell of the warm stone in her nostrils, the gentle brush of the prairie wind along her back, she quivered in an ecstasy of religious fervor that intensified as she felt the sudden jolt and roll of the tower as a tremor shook the ground beneath it. Earthquakes were becoming more common everywhere on Saffroa—the footsteps of the Prophet pacing toward the Corruption and the Cleansing.

When the roof was still again, she got to her feet, a long thin woman with long thin hands, a handsome, austere face. She walked to the ring of merlons, stood leaning on one of the stone teeth, looking out across the Domain. Rolling prairie lands stretched to the horizon on three sides of her, some of it plowed and sowed to grain, some growing the long narrow lines of siotha threadplants, yet other fields plowed and waiting for seed, the heavy black soil glistening in the slanted sunlight as the sun descended toward the western hills. Near the river there was a patchwork quilt of greens and browns, the farms of the darocs. The rest was left to pasture, with herds of black tribuf grazing across the grass with the slow inevitability of a pool of thick oil flowing down a shallow slope.

The Lynhouse itself and the area around it swarmed with darocs and Lynborn, bantars and Seers, preparing the place for the Wedding Feasts. The Guesthouses had all windows and doors opened to air them out. The slaughtering ground was already busy, with tribuf carcasses hanging on hoists, the offal cleaned from them wet and greasy in half-barrels, waiting to be carried off, the usable parts separated out, the rest put in the drying sheds to be ground up for fertilizer. The vao seyl arena and the stands were quiet; the ridos and bantars had not yet begun the ritual clean.

Radayam looked down at her hands, rubbed her thumb across the bump on the middle finger of the right hand, a mark set there by all those years of holding a pen. Ten years ago she was Seer/Historian, a place that was suited to her temperament and her interests. Then Traiolyn Drannach ait é Eadro-Carlach died from a stroke before she had named her Heir. All the children of her body and those of her long-dead Wife were also dead so a Seer's Convocation was called and the Seer's Lot fell to Radayam. She would have refused the call if that possibility had been open to her. Instead, she took on her shoulders a role she did not want and did not like and kept her unhappiness to herself. The coming of the Messengers gave her a reason for what had been done to her. And she embraced that reason with all the passion in her.

The Time of Corruption could also be a time of cleansing and renewal, a return of the Pure to the pure worship of the All-Mother and a humbler bowing to the commands of her Prophet. Cleanse the Land. Cleanse the soul. That was her task and this wedding was the first step toward realizing it.

She tilted her head back, staring into the heart of the sky, drowning in blueness.

For a moment she stood there, blinking rapidly, then she turned and walked briskly to the trap door laid back onto the stones of the roof. She pulled it shut after her and descended to her cabinet and the multitude of business details that waited for her.

[2]

Her contempt thinly veiled, Mirrialta stood with the worktable between her and the woman she had once schemed to marry, waiting for Obayr to speak. It had been years since she'd been here in this room, but nothing much had changed. Traiolyn Obayr was a stupid, gutless woman still in her mother's shadow though the old Traiolyn was five years dead.

"So you've got what you wanted." The new Traiolyn's hooded eyes were on the long thin hands like birdclaws spread on the worktable before her. "It won't be easy, but you'll have a well-furnished chest to take with you to Eadro. Tiolan won't be shamed before the Domains. However, all unnecessary drains on our coffers must be eliminated. Your . . . affair, business, whatever you want to call it . . . in Valla Murloch must go on hold until you can find other sources of funding. I hope you understand that this is done from necessity, not malice."

The Traiolyn raised her head. A muscle at the end of her right eye twitched repeatedly. She waited.

Mirrialta smiled. "Not malice? But aren't you enjoying this, Obayr? I won't forget." She rose from the chair, laughing as she watched the Traiolyn's carefully expressionless face.

After a moment, Obayr nodded. "I know. You never do."

[3]

"Ké ké ké!" Herdgirl Mianu cracked her whip against the rump of the yearling steer and sent it trotting back into the pod of young tribufs she and her triad were driving toward the nearest of the five corrals set up to supply the Wedding Feasts. "Ké ké ké," her tria Dreolu chanted on the far side of the little herd. Mianu laughed and shook her whip, then clicked her tongue as she saw a familiar shape edging toward another break for the hills. She started after him, heard giggling.

A small dark form dived under Tukka's belly, slapped her on the foreleg, and he nearly lost a mouthful of buttock as the cayoch's meat teeth snapped together just short of his ragged drawers. Tukka's temper was uncertain at the best of times and the Song of the Messengers had left her still twitching after the vision was long gone.

The third of the triad riding point cried out, "Get away, you young idiots." Staleu raced back, the tip of her drover's whip cracking against whatever flesh she could reach, driving the young darocs out of danger. Cursing them at the top of her voice, she swung her cayoch around and went kékéing back to the point where it was blunting as the pod began to waver and the steers to think about diving into the brush.

[4]

Urs wriggled through the brush and emerged on the bald top of the knoll. He did a mockerjig at the herdgirls, tongue out and fingers wriggling, stopped that with a startled urk as a hand caught him by the back of the neck and shook him. "Airhead. Your Mum would skin me in strips if I brought you back in pieces."

Urs twisted around. "Ahh, Laod-ca, I din't do nothing."

His uncle snorted. "Don't you know cayochs eat tadlings like you for breakfast? And that's no poet-talk, you young baöd. They got a liking for man meat. Herdgirls feed them on runaways they catch hanging round their herds." He gave Urs another shake. "Now you get back over to scrubbing those tubs. With so many hoists still to go up, Gara wants to keep on with the butchering until the sun drops too low."

Urs watched his uncle stalk off, hunting for the rest of the truants. "Yeh," he muttered. "Like I believe that." He kicked at a clod of dirt, grinned as it slammed into the gnarled trunk of a tumba bush and exploded into grains of sand. Then he went slouching back to the slaughter floor and the offal tubs he was supposed to be scrubbing till they were clean enough to eat out of, though the thought of eating the guts and stuff that came out of the insides of tribufs made his belly churn. Then he thought of winter sausage and head cheese and pickled hocks and walked a bit faster.

[5]

Gara snorted with disgust as she saw her recreant nephew slide out of the scraggly brush beside the stream at the edge of the slaughter floor. "You wait till your Mum gets hold of you tonight, you scrimpsy little baöd." She watched a moment longer until she saw him drag a tub into the scrubbing pool, then she turned back to the men raising the hoists and trying to foot the poles into the worn seating holes cut into the slate floor. Half the hoists were finished, with carcasses hanging from them, but those were the easy ones to fit.

She clicked her tongue with disgust at herself and the rest of her team. Because there'd been no big feasts for more than ten years, they'd forgot half of what they'd needed to do and no one had thought to bring quickset along to repair the holes that needed it or shaving knives to work on the butts of the tripod beams that were too big or the wrong shape to fit into the good holes.

The daroc nearest to her was seated on the slates with the end of a beam braced on his knee as he tried to whittle it into shape with his utility knife. The low-grade steel of the blade couldn't keep a sharp enough edge to get very far with the tough, seasoned wood.

"Maol, what happened to Siun? I thought you went to fetch him."

"Bantar got to him first, Breigga, I think it was. Hauled him off to oversee the stone wash and to shape stakes and shoring-staves for the roasting pits."

"Hunh! If we can't get the rest of these hoists up and set firm, meat to roast in those pits will be scarce as snow in a grass fire."

Maol shrugged. "Wan't going to argue with no bantar."

"Sssa!" Hands on hips, she looked round. "Aron, come over here. I need you."

Aron gave his assembled hoist a shake to make sure it was set solid, then he ambled over to Gara. "What you want?"

"Seeing as how you're done, go find Siun. He's probably over at the pits resetting the stone linings. Tell him to send his girl Cis over here with some quickset to mend the busted holes. And one of his shaping blades so we can cut the cursed wood on these beams they give us."

"Gotcha."

"And don't take till next week to do it. Achtaim Orduïl was getting nasty sweet the last time she came by and you know what that means."

He grinned and waved a hand at her, then ambled off.

"T'k. That daroc wouldn't run if his shirttail was on fire." She looked down. "Do what you can, Maol, till he gets back. I'll be round in a while, after I go beat on the kids and see that they're getting those tubs clean as they should."

[6]

Achtaim Orduïl set two sheets of paper on the worktable, sheets covered with her small precise writing. "The last of the acceptances came in this morning, so you can consider this list the final one."

Radayam glanced at the lists then laid her hand on the paper and smiled at Orduïl. "I don't envy you the task of sorting all this out and making sure everyone gets her due. There's no way you can satisfy all those prickly prides."

"Ah, my Traiolyn, it is the challenge of trying that gives me pleasure. Measuring myself against them and seeing how close I can come to perfection. You have a role that is far more trying. You have to stand and smile and do nothing." Orduïl chuckled. "Five marks of such concentrated boredom would drive me madder than a cayoch in must."

*   *   *

When the Achtaim was gone, Radayam shut and moved aside the dusty, worn volume she'd been reading—the Lyn Book of Days written at the time of the last Corruption. She had read it so many times she did not bother to mark her place. That long-ago Lyn Historian spoke directly to her heart in words she herself might have written.

She wiped the dust and the crumbles from the leather binding off her hands with the old huck towel, washed so many times it was little more than a rag but soft as velvet against the skin. "A time of Chaos," she said aloud. "A time of change. We must be worthy. Pure. Or the Prophet will not bless us. That's what went wrong in Oryamaya's time. Her will failed and the Cleansing was not complete."

She scowled at the map pasted on the wall across from her. The Domains were marked on it, painted in different shades of gray, with the towns of the Riverine Confluence and the lands they held painted red. Bloodred where they were old and strong and a pale translucent pink where they had just recently taken new land under their control. Bloody fingers closing round Saffroa and reaching into her heart wherever rivers ran.

Her scowl deepened as she contemplated the black dots swimming in the darkest red, the Riverine Citystates. Slack, unhallowed lives, runaway darocs acting like free persons, outcasts from Ascal owning Siofray land, Dyar from Glandair who had no business here, excrement from that foul world— and all of them breeding like rats with no thought to the bloodlines they desecrated. Dyar! Animals.

This was what she was born for. "I will wash Saffroa clean with the blood of heretics and apostates. All that is not Pure I will wipe away until it will be as if they never existed. And when this is done and we are Blessed, I will gather the Seers and together we will find the strength to separate Iomard from Glandair forever, even till the end of time."

She had said this before, but the words rolled so sweetly off her tongue that she couldn't help repeating it whenever the occasion arose.

Then she sighed and pulled the list of names in front of her, dipped her pen in the inkwell and began circling those names she was sure of, the Traiolyns, Seers and Historians who felt as she did. The others would come around. They would see the Truth and embrace it. But that had to wait for later, until she had the weight of others to give gravitas to her words.

[7]

Mirrialta threw her shutters open and leaned on the sill, staring into the bright, chill night. The moon was low in the west and soon would be gone, but the air was still and the stars burned like phosphorus against the velvet black of the sky. The Tiolan Seers watched her all the time now, those wrinkled old bitches with sludge in their veins. *They can't wait to see the back of me.*

She shook her head, sending her thick black hair tumbling forward over her shoulders. She drew her fingers through it, taking pleasure in the softness and the way the curving strands clung to her fingers. *Malart's get, that perversion on two feet in Valla Murloch, he can rest easy for a while, but I won't forget him. And I won't forget them. I can wait. I'm good at waiting.*

A light shone suddenly—out past the oilfruit groves where the inlet came to a crumbling point. It vanished, reappeared, vanished again. At the third flash, she straightened, pulled the shutters closed and walked from the room.

Thador was waiting in the grove of cenams, small mud-gray trees tormented by the sea winds into twisty, thrusting shapes. When she saw Mirrialta coming, she dropped to her knees and bowed low, banging her head on the short grass.

Mirrialta squatted beside the thin, intense woman, slapped at her head. "Well?"

Thador rose, sat on her heels, eyes slitted so their glitter was obscured by the tangled brush of her close-cropped hair. "The Traiolyn Radayam is a woman of middle years, on the farther edge of her bearing time, a woman of austere habit with no interest in the pleasures of the flesh. She expects you,

O Damya Mirrialta, to bear the heirs to Eadro and to take over the administration of the Domain while she raises an army and marches on the Riverine Confluence to purify Saffroa of the taint of mixed blood and to reclaim runaway darocs and their children, even those children whose parents, grandparents and so further have lived in the Confluence for generations upon generations.

"It was difficult to discover even this because the Traiolyn holds herself apart from the bantars and the ridos, consorting only with the Seers and the cadre of cantairs. She is a woman who holds her secrets close and she will most likely not speak to you of these things, thinking that as a Wife you have no need to know them. You will probably see nothing of her except on those formal occasions when the Wife's presence is required. She treats all with a stiff courtesy, but there is no difficulty seeing that she holds low those without interest in the pursuits of the intellect and those whose piety is form without fervor. She has little mercy to show those who offend against rite or law, but she is rigorously just in her decisions and often clever in how she chooses to implement them. She keeps the bantars in line and those who offend from arrogance or ignorance do not do so twice.

"Eadro is a Domain without restlessness among the darocs and the lesser folk who are content with the distant rule of the Traiolyn, though there is some muttering among the bantars and the ridos."

Mirrialta heard the warning behind the words; it made her angry, but she concealed that. "Who's doing that muttering?"

"I have the names of five who complained in whispers from the corners of their mouths, but it would be best to know more about them before putting any trust in their support. Three more had hungry eyes. I think they could be bought either with promises or gold. No doubt there are more, but my access was limited."

Mirrialta tapped a fingernail against her front teeth and stared out over the star-silvered water. It wasn't going to be easy to establish herself at Eadro and wield the power there she'd held in her hands at Tiolan. Better not to take anyone from here but Thador. The woman was bound to her by chains of pain and habit. Thador would never betray her and she was a clever spy. She got to her feet. "You've done well. I'm pleased at what you've gathered for me." She reached down, stroked her hand across the coarse, shaggy head. "Come. I'll show you just how pleased I am."

[8]

Aron stopped in the shadow of the tall thin leocas, their stiff, spearpoint leaves rustling like starched linen. He leaned against the nearest trunk, folded his arms and, with a leisurely turn of his head, scanned the swale opening out below.

After ten years of neglect—since the funeral meats for the last Traiolyn were roasted here—the pits were little more than dimples in the dirt; the walls had collapsed, years of wind had blown soil in over the stones, weeds and grass had grown in the dirt. Two bantars were striding from pit to pit, yelling at darocs digging out the weeds and grass, retrieving the stones and piling them up beside the pits. It was slow, slogging work, meticulous and backbreaking at the same time. Aron snorted. They were both of them pissed because the work was taking so long and the workers looked as if they were dogging on the job. That was something the bantars didn't understand, they didn't work with their hands and didn't know the rhythm you fall into so you don't break your back and tear your knees up.

He looked for the carts bringing wood from the piles that had been seasoning since Traiolyn Radayam had announced her contract with the girl from Lyn Mullach, then saw that the cart lane hadn't been cleared yet. Bantars would be looking to grab more hands for that and he surely didn't want to be one of them. Which meant he had to do some thinking about how he was going to go when he did go and keep his tongue nimble for talking his way out of trouble.

It took him several minutes to find Siun. The builder was on the far side of the swale, standing over a clot of youngsters cleaning the stones as they were lifted from that pit, talking at them in the singsong beat he brought with him when Domain Fokklarno traded him for two lacemakers. He talked like water ran, not all that loud but never stopping. Aron sucked on his teeth, then slid behind the line of trees and began making his way around the rim of the swale. With a little care he could keep himself out of sight till he was almost at the pit he wanted.

"Cis, if you leave the roots on like that, they will lead the fire into the heart of the stone and the stone will crack and the wall will tumble down and smother the fire and the meat will be ruined and all because you are a lazy little leiscu."

"Ahh Paaa, was good enough."

"I do not hear good enough. You hear that, Cis? Fan, that stone is a web of roots, take it up again and strip them all away. And the rest of you sharpen your ears and hone your eyes or you will be spending the night right here and all day tomorrow too. You will not be moving until you do the work the way it ought to be."

The second small girl wrinkled her nose and looked at the stone she was about to put on the pile. "Ahhh, Siun-ca."

Aron laughed. "Ahh, Siun-ca. Don't you get tired being the same old tight arse?"

Siun twisted round, lifted a hand in a minimal gesture of greeting. "Aron. Thought you would be over messing up the hoists."

Aron dropped to squat and sat on his heels beside the pile of rocks, his head pulled down like a turtle's. "Messed up is what they are but not my doing. Gara says would you send your Cis for some quickset? There's some seat holes with part of the sides busted out. And your shaving knife. Beam butts, some of them, are the wrong shape and that's cursed hard wood."

"Cis, put the stone down and come round here. I've got something I am wanting you to do. Aron, you must go with her to haul the quickset. I do not want my girl messing her joints by carrying too heavy.''

"You! Come here.''

Aron swore under his breath. As he turned slowly to face the bantar, he whispered, "Play the game, Cis, mouth shut. You know how it goes.'' He finished the turn, stood with shoulders rounded and eyes on the ground. "Your wish, Bantar?''

"What are you doing strolling around like this is a holiday? This isn't a holiday, or hadn't you noticed?''

"Pardon, Bantar. We do work. Not arguing, just saying.'' He spoke with slow care, pandering to bantar prejudices by slurring his words and keeping them simple. "I work slaughter floor. Daroc Gara sends me to fetch stuff from Builder Siun. His girl Cis, she taking me to house to get it.''

He kept his eyes down so he couldn't see more than the toes of her boots, but from the way they moved he could tell she was angry but not going to do anything about it, at least nothing more than keeping him standing there as long as she dared.

After a long moment the boots shifted again. "Well, then, get on with it. I see you dawdling along like you were, I'll set an encourager on you.''

"Pardon, Bantar.'' Hand on Cis's shoulder, he backed off then eased around and set off along the overgrown lane, moving at a quick trot until he was out of sight behind the line of leocas. Then he slowed to his usual amble and headed for Ead Village. The only people left there would be the grannys and grandys tending the crops and Ead livestock.

As he walked the poisons of resentment churning in his belly began draining out of him. "High-nosed bloodsuckers . . .'' He blinked, glanced at the young girl walking silent beside him. Her round solemn face flashed into a sudden grin, then she was looking straight ahead as if nothing had happened. Good kid. He felt even better as he savored that grin.

[9]

Bantar Breigga watched the mismated pair go trotting off, then she shook her head. Trying to get work out of these animals was worse than flogging a dead dog to get him to point. She kicked at a clod and scowled as it broke apart and smeared her boots with dust. "Like everything else. Sssa!"

This was her real chance to make a show and pull out a recommendation for Seer training. I can do it, she thought. If I can just get a chance to prove it. She'd tested Pure, with a strong Gift, but was only Eadro-Limda, not one of the elder lines. And there was a blot on her descent tree; the vao seyl who'd fathered her great-grandmother had put bi-colored eyes in his male get and a hot wild Gift. He was killed and they were gelded, but since then Limda was tainted and none of the males born to that line were allowed to live and none of the women went beyond bantar.

Why Radayam had taken notice of her, Breigga couldn't guess. Maybe she knew ambition when she smelled it. She certainly knew how to use it. Fine with me. I'll dance to her strings and use them to jump high high high. This was not one of the plum assignments, but it could have been worse. She could have been assigned to the work force in the vao seyl arena. That was blessed ground and darocs were not allowed to set foot on it, so bantars had to repair the pit and the tiers, pull the weeds and sweep the debris away with their own hands. At least she was spared that.

Breigga looked angrily around, saw a clot of daroc children crouched over a bit of sand. Games. I'll put a stop to that right now.

She charged toward them, then slowed as she saw her cousin Slears come round a pile of brush and send the children scurrying.

[10]

Radayam shuffled the strips of paper, put the list of names she wanted for her inner circle at the top. It was a shorter list than she had expected, the shortest of them all, only four names on it, Historians whose bone-deep beliefs matched her own. This was going to be a difficult negotiation. Traiolyns were not going to line up to defer to her leadership; they were prickly, suspicious and reluctant to yield the slightest part of their power no matter how tempting the goal. It was going to take some delicate negotiations and careful management to get the army and the backing she wanted.

She touched the pen point to the first name.

TEANNAL ait é PIOCA-SPADHAR

When they were students together at the Scribe School in Gabba Labhain, Teannal was a plump girl with pimples and wispy brown hair, but her brown eyes glittered with intensity when she slid into one of her fulminations about the corruption of the Siofray and evils of blood-mixing. Her deep and pleasing voice made music even of curses.

That was nearly fifty years ago and Radayam had seen her only twice since they finished school—at the funeral and at the Rites celebrating her installation as Eadro Traiolyn—but from Teannal's letters and those meetings, it was quite clear she hadn't changed her views. She still had that Voice, but the fat and pimples had vanished. Radayam tapped the pen by the name, ignoring the splatter of ink. Teannal's mind had got distressingly rigid over the years and her interests had narrowed to the niggling trivialities of daroc sins and the lack of fervor among the younger bantars.

With a click of her tongue, she wrote beneath the name:

ASSETS   strong gift for oratory, conviction, loyalty, will follow whoever can evoke the latter

DRAWBACKS   stubborn, can be clever, but is often blind to the obvious, hard to shift when she sets down the wrong path, can't trust her evaluation of others

CLUAYN ait é FUASCALA-COLAI

Domain Fuascala was at the northern edge of the Settled

Lands, up near the Riverine Citystate Soriseis. Cluayn was twenty years younger than Radayam so they didn't share schooling. Fuascala's Wife was a vigorous woman filled with indignation at the scaff and raff who lived in the hills above Fuascala and stole everything that wasn't nailed down—which the mongrel merchants in Soriseis bought from them without embarrassing questions. Her indignation reached such a pitch that she even managed to spark a special session of the Council.

Radayam snorted. For all the good that did her. A letter of protest sent to the Riverines, a few Seers and some bantars and ridos to add two extra patrols sent on a summer's loan to Fuascala—then everything was back as it was before. The only good thing to come from that exercise in futility was that Fuascala's Wife had dragged the Fuascala Historian about with her as she raged from Domain to Domain trying to stir up some kind of reaction against the Riverines and the Hill Lice.

Under Cluayn's name, she wrote:

ASSETS	apparently has as deep an anger against the Riverines as Fuascala's Wife, quiet but quick and clever, managed to guide the Wife through the complications of the negotiations without appearing to interfere, would make an admirable Aide
DRAWBACKS	too young to be accepted as an authority, too clever to be fully trusted and too ambitious. Made it subtly apparent when she was here that she could see herself as Eadro's Wife, would have to be watched all the time. Does she have any true beliefs beyond her ambition?

SHONEYN ait é PLANDA-PASSAN

Domain Planda was one of the largest and richest of the Domains in the Western Lobe of Saffroa and for the first time in Planda's long history it had lost control of the port city

Fasalla. Fastidious and shortsighted, the Traiolyns of Planda had set up barriers between that festering pustulence and themselves and had laid no claim to the land, though they had extracted a tribute from the landholders and merchants in the city, which was called a tax but was in truth an extortion of money for threat. It was a comfortable sum and grew as Fasalla grew. And Planda did not seem to notice how much of the Domain's wealth came from the trade that flowed through that port, nor did any Traiolyn, Wife or Seer think through the consequences of that fact.

Then Fasalla declared itself a free port, affiliated itself with Valla Murloch and the Eastern Riverines and put a tariff on all goods passing through the port. It was only a few coppers for every pund of goods weight, but it was a slap in the face to Planda and the other Domains that had before this treated the Fasallats like darocs and the city as their own. Almost at the same moment Teyas Brotta farther south and Mionach in the north declared their alliance with Fasalla, and the Western Confluence was born. These were the only three storm-sheltered deep-water ports along the western coastline.

Radayam felt a dour satisfaction as she contemplated the events of the last five years. Shortly after her installation here she had sent out a warning to the other Traiolyns about the ambitions and the encroachments of the Riverines along with a plan for acting against them.

First step: simply ignore their pretensions and deal directly with traders at the ports, protecting ourselves with a large force of armed ridos, but not attacking, something all the western Domains would have to do in order for it to be effective.

Second step: take control of river traffic by setting nets across the water at strategic points and assessing fees for boats that wished to pass the toll points. This could be used for a double purpose—to punish *and* reward. All those boatmen and merchants who swore allegiance to the Domains would have their fees lowered step by step as they proved their loyalty and subjected themselves to Domain Law.

Third step: Seizing the harbor area of each of the port cities. This would have to be done by force of arms and would mean a guard troop would have to be left there until the Riverines had capitulated to Domain pressures. All trade could be halted except for Domain goods and Domain-sanctioned enterprises.

"If the Domains East and West had followed my plans . . ." Radayam drew a thick ragged line under Shoneyn's name. "We wouldn't have a Riverine problem today."

She'd got answers from several Domains essentially saying *this is your problem, not mine; deal with it yourself.* Fuascala's Wife wrote that Radayam was too tepid; *we should take an army and burn the cities to the ground, hang all merchants and misbreeds and turn the rest into darocs.* The sentiment pleased Radayam, but even then she could see that very few of the other Domains would agree. From most she got no response at all and suspected her letters had been used to light kitchen fires. In hindsight it had been quite a valuable lesson, though she had been very angry at the time.

And it had brought her Shoneyn. Shoneyn the Beautiful. Shoneyn the Visionary. Sent by Planda's Wife to get a copy of the Plan and any other thoughts Radayam had about dealing with upstart riverines.

ASSETS   beauty of a rare and wonderful kind, like one of the Prophet's Messengers made flesh, deeply religious, deeply committed to restoring the purity of the Siofray and reaching for the perfected worship of the All-Mother, a singing voice as beautiful as her physical being, a soul so immaculate and glowing that it was apparent even to the most vulgar that here was a rare and wonderful being

DRAWBACKS   essentially none, though perhaps Shoneyn
             is a bit vague about the practical aspects
             of her dreams

MYCILL ait é ARRAIN-DORSEH
Radayam wrinkled her nose. From the sublime to . . .
The bell on the wall behind her jerked, then tinked with that
cautious diffidence that always irritated Radayam, but told her
without doubt who stood on the other side of the door fiddling
with the bellpull. Cantair Hogtha was a woman of genuine
piety but unfortunately also of limited intelligence, with a ten-
dency to dither. She lifted the papers from the worktable, set
them in a locking coffer and turned the key. "Come," she
said.

[11]
"I heard . . ." Bett broke off as Ama poked her. When she
looked round, she saw bantar Eirim standing in the doorway,
scowling at them.
"Less talk, more work," Eirim said. "Wedding parties will
start arriving in two days and if the Guesthouses aren't ready
for them, I'll see you know what that means."
Bett waited till she heard boot heels clumping off, then she
primmed up her full mouth, wagged her arm. "What that
means . . ."
Ama giggled, then she caught hold of the end of the bed
pad. "Gimme a hand, Bett. I hear creaking and that means
Keml's on his way."
They rolled the pad into a tight cylinder, tied it with a bit
of cord and carried it into the hall just as a daroc in a headband hauler snaplinked to a broad-wheeled cart came around
the corner at the end of the hallway. He stopped by the first
door, dropped a rolled-up bed pad there, came on toward
them.
He stopped when he reached them, pulled the band down
and wiped his sleeve across his sweaty face, smearing yet
more the gray streaks from the smoke in the slathouse.

"Bantar catches you doodling round, you get backside her hand."

Bett ticked her thumbnail off her front teeth. "That for bantar. She gets my backhairs up, she can do the cleaning with her own lily-whites."

Keml snorted. "And you say it to her face, huh?" He tossed a fumigated pad off the back end of the cart and put the one from the room into the box at the front. "Be making my last round middle of next watch. Anything after waits till tomorrow." He settled into the headband and went trudging off without waiting for an answer.

Bett and Ama hauled the new pad into the room, unrolled it on the bed, fetched a pair of sheets and a pillow from their cleaning cart and snapped a sheet across the pad, tucked it under, and with smooth efficiency finished making the bed.

Bett gave a last tug to the coverlet, straightened and stood with her hands on her hips. "I'll get the commode set up if you'll take care of the windows."

"All right, but I did them last room. Next room they're yours."

"Oh, all right." Bett opened the doors to the commode, clicked her tongue at the spiderwebs, dust and ten years' worth of bug droppings. "What I started to say, I heard some shlacty dirt about the Bride."

Ama squeezed out the rag she'd dipped into the vinegar bucket. "Took you long enough to get to it."

"Wasn't gonna say at all, but this is too good. You gotta promise you won't tell where you heard it."

"That good, huh?"

"Uh-huh. And 'twouldn't be hard for bantar to pick up where you got the word, then it's me hauled up 'fore the Seers and babbling like a baby reaching for a lolly."

"So I promise. So what *is* it?"

"Swear by Prophet and hope of heaven."

"I swear, I swear. So tell me."

"Come here, I don't want anyone else hearing this." Bett dropped to her knees on the bare boards of the floor. When

Ama was kneeling, she said, "One of the haulers that come up from Domain Ullord with the plums and berries and the yams, she brought word to me from Teyas Brotta—my cousin Immer, the one who ran last year, he's living there now-anyway we got to talking, the hauler and me, and she told me stuff, swears it's true. Mirrialta, she's a Mullach fostered to Tiolan and you know what Mullachs are like, crazy mad all of them, well, from what I hear she's worse than any of them. Likes whips and knives and does weird things with pliers. There was this daroc boy . . ."

[12]

Keml unrolled the last of the bed pads on the smoking racks, weighed down the ends with two half-bricks. He paused a moment to scratch the places where the bugs from the pads had found a home on him. Then he shrugged, stirred up the fires in the pits and heaped on fresh-cut stinkweed. As the long thin spears of the weed began to burn, thick yellowish smoke came pouring off the firepits. Keml closed his eyes and held his nose while the smoke coiled around him.

He could feel the tickling of their tiny feet as the bugs ran through his hair and across his skin, trying to escape the smoke that would kill them. He stood where he was until the tickling stopped, holding his breath because that smoke wasn't all that good for people, either. He tossed a few last handfuls of stinkweed onto the fire and trotted for the door.

Outside, he flopped against the side of the smokehouse, sucked air into his lungs. He had to go back inside in a little while and burn some sweet resin to get the stink out of the pads. But even with all those girls working their gums like there was no tomorrow, they'd got through the cleaning by sundown and this was the last of the fumigations for this year. Next year he'd have the spring turnout to take care of but that was nothing beside this upheaval.

He dropped onto his heels and sat with his back against the wall, the warmth from the three-day fire inside seeping into him. There were worse jobs. He could be over on the slaughter grounds sorting through tubs of steaming offal. Another bonus of the burning stinkweed—bantars stayed well away from the smokehouse. Eirim the high-nosed wasn't about to show up and boot his rear for lazying around. He took out a comb and ran it through his head hair, then his beard, grimacing at the black dots that fell on his shoulders and the front of his shirt. Hefty crop of vermin.

He got to his feet, stripped off his shirt and trousers, shook them out, then got dressed again and went inside to beat the dead bugs out of the pads and smoke them a last time to sweeten the smell.

[13]

Urs flung himself down beside Saml and Argy and settled himself to enjoy the sight of bantars working like darocs.

The vao seyl arena was on the side of the Lynhouse opposite the daroc village and the slaughter floor. Earthen walls were built up in an oval about the fight floor, the Pit it was called, a floor of slates laid out on hard-packed earth, grass growing between them though the Pit was used all the time for the arrthoïr who showed up, one or two or even five at a time to challenge the unseyled males for places as ridos inside the Lynhouse. Even with that steady usage, though, the arena needed some hard work to get it into shape for the solemn occasion of the Wedding.

The arena was quiet, almost somber. Those bantars who were religious were into the symbolism of the clean, those who were not were annoyed at having to do physical labor, the kind of work they thought only suitable for darocs.

A line of bantars moved along the earthen banks, scrubbing the planks that were set as sets on the stepped slopes, cleaning up the sprays of dirt where the steps had given way, setting in bricks and fieldstones to level the planks again. Others were pulling grass and weeds from between the slates that paved the Pit. A third group followed behind them, dragging mops across the slabs of stone, wielding them awkwardly enough to make the watching boys giggle.

When the sun was almost gone, only a red bead showing between the peaks of the distant mountains, and the shadows were thick in the arena, the bantars gathered their cleaning tools, piled them on a cart and went marching off, maintaining their silence until they vanished from view.

Urs crawled from under the bushes and rolled onto the top round of benches. "Eh, Argy, bet I can piss farther'n you."

"Arrr, Urs, you eeevil."

A moment later three pale streams hissed through the air and splattered on the planks the bantars had washed so carefully such a short while before.

[14]

The Wedding Galt was a dome of carefully woven strips of wood cut green from sellach saplings, cured and made supple again by steaming them. Cantair Hogtha began work on the Galt the day Radayam informed her that the contract between Eadro and Mullach had been drawn up and would be signed on the Feast of the Holy Mauralt, the date chosen to honor the Bride whose name was a variant of Mauralt.

Hogtha ait é Brisim bond Eadro was a deeply pious woman and clung passionately to the old ways. Where many less rigorous cantairs would have darocs doing the rough work, she would not allow herself such laxness. She rode about the Domain with a guard of ridos, cut the saplings with her own hands, brought them back to the Lynhouse, peeled the bark carefully away and saved it to weave the cords, then used a carpenter's wand-cutter to split out the slats. When she was finished, she took the wood to the drying shed and left it for time and the directed flow of air to cure it properly. It would be steamed into flexibility when it came time to weave the Galt.

She twisted the inner surface of the bark into the special cords, dyed them red and hung them to dry also.

When the time came for the Purification before the wedding, everything was ready. The specially chosen stones fitted together to form the fire pit, the dome of the Galt woven from wood only her hands had touched, tied in place with cords that she herself had made. The wood for the fire, the scented grasses, the scya whisks, the stone scrapers, even the special oils, Hogtha had gathered herself, made herself, and all these things were as pure and blessed as anything done by Siofray hand could be.

Her hair plaited into the three braids of contrition, her body glistening with the aromatic oil, Radayam lay stretched out upon the springy frame made from the stripped branches of mountain conifers. Steam from the fire pit rolling around her, her hands folded on her breasts, she listened to Cantair Hogtha chanting the Be-Mindfuls and meditated on the deeper meanings of the Wedding that was nearly on her.

The marriage of a Traiolyn was another link in the long history that secured into one family all who lived within the boundaries of a Domain, whether they were joined by blood or simply by place. More than that, it was a treaty in a web of treaties binding Domain to Domain. The Wives brought new blood into the lines, they brought youth and vigor and a breath of strange air that opened up pores clogged by years of unchange. And most of all, each such marriage was a caught-in-time symbol of the eternal bond with the Prophet and through Her sanctity with the All-Mother.

Be mindful that you are Mother to the children of the Oath.
Be mindful of daroc and Lynborn.
Be mindful of the herdgirls and the beasts they serve.

Cantair Hogtha had a deep rich voice that in this Galt of her weaving was curiously without resonance. The words touched Radayam's ears and slid away like the sweat that gathered on her body and dripped from her edges.

Be mindful of the words of the Prophet and the duty
  you owe to her teachings.
Be mindful of the state of your soul, for a clean soul
  means a healthy and contented Domain.

> *Be mindful to avoid sin and the occasions of sin.*
> *Be mindful that justice is yours to give, that you in all*
>   *things submit yourself to the will of the Prophet.*

Cantair Hogtha sang the words simply, without flourish or ornament. It was comforting to Radayam's ears to hear those ancient forms come so easily off the tongue. In her years as a librarian she had become very fluent in Oldspeech and though her duties as Traiolyn left her with little time for reading, she still gave herself permission to plunge now and then into the ancient records of the Domain.

The chanting stopped as Hogtha got to her knees and crawled over to tend the fire. Radayam heard soft chunks as she added sticks of wood, then a sudden increase in pungency as she set another handful of aromatic grasses on the fire.

A sudden sharp stinging on her thighs.

Radayam let a small sound escape her, though she'd been expecting this. The scoriation was part of the ritual, coming immediately after the Be-Mindfuls.

The sting came again and again, the slap of the whisk harder this time as it moved along her body, its needles scratching her skin. And the chanting resumed.

> *Examine your soul, Oh Daughter. Find out your sins of*
> *commission and omission and confess them into the ears*
> *of the Prophet, the All-Merciful, All-Comprehending.*

Sins, Radayam thought as her body responded with a prickly pleasure to the light beating of the wisk. I've had no time for sins of commission. Omission . . . I have been lax with myself and my Oath children . . . I have not seen to their discipline or mine . . . I have let the darocs slide out of prayer call . . . work in the fields seemed more important . . . that is not right . . . I will do better . . . I should have married before this . . . I did not want the intrusion . . . was it pride . . . did I covet this power and not wish to diminish it . . . I don't know her . . . the intermediaries say she does well at organization and control . . . the ties with Mullach and Tiolan are necessary . . . I'll need backing there . . . I really don't want this . . . face the truth . . . I don't want calls on my time that I cannot refuse to answer . . . I don't want anyone inside my rooms . . . inside my head . . . don't want . . . no, not just that, I loathe having her here . . . Mother, Great Mother, you see my sin . . . Prophet, you see my sin . . . always my will, not Yours . . .

The light swats of the whisk grew more painful as the cantair moved along her body, chanting and striking the same spots over and over. The Galt filled with the smoke from the burning grass.

Her head swam.

Without opening her eyes she could see herself lying there, the oil glowing on her body as if she were dressed in golden light. Suddenly she was lying in open air, raised up on the backs of a flock of white clurs, their cooing in her ears, more clurs walking on her, their talons pricking her, their beaks pecking at her, leaving behind flecks of blood though whether it was hers or theirs she couldn't tell, and the song of the Messengers that she had heard earlier in the day swelled round her again. . . .

She was buoyed on light, bathed in light, warm light, tender as a mother's hands.

Words in a voice too sacred for sound formed in her mind.

YOU ARE MY BELOVED.
SPREAD MY BLESSING TO THOSE WHO HAVE FORGOT BELIEF.
GO FORTH AND PURIFY THE WORLD.

Cold water splashed over her.

She woke with a cry of anguish as the chill wrenched her from communion with the Mother of All and brought her back to the endless complications of her life.

The cantair knelt beside the frame, holding out the thick warm towel. When Radayam took it, Hogtha said, "Traiolyn-

Ca, your bath is prepared and waiting. For your health's sake, you must go now.''

Radayam drew her hand across her mouth, then looked at it. The hand was shaking. She stared at it as if it might belong to someone else, continued to stare until the shaking stopped.

"Yes," she said, then cleared her throat and spoke without the harsh edge to her voice. "Thank you, Cantair Hogtha. This was well done."

3

Cymel's Rebellion

By the secret calendar of the Watchers of Glandair, events dating from the 27th day of Ailmis, the second month in the 737th Glandairic year to the 9th day of Pedarmis, the third month in the 738th Glandairic year since the last Settling.

[1]

Cymel brought the heavy mallet down on the strip of meat she was tenderizing and imagined it was Raffyn lying there. "Riff raff Raffyn, nasty tongue, filthy mind, arrogant snob," she muttered, then grinned as the mallet thudded down again, flattening the strip yet more.

The birdhouse was quiet and dark outside the workroom where she was getting ready to feed sick Creulo, moonlight a pale glow through the lattices. The nights were warm enough now to leave the shutters open and the tullins and colos were healthier with a fresh flow of air through their perches. Creulo was in premature moult, skin and bones, dull eyes, huddled posture, a sorry-looking creature, but he was recovering quite handily, already past the need for bran mash and cooked meats, but still needing small meals every four hours so he could rebuild his strength without straining his body. She had permission to be out until dawn without constraints on her comings and goings, something that got Housemum Amys Tyrfaswyf's nose in a twist and sent the other boarders whispering nastiness behind Cymel's back—and sometimes to her face.

It just wasn't done to let young virgins off the leash, but Cymel had her permissions because of who she was and the task she'd taken on, tending the sick birds so old Derdo could get some much-needed rest. There were not all that many students with the time or interest in the trivial drudgery involved in such work and even fewer that Derdo would trust with his birds; since the Watchers were paying her room and board they were pleased to have her services in return. Tyrfaswyf could go sit on her thumb and bide her bellyache with her mouth firmly shut.

"And Raffyn should bite her tongue and taste her own venom." Cymel poked at the flattened strip of rabbit with her thumbnail. A harsh sound like a rusty hinge came from the corner of the room where Creulo crouched on his perch; by now he knew that when the thudding of the mallet went silent, food was on its way. "Smart, aren't you, silly bird. All antsy for your dinner." She laughed, wadded up the rabbit meat in one hand and reached for the feeding prong with the other. "It's coming, bach."

Using the prong, she fed the tullin small bits of meat, watching him carefully to see how he held himself as he ate.

At the beginning of winter last year, when Cymel first came to Cyfareth, she stayed with a Scholar's family. Scholar Hellydd was a historian so lost in ancient times that he barely noticed the present; by necessity, his wife was considerably more alert though she had her own craft classes to teach. She was a weaver of some renown with apprentices sent to her from the length and breadth of Nyddys. They had one daughter still at home, a small pretty girl with an abundance of golden brown curls and cold brown eyes. Bolryn Hellyddsdattar took one look at Cymel and fell into instant hate.

By the end of the year it had become obvious to three of the four people in the small house that Cymel would have to find shelter elsewhere.

Tyrfa Beichson was employed by the University as a sub-historian. He was addressed as Scholar but was really little more than a scribe in one of the vast array of copyrooms attached to the many Schools of the University. He was proud of his position to the point of arrogance, but the pay was small. To live with the kind of style they felt was due them, Tyrfa and Amys needed an addition to their income. Amys arranged this by opening a boardinghouse where she took in Broon daughters and occasionally a girl from the merchant class if her parents were wealthy enough with the proper sort of connections, girls for whom the rougher life of University dormitories was not considered suitable.

The Watcher Council moved Cymel into this boardinghouse despite her vehement protests. She preferred the dormitories, being quite aware that life there would be a lot freer and probably more to her liking. Shut in with a lot of snotty, hateful and above all uninteresting Broon daughters didn't seem like any sort of improvement to her. But she was simply too young. Neither the Watcher Council nor the Governors of the University would permit her to live unsupervised.

"That's a good Creulo, nice bach, eat up your meat, eat it all."

As she was finishing the feed, Derdo came in and stood watching.

"Another week and he'll be eating regular meals," he said.

She nodded as she took the prong from the withy-cage. "Yes, I think so."

"Where's that boy Tyrfaswyf sends with you? I didn't see him where he usually bides."

"Raffyn and Yllys needed escort to some do over the other side of University. Well, needed someone to fetch and carry for them, so Housemum agreed to send Gwaur with them. She wanted to make me stay in, but I wasn't having that. I can take care of myself."

"Hm. You go home right now, Cym. Keep your eyes open and stay in the light. There's leavings from Yabbernight up to no good round every corner. Wine in their heads and a roil in their trews." He hesitated and for a moment she thought he was going to offer to escort her, but Creulo started stamping on his perch and looking unhappy. "Saaa, old bird, ate too fast, did you? That's no sin of yours, Cym. He's a greedy young'n and he's always outdoing himself. Go on. Git! And like I said, keep your eyes wide."

Cymel stepped from the birdhouse into a thick darkness, the tiny sliver of moon about to slide behind the mountains. The air was still and cold and the night should have been quiet but it wasn't. Here and there in the Schools and the dormitories, windows showed yellow strips where students or ambitious would-be Scholars were working. Off to one side she heard the beat of feet—several people running hard, in the distance, shouts and laughter and a few squeals and squawks. The lamps on their standards had burned so low that only a pale flicker of light remained, enough to make shadows darker and kill nightsight so the places where cobbles were missing were traps for her feet.

Yabbernight. She'd heard the Broon daughters talking about it in scandalized whispers that stopped the moment they saw her, and when she asked Amys Tyrfaswyf what it was all about, she got a scold for taking an interest in sordid things. It was another one of those maddening things that adults did to youngers. She sighed and thought about the farm. She didn't really want to go back there, but it was hard getting used to being with all these people and learning the rules that let them stick close together without going crazy and beating on each other.

More garbled voices, beat of feet against the cobbles— nearer this time. Cymel looked nervously around, but saw no one. There was a narrow frill of buildings between the bird-house and the several boarding houses at the rim of the University grounds; these were mostly offices, lecture halls and workrooms and were deserted now.

Tyrfahouse was just beyond these. The wooden lace painted white that acted as snowcatchers on the roof shone in the remnant of the moonlight and she knew she'd be home and safe soon. She'd been impatient before this at having to put up with Gwaur trailing around after her, but it'd be a comfort to have him with her, though he'd be no sort of help if she got in trouble. He was a weedy, adenoidal creature with the wit of a slowworm; a breath of air would knock him off his feet. She walked faster.

As she passed the corner of the last of the buildings, four students came running from the shadows to circle round her. Hands grabbed her, whirling her round, passing her from one to the other round and round the circle. The smell of rough, harsh calda was strong and sickening, the voices slurred, the hands hot and sweaty.

"Chicka chikee, look what we found."

"Pretty pretty townee babe."

"Who slipped you in, tender bit? Which ol' lecher found you out?"

Hands snatching the scarf from her head.

Whistles as her long black hair spilled down, caught the wind and blew about her head.

Hands fumbling at her breasts, tearing her blouse.

Hands pulling at her skirt.

It happened so fast that at first she was too startled to do anything, then she was furious. "Leave me alone," she screamed at them and clawed at the hands fumbling at her. "Go away. Leave me alone."

A hand cracked hard against her face. "Craza bitzh, she got me good. Grab 'er, Edil. Who the whore think she iz?" He had an odd slurred way of speaking, the way people from the west coast stretched their words and hardened their vowels.

Hands snatched at her hands and one of them grabbed a fistful of her hair, jerking her head back. For the first time she was frightened. They were stronger than she was and they were going to hurt her. The man she'd scratched forced his hand under the waistband of her skirt and pulled, ripping away the buttons and tearing the skirt off her.

She reached for the Pneuma. "Let me go," she said. She wasn't screaming this time, just speaking loudly and firmly. "Or I'll burn you dead."

The man slapped her again. "Shut you mouth, whore." He stepped back and stood slumped in shadow, a fugitive faint gleam from the whites of his eyes. "Or itz my fist you feel next time." A quick, violent gesture to the men holding her. "Put her on the ground. When I finizh, you get your turn. We teach the bitzh to mind her betters."

Suddenly cold and calm, the fire-call clear in her head, Cymel gathered the Pneuma knot to hurl at him.

"No!" Another man emerged from the shadows, a thin, bony figure, round spectacles glistening in the moonlight. "Let her go, Mayrt. She's no towngirl, but a Watcher's daughter. Mess with her and you've got big trouble."

"You lie. I know you, Mole. Cry like a baby over these miserable brefs."

"I said no to her, not you, Mayrt. Hadn't stopped her, you'd be a torch and dead. Show him, girl."

Cymel stored the name Mayrt in her mind just in case, then opened her mouth wide and breathed out, letting the breath carry fire a man height into the air.

The hands that held her jerked away, she heard muttered curses, then feet running.

"You'd better follow your friends, Mayrt. Before the young lady loses her temper and gives you a taste of what you've earned."

"I'll remember this, Mole." He glared at Cymel. "And I'll remember you, whore." He went striding off into the shadow under the trees.

Cymel started shaking. She tried to say something to Mole, but she could only gulp and clutch at herself.

"Firill," he called. "Your work now."

A young woman came from the shadows, tapped her fingers against Mole's cheek as she moved past him. "About time," she said. She set her hand on Cymel's shoulder, turned her head to look back at him. "What's her name?"

"Don't ask me."

"I thought you knew her."

"No. But who else could she be and call a vortex like that?"

"Well, you can still make yourself useful. Give me that coat. The child can't go anywhere all messed up like that."

Firill set the coat around Cymel's shoulders. It was warm from Mole's body and the kindness of the woman and the man warmed her even more. She was suddenly so tired she was shaking and weak tears were rolling down her face. "M-M-Mela," she said. "M-my name."

"Mela. Good. What we're going to do is take you to my rooms. You can have a good washup there and I've got a skirt and jacket you can borrow. They'll be a bit too big, but we can fix that. Once we get you pulled together, then we can get you home again. Hm? That sound all right?"

Cymel gulped, then nodded. Anger and impatience were crawling back inside the hollow they'd left when the expelling of the fire burned away the passion that had begun to drive her. For the moment she was still content to let these strangers be kind to her, but they had interfered, especially that Mole. She could have got herself out of this mess and it would have been really satisfying to burn the hands off that loorf.

As the pair led her past Boardinghouse Row, toward the smaller buildings where townsfolk rented out rooms or room sets fitted with bathroom and a hole in the wall they called a kitchen, she went sullen and simmering with the injustice of what had happened. Raffyn and Yllys were bound to see her when she got back to Tyrfahouse and would make her life a misery as far as their tongues could reach and that was farther than she liked to think.

In the short time it took to reach the room set, her anger drained away again and she was simply tired, so tired her bones had lost their stiffening, and a cold sweat clung to her skin. She stumbled up the stairs with both of them lifting her and she wondered with a kind of leaden curiosity why she was letting them bring her here rather than taking her home.

* * *

Firill's room set was cluttered, piles of clothing, scattered books, bits of paper everywhere with bits of brush drawings and scrawled notes, sometimes a wash of bright color, a worn velvet throw pulled over a bed that doubled as a couch but couldn't hide the sag in the middle that marked it as what it was. Guttered candles and battered old oil lamps were scattered about in wall clips and standing on the several small tables placed here and there amidst the clutter. Firill lowered Cymel on a scuffed hassock bleeding its stuffing through cracks in the leather cover. "You sit here. I'm going to start water heating so you can wash and so we can have some tea. And Mole, you're not to fuss at her, you hear?"

He grunted, lowered himself on the edge of the bed, the velvet throw puffing up around him. He sat staring at Cymel till she wanted to scream. He was a thin, neat-looking man with short plushy black hair and wide gray eyes magnified by the thick glass of his spectacles. He was dressed in fine gray wool from head to toe. Even his boots were gray. He'd taken the name Mole and made it his in a whimsical way that would have delighted Cymel if she'd been capable of delight at this moment. He waited until Firill passed through the narrow arch into the tiny kitchen beyond, then he said, "Well, was I right?"

Cymel laced her fingers together to stop her hands shaking. She glanced at him, then deliberately turned her eyes away. "About what?"

"About you being the Watchers' Ward."

"I thought I answered that."

"It's always good to have the words spoken. You know where you are then."

She shrugged. "You're right. My name's Cymel Ellarsdattar. My father's Court Poet and the Watchers are warding me here."

"How old are you?"

"Is that your business?"

"I could guess. Fourteen at most. Hm. Ellarsdattar. Your mother was an Iomardi Walker, right?" He chuckled as she shrugged without answering. "Potent mix, it seems, Walker and Watcher. No, I'm not a Watcher but people talk to me." He sobered, shook his head. "I know you're wondering why I stopped you protecting yourself. Thing is, while I wouldn't mind a whole lot watching you torch that Mayrt and singe his lapdogs, they're Broon sons. A collection of louts and morons, but powerful louts and morons. Doing them any kind of hurt no matter the reason would bring more trouble down on you than you would want."

"So they just get away with what they did to me."

"You wouldn't be here if your father didn't think you could handle the requirements, Mela. So listen to what I'm saying. Weigh costs. And don't pay too dear a price for something so trivial as Mayrt Gyldson."

"Trivial! He was going to—"

"I know. That's not what I'm talking about. I'm talking about the cost to you and probably to your father. Broon Gyld gan Tomen is a wealthy and powerful man, not someone Tyrn Isel would ignore. And the loathsome Mayrt is his Heir. Wrapping him in a fire vortex, while satisfying, would guarantee that the hurt he tried to put on you would keep on working even after he was ash and cinder." He took his spectacles off, pulled a handkerchief from his sleeve and sat polishing them, his face curiously naked without the protection of those heavy lenses. "Thing is, Mela, it's simpler not to roil folks up, just give them a sop so they can tell themselves they're in charge, then go your own way. Softly softly go little mole feet and who knows where they take him."

"Why're you bothering with me, telling me all this?"

"Good question." He fitted the glasses back on his rather beaky nose, tucked the curled ends of the sidepieces around his ears. "Not sure I know the answer."

She made an exasperated sound. Behind her Firill laughed, a low breathy in-out like pillow down in the ears. "Makes you want to slap him silly, doesn't it." Balancing the tray against her hip, she brushed a pile of paper off one of the little tables, then she nudged it over to Cymel's hassock. She put the tray on the table, lifted the pot and held it poised over one of the cups. "You take honey or sweetsour? And don't tell me you take nothing at all, because you need hot and sweet in you to chase the glums away."

"Honey'll do."

"Honey it is. Don't pay no mind to Mole. He's apt to chase a thought in circles till it's biting its own tail." She took a cup to Mole and thrust it at him with an angular gesture that made him smile tenderly up at her. She scowled at him. "I told you not to fuss at the child; she has enough to cope with without you prying at her." As if she couldn't help herself, once he'd taken the cup from her, she brushed her fingertips along the line of his jaw. "Fool man."

Cymel sipped at the tea; it had an odd flavor, one she didn't know if she liked, but the heat flowed down into her and dissolved the knots the loathsome handling had left in her gut. The need to sleep rested all the heavier on her as the need for wariness vanished. Her eyes drifted shut and she missed the question Firill asked her. "Wha?"

"Where you're staying—will you be able to get in all right? Or will we have to sneak you in?"

Cymel wrapped her hands round the cup and flogged her mind into a transitory alertness. "I've permission to be out. Doorman. Porth's his name. He'll let me in. Isn't the first time. I help Derdo with the tullins and colos, 'specially when one's sick like now."

"I see. Water's going to be hot enough in a minute. We're going to have to do something about your face. Hm. You're going to have one grand black eye for the next week or so, till the bruise fades."

"Oh." Cymel reached up, touched the place where the man had slapped her. She winced. "I must look like . . . what am I going to do? I can't . . ."

"Derdo willing to back you if you cook up a story?"

"Uh-huh. He doesn't like Amys Tyrfaswyf."

"They put you in Tyrfahouse? Poor baby." Firill clicked her tongue. "I see your problem. How's this? One of the tullins had a fit and knocked you in the face with his wing and scratched you up a bit. You said one of them's sick."

"Creulo wouldn't—"

"I know and you know. Would Amys and the rest?"

"I don't know . . . no . . . I suppose not."

"Mole will go see Derdo after we walk you home, won't you, hm?"

"Indubitably, Mistress."

"Hmp. If any of that lot at Tyrfahouse go snooping around, Mole will make sure your stories match. Give me your cup. I want you to drink down some more tea then we'll go deal with your face."

As they walked through the winding narrow streets heading for Boardinghouse Row, Mole said, "Have you had any serious teaching in the craft of Flow handling, Mela?"

"I don't know what you mean by serious, Mole. My father has been giving me lessons on avoiding distractions and word power and like that. Before he was made Court Poet he was going to start me on spells, but he never had a chance to do that."

"Have your Wardens said anything about teaching you?"

"No. I think they think I'm too young. They're all *so* old."

"Foolishness. You need to know how to handle this power you have. With a little finesse you could have used those louts' clothes to hobble them and turn them into clowns with their pants round their ankles. I'm working on some extensions of basic spells right now. Like me to tutor you?"

"Why?"

"You interest me. I've never seen that configuration and degree of power in the hands of someone fundamentally untrained."

"If you can convince Watcher/Scholar Henannt, I'll play. Otherwise, no." As they came round a bend in the lane, Cymel scowled at the elaborately ugly building at the corner of two of the lanes. Tyrfahouse made her wince every time she looked at it. She pulled Firill's cloak closer about her body. "Maybe you should stop here. Amys will make a big stink if she hears about you.''

He grinned at her, snapped his fingers. ''That's the girl. Don't roil the bottomfeeders.''

[2]

Scholar Henannt drew his brows down and stared irritably at Cymel. Those brows were as tangled and prickly as sun-bleached thorn hedges. He was the oldest man Cymel had ever seen and one of the craggiest; his skin was old and crêpy and hung on massive bones. His nose seemed to get bigger and more like a great promontory every time she saw him. ''What happened to your face?''

''Drunk student.'' She knew better than to lie to him. ''It's nothing.''

''Gylas Mardianson thinks it's time to start your formal teaching. You're what? Fourteen? That's absurdly young. Were it anyone else, I wouldn't bother listening. Hmp. He is doing some rather remarkable work with the Flow and seems to think you will be useful so I might as well allow this. I will inform your Housemother of the new arrangement. Because of this . . . incident, you will no longer be permitted out after sixth watch so arrange your hours with Ser Derdo to reflect this change.''

''You're going to tell Amys Tyrfaswyf about it?'' The words rushed out before she thought. She would have called them back if she could, but that wasn't possible. She ran her tongue across her lips and waited for his response.

He cleared his throat, a loud harsh rasping, and his tangled brows dipped lower over eyes the color of ice. ''You didn't?''

Cymel clasped her hands in her lap and told herself she was an idiot and should learn to keep her mouth shut. Aloud, her voice soft and trembling a little, she said, ''I told her it was a tullin's wing that hit me. The other boarders—they're Broon daughters and they never have liked me. If they knew what happened, they'd be really ugly to me.''

''I see.''

She was careful to keep her face quiet, though she was startled by the sudden sympathy in his voice. She didn't understand it and set it aside as something she should ask Mole about.

"A habit of lying to your elders is not a good thing, girl. However, I will pass over this breach of courtesy because I suspect you have had considerable provocation. Hm. We have to lodge you somewhere until you're at least sixteen and the choice is not an extensive one. Do you wish us to transfer you elsewhere?"

Cymel stared down at her hands. She'd love to get away from Raffyn and her shadow Yllys, but these were only two of the six other boarders in Tyrfahouse. The rest weren't friendly but nowhere near as malicious. She thought about the way things were in Carcalon, about Bolryn Hellyddsdattar. Until she was old enough to move into one of the dormitories or into a room set like Firill's, it was likely that any other place the Watchers would put her would probably be just like Tyrfahouse. Besides, if she ignored Raffyn and Yllys, she was quite comfortable where she was; she had a nice big room, the meals weren't bad, the maids kept the place clean and neat, did her washing and ironing so she didn't have to fool with that.

She lifted her head. "No, I can ignore the spite if I've got something else to do."

"Your head is older than your seeming, child. Patience is a weapon if you use it properly."

Cymel dipped her head in a respectful bow, though she was annoyed at the sententiousness in his voice. Amys Housemum was full of little bits like that and dispensed them all too readily to anyone she could make listen.

Scholar Henannt rubbed his hand across his chin, his wrinkled palm rasping across the short white stubble growing there. "Keeping busy. A good idea. Hm. Music and the arts. Yes, I'll see about arranging tutors for those. Students perhaps, not lecturers. You won't have had sufficient grounding for formal classes. Natural philosophy and rhetoric? Not yet, I think. Your age presents a problem, child. It will be difficult to find the right . . . um . . . guides." He leaned forward, positioned his hands carefully on the arms of his chair and grunted himself onto his feet. "Walk with me in the garden. I want to hear what happened when you got that bruising, who was involved and why it was allowed to happen."

[3]

Mole grinned at her. "First lesson. We go visit some friends of mine. I want you to watch and tell me what's going on when we get back here."

The long narrow workroom had astonished Cymel when she walked in to meet her tutor. There were large pillows scattered about on the white glazed tiles of the floor and a few black painted stools pushed up against white-tiled counters. There were huge rectangular mirrors hanging along one side, bigger than any she'd ever seen before. They caught the light from clerestory windows and reflected it onto the odd crystal shapes that were sitting on every surface. The room was alive with light and there were places where it seemed almost solid, as if a being of some sort stood there though it couldn't quite be seen.

Pneuma poured like smoke from crystal to crystal, broke against the mirrors on the wall into the curdles that were like the white water of the stream that had flowed past her house. The room made her uneasy and she was glad when Mole led her out again and started with her across the enclosed garden.

They passed through several other arcades, then turned into an oddly shaped building that seemed to be made from shutters and small round windowpanes.

Mole opened a door and waved Cymel inside.

A sturdy old woman with an abundance of white hair plaited loosely into a single braid looked up from the table where she was working with a stick of charcoal and some ragged sheets of paper. Behind her a waist-high bench ran along a window wall, the light coming through the small round panes playing erratically over hundreds of small clay figures. A short distance beyond the table was a wheeled platform with a big lump of stone on it, pale gray with veins of green running through it. Over in one corner were canvas-shrouded forms that stood like dusty ghosts, shapeless and enigmatic.

"Greetings, Marga."

The old woman acknowledged him with a brisk nod, but she seemed more interested in Cymel. "So you finally caved to the Governors and took a student. I say student because this one is too young to be one of your consorts."

"Cymel, meet Marga of the Bitter Tongue. Well, Master Sculptor Rynnat Margalan Wyldindattar, if one must be formal. Dabbler in the plastic arts, possessed of wit and charm beyond her years."

"Dabbler! Hah! And you say *my* tongue is bitter." She frowned at Cymel. "See that hassock, girl?" She pointed. "Go sit on it and don't move till I say you can." She rooted among the sheets of paper, found one as yet untouched. When she looked up, she saw Cymel hadn't moved. "What are you waiting for? Mole, get her over there. If you're going to use me to illustrate some point or other, you're going to have to give me something for my time. Her."

"What!" Cymel took a step toward the door.

Mole chuckled and caught her wrist in a gentle grip. "Calm down, Mela. You sit, Marga draws. That's all." He tugged at her. "When she's finished, we'll have a look round the studio."

"Why?" She heard how rude that sounded and felt the heat of a blush, but she couldn't think of anything to make the question sound better so she didn't bother trying as she let him pull her over to the hassock.

"Ah! That's what you're going to tell me."

Cymel scowled at the paper and the sketches on it. They were all pieces of her, but nothing was put together.

"Studies," Marga said, and took that sheet away, uncovering the second sheet.

Cymel's head was there, facing forward, right profile, left

profile. She stared at those wiry simple lines that somehow enclosed space in such a way that she could feel the weight of her own flesh existing within their curves. The drawings were quick, simple and astonishing and she knew in a confused way the years of craft that went into that simplicity.

Marga took the sheets from her and handed her a towel. "Charcoal is treacherous stuff, it gets onto the most impossible places. You've smudges all over your face."

Cymel examined the crude clay figures ranged in armies along the countertop. Maquettes, Marga called them. "Why make so many just about alike?"

"Ah! The reason is in that 'just about.' When you put chisel to stone, you have to know where you're going. Shape. It's a thing that must be searched for in the hands, not in the mind. I ring the changes in clay until I have exhausted possibility, then I know what I am looking for and I can ask the stone to give it to me."

"I see. When my father writes his poems, he tries phrases and rhythms almost the same way."

"Hm. Interesting." Marga examined her strong bony hands. "I'm not much for words. Though I admit I'm fond of Mole's dramas. Take you out of yourself, they do." She reached out, took hold of Cymel's right hand, ran her hands absently over the palm and along the fingers, a musing look on her face.

Her touch was curiously impersonal, as if the old woman were a surgeon exploring how the bones fit together. It was an odd feeling. Cymel felt for a moment like those sketches on the first sheet—as if all she was to the sculptor was a collection of body parts, though a collection articulated in a pleasing and interesting fashion.

"Behave yourself, Marga." Mole freed Cymel's hand. "See you later. Mela, we've another visit before we go back to the workroom. Come along."

The building he took her into this time had thick walled corridors with ranks of quilted doors; the builder had done something to the interior that muted sound so that even footsteps on the thick reed mats were silent and words faded inches from the speaker's mouth.

When Mole opened one of those doors and urged her through it, the sudden burst of sound was almost painful and she was in the room before she recognized it as harp music. Despite the pressure of Mole's hand, she stopped and stared. The harp was bigger than the man playing it. She had never seen one that size.

The man hugging the harp was wide across the shoulders with long arms, but his legs were meager and his feet set oddly on the floor. He had an abundance of white hair and a face so deeply lined it looked as if the skin were pleated. He paid no attention at all to them, and though he stopped playing, she understood clearly that their entrance had nothing to do with that.

There was a table beside the harp and on it a soft sort of book made from vellum sheets stitched together at one side. It was curled open and on it were lines of small black squares with tails of varying lengths; some of the tails had slashmarks cutting through them, some had bars, though most were simply unbroken black lines. He leaned over, ran his finger along one of the lines, scowling at the march of the squares, then he straightened, leaned into the harp again and began playing the same notes she'd heard when she came in.

She listened as she let Mole lead her to a bench at the side of the practice room. Same notes, she was sure of that, but he was putting them together with a difference, a shift of rhythm maybe or something subtler. She turned to Mole, started to speak.

He put a finger on her lips, shook his head, then he leaned close and murmured in her ear, "Just listen. Too much talking disturbs him."

The harpist played over and over the same snatch of music until he was satisfied, then he played it over yet more as if to wear it so deeply into his ears and his fingers that he needn't think about it ever again. Played it over and over until Cymel felt like screaming. Instead, she reached over to Mole's arm and pinched him hard.

He grinned at her, trapped her hand and held it away from his arm. "Listen," he whispered. "This is your tutor speaking to you, the voice of Dyf Tanew."

The harpist shook his hands, then dropped them on his thighs and sat back. He seemed to see them for the first time. "What you doing here, Mole? Haven't seen you outside your mole-hole for ages."

"I have taken to myself a pupil, Cys. And I'm using you for a lesson."

"Hah!" He turned his upper body so he could stare at Cymel. "Young, isn't she? Nursery bait. Not like you."

"I'm not sleeping with her, I'm teaching her Flow. Cymel, this evil-minded old gafr is Master Harpist Ryn Cystal Oerison. Cys, invite her to your recital. Least you can do after torturing the poor child's ears the past hour."

Cystal inclined his torso in a seated bow, then smiled at Cymel. "Since we share the first letters of our names, we are fated to be friends, Cymel. Not because this crazy youth demands it, but because it pleases me, I bid you come and hear me play. I'll leave a pass at the door, Mole. Now the two of you, get out of here and let me work."

Mole led her through his glittering workroom and out into a tiny garden with an even tinier fountain playing in the middle beneath a cau tree putting out new leaves, pale green and fragile as bobbin lace. He pointed at a stone bench by the fountain and leaned against the tree's gray trunk.

"The pass to Cystal's recital is more of a favor than you know, Mela. When he plays the room is filled even to standing room in the corners. His health keeps him at Cyfareth these days and those who want to hear him come from everywhere, even halfway round the world, for the privilege." He was silent a moment. "And you see how he takes time and spends his energy perfecting what to other ears is already perfect."

Cymel wriggled on the bench, feeling more than a little impatient. She'd enjoyed the visits and liked both of the Masters, but she didn't see the point. She wanted to learn magic, not drawing or music.

He dropped his seriousness and smiled at her again, that slow, happy, utterly charming smile that dissolved anger like sun melted ice. As if he'd read her mind, he said, "You're wondering what all this has to do with the Sight."

"Yes." She thought about saying more, but didn't.

"Tell me the most important thing you noticed about Marga."

Cymel thought about that a moment. "Shape lies in the hand, not the mind. I think that's not true, though. I think you need both, the mind to look and the hand to feel." She brooded over this, not satisfied. "And the eye to see," she said, the words rushing out. "To override what the mind knows and really see what's there. No. That's not right either. Eye and hand working together to override the mind. The mind there to recognize possibility so hand and eye can do their work. That's all confused, but that's what I learned from watching her, not from what she said."

"And the next most important?"

"Hm. That it takes time and lots of practice to learn to do this."

"Good enough to begin with. Now, what about Cystal?"

"That there's no end to learning. Even when you're the best in all the world at what you do."

"Not bad for one afternoon. You're a clear-eyed child and smarter than most. Do you disconcert yourself sometimes? I suspect you must upset more commonplace folk even more." He cleared his throat, folded his arms across his chest. "It is my contention that work with the Flow is more an art than a craft or a science and to do it well you must develop a feel for it as Marga has for line and volume, as Cystal has for melody and rhythm. What you've been taught so far, maybe whatever you've worked out for yourself, it's all tricks. Same with your father and the rest of the Watchers, the war wizards and even the Mages. As if they pressed the Pneuma into a colander and collected the strings that passed through the holes. Some very powerful tricks in those strings, of course, but with no sense of them being connected to each other as part of a whole. I haven't taken a pupil before this because I have never found any with the capacity to reach beyond the known. I think you have that, Cymel. Perhaps because you're a braid of two worlds.''

Cymel tried to hide her disappointment, but he must have read it in her face or the pose of her body, because his eyes went sad.

"Oh, I *will* teach you tricks, some very clever ones, but I need to show you how they fit together so it will be slow and difficult." He shook his head. "Very difficult. I'll have you practicing till your ears bleed."

"Until I'm bored out of my skull and ready to bite?" She grinned at him. "That sounds better than that other stuff. As long as we *do* something and you don't just talk at me all the time. Look, Pa made me memorize the old-time History Chants and give them back to him without a misplaced halt. I can do boring stuff if there's something there in the end."

He shouted laughter. "Mela, my Mela, I will try not to be as boring as all that."

[4]

Two weeks after her visit to the studio and the practice room, Cymel lay on her back on a low couch, watching as Mole finished tying a crystal to one of the thin silver chains that hung like icicles from the ceiling. The crystal was irregular in shape, rather like a water-polished pebble with a hole through one end. The light reflected from the mirrors touched it and seemed to flow along its hollows and knobs, an odd and enticing effect.

Mole tapped the crystal and sent it swinging gently back and forth, then he stepped off the short ladder, collapsed it and took it across the room to the niche he'd fetched it from. He kicked one of the floor pillows across to the couch and settled himself on it. "I'm going to put my hand on yours, Mela."

His hand was warm, at first disturbing, then merely comfortable. She let out a breath in a long sigh.

His voice muted, as liquid as the light, he murmured, "I'll be guiding you through this so you can't possibly get lost. Just relax and watch how the light flows through and around the moving crystal. See that and only that. Let yourself flow with it. You can trust me, you know that, you feel that. I won't leave you, I won't let you be hurt. See how the light gains form from the crystal, how it slides so smoothly about it, always changing, yet always the same. Let yourself know that without thought, always changing always the same . . ."

He was a warm, enveloping quilt.

He was her father, standing in a pool downstream from the house, hands strong, holding her up, teaching her to float, teaching her to swim.

He was himself, her friend, a man she trusted above all others, a man she was beginning to love in a way that sometimes frightened her, sometimes made her angry because she knew he would never acknowledge it.

She watched the light slide over the uneven curves of the crystal, watched it go round and round a while, then spill over, dropping down around her, a waterfall of light, a pool of light, she floated in light. She could feel it rippling and lifting her.

Mole's hands held her. He wouldn't let her drown.

She breathed light and tasted it. It tasted like cold water.

Mole spoke. She was inside the words. At first she couldn't understand them, then she did.

"You are inside the Flow, Cymel. Experience it. Learn it. Use your senses not your mind. Shape is in the hands, not the head."

She scooped up a handful of light, poured it from hand to hand. Watched smoke feathers sublime away from the Flow, like her breath on a deep winter morning—but it was neither cold nor hot. It came to her that there were no words for what it was. For the first time she caught a glimmer of what Mole was trying to teach her. Then she let that thought fade with the first handful of Flow.

She dipped her hand into the swirling light and shaped what she took into a crude representation of a bird, a tiny tullin only as long as her pointing finger. She perched it on a crooked forefinger and watched, amazed, as the creature took on detail, eyes and feather and delicate pink legs. A moment later, it flapped its wings and flew away.

Her hand was still raised. She stared at the suddenly unweighted finger. Interesting. One need only point the way. Dangerous too. If one doesn't understand what one's doing.

She shivered with a sudden chill.

Mole's hands grew warmer, the warmth spread through her body. He spoke.

Once again understanding was late in coming but at last she puzzled out his words.

"Cymel. Cymel. Mela. Close your eyes, think of the workroom. Remember . . ."

She followed the sound of his voice out of the Flow. She didn't know the workroom well enough to use it as an anchor, he should have understood that, it bothered her like a fugitive itch that he hadn't understood that, but his voice and the warmth of his hands—or was it his hand over hers—just one hand—she remembered that, focused on that, the long, rather bony hand with the flat fingernails and the thin pale hairs on the backs of the bottom joints of the fingers. There was a small scar in the ball of his thumb with the lines of the thumbprint springing away from it like hair from a part.

She opened her eyes. Blinked up into Mole's rather worried face.

He helped her sit up, brought her a glass of water. As she sipped at it, he said, "I rather seriously underestimated your capacity, Cymel. You went farther on this dip than I managed in a year of trying."

Cymel patted a yawn, took another sip of water and wondered how she was going to manage to get home. She was exhausted. Even the time when she forced the Bridge on Aunt

Cory and rescued Lyanz hadn't left her so wiped out. "I have a guide," she said drowsily. "You didn't."

"Perhaps so." He took the glass away from her and pulled her onto her feet. "You need to go home and take a nap. I'll walk you to Tyrfahouse. Never can tell when one of these sessions is going to kick back on you. No harm to it." He frowned. "Or at least, I thought there wasn't." He slipped his hand under her arm and eased her toward the door. "You surprised me, you know."

"You aren't the first." She sniffed and moved away from his hand. "I'm not going to run away or fall on my face."

He didn't bother explaining or arguing with her, he just moved himself a pace away from her and strolled along chatting as easily as if she hadn't snapped at him.

Cymel sighed, suddenly missing Breith. At least he took her seriously enough to yell at her. Then she thought about the next time he popped his Window through and grinned to herself. I'm going to show him some spells! She giggled as she remembered how irritatingly smug he'd been when he made the Window the first time.

Mole reached over, tapped her arm. "Put what you're thinking right out of your head, Mela. If you try using what I teach you before you're ready, I'm going to shut you down till you learn some discipline. And if you don't think I can, you're as much a dreamer as those Broon maids coming here for polish and husbands."

"What do you think you are, a mind reader?"

"Who needs to read minds to know what's written in large letters across that pretty face of yours?"

"You think I'm pretty?"

"Hm. Not really. I think in a few years you're going to be beautiful. Pretty is a thin gloss that wears out fast." He stopped in front of Tyrfahouse. "I want you to get a pot of hot tea and load it with honey. Chug it down. Take a bath. Crawl in bed and wrap your quilts around you. When you're warm and relaxed I want you to think about these two weeks of lessons. Replay them until you're too sleepy to think anymore. Then you sleep till you wake up. No nonsense about meal call or work in the birdhouse.''

"All right. When's the next lesson?"

"In a fortnight. Not before."

"And I'm not supposed to do anything?" Her indignation turned her voice shrill and loud enough to attract attention from Duryn, who was coming through the door, pulling on the pastel silk gloves that were high fashion for afternoon calls; she had many pairs of these gloves because she was vain about her small delicate hands. She was a plump, soft girl with fine brown hair that she twisted into the wiglets she used to give it some body so it wouldn't hang lank and wispy about her round face. She was playing at music and poetry with few signs of talent at either.

Duryn stared at Mole, then came smiling over to Cymel. "Mela, you have hidden talents. Introduce me to your friend."

Ignoring Duryn would just make things worse. Her face carefully blank, Cymel said, "Broona Duryn gan Pallu, be pleased to meet my teacher the Craft Master Gylas Mardianson of the College of Natural Philosophy."

"Craft Master Gylas? Oh, I adore your dramas, the last one was so . . . so moving." Small lavender silk hands fluttered. "Where do you get your ideas? I could never think of anything so clever."

Cymel smothered a grin at the quickly erased exasperation on Mole's face.

"How kind of you," he said. He turned to Cymel. "I'll see you later, Mela." He nodded to Duryn and walked away.

Duryn looked annoyed, then she went on her way with a fillip of her skirt and a sniff that were meant to inform Cymel once again that she was lower than a worm's belly and less worthy of notice.

"Sweet."

She started as Mole's voice sounded in her ear. "Coward," she said.

"Fervently. When it comes to dangers like that one."

She giggled.

"You haven't been to any dramas, have you."

"Only way I'm let out at night is to go to the birdhouse. And Scholar Henannt has axed that now."

"Hm. That's a problem. Firill told me I should be sure to get you to the new one. She wants to show off. She has the prime role, you see."

"Well, if I take your advice and don't roil the bottomfeeders, there's a tree outside my window. I could get down it, but I couldn't get back up without help. And where's this drama supposed to be?"

"I'll send someone to collect you. I'll be having nervous fits at the time and screaming at people so I can't come. Hm. Paffra, I think. She's a friend and owes me a favor or two. Come over to the workroom tomorrow and we'll work it out."

"Won't you get in trouble over this from the Watchers?"

"You want to come or don't you?"

"Yes." The word was a squeal. She slapped her hand over her mouth and looked around to see if anyone had noticed.

Mole grinned at her. "Mela, I walk the road I choose for myself. If I get booted from here, I'll find another place. I don't worry about that kind of thing. Just wastes time and vigor on stupidity. I'll see you tomorrow, first watch after noon."

[5]

Cymel backed onto the sill, balanced on one knee and felt about with her other foot for the crotch where the limb joined the tree. She grunted as she found solid footing, pushed away from the window and began swinging down the tree.

There was a chirrup from the bushes as she hit the ground and she hurried to join Paffra who was waiting there, carefully hidden from the windows.

"Come on, Mela," Paffra whispered. "We've got to hurry."

"Is it starting earlier?"

"No, but Firill and me, we've fixed up a present for you and we have to drop by her place and pick it up."

* * *

On the rumpled bed there was a black leather skirt, a black knitted silk top with long sleeves and a rolldown neck, a beaded black and silver vest, with long beaded fringes around the bottom, a silver beaded hair tie. On the floor beside the bed sat black and silver beaded slippers.

"Oh!" Cymel crooked a finger and smoothed the back of it down the vest.

"We wanted your first dramá to be special. Now, what you do is go wash that tree off your hands. When you're dressed in the new stuff, I'll do your face paint then we're off to see the show. You like my paint?"

Cymel turned. Paffra had outlined in black a spray of five pointed stars across one cheek and painted them silver. On the other cheek she had a full moon with the Moonconey as a black silhouette within the silver disc. "Yes," she said, and began taking off her skirt. "I like that a lot. You did them?"

"Lefel did them for me. He's going to be a shipbuilder so he's got nice steady hands. We're a thing." She collected Cymel's discarded clothing, folded it and put it away in a cloth bag with a shoulder strap. She raised her voice so Cymel could hear her over the rush of the water. "That means we go round together and might end up lovers but we haven't got that far yet."

Cymel dried her hands and came back into the bed-sitting room. "I thought you were Mole's friend."

"Oh Mole, he has more girls than a farmyard rooster. And he changes them when he pleases. He's easy to like, you know. It's because he has eight sisters, all older than him, so he knows a lot about women and it's because he likes you back. But you should understand right away he's a slippery slidy sort, not one to lean on for more than a little while."

"You warning me?"

Paffra wrinkled here nose, sighed. "No. Talking to myself. If I say it often enough, maybe I'll start believing it." She inspected Cymel. "Firill was right, you look great. Time for paint. I think a silver butterfly on your right cheek and leave it at that. Sometimes less fuss makes a louder shout.''

The cellar was a vast space beneath one of the History School's buildings. The room was packed with people, all of them talking loud and fast as they sat around smallish tables from lots of different sources, old and battered from years of use. They sat in backless folding chairs with canvas seats, leaning forward, elbows on the tables, their faces lit by the short fat white candles that stood in their own grease in the center of each table. The walls were muffled with black hangings from some anonymous source, hangings that fluttered constantly in the drafts that crawled about the walls and curled about the feet of the spectators seated at the tables.

In the middle of one of the long sides of the cellar there was a low stage, just a wooden platform raised waist high above the concrete floor with a line of reflector lamps providing a strong orange light. There was a backdrop rising behind the stage, half of it painted with an outdoor scene, trees, a stream, a line of snowcapped peaks in the distance, half of it an interior setting, a parlor with windows looking on a garden and paneled walls. On the stage itself there were potted bushes and a sort of gravel path, a low divan and several chairs.

More black curtains of some kind fell about the sides, providing wait-spaces for those putting on the drama, and at the front of the stage near the left side was a lower dais, where three musicians were seated, chatting, their instruments at hand, a harp, a lute and a tweekhorn.

Agitated by more than the drafts, the offstage bulged and fluttered while fragments of curses, demands, nervous laughs leaked from behind them.

Having wriggled her way through the crowd with Cymel keeping close behind her, Paffra tapped the shoulder of a man seated at one of the tables near the front. ''We made it, Leff.''

The man swung round, his brows coming up as he saw Cymel. He waved a hand at the chairs, turned to Paffra. ''Got some good glares waiting for you to show up.''

Paffra snorted. "And you were oh so sorry. Right?"

He mimed a cat licking its paws, grinned at her.

Mole thrust his head around one of the edge curtains; his hair was clumped into spikes and his face shiny with sweat streaks. "Time," he said.

The musicians took up their instruments and, after a few moments of fiddling with them, began playing a lively dance tune.

When the noise in the cellar faded to silence, the music changed, softened, took on a musing note.

On stage the curtains at both sides bulged and two sets of dancers moved onto the stage. In the garden four women in silver gauze circled each other with dreamy smooth gestures and slow stretches, hands grazing for momentary support, moving apart again. The lute played for them, liquid purls of sound. In the house four men in black leather danced an angular reel as if each were alone on that part of the stage. They carefully did not interfere with each other and equally carefully cultivated the impression that this was merely by chance, never by design. The tweekhorn played for them, sharp bursts of sound cutting through the flow of the lute. And the harp bound the two together in a way that Cymel could not understand, disharmony made harmony by this third force.

The music broke off suddenly and the dancers stopped moving as if it were their life force and without it they were turned to stone. Black curtains slid across the stage. A woman walked with them, one hand on the edge of the left-hand curtain, as if she drew them shut. She was dressed in an odd long robe, the cloth of the robe black and white squares of differing size so they seemed to swirl, dip and thrust outward even when she was still. The robe was cut to display her slim figure, with a high collar that served as a frame to the sparely detailed porcelain mask that covered her face—a face worn on a face, as it were.

She turned to the audience, her arms bent, the palms shoulder high and turned outward. "I am prologue," she said, her rich warm voice projected outward, seeming to fill the cellar.

Cymel started. It was Firill. She hadn't recognized her at all until she spoke. She turned to Paffra, but let her questions die as the woman set her finger across her lips and shook her head.

I bring to you a tale of seduction and betrayal, of despair and triumph and ultimate sadness, for that is the human condition. All things pass, the good often more swiftly than the evil.

Let me tell you how it was.

In the days of Tyrn Dorallin when raiders rode the spring winds out of the Northlands and harried the Halsianel Coast without let or surcease, Broona Serinth gan Turma rode on an errand of mercy to the Broon farm of Horwad Uchelsson.

Prologue lifted her mask and bowed. "I will present the Broona Serinth."

She fitted the mask in place again, repositioned her arms and hands and went on with the prologue, introducing the actors as they were mentioned.

Cymel was a little restless at first. The prologue seemed overlong and there was so much in it which she thought she had to remember that it felt like one of those study sessions with her father when he chanted history verse at her and tested her on the details later. Once the drama began to unfold, however, she found herself laughing and crying, gasping and blushing, utterly absorbed by what was happening in front of her.

[6]

Mole stopped her in the bushes. "Have a look round, Mela. Any trouble waiting?"

"How do I do that?"

"Think on it, I'm sure you'll figure a way."

"You're my teacher, tell me."

"Right. Teacher not puppetmaster. Think."

"I'm tired."

"So?"

"You're not nice."

"If I were a nice person, I'd be treating you like the child
your years say you are and you wouldn't be here."

Cymel sighed. She'd drifted in a pleasant haze as Mole
walked her home from the after party. She was drained and
yet filled with delight and a vague sense of the joys that were
waiting for her in the following months. She didn't want to
come to earth, but he wasn't going to let her go in until he
was satisfied it was safe, so she'd better get to work.

None of the Broon daughters or Housemum Amys had
enough Sight or skill to light a match, so she didn't have to
worry about them feeling her nosing about. Nosing. Smell . .
hm . . . no, that won't work . . . scrying . . . I'd need a mirror
. . . but I don't know how to use it yet, Mole wouldn't . . . but
maybe not . . . maybe I can make a mirror and send it . . . if I
can't bring pictures to a mirror, I can send a mirror to . . .

Cymel dropped to a squat, arms draped over her knees, her
fingers touching the cold, dew-wet ground, the touch steadying
her, letting her feel the earth as a hand cradling her, keeping
her safe. She focused on the Flow, teased a bit of it apart from
the rest and began kneading it, shaping it as Master Margalan
worked her clay, shaping it as she had when she'd formed the
miniature tullin.

When she finished, she had a scrying mirror, round and
curved like a shallow bowl. She contemplated what she'd
made, thought about how to use it, then sent it skimming at
the house.

The mirror slipped through the walls without hesitation,
then hung in midair outside the Doorman's niche, waiting for
her to send it on. She concentrated and found she could see
what the mirror reflected, a tiny image but very clear.

Porth was seated in a stuffed chair, his feet up on a hassock.
He had a book open on his lap, had been reading it in the
light of the small lamp on the table at his elbow, but the

limpness of his hands, the slow rise and fall of his chest, told her he'd fallen into a doze.

Satisfied, she sent the mirror slipping through the house, then let it dissolve. She lifted an arm and with a distant wonder watched it tremble with the effort. "Give me a hand up," she murmured, groaned as Mole pulled her to her feet.

"Well?" he said.

She yawned. "You see what I did?"

"No. You can come tell me tomorrow."

"Mmm. They're all sleeping. My room's like I left it far as I can tell."

"Hm. I can show you some knots tomorrow that will yell warning about intruders." He tucked his finger under her chin and lifted her head so he was looking into her eyes. "Tricks, yes. Why change my mind? Because you don't know how strong you are, that's why. When you hatch, little butterfly, and emerge into the world full grown, it won't know what hit it." He took his hand away. "Come on. Time I boosted you into your tree and got you home to bed."

[7]

Eight months later, Cymel crawled into her window after another night out and smiled to herself as she saw Breith's Window waiting for her and felt his frustration and impatience. He deserved a little frustration, leaving her alone so long.

" 'Lo, Breith," she said. "Give me a minute till I light a lamp."

4

Dur's War

By the secret calendar of the Watchers, events dating from the 21st day of Degamis in the Glandairic year 736 till the 19th day of Cyntamis, the first month in the 738th Galandairic year since the last Settling.

[1]

The Mage Mahara stood on an outthrust of rock above the mountain pass, his black robes blowing in a suddenly burning wind, great gouts of steam swirling before him as he melted the snow on the slopes ahead.

Dur watched Mahara as long as he could see him. He'd carefully noted the pattern of Flowlines as the Mage cleared the passes and itched to see if he could play fire like that, but he didn't try to light as much as a match. If Mahara felt another Mage active in the vicinity, he'd dig him out fast. And Dur knew only too well how vulnerable and ignorant he still was.

As his askerit turned the last corner before the descent into Tilkos, he nearly walked onto the heels of the man in front of him who had stopped dead in the middle of the road.

On the vast field of snow below them the rebel army was drawn up to meet them. Before and behind that army, two great forms of painted light rose from the valley floor, confronting each other.

Rueth, the Serpent of Kale. Winged dragon, mouth open, hissing, great teeth whiter than the snow on the peaks, scales glittering like plates of emerald, ruby and topaz. Body arched. Forearms lifted, ebon claws ready to strike.

The Dread Wyrm of Tilkos. Rising from coil upon coil of body, hood extended, poison teeth dripping ocher fire, eyes hotter than the sun at midsummer.

The Gods of this world walk, Dur thought. And join battle like their worshipers. Part of the Settling, that was. Fanach had read him something like that from the books stored at the caves. He scowled. He was going to have to replace her as soon as he got back to Iomard.

Tegmal Mikal came stomping back along the line, cursing them and using his baton to punch the askerit back into marching order.

They moved on.

As they crossed from Kale to Tilkos, heading for the plain where the rebel army was in place and waiting for them, Dur grew increasingly nervous. He needed still to watch strategy and tactics in a real war situation, but he didn't relish the thought of getting killed or maimed on a strange world in a war that had nothing to do with him or his desires. The Pneuma was swirling and seething, the currents wild as a river in spate. The Flux was so disturbed that it seemed unlikely that the Mage would sense a further disturbance so he risked tapping the Flow to draw a store of power into himself in case he needed to vanish from disaster.

The enemy was camped in a wide, shallow curve, tiny bright figures on a ground of white, about half a foot of snow laid about them in a soft white blanket that concealed the irregularities of the land. Pavilions bright with saturated color and circles of fire, the dark amoebas of the horse herds and the angular shapes of feed wagons. Pennants on lance poles snapping in the wind, the green and gold of Tilkos. As Dur paced downward, the whole Kale army confined to that rutted narrow road that led from the pass, the army that waited for them appeared and vanished, appeared and vanished, as the road turned and twisted through the mountains.

To his mind this was stupid. Worse than tribufs in a slaughter chute. Were he leading that rebel army he'd set on these invaders as they came through the chute, before they had a chance to get themselves set for attack. He didn't understand why they were just standing there, waiting. *I need to know* he thought. *There's a reason things are happening like this Mahara? That roaring storm in the Pneuma?*

Mahara couldn't keep this up long. After the enormous expenditure of force to clear out the pass, he'd be burning so hot now that he'd burn himself out if he didn't shut down soon and do his reordering exercises.

As the snow melted at the touch of the furnace wind, great rolls of fog billowed upward, hiding the rebel army, swallowing finally the immense forms of Rueth and the Wyrm of Tilkos.

By the time the sky cleared again, both gods had vanished

The Kale army was only halfway through the mountains when the sun went down. They camped at several levels of the twisty road, tramping into mud the glades and meadows, shattering the chill silence of the forest with shouts, curses, complaints, yelps. Cords of wood came thumping down every few moments, flown by war wizards from the places where woodcutters had been working all day. Sacks of grain for the livestock came off the wagons. Water in white sheets filled the tanks. Hammering from the foot-soldiers pegging in their tents. Organized confusion.

The noise gradually quieted as the setting up was completed and the thickening aroma of the inevitable trail stew began drifting on the nightwind that wound between the trees. The stew was hot and filling though boring and bland as Rueth's holy farts, and the cook who managed to score and hoard a few spices was a pampered prize in those askerits that were fortunate enough to have them. Tegmal Mikal was a man of experience and forethought, though he never talked about exactly where he'd got that experience. He had his own store of spices and managed to see that the cook got time and coin to

tock up on this and that. Askerit 502 ate well and slept dry.
Dur was increasingly pleased with the lot that Luck had dealt
him.

The Third Prince moved that night among the askerits, stopping for a word here, a joke there, a name remembered, a bit
of praise.

Dur watched the flow of the torches that accompanied the
Prince, listened to the swell of the voices in the other camps
and felt the lift to the spirits of his own askerit when the Third
Prince rode his Aygirsade black into the circle of firelight. He
made a note. Morale is important and it has to be cultivated
assiduously but also with skill. The light touch, slightly coarse,
is best.

The side of the mountain and the thick stands of brush provided some shelter, but wisps of fog were caught in the tree-
tops and dripped endlessly on them. The wood they used was
wet and smoky, though it provided light and enough heat to
warm food and take the edge off the chill.

A water wizard had kept the tank wagons filled on the
march across Kale, now another wizard had taken up a supply
role. Interesting. These wizards gathered like a flock of crows
about the Third Prince and his Guard. Their range was narrow,
but within that range they were formidable—all the more so
in Dur's estimation because he had not yet managed to untan-
gle the knots they used to force the Pneuma to fetch and carry
for them. It was as if wizardry were so alien to a Mage's
thought that he couldn't even perceive what a wizard did.
There was nothing on Iomard to match them.

As Dur came back from the woodpile with more wood for
his askerit's fire, he brooded over the wizards. Might be a good
idea to round up several of them and somehow Bridge them
over to Iomard. He unloaded the wood in the circle of tents,
carried a few splits to the fire and laid them across the coals
between the legs of the tripod. The kettle was already filled
with water and heating slowly toward a boil. In a short while
he'd be cradling a can of the hot strong tea he'd learned to
like after a long day's march. Bridging wizards. Hm. At the

moment he couldn't get himself back home, let alone a gaggle
of wizards. I'll worry about that when the time comes, he
thought. I still have a lot to learn about actually fighting a war.

[2]

The battle began at mid-morning.

The askerits marched back and forth across the snowplain
as the two armies shifted position, rather like two large amoebas feinting at each other, then they stood where they'd been
put in a field of trampled, melting slush, the askers leaning on
their pikes, waiting for orders to move again.

Dur's askerit was stationed at the rear of the left wing of
the formation. He couldn't see anything from where he was
standing except the backs of a lot of heads and the flags around
the Third Prince. And occasionally a flag on the rebel side.
The sun was bright and warm, the sky clear, but the wind was
sheer ice and cut him to the bone, especially as the slush and
muck from the melting snow soaked his feet and he was no
longer moving about enough to keep warm. It seemed ludi-
crous to him to come so far and spend so much time educating
himself only to find himself dead of pneumonia.

Overhead, the Pneuma Flow seethed and churned, as stormy
as the wildest white-water slide on an untamed river. He took
a chance and bled a tiny trickle into himself, just enough to
warm him and smooth over the chilblains on his feet. He heard
a grunt to his left, then sucking noises as Bakuch the Myndya
smuggler shifted his feet.

Bakuch met his eyes, grimaced, muttered from the corner
of his mouth, "Stupid shimuks, gonna kill us all."

Dur glanced around quickly. The tegmal was standing at the
front of the askerit, his body slumped into his pike, and the
rest of the askers were too concerned with their own miseries
to bother listening to someone else's. "What's happening?"
he whispered.

"Fug 'em all, you know as much as I do. Know-all Jorr
says he heard the wizards do their thing first, then they send
us in."

"With our feet froze."

"You said it."

Dur shivered as he felt an organic spikiness creep into the Pneuma, as if it were yeast on a growth spurt. It was not a form he was accustomed to, nor even one he'd seen before. A black figure suddenly rose high in the air above the rebel army. On the Kale side, their war wizards also rose and fell like toys on a string. This looked so absurd that at first Dur wanted to laugh—then there was a sudden odd *!crump!* from somewhere round the front of the army and a moment later black smoke began billowing upward. It tried to spread out over the Kale army, but seemed to be battering at a shield of some kind—if smoke could be said to batter anything.

Wisps of the smoke managed to break through and travel a short distance before they dissipated, leaving behind an appalling stench. But it didn't last long enough to feel dangerous.

The wizards' rise and fall continued.

A moment later something with the effect of a huge fist gathered the cloud and flung it back at the rebel army.

Before it reached the front ranks, it melted into the air and was gone.

Nothing happened for several breaths, then Dur swayed as the earth shifted under his feet.

A jagged crack came racing across the ground toward them, gouts of thick, stinking smoke billowing from it—one of many such crevices that struck inward into the heart of the Kale army. Without stopping to think, Dur flung a shield around the askerit and drove a shunt into the ground between him and the advancing fault.

An instant later, the signal horn sounded the two-note call of the Down. Dur dropped onto his stomach, heard Mikal yelling at the pair of Yuskova herders because they were slow to follow the Call. He got his own nose out of the mud and saw the tegmal crouching low, his head turning, his eyes scanning the askerits around them and lingering briefly on the chasm close beside him.

A gale-force wind came sweeping suddenly across the prone

figures, blowing the fumes from the crevices back toward the rebel army.

Shivering with cold and with the stupidity of what he'd just done, Dur watched the earth close up. With no time to think, he had protected not just himself but the whole askerit. Which was both appalling and interesting. Something to remember. Training can create bonds between men even when they don't realize what's happening. Small groups, not big ones. And those bonds operate on an instinctual level.

He felt carefully about, touching the Pneuma Flow, trying to read any disturbances tied to him.

As far as he could tell, there were none. He'd got away with it. This time. Probably the war wizards had kicked up enough turmoil to mask his actions.

The sky darkened suddenly. He twisted his head around and looked up. Clouds. Thick and black.

Abruptly, lightning speared downward into the mass of the rebels. Again and again it struck. One of the floating enemy wizards flung out his arms and fell without a sound onto the heads of the army below. Dur heard screams from horses and men, sounds of confusion, stampede. And mingled with these, the horn again, cutting short the Down. Dur scrambled to his feet, hit at the mud on his front, knocking as much of it off him as he could. As he worked, he heard the horn sounding again, the calls meant for the front ranks. He and the others back here were in the reserves and had nothing to do but stand and wait until it was their turn to mount an attack.

He could still see little but the heads in front of him, but he could hear the ululations of the charging askers and see the walk of smaller lightnings across the gap between the armies.

By sundown the Third Prince had taken the ground where the rebels had camped and scattered them into flight. Dur had done nothing, seen little, spent the time leaning on his pike, bored and frustrated. When the order to march came, he picked up his pack and walked with his askerit across that broken bloody ground then marched back to bury the dead and collect the wounded.

[3]

Tegmal Mikal stood with his hands behind him, the campfire turning his face to a red and black mask. "I guess you lot figure we whomped the Tilkers good and it's just a matter of cleaning up, then we go home. Yeah, I see you do. Get that sappy grin off your face, Sohluc. You haven't a clue in that dome of yours. We hit 'em hard today. Cursed chisms hit back too. They wasn't roots you was out burying not so long ago. So we got patrol tonight. You know patrol. Keep your eyes open 'n your mouths shut and you spot any Tilkers you yell loud, pull square and do your chismin best to stop 'em coming and wipe 'em out. I'll take first squad. Bakuch, you make second. Now to moonset then moonset to dawn."

Dur moved silently through the dark, his senses alert. He could feel hostility around them. They were being watched. The attack would come soon. He figured that was why Mikal took the first patrol. The tegmal expected the Tilkers to hit them as soon as it was dark enough.

Made sense that way. The Kale army would be tired and triumphant enough to let down its guard maybe just a little. Enough to give an edge to men well-known for their horsemanship and their daring. He expected it to be a mounted attack, hit, slash and retreat. And was rather eager for it to happen since that would vindicate his judgment and give evidence that he was really beginning to learn this business.

He was two men back from the tegmal as the patrol moved at a steady walk along the perimeter of the camp. The section they were responsible for was on the northwest side, an hour's walk over uneven brushy ground where visibility was limited and a strong wind blew debris and dead limbs about, making such a noise that it was hard to hear even their own footsteps.

The Flow was quiet now and he didn't dare touch it, but he had enough Pneuma stowed away that he could use it to enhance sight and hearing. If he chose to use it. He was puzzled about how to go. The days of steady march across the Yuskova, the high plain of central Kale, had settled into a comfortable rhythm. In spite of the secrets he held, he had real friends for the first time since he was a boy. He liked the easy back-and-forth, he liked the shared life. He didn't want it to end.

Then they hit the mountains and the blocked passes. Mahara sank his fists into the Flow and turned it to fire to burn the passes clean. And everything changed. The big sloppy worm crawling across the dusty plain went jittery, as if it had just rolled onto a griddle.

He thought about that and about why the Third Prince hadn't gone after the rebel army when it broke apart and fled. And about what the tegmal had said. There was something there . . . the worm wasn't ready yet . . . it needed settling . . . the parts glued together again, askerit to askerit. Interesting. When you started on a new phase, you had to reintegrate your army, shake it down into another sort of whole.

It was not something he'd had to cope with while he was leading his band of raiders and he preened a little at his wisdom in coming across the membrane. However, if he got himself killed while he was here, all his accumulated learning would be worth no more than the dirt that buried him. So. Take a minor chance that a probing wizard wouldn't pick up on his tricks. Mahara would still be in rest phase, more concerned with his own inner workings than the antics of the arm. No need to worry about him.

Wait. Another possibility to factor in.

If there are Tilkers out there prepared for ambush, they might have Flow readers with them, or someone with a touch of the Sight. He walked in the footprints of the man ahead of him and thought about that.

Though the Flow had smoothed out considerably once the war wizards had stopped their manipulations, there were still free-floating pockets of Pneuma about and smaller bits clinging to tents and other gear—perhaps enough to blur perception. Mikal was convinced there'd be rebel ambushes tonight; he'd made that very clear. *Better to know where they are even if I attract interest I don't want.*

He shaped Pneuma. A moment later he shivered as sounds that had tickled at him now crashed in his ears; the rustle of dead leaves and the rubbing of bare branches were shouts, not whispers, and his eyes watered at the suddenly enhanced moonlight.

A moment later he heard dull rhythmic sounds coming from the darkness out where the plain broke into low hummocks crossed with shallow ravines. The whuffs of horses' breathing, the thump and scrape of their feet against the frozen ground.

He ventured a fine and fragile probe, touched anger and determination and let the probe melt into the air.

Now what do I do?

He chewed over possibilities for a moment then he moved from his place and walked faster so he caught up with the tegmal.

"Ambush out there," he murmured.

Mikal turned, eyes narrowed, the lines deepening in his face. "How?"

"Heard horses, sir. Over there." Using his body to conceal it from any watchers in the ambush, he lifted a hand and pointed. "Think maybe nine, eleven. Like that."

The tegmal strolled on, his hand closed round Dur's arm, his voice pitched to reach Dur's ears and not beyond. "You're a thinker and a wanting man scratching for a way to climb. I've seen you taking in and not saying much. Measuring. Nothing wrong with that long's you don't go selling what isn't yours to buy that ladder you're looking for. Just how sure are you?"

"Solid sure."

"Bet your hide on it?"

"What?"

"This a cloud's tale, twenty strokes of the bokhir. Your back's hide, asker."

"No risk of that. They're out there. What happens now?"

"You drop back in line till we hit those trees up ahead. Then we take 'em out."

Dur moved quickly through the brush and snow, shifting his feet as silently as he could, keeping a screen of brush or the tangled thorn trees between him and the hollow where the rebels waited for the camp to quiet down and for the patrols to get tired of vigilance; the rest of the patrol followed behind him, spread out, moving with an equally careful silence. He could feel them though he couldn't hear them, feel the jags of fear and excitement. Just in case the rebels did have a Reader or even someone with just enough Sight for a hunch, he'd thrown a thin shunt ahead of them, not as a concealment, but a simple shift of perception that ought not to alert anyone to how close they were or precisely where they were going.

There was a musky, acrid scent on the wind, a mix of man sweat and horse, strong enough that the others in the patrol without his enhanced senses would be smelling it now. Moving more slowly and yet more cautiously, he pulled the carrystrap of the crossbow over his shoulder, unhooked the bow, clawed the cord over the trip and dropped a bolt into the slot.

Crawl to the top of the rise, too excited to feel the snow creeping inside his clothing and down his boots.

Odd feeling as if this were something he'd done before.

Recognition. Yes. Very like any of a dozen raids he and his band had made on Iomard.

Relax. Yes. I know how this goes. No sweat. We've got them pinned.

Dark shapes moving nervously in the hollow, whispers, rasp of gloves as they calm the horses.

Choose his target.

Signal.

Stand. Shoot. Got him. Charge down the slope, sword ready.

"How many got away? Anyone see?"

Dur looked up from the dead man he was stripping. "I saw

three running." He listened. "Rider coming. From camp. One of ours, I think."

"I like those ears of yours, Northlander. Rest of you, get that gear packed on the hop and head back to the fire. Then get out and take over patrol from Bakuch and his squad. Dur, you stay. Want a witness with a brain in his head."

The rider was one of the Third Prince's couriers, a young Born with a pale pink face and an unpolished arrogance that turned the tegmal blank-faced and stolid and slowed his speech to an incomprehensible drawl meant to irritate without giving an excuse for reprimand. Dur stood silent behind him, trying to be as inconspicuous as possible.

In the distance he could hear shouts and horns as other ambushes came down on the fringes of the army, intent on doing as much damage as they could before they took off for the horizon again. The rest of the patrol was out of sight, though he could still hear them. They'd got off lightly, no dead and only one man seriously wounded. And that was Hantal, who was strong as a horse, but could trip on the edge of a shadow without half trying.

The courier slapped a long narrow hand against his thigh and scowled at the tegmal. "You had no orders to attack."

Mikal gave him the slow stupid gaze. "On patrol, sir." Dur found the words almost unintelligible they were so distorted by the Yukosa drawl. "General orders, sir. Capture spies and defend the perimeter."

"That's if you're attacked, numbhead. Going on a rampage and leaving the camp vulnerable. Explain that if you can."

"Sir. Didn't leave camp without a patrol. Second squad was working afore we left." His stone-dull eyes fixed on the courier's face, he went on. "And scout tells us the Tilkers was getting ready to come at us. So we go at them. Sir. We get nine. Three of 'em run off. Sir. Might bring friends back to pick up dead. Best we get back to camp. Sir."

Though it was hard to tell in the clouded moonlight, it seemed to Dur that the courier's round rosy face went pale.

Watch out for tailburners, he thought as he watched the Born kick his horse around and take off for the camp. They make trouble and muck up your plans. He looked around at the scattered, plundered bodies of the rebels. No, his raids weren't like this. No such harvest of death. Get used to it, he told himself. That's what war is.

[4]

For the next two months the Kale army crawled back and forth across Tilkos, trying to pin down the rebels to a fixed battle, being hit repeatedly by raids, the supply lines cut again and again until Mahara gave most of his attention to maintaining them. He was being stretched between that tending and clearing away snow so the army didn't freeze in its tracks, driving away blizzards and ice storms.

Don't start a war in winter, Dur thought.

He knew why the Mage had broken this rule. Mahara and the Third Prince wanted to break the Tilkose, starve them into submission, turn their farms and estates into muddy rubble and send the people fleeing to cities that had no way of feeding them. They were doing all that with admirable efficiency, but they weren't doing so well with the fighting.

After the first debacle on the plain below the pass, the rebel army changed tactics to lightning raids, sniping at the rim of the Kale army, killing askers, hitting at supply wagons with the army, doing what they could to harass the lengthening supply line. The horsemen of Tilkos were doing real damage and not taking much hurt in their turn. And the longbowmen standing off in the distance did yet more damage, with a seemingly inexhaustible supply of shafts. The war wizards fought this with earth shakings, wind gusts and a bouquet of stinks, but the sudden spates of arrow rain were deadly. And the Kalemen died like wheat before a scythe.

When they were over halfway to the walled city Kar Markaz, the Citadel of the Farmyn who governed Tilkos, the Third Prince stopped the sweep across the valley and swung the Kale army toward the mountains that marked the boundary between northern Tilkos and Faiscar. In the rocks and ravines, the brush and woodlands of the foothills, the rebels didn't have nearly so great a surplus of mobility and the bowmen lost a part of their effectiveness.

And the Prince began hitting back at the rebels, sending out roving askerits to ambush and harry them. A man on foot, used to fighting in small bands with a minimum of supply, had the advantage here. The askerits tramped across mountain farms, burned and looted them, drove off any livestock they came across. Dur listened to the talk in his askerit and noticed that Mikal and a few others were silent as the rest boasted what they and the Third Prince were going to do with this lot of Wyrm kissers and praised the Prince's war wit, how he'd got them away from the Tilker bowmen and slowed down the riders.

Night after night, Dur brooded over that silence as he sat staring into the coals of the supper fire. His conclusions were not pleasant to contemplate.

One: Within a week or two, the Third Prince was going to have to take the army back out of the broken lands and start his drive for the walled city Kar Markaz. That was the Administrative center for all Tilkos, and without that, he could not claim victory or even hold on to the lands he had taken.

Two: The Third Prince had to trap the rebel army somehow and break it. Out on the open ground Kale had been losing more than ten men to the rebels' one. The ratio had improved considerably here in the broken lands, but the rebel army was now more nearly equal to Kale in strength and it was relatively intact. To leave such a force on the loose was to invite years of grinding attrition and to lose everything gained so far.

Three: The next weeks were going to be bloody, futile and possibly deadly. Luck was a fickle charmer. He could get killed out there. And he wouldn't be learning anything new.

Four: It was time to go home. Or rather, time to leave the army and head for Nyddys as fast as his legs could take him. Time to search out Cymel and use her to call her aunt the Bridge to come for him. Or perhaps . . . a new idea came to him. The girl was young, but powerful, her skills undeveloped. Easier to deal with her than that Scribe who had impressed him as tough as a three-season gull. He could do with Cymel what he'd done with Fanach, force-grow her mind, take her to the Sanctuary Isles and use her to replace Fanach once he'd got her thoroughly tamed.

[5]

Rain fell with sullen persistence, dripping from the leafless branches of the winter trees and turning the red mountain clay into a treacherous porridge that alternately trapped Dur's feet or slid from under them, threatening to send him sliding down the slope of the hill he tramped across. Time, he told himself. More than time. Make the break tonight. No more waiting.

He glanced at the peaks as they moved into a small meadow. It wouldn't be easy, getting through there, but living on Isle Tuays had taught him more about ice and snow than he'd learned in all his wanderings farther south. He could do it. Find a mountaineer's camp and steal gear, pick up as much food as he could, dried meat, nuts, that kind of thing, use the Pneuma when he had to. He could get across those mountains with fingers and toes and the rest of his hide intact. It was just a matter of finding the right time to start.

Yet—he found himself oddly reluctant to leave. It bit at his pride. He was part of this askerit and valued for his skills. Not because he was a Mage, but because he was a quickhanded and able fighter. Leaving them felt like betrayal. It made him little in his own eyes and he didn't like that.

It was stupid, of course. His true loyalty was to Iomard and the thousands of darocs tied to the Domains in something close to slavery. He owed them what he'd promised them. Freedom or death. And it was time he made his way back there so he could start fulfilling that promise.

Tomorrow, he told himself. When the rain stops. Tomorrow night I run.

Breith on the Run

By the calendar of the Domains of Iomard, events dating from the 15th day of Trairin, the fourth month in the Iomardi year 6535, the 722nd year since the last Corruption.

1]

The shallow bowl was two spans wide, the silver surface polished mirror-smooth. When she gave it to Breith as his fifteenth name-day gift, Mam Fori had told him, "Keep it bright. The better the mirror, the clearer the vision."

He looked into the bowl and winced at what the reflection showed him. The brown was almost gone from his right eye; except for a few flecks it was green as the new leaves on the trees outside. Even though he was using Sight a lot, both his eyes stayed brown all the time he was in school and he'd thought maybe they wouldn't change after all—or so slightly people wouldn't notice. His father's eyes were indeed bi-colored, one a greenish-brown, the other yellowish-brown, but unless you were really close, you couldn't tell. Wasn't going to happen; that green eye really popped out at you. He twisted his face into a clown's grimace. Nothing like being branded as Weird.

He poured the water carefully until the bowl was two-thirds full, then carried the pitcher to the washbasin in his bathroom. "You'll find it easier to work with water that is isolated, Bré,"

Mam Fori had said. "When you've had more practice at scrying, you can use any still pool, but in the beginning, make sure the distractions are few."

He checked the dropclock. Nearly fourth watch. The delegation should be here soon. As he murmured the charm that Mam Fori had taught him, chanted it over and over, he narrowed his vision to a point at the center of the bowl, held focus for a moment, then watched the water suck in a film of Pneuma. A moment later the formal parlor opened out before him. A second charm and a moment's fierce concentration, then he could hear the small sounds of the empty room—the rustle of papers in a draft, the creak of the drapes as a breath of wind through a partly opened window stirred them and set the rings scraping over the rods.

He pulled up a chair and settled himself with his arms folded so he could lean on them while he watched the image in the bowl. "You've become good enough with the scry bowl not to intrude on our visitor's Sight, Bré. I want you to watch and listen," Mam Fori told him when she sent him to his rooms.

Scrying was also a lot harder work than opening a Window. A Window you could lock in place and forget till time to close it. If you let your attention wander too much when you were scrying, the· image broke up and sometimes even went away with such stubborn resistance you couldn't get it back.

He took a boiled sweet from the bowl on the table, slipped it into his mouth and prepared to wait.

The door to the formal parlor opened and Mum Yasa walked in, her staff reading the floor before her as if it had the eyes she'd lost. Even though he was not even in the same room he could feel the odd whorls of Pneuma that moved with her, as if she were anchored at the heart of a never-ending storm. She had put on her formal face and walked with a powerful, blind inevitability two steps ahead of Mam Fori and the unwelcome visitors she brought into the parlor.

Trailing behind them were three cantairs in stiff black robes and inquisitors' masks. Breith wrinkled his nose; the Prophet

ales he'd read when he was a child were filled with those stiff
black figures always lecturing and punishing the thoughtless
boy and heedless girl who neglected religious duties and
assed their Mams and Mums, then ran away from home and
got into serious trouble until the inquisitors restored them to
home and faith.

That triad was the reason Mam Fori didn't want him messing with Pneuma. They had to be Readers and Sighted, otherwise they wouldn't be inquisitors. And he knew suddenly
that they were here for him. Mam hadn't told him that, just
ordered him to watch and listen, but he was sure they wanted
to take him away from the House and do something to control
him, something probably near as bad as what Mirrialta wanted.

At Mam Fori's right hand was an Enforcer from the Riv-
rine Council and at her left there was a Legalist from the
Sinne Council that ruled the Scribes. This was going to be
bad.

Mam took them to the middle of the room and sat them in
armchairs about the oval conference table. Mum Yasa was
already seated there, her staff held upright in a springclip
screwed onto the side of her chair.

Mam stood beside her sister/Wife, her face stern. No wel-
coming smiles there. She didn't like anything about this and
was going to give them the courtesy due any visitor and nothing more. "I bid you welcome to Urfa House, Legalist Gyure,
Enforcer Synoïm and You Who Are Nameless. Tea is being
prepared and will be served shortly. Unless this is so serious
an occasion that you refuse the bread of my House."

Breith's brows went up. Scande! Mam, that's putting it to
them.

The Enforcer lifted a graceful hand, let it fall; there was a
fake sorrow on her long thin face that made Breith want to
kick her. "Cay Faobran, I am saddened to see you so mis-
understand our visit. We come in amity, seeking only a clar-
ification of rumors that have reached our ears. Insofar as we
are able, we will be pleased to accept the bread of Urfa House.
There are those among us who are constrained by rule from

eating or drinking that which is not prepared by their own hands. This has no meaning here.''

Breith saw his Mam's mouth tighten and her brows draw together at the condescending explanation of what she already knew, but she said nothing, simply took up the small silver bell at her right hand and rang it.

He sighed and closed his eyes as the dance of courtesies went on, nothing happening, tea being sipped, wafers eaten, everyone end-of-the-teeth polite. Boring boring boring.

The image wavered, but steadied again when Breith whispered the focus chant. He forced himself to watch.

Legalist Gyure set her cup on its saucer, folded her hands before her on the table. ''Cay Faobran, it is known that your seylmate Malart has the Sight.''

''We have never attempted to conceal it. There are no geld laws here as there are in the Domains so I don't see what business it is of anyone other than my Wife and myself.''

''The Confluence was formed to fight such barbarisms.''

''So I have always believed.''

''However, there are . . . difficulties . . . that can arise from too much laxity in the pursuit of that life of devotion which the Prophet sets out for us. You have a son.''

''That too we have not attempted to conceal.'' Mam Fori's voice sounded brittle as ice on a puddle in midwinter.

One of the inquisitors moved forward half a step. ''It is written: The sport is poison to the stem. Cauterize the join so the infection cannot spread.''

Mum Yasa slapped her hand on the table and even the inquisitors started at the sudden violence of the sound. ''That is not in the canon, but only in the commentaries, commentaries scribed in the Domains before the Riverine States existed. Whoever invokes these is not welcome in my house.''

Mam Fori got to her feet, moved to stand beside her sister/ Wife, her hand on Yasayl's shoulder. She said nothing, but her body shouted her agreement with Yasayl.

Breith shivered as he saw his Mam's face. There were white

spots beside her nostrils and her mouth was reduced to a pale line. She was so angry she frightened him.

Legalist Gyure waved the inquisitor away from the table, then leaned forward, her mouth curving into a charming, rueful smile. When she spoke her voice was sunwarmed honey. "Let us approach this calmly and with reason, not emotion. We come inquiring, not to sit in judgment. Sit down. Please."

Breith decided he trusted the Legalist about as far as he could throw her and she was a tall, big-boned woman with wrists to match his father's so that wasn't very far at all. He watched his Mam move stiffly back to her chair and felt sick because under the anger that robbed her of her grace was fear. Fear for him. Fear for Urfa House and the housekin who worked here. He drew his hand across his mouth. Mam was annoyed at Mirrialta and her hired men, but she wasn't afraid. This was much worse.

"When you bring a parade into my house, Legalist Gyure, what am I to think? This is not a friend's way."

"This could be a serious matter, requiring counsel from faith, law and custom, Cay Faobran. View us as speaking for these—They Who Are Nameless for faith, the Enforcer Synoïm for law, and I for custom. No parade, only seekers for truth. And the truth we seek is this: Has your son inherited his father's . . . gift?"

"That is a family matter and no concern of faith, law or custom."

"These are perilous times, Cay Faobran. You know as well as I—perhaps better, since your seylmate concerns himself so extensively with the historical record—that a time of Corruption approaches. We must seek the strength to hold the Confluence together and we must become punctilious in our observations of the Prophet's Strictures that we may survive what swims toward us. Weakness of purpose, moral laxity, these things endanger all of us. It is well documented that danger comes most terribly from a man with the Sight. We only wish to safeguard the Confluence and to protect those with that . . . um . . . weakness, that dangerous gift from the anger of the ignorant. Nothing more. No threats. No gelding. No brainburn. Simply a life of service and quiet as a Brother in a teaching order. The Riverine Council, the Order of Scribes, the Synod of the Cantairs, have met and spoken of this. It was decided that we must impose these gentlest and most maternal of controls over those who are in danger of losing perhaps even their lives but certainly their souls in the chaos of the Corruption. I have the authority of all three to ask you this question: Has your son inherited the gifts of his father?''

Mum Yasa straightened and the whorls of Pneuma swirled more violently about her. ''What you have claimed has not been delivered in writing to the Houses nor has it been cried in the market-places. It cannot be lawful until this has been done. You call it a decision. I say it is not-law. I say the authority you claim is a phantasm that exists only in your minds. We are not scurds squatting in hill camps counting over the booty from raids. We are a House of good repute. We tithe to the Service of the Prophet and pay the House tax to the Riverine Council, we buy and sell prudently but with honor, we govern our household justly, paying heed to this faith, law and custom you have invoked. Shame to you who come to us with such disregard for our dignity.''

Her head jerked up, her mouth worked a moment, her hands trembled. After a moment, she drew in a long breath, then turned her blind face toward the inquisitors.

Breith saw them stiffen though the masks hid their faces.

Yasayl nodded, then swung her body till she faced the seated pair. Her voice when she spoke was soft, barely more than a whisper, but it compelled them. The Legalist and the Enforcer pulled their heads back, but they couldn't look away from her.

''You know so much about our House, you will know my gift. Legalist Gyure, do not try to tie the Scribes too closely to the Society of Inquisitors. Many among them will give allegiance to the Domains and will work against the Confluence. I see Scribes brought to burning and others on their faces, surrendering their will to the Society. Enforcer Synoïm, a warning for the Council. In your attempts to tighten control over the cities of the Confluence, you risk destroying it. I have seen war and rebellion, fires burning cities, trees with Siofray fruit swinging from their branches. Take care.''

She reached out her hand. Faobran took it, helped her onto her feet until she could steady herself with the staff.

In his room Breith sighed with relief as the itch under his skin subsided. He was uncomfortable around Mum when she had one of her visions. It felt as if something were chewing on his bones and eating at his head from the inside.

He calmed the scrywater and watched Mam Fori send the delegation away with an exaggerated courtesy that he could see made them angry but gave them no room for complaint. They left without further protest and he almost felt sorry for them, remembering the times his Mam had torn strips off him and left him feeling like scum on her feet. Not too much sympathy, because they scared the stiffening from his bones. Mam and Mum and Da could protect him from Mirrialta and her lot, but he knew enough from school about what would happen to them if the Council and the Scribes turned against them. House Urfa could be put under a Ban. Which meant Mam's riverboats might as well be left to rot because no one would do business with them. And the housekin couldn't go to festivals and seyling matches. And if someone got sick, a cantair wouldn't come to sing his soul clean. And . . .

Faobran came back into the room. ''Breith, you can stop watching now. We'll talk later.'' She moved her hand as if she wiped something away and the image vanished from the scry bowl.

Breith carried the water out into the court and poured it on the grass. He looked up at the sky. It was so blue it was almost purple, the color intensified by the puffs of white cloud wind-driven across it, the color of high spring when summer's heat and dust were still last year's memories, when the ships were thick along the wharves and Ascal tongues were heard in the streets almost as often as Siofray.

He shook the last drops out of the bowl and took it inside.

Restless and unhappy, knowing he had to do something, though what was beyond him, he wandered around his room set, just looking at his things, picking them up and putting them down. He poured himself a glass of water, took two sips, put that down too. After a while, he went outside again, picked up a stick and whistled for Gath. He played fetch with the dog until he couldn't push away the thoughts any longer. He thumped the dog on the shoulders, scratched behind his ears then shoved him away. "That's it, Gatha, no more. Go chase some squirrelmonks or dig a hole. I have to figure out . . ."

Gath tried to follow him into the room set, but Breith used his foot to keep him out of the doorway and snatched the door shut before he could wriggle past.

He dropped into the chair at the worktable, sat with his head down on his crossed arms. Mam and Mum won't give in, whatever the Council says, he thought. Da doesn't have a say, but he'd be with them all the way, even if it did mean a Banning. If I weren't here, there wouldn't be any problem. If I went away . . ."

It wasn't a new thought. Being kept like a prisoner inside these walls had pushed at him and squeezed him until he felt ready to burst like a ripe puffball someone had kicked. Months and months. At the same time Cymel was running around having adventures, enjoying herself at Cyfareth, turning into somebody he could barely recognize. And she was three years younger than him. And his father had run from his Domain when he was the same age as Cymel. So why couldn't he take off and see something of the world when his being away would be a big help to his family?

Mirrialta's spies had vanished a few days ago, though Mam Fori still wouldn't let him go beyond the walls just in case his cousin was trying something sneaky. I'd better go see if there's anyone out there. Don't want to stick my head out and get it kicked off.

He grinned as he got to his feet. At least Gath would be

happy. All the dog wanted was someone to throw things for him to fetch.

Breith left his rooms and whistled to Gath. The dog beside him, he began walking as casually as he could manage about the public court near the front gate. He bounced a ball off the wall and laughed as Gath went scrambling after it. Slowly, casually, the two of them moved away from the family quarters and edged toward the main gate.

As he sent the ball bouncing off along the gravel path, Breith glanced out the gate, looking through the narrow spaces between the bars.

A band of Enforcers and a cantair were squatting on the far side of the road, pretending to play the stone game but actually keeping watch on the gate.

He took the ball from Gath and threw it toward the family quarters. No point in checking the other gates. It'd be the same thing at each of them. That Legalist and the others, they weren't giving up. They wanted him and, one way or another, they meant to get him. Stomach in knots, sweat popping out on his face, he thumped Gath, tossed the ball again and followed him through the arch in the inner wall.

Breith sat on his bed and opened the carved box where he kept his treasures. He counted out his gift money and grimaced with regret because he'd spent such a lot of it last year on new modeling tools. There was enough to buy food for a month or two, but not enough to pay for transport, not if he wanted to leave Valla Murloch and get far enough away so the Enforcers and inquisitors couldn't come after him.

There was the medal he'd received last year for winning his races. It was heavy, supposed to be gold. Probably worth something if it were melted down. He picked out two thumb-stones. They were smooth and soothing to the touch. No value in money, but worth hauling along if only to help him calm down and go to sleep.

He dug out the backpack from the time three years ago

when his father took him north along the river to see Gabba Labhain and the great Central Library of the Scribes. He filled it with a change of clothes and other things he thought he might need. He'd like to open the Window and talk to Cymel, tell her about what he meant to do. She'd agree he had to get out, she'd tell him he was doing right, she'd argue with his plans and this sick feeling he had in his gut would go away. He didn't dare. That cantair outside the gate wasn't wearing an inquisitor's mask, but she was probably able to read the Flow and follow his drain to him. All the evidence the inquisitors would need to march into Urfa House and march him out.

He looked at the pack in his hand, dropped it on the bed and sat beside it, staring at the wall, suddenly overwhelmed by the impossibility of leaving. Where could he go? And how would he get there?

If it weren't for the Mage—Corysiam's warnings a couple of years ago had frightened him more than he wanted to admit—he could go to the Sanctuary Isles and be safe from both Mirrialta and the inquisitors. He wasn't overly dismayed at having that possibility canceled out. What he'd read about the Isles in his geography lessons didn't sound very appealing.

He drummed his fingers on his thighs, scowled around the room he'd slept in since he left the nursery. His maps. His models. The book his father had given him his first day of school, an old history of sailing ships and sailors' tales that Malart had got from the Scribe Archivist Slionn when she was about to send it to the page cleaners so the parchment could be used again. He'd made his models from the ship plans drawn in there and labeled in tiny, crabbed handwriting he could barely make out.

He'd thought about taking the book with him, even picked it up several times when he was packing, but it meant too much to him to take a chance on losing it. It'd be safer here. And sort of an anchor. A promise to himself that he would come back. That this was his home still and always would be, no matter what happened to him.

Ascal, he thought. Stow away on a merchanter and cross the ocean to Ascal. Who'd bother following me all that way? I know those ships. Plenty of places to hide. I can get at the water barrels and the food stores.

He jumped off the bed and ran to the wall where he'd pasted up his maps. Now that he had a plan and a goal, the excitement came rushing back and smothered his misgivings. He used a pocket knife to peel away the map of Ascal, folded it into a small packet and pushed it into the pack. He stood with his eyes closed, whispering the things he'd need to take with him. "Water bottle. Bread and cheese. Cord. Prybar. A bronze mirror for scrying; can't take glass, too easy to break. Can't take the bowl, it's too big and needs too much water. . . ."

[2]

Breith stopped in the shadow of a tree growing beside the flag tower. The bulk of the tower was between him and the gate so the watchers across the court couldn't see him. But that cantair out there wouldn't need her eyes to figure out that someone in here was up to something. Unless he was very, very careful at what he did. He glanced back at the court and the building where he'd spent all his life then looked quickly away. Getting soppy about this wouldn't help him do what he had to do.

He lowered the pack to the ground and settled himself on a root. Take your time, he told himself. There's no hurry. You've got till supper at least. Four hours. He leaned against the trunk and closed his eyes. Mirrialta had done him a favor by teaching him how to be sly about accessing the Flow. He grinned. Would probably make her mad as spit if she ever learned about it.

He began bleeding a thin trickle of Pneuma from the Flow, storing it within his body until he had enough for what he meant to do. It was hard to force himself to be patient, to sit there acting like a milk bucket under a cow that didn't want to let down. He began thinking about Ascal.

No one had much magic over there. They weren't Siofray.

They didn't have the Sight. He'd be the one with power. People would have to jump when he said hop, or he could . . . he didn't know exactly what he'd do, but it would be awesome enough to make them tremble in their boots.

When he had enough Pneuma in hand, he kneaded it and worked it into a thin sheet, then used it to make a pocket like the one he'd taught Cymel about. He pulled it round him and sealed himself inside. He stood a moment twitching and arranging the film into a lumpy bubble, then started walking slowly around the tower, heading for the gate.

The first few steps were difficult; he nearly tripped and fell flat several times. But by the time he was on the walkway leading through the gate, he had got used to maneuvering the bubble. Though the heat was already beginning to build up until he felt like a tuber being baked in its skin, he forced himself to take small, deliberate steps.

He couldn't see very well either; he had to strain to make out blurry shapes he could only guess at.

He felt a spike of uneasiness.

It wasn't his.

Must be the cantair.

He kept putting one foot in front of the other, creeping along slower than an eiler worm.

Darkness. This confused him until he realized that he must have passed through the gate into the shadow from the tower. He turned into the shadow. Somewhere to his left he could hear the voices of the Enforcers, the click of the stones as they shook and threw them, voices again as they counted off the points.

Red light diffused through the film.

Out of the tower shadow, into the full light.

Out in the middle of the road. Prophet grant no cart comes along.

Hot. Can't think. How much longer?

Keep on.

Roughness underfoot. He stumbled, nearly went down on his knees. The road curves here. Scande! Need to watch it or

I could go over the cliff. Edge back. Find the wall shadow. Find the place that's half red, half black and walk the line.

Keep on.

Sweat rolled down his face, down his back and arms. Tongue swollen. Thirst. Mouth dry as a lime kiln.

Keep on.

Voices faded behind him. They weren't following. They hadn't seen or sensed him. The cantair felt something, but not enough something to worry her.

Keep on.

He stumbled and this time he fell, crashing down onto hands and knees. For a heart-stopping moment he couldn't remember who he was or what he was doing, couldn't feel his own body.

He knelt like a beast, feeling the rutted surface of the road under his knees and his palms. Palms not paws. I am . . . I . . . I . . . I am . . . Breith. I am Breith na Faobra-Yasa.

Slowly he recollected himself and started to crawl deeper into the darkness of wall-shadow because that promised at least the illusion of sanctuary.

The Pneuma film came tight against his head and he stopped.

He flogged his feverish weary mind and managed to remember enough to dissolve a fist-sized portion of the Pocket.

The sudden burst of air that blew against his face felt like ice-melt; shivers ran along his body, his arms and legs lost their strength and he collapsed on his face.

The hole frayed slowly into nothing as the Pneuma sublimed back into the Flow.

As he staggered onto his feet, he glanced along the road. He was two houses away from Urfa and the curve in the road had concealed him from the Enforcers. It wasn't market day, so there wasn't much traffic on the road most hours and he'd been lucky enough to pull his escape at a time when none of the neighbors were going anywhere.

He hurried along the road. If Mam missed him, she'd find the note he left, scry for him and that would be the end of that. He didn't want to think about the heat, he didn't want to recognize how close he'd come to doing himself serious damage, but he couldn't stop coming back again and again to that heat buildup. He'd played Mouse in Pocket with his father since he was a baby. He'd taught Cymel how to play it and she had no problem with it. He thought back to the last time he'd dared talk with Cymel, to the anger he'd felt and the heat it summoned. What his father called a vortex.

His father had promised to show him how to dissipate the heat, but all he'd done so far was give Breith some exercises. He didn't explain anything, just said, "Do this. And when you've got everything right, you'll understand what happened and why." If he had just told me right out, I could figure out how to deal with it. If he'd just told me. . . .

Breith trudged along the road, thinking and thinking, considering what he knew about fire and Flow, trying without enough learning to work out a way of venting heat yet keeping the Pocket around him. It was too useful a trick to lose, especially since he was going to be on his own in a world that he didn't know all that well. Yet how could he find a solution when he didn't know what caused the problem? If he'd just told me what was happening, if Da had just told me. . . .

When he reached the wharves, the tide was on the point of turning and already several ships were curving out away from the wharves, heading for the mouth of the bay. He threw himself on a butt and scowled at the water. "Prophet's hairy toes," he muttered. "I forgot about the stinking tides. Scande! I'm going to get myself killed if I don't shape up."

This turning of the tide meant his choice of transport was thinned to the danger point. No matter how well they behaved at Valla Murloch under the eyes of Siofray merchants and Council Enforcers, a lot of these traders were pirates and slavers once they got where Siofray magic wouldn't touch them. And some of the captains ran dirty ships with muck in the waterbarrels and worms in the biscuit. Since he planned to live off ship's stores, he wanted a merchanter with tidy habits in the crew. His Mam wouldn't let any of the Urfa riverboats get so cluttered and grimy as some of those ships. She'd have the hide off a Master the first time and boot her off the boat and out of Urfa's hire on the second offense.

He also wanted one with a full cargo, laden to the limit with Saffroa goods. Less temptation to stop overlong at any of the island supply ports that dotted the ocean and less chance the crew would be messing around down in the hold.

He left the butt and slipped into the crowds moving along the wharves. Even with several ships already gone, they were busy, crowded with ladesmen hauling bales and barrels on and off the ships, sailors dickering with furtive street sellers, most of whom were women who looked as timeworn as the wind-blown conifers out near the mouth of the bay. Others listening to the whispers of shills for the Houses of Assignation where Siofray women looking for thrills came to bed the foreigners. At least that's what Breith thought they were. He and the others had sniggered when Gloy told them; they'd sneaked around to watch a house that Gloy said he knew about, but they hadn't seen much. He'd never dared ask his father whether what Gloy said was true or not. Because if Da told Mam . . . Even now the thought sent a chill along his spine.

He slipped through the lengthening shadows of the warehouses and the boxes, barrels and bales piled on the wharves, grateful for once that being skinny and short for his age made folks see him as a child and ignore him as long as he didn't try to go on one of the ships. They'd chase him fast the minute they saw him trying to slip onboard.

He saw several boys he knew, down here playing instead of in school. A quick dive behind a pile of crates kept them from spotting him: He didn't want questions he couldn't answer flung at him.

Shadow to shadow he went, inspecting each of the ships getting ready to raise anchor, knowing that he couldn't spend too much time on making his choice, or it would be made for him. There was a trim three-master, but the crew were gaunt with furtive eyes and a habit of looking over their shoulder even when no one was watching. The smell from another ship

was so bad he held his breath going past it. Hides and other
things he didn't recognize and didn't really want to. A third
made odd jags in the Pneuma Flow for some reason.

Two more boys from school. He edged into deep shadow
between two tiers of crates and waited until Hanas and Daol
trotted past. Brother Bullan would have their hides tomorrow
if they didn't come up with a foolproof excuse. He listened to
them arguing until their voices were lost in the rest of the
noise, then leaned his head against the side of a crate, his eyes
squeezed shut. Seeing them brought home just how much he
was losing, how much he was going to miss these streets and
his own people.

After a moment, he forced himself from the nook and went
on looking for the right ship.

She was old, but even from his hiding place in a stack of bales,
he could see that she was lovingly maintained. The slightly
different coloring of patches showed where damaged and rotted wood had been cut away and replaced with meticulous
care. The cordage was smooth and new and so were the tar-
paulins stretched taut over deck cargo. She was smaller than
most, only two masts, and her hold would be cramped. He'd
have a hard time finding a hiding place, but once he did, he
should be safe enough from discovery unless he did something
really stupid. He sniffed cautiously at the ship's aura, but as
far as he could tell, there were no Readers on-board. That
matched what he'd read and what Tel told him. Ascali didn't
like being around the Sighted. They thought it unfair and dangerous for others to have power they couldn't match, and they
had a lot of superstitions about Siofray magic that had nothing
to do with the reality of the Flow.

Breith eased himself down until he was half squatting, half
sitting on a bulge in a bale. The ship had a waiting air, as if
one last item were expected before the crew cast off and
started out into the bay. Careful to disturb the Flow as little
as possible, he drew Pneuma into himself until he had what
he needed, then he severed the connection, shaped the Pneuma

into a thin sheet as he had before. But this time he only draped the sheet around him, leaving the edges to trail on the ground, and he opened slits in the sheet to let the outside air filter in.

Stay quiet, he told himself as he got carefully to his feet. No hurry, no fuss, no danger, just stroll along, small steps. Let the scrape of your feet merge with the noise on the wharf. Watch out. They can't see you. If they bump into you, they'll feel you. Swerve, dodge. There's the gangplank. Be careful now, man on watch, looks alert. Keep the pocket tucked round you. It's working; letting air get through the punctures bleeds off the heat. You can stop worrying now. Easy. Don't look at him. Some people can feel you looking at them even if they can't see you. Good. He didn't feel a thing. Hatch. Forward hatch, yes, that's the one. Hope they haven't piled cargo on it. No. Here we are. All right. Look around. Any one watching? Hm. Not dogged down yet. Wonder why? No time to fool with unanswerable questions. Get below and fast. You're riding Luck but it could collapse under you any minute.

He lifted the hatch, went down the ladder and found himself in cramped space with almost no room to move about. He listened, felt about for life fires, but the only ones he noted were small rat-fires scattered here and there among the boxes and bales. With a sigh of relief, he dissolved the Pneuma and started wriggling over the cargo, hunting for a niche where he could hide.

Half an hour later, teeth clamped over his lower lip, he felt the ship's movement change as it moved out into the open water of the bay, picking up speed and thrust. He closed his eyes and thought of Bauli. I didn't even go tell her goodbye, he thought. Bauli, baby, this is for you. This is to keep you safe. To keep everyone safe.

Exhausted by his exertions and the strain of the day, he stretched out on the top of a bale of hides, pulled his blanket over him and went to sleep.

6

The Wedding

By the calendar of the Domains of Iomard events dating from the 1st day of Seyos, the fifth month in the Iomardi year 6536, the 722nd year since the last Corruption.

[1]

"Wasn't I right, huh? Isn't this a good place to watch?" Bett slapped her hand on the stone of the curtain wall that enclosed Eadro Lynhouse. She and her friend Ama sat behind the wall's ornamental baluster, protected from view on the house side by the wall of a tower and a low parapet, on the outside by the carved encrustations that disguised utilitarian arrow slots. Though it was almost noon, the Bride's party was not expected for hours, so they were early indeed for the viewing, and only a few others had shared their idea and their aversion to the finicking work of last-moment preparations.

"Well, it was me thought of getting here early and making a party."

"And a Prophet-blessed thought it was. Pass me the jug. The tea still warm?"

"Warm enough. Almost gone, though. In a while I'd better see if I can fetch more." Ama filled Bett's mug, got to her feet and went to stand looking down into the Grand Court. "The fanai are starting to get set up. Looks like the Bride will get here sooner than we thought. Oooh! Bett, come here and look."

When Bett reached her, Ama whispered, "Look at that one. There with the guitar. I don't want to point, do you see him? Isn't he the most gorgeous thing you ever laid eyes on?"

The young man was tuning his guitar, so intent on listening as he plucked the strings and turned the pegs that the chaos around him didn't touch him. He was daroc dark but his brown hair gleamed gold where the sun touched it; his face was lean and angular but his mouth had a tenderness that made Ama sigh with pleasure, and his hands were beautiful both in shape and grace of movement as he worked.

Bett giggled, whispered, "Almost makes you want to take up the flute and get adopted fanai. Still, they're going to play for us at the Posha in the Village. Let the Lynborn have their feasts, my feet want to dance."

"You right. Oooh, all that tea is resting heavy. I've got to water the munta. You hold place here, I'll be back and bring more tea while I'm at it."

2]

Alainn frowned. He was going to have to find some seasoned wood and make new pegs, thicker ones. He wasn't sure what effect that would have on the instrument, but strings continually losing their tuning while he was trying to play wasn't something he could cope with. Maybe Master Bayn could play such an instrument but he hadn't the skill. And he hadn't yet passed the exams that would bring him a new instrument, rather than this ancient hand-me-down.

No time now to whittle pegs, though. He rummaged through his gear, found an old pair of leather gloves and cut small squares from the palms; one by one he dealt with the loose pegs, using the leather as wadding. It would last a day or two at least and he could put off the worry till then.

"You've got admirers."

Alainn looked up. Bayn's daughter Fonn was standing on the wagonstage downlaughing at him, her missing tooth add-

ing a touch of the raffish to her triangular grin. She carried
the baby tooth in a sighla pouch dangling from a thong round
her neck.

"I can see white in the gum," he said, grinning back at
her. "Shall we bury the tooth here or out on the grass?"

She clutched at the tiny pouch, wrinkled her nose at him.
"Inside walls? Prophet avert!"

She jumped down beside him, looked at the pegs. "I'm
thinking we'll be burying that too after the Wedding's done.
It's falling apart."

"It's good for a few more years. Though I wish not for
me."

Fonn patted his shoulder. "You'll do. Next Commorta
you'll make journeyman first for sure." Then she went back
to helping the other children hang the swags of bright red sarol
cloth around the edge of the stage and drape more of it over
the stools where the musicians would be sitting as they played
the Bride in. As was custom, the Traiolyn had provided the
cloth and the pushpins to hold it in place.

When Alainn finished tightening the pegs, he set the guitar
aside and began work on the other instruments, doing apprentice work because Fanai Spriocha hadn't adopted in any apprentices for more than six years now. The Banria was always
going on about that, scowling at him when she voiced the
complaint. Seemed like very few daroc on the Spriocha Round
either had talent or any desire to leave home. He was the last,
taken into the clan from Domain Dorseh, down south near the
swamplands. Sometimes, late at night when his bones ached
from the work the Spriocha Banria demanded of him and the
Bone Devil's claws were sunk deep in him, he suspected that
his adoption had been a farce and that the real fanai were
making a fool of him, keeping him as worse than a daroc to
do all the scut work they didn't want to touch.

He never told anyone because in daylight he was ashamed
of such thoughts, but they haunted him as that day when he'd
reach journeyman first and join the ensemble of the Masters
kept receding into the future. He gloomed as he sat rubbing

he Banria's secret cream into the instruments, working with
his fingertips only to keep his touch just right. Even little Fonn
had noticed and she'd only made five winters since she was
born. He sighed. Even if his darker suspicions were true, life
was still lots better traveling with the Fanai than grubbing in
the dirt as a Dorseh daroc.

As Banria Marasc came striding toward the group of workers, the white streaks in her black hair seemed to crackle with
energy and anger. She stopped in front of him, set her hands
on her hips and glared down at him.

He clutched at the reed pipe he was polishing and wondered
what he'd done now.

She snorted. "Pretty face. Someone took a look and said I
want that one. You're to play the Bride through the Gate.
Toma the Wise, she says you'll do fine. Fine or no, you'll be
representing Spriocha. You make us look good, you hear?"

"Yes, Banria." He was confused, but didn't dare ask any
of the questions swarming behind his teeth.

"Hmp. Find Bayn and have him go through the routine with
you. Cursed bantars. They go into heat and good sense blows
right out their heads." She snorted again and went stamping
off.

Behind him, Fonn giggled. He heard the whispered chant,
"Aly's got a girlfriend," and writhed with embarrassment.
Without looking round, he set the pipe aside, pushed the cork
into the wide mouth of the porcelain jar, got to his feet and
went to find Bayn.

3]

By the time the cloud of white dust from the Bride's Party
puffed up and spread across the empty sky, the red-dyed grass
carpet had been unrolled along the road that led through the
main gate of Eadro Lynhouse, the Lynborn bantars and ridos
positioned on either side, their fertility wands in their left
hands and their rolls of red ribbons in their right. An honor
guard of bantars and ridos in red-dyed leather, tunics and trou-

sers made of spring-harvested siotha glimmering like wet blood in the sunlight.

Bett and Ama had maintained their claim on the favored spot next to the gate towers; the rest of the front wall was packed with darocs and herdgirls, while the visiting Traiolyns and their entourages filled the Great Court inside the wall.

A few moments after the dust blew up, the Bride's party came through the grove of weeping sayls down by the river road. The Bride rode in an elaborately carved litter between two large cayochs. Each cayoch had a herdgirl from Tiolan holding the straps of its halter and keeping it to a mincing walk. In spite of this the box that enclosed the Bride swayed and bounced.

Bett nudged Ama, whispered, "She'll be ready to toss her lunch."

Ama grinned. "Like to see that, I would." She shook the jug. "Want some more tea?"

"Nah. Had enough. Was talking to Urs this morning before I come over to dust and pick up . . . ooh-eee, those bantars leave a mess worse than a scritchscratchy squirrelmonk."

"Couldn't be worse'n my floor. This bantar from Fuascala, she must have got way drunk last night, spewed all over the floor round the pot, missing more'n she hit. What a stink! Urs? I thought you couldn't stand the little pest."

Bett made a face. "Little brothers are the curse of family life. He's such a sneak, sticks his nose into everything. Anyway, he was telling me a Runner had got in last night and spent half the night talking with the Elders. You know what I was telling you when we were cleaning out the Guesthouse? Well, Urs said he heard the Runner say he was all the way up from Domain Mullach. And everything the haulers were saying isn't as bad as what's really true. Runner said don't do anything to make her look at you. And never ever talk back to her. She's mean. Really mean. And she never forgets you."

"Ouch, Bett. Sounds like a good time to go back to the farm—while the Bride's showing her best side, I mean. Mac is sniffing around me again, maybe I'll break down and ask him to jump the wand with me. Or maybe Jory. Mac's the sweetest, but Jory's a good 'un and he likes kids. There's worse things than hoeing weeds.''

"Hunh. You're oldest daughter so it's easy for you. Me, I'd have to get permission to break new ground from the Grass and guess who I'd have to ask for that. Look! She's about to get down.''

The herdgirls stopped the cayochs at the foot of the avenue. Two of the ridos dismounted and stood by the sliding door to the litter, hands out to give support to the Bride as she dismounted and began the ceremonial walk to the Gate.

Mirrialta ait é Mullach-Tiolan descended with grace despite the awkwardness of the litter, her hands clasped in the ridos', her back as straight as if someone had shoved a rod down her spine.

Bett clicked her tongue against her teeth. "Wouldn't you know, she's gorgeous. Who's going to listen to a daroc's complaints against someone who looks like that?''

Ama sniffed. "Seems the Holy Radya is like the rest of us, a sucker for a pretty face. Thought she was above such earthly things.''

"Nobody's above stuff like that, I don't care what they say. Hey! Talking about pretty, look who's playing the Bride in.''

The moment the toe of Mirrialta's red-dyed boot touched the grass carpet, one of the fanai stepped from the silent watchers, bowed and began walking backward ahead of her, nimble fingers sliding along the guitar's strings, playing the Bride's Walk. He wore a white tunic and trousers and white sandals, with knots of white ribbons fluttering from his shoulders and the neck of his guitar. He was as beautiful as a Prophet's Messenger, an image from a chantstory, not a breathing man.

The Tiolan bantars and ridos paced along the sides of the grass carpet, the crimson ribbons they wore fluttering in the light wind.

The Bride's long black hair fell to her waist in a gleaming, rippling mass. She wore a dress of white siotha, so thickly beaded around the hem of the bell-shaped skirt it glittered red as if splashed by fresh blood. An embroidered baldrick crossed the fitted bodice; from it hung the Tiolan Bridesword. This was an ancient object, passed down in Lyn Tiolan from before the Prophet, only borrowed for the occasion. When Mirrialta's escort went home, the sword and baldrick would go with them.

Ama leaned closer and breathed a whisper into Bett's ear. "I'd *kill* for a dress like that."

"Yeh. Me too."

When the procession of two reached the curtain wall, the fanai stepped aside and stood in the shadow of the wall, his hands drawing a soft, insistent beat from the guitar strings. Mirrialta drew the Bridesword from the hanger; she flourished it at the house and cried the formal challenge. "By the Prophet's Law and Precepts I claim Bride's Place within this House."

The dark red of her robes unbecoming, making her look older than time, the Traiolyn Radayam waited just inside the archway of the Gate. "Who is it who demands Bride Place in the House of Eadro?"

"Mirrialta ait é Mullach-Tiolan stands before you and speaks those words."

"Let Mirrialta ait é Mullach-Tiolan enter. The Bride is welcome in the halls of Eadro." Radayam took her place beside the Bride, offered her arm, then together the two of them walked along the grass carpet between the ranks of visiting Traiolyns and their entourages. The fanai youth strolled behind them, playing the Bride's Walk again, though this time it had a sensuous rather than martial tone with ornamental trills and fingers thumping on the body of the guitar that sounded like a dancer's feet.

As Radayam and Mirrialta—with the fanai musician four steps behind them—went up the wide steps to the great front doors of Eadro House, the guests moved from the viewing stands and followed them inside.

"You serving at the Feast?" Bett reached for the basket and began putting the plates and mugs in it.

Ama shook the lunch cloth over the outside of the baluster. "Handing off at the kitchen door. The Achtaim says no darocs in the Hall." She grinned. "Baby bantars will be hauling grease tonight."

"Me I'd rather scrub floors. Only took dropping two full platters and tipping a pot over Cook to get me out of the kitchen gang."

"I remember that. Whoo-ee, your tail must've been sore for a month after your Mam got done with you."

"Sore goes away. You just make up your mind what you want and do what you must to get it." She got to her feet. "Not that I really want the laundry shift, but at least I don't have to bite my tongue round a clutch of bantars. Let's trade, hm? You take the dishes and I'll carry the cloth to the laundry." Bett sighed. "I'm going to be wrinkled as a year-old windfall before this mess is over."

[4]

Urs eased himself flat on the broad limb of the wyllan and pulled the old horseblanket over him; it was tattered enough to look like summer leaves and dark enough to make sure his arms and legs didn't shine in the moonlight. This was an ancient grove and one where Ead daroc elders had been meeting as long as there were Domains and darocs. He supposed the Traiolyn knew all about this place, but his Mam said she was one for honoring the old ways, so she left darocs alone as long as they did what darocs should.

After the long talk with the Runner last night he didn't expect them to come here again, but just before supper Healwitch Cheaasa's Beati came by. She giggled at him and pretended she had come to court him, but he saw the sign she made to his Mam and knew there'd be another meeting tonight.

He'd barely got himself settled in the tree when Cheaasa and Beati arrived and began setting up the looids that would ward the clearing from overlooking by the Seers and turn away lovers seeking privacy for some snuggling. It was why he'd got here early and climbed into this particular tree. He'd be inside the ring when Cheaasa fired the knots and safe from discovery unless he did something really stupid like sneezing.

His Mam and his aunt Gara were the first to arrive. They nodded to Cheaasa, but didn't say anything, just went to one of the logs arranged in a triangle about a small firepit and sat down to wait for the others.

Urs's nose tickled. Shouldn't have thought about sneezing. Called it down on me, I did. Cautiously he brought his hand around and pinched his nostrils together, moving his thumb and forefinger up and down to try and scratch away the tickle. When he looked down again, Siun was there with Aron. Seeing Aron surprised Urs. Aron was Ead Village's layabout; he ran errands, did little finicking repairs, but mostly sat about like an old lizard basking in the sunlight. Urs's Mam Reyar was head Elder, Siun, Gara and Plesc were the others; Aron definitely didn't belong with that group.

A moment later Plesc arrived with the Runner.

She was a tall, lanky woman, in a faded shirt and trousers that looked older than she was. Her face was weathered and lined, her hair a brown-gray mix like old dead leaves. Even when he was looking right at her, his eyes tended to slide away. It was part the way she looked and part from the charms she wore on a thong passed round her neck.

She moved her head when he looked at her. It was almost as if she were like a hunting dog and could smell the tracks his eyes made.

He snapped his lids down and lay very still, relaxing only when he heard Plesc's voice. He eased his eyes open but was careful not to look at the Runner.

". . . wanted to wait till the Bride was here and the Seers too busy with upping at each other to bother with darocs. That's why this second meeting. There's more than the Bride's little games to talk about." The old woman's face was weary, the flesh sagging on the bones, and a muscle twitched at the end of her left eye, which meant she was really worried.

Urs lost the sense that this was a game. He lay very still

and listened as hard as he could, so he could remember every word.

The Runner leaned forward, elbow on her knees.

Urs watched her from the corner of his eyes, but fixed his gaze on Aron so the strange woman wouldn't get nervous again.

"You've got some time to get ready. Once the Bride is seyled and pregnant, she won't have access to privacy and her habits need that. Ordinarily that would be a blessing. Not so, at this time. At Domain Tiolan a daroc boy, the Rememberer's apprentice he was, he followed Mirrialta when she went to meet one of her spies. It was a dangerous thing, but his Master had taught him the sliding ways and he was not caught. I was there, up from Mullach, and what he saw is why I bring you warning and will carry warning along my Round."

"Warning?" Urs's Mam frowned. "What could be worse than having a whipmistress as Bride and why should other Domains care?"

The Runner didn't answer her directly. "If you did what I asked, one of you is the Ead Rememberer. Tell us of the time of Corruption." She clicked her tongue. "No. Wait. I'm wrong. Tell us what the Domains do in the Corruptions, time after time."

Urs blinked as his Mam and the rest of the elders fixed their eyes on Aron, then waited in silence for him to speak.

Aron was sitting with his eyes on the ground, his clasped hands dangling between his knees. He stayed that way for several moments, then he lifted his head, his face gone stiff. "War," he said. "They march against the Riverines, kill all mixed bloods and bring the runaways back to the Domains."

"And who fights that war for them?"

"Bantars, ridos and darocs."

"Darocs," the Runner said. "Fight because they have no choice about it. Die so that their cousins are killed or tied back to the land. This is the word the boy brought to his Master: 'Radayam ait é Eadro-Carlath is a woman of middle years, on the farther edge of her bearing time, a woman of austere habit with no interest in the pleasures of the flesh. She expects you, O Damya Mirrialta, to bear the heirs to Eadro and to take over the administration of the Domain while she raises an army and marches on the Riverine Confluence to purify Saffroa of the taint of mixed blood and to reclaim runaway darocs and their children and their children's children.' Those are the very words of the Bride's spy.''

The Runner cleared her throat. ''There was more, but that's what matters now. The Rememberer of Tion spoke to me of the Corruption, and I say to you, ask the Rememberer of Ead to tell the beads of time and listen to what he says. The signs are clear. It comes soon and when it comes the Powers of the Seers will be increased and the Powers of the Traiolyns will be terrible.

''Daroc magic is subtle and slow. That's as it must be for were the Lynborn to suspect its presence they would destroy it as they destroy all boy children with the Sight. But it means we must act soon or we can do nothing. I carry this warning while there is still time to think and choose, still time to weave our defenses and preserve our own.''

She got to her feet. ''Ask the Rememberer while Radayam and her Seers are distracted by the Wedding and the Seyling and let no time be lost before you begin the weave.'' She bowed and slipped away, lost among the shadows before she'd gone more than two steps.

Plesc stayed where she was. So did the others. No one said anything. Urs scowled through the leaves at them and wondered what they were up to.

Finally Plesc sighed, drew her hand across her face. ''When the Messengers sang the first time, I asked Aron if this had happened before and what it meant; he told me what he told you tonight, but I didn't know it would start here. And I didn't know it would start now.''

Cheaasa cleared her throat. ''I think we need to know more, especially about the strengthening of the Seers. And what is this Corruption? Does it affect our magic too? Or only those who tear fistfuls from the Flow?''

Gara nodded. "I agree. First though . . . Aron, have you chosen your apprentice? If not, you must. You can't put it off any longer."

"He's chosen himself. As I did, do you remember, Plesc?" Aron grinned, then he lifted his head and stared straight at Urs. "Urs, come down out of that tree and join us."

[5]

Watching as the guests filed into the vao seyl arena, separating to find the seats allotted according to carefully worked-out precedence, Argy lay in the brush at the top of the hill behind benches, scratching his snigga bites and wondering what had happened to Saml. He turned as he heard a rustle in the dead leaves and dry grass. "Where you been?"

Saml stretched out beside him. "Seeing if I could find Urs. He's gone off somewhere, I dunno where."

"He was acting real funny when I saw him this morning. Wonder what's got into him?"

Saml shrugged and the bush arching over him shivered in response to the movement. "You see how many arrthoïr got past the doorkeeper?"

"More'n twenty last count. Hard to tell the way they're milling around down there. Just 'fore you come, doorkeeper booted ol' Liom. So drunk I could smell him from here. It's only the best get in."

"Yeah." Saml wriggled forward a bit more. All around him he could hear rustles and whispers, the glug of water jugs, the crunch of hard candy. "I wonder what happened to Urs. Everyone else is here."

"Maybe he was doing some fool thing and got caught."

"Yeah. Any daroc-born among the arrthoïr?"

"They been milling around so much it's hard to tell, but I think there's three. Anyway there were three darker than the others."

" 'S Teeth, that's not bad. Three out of twenty in a big Do like this. Show me."

"Can't. They went inside the waithouse just 'fore you came."

"Bonedevil take that slachhead Urs. He gone ferkier than a herdgirl with the itch. I wanted to see them marching in."

· "You didn't miss much. They just walked 'cross the slates and went inside."

The two boys went silent and rested their chins on their crossed forearms as the horns sounded, announcing the Bride and her entourage. They weren't interested in her, just wanted the fuss to be over so the fights could begin. They were wondering if one of the adopted darocs would win the Seyl. Wondering if maybe he or one of the other boys among the Ead darocs would have a chance to break free of the laws and customs that tied them to the soil.

[6]

Mirrialta took the hand that Thador extended to her after the servant had brushed off the leather-covered bench; she settled herself on the cushions, the beaded white siotha of the Second-Day dress billowing about her. Thador knelt beside her and handed her the speaking rattle, a bronze U on a handle, strung with wires of silver, beads of bronze and crystal threaded on them. When it was shaken to show approval, the beads made a rushing sound like whitewater rapids.

She sat alone in the Host's bosc. Alone, because this first day was dedicated to her, not to the Traiolyn. In the other boscs, the guesting Traiolyns were watching her, critical, appraising, wondering what she meant to the power of Eadro. That was good, though there were other things about this business that she found less good than she'd expected.

Radayam had made letting her come alone a point of courtesy, but Mirrialta had a strong suspicion that her newly made kinswoman was pleased to be able to escape this particular part of the wedding celebration. Behind the smiling mask she was careful to keep in place, she was uncertain about how this was going to work out. She had plenty of confidence in her own abilities, but something about Radayam chilled her; the woman's eyes seemed to read her inmost secrets and having read them, looked at her with cool disdain that made Mirrialta feel about two years old and stupid besides.

She thought about the word that Thador had brought her and found herself hoping that Radayam's plots prospered. That would take her away and leave Domain Eadro in Mirrialta's hands.

With any luck the old woman will get herself killed, and if I'm carrying the Heir, the Domain Council will wait for the child to be born before jumping up another Traiolyn. If it's a girl, I'll be Regent until she is thirty and if I can't tame her in all those years, I don't know myself.

A drum boomed.

Mirrialta emerged from her daydream and the smile on her face turned real as she watched the rido drumming the double line of arrthoïr onto the slates of the arena floor. When she saw the three darker ones at the end of the line, she almost forgot herself and scowled. Jumped-up darocs adopted into the Lyns of minor Domains who didn't care about purity of blood, only about the chance of bonding through a Seyl-match to a major Lyn. If one of them wins, I'll poison him before I'll let him into me.

The Ead rido stopped his march in front of the Host's bosc. He lifted the strap from round his shoulder and raised the drum above his head; it was a tambourine, long as a tall man's legs and shaped like a truncated cone with a single drumhead, the small hole at the bottom open to the ambient air. He tapped the head twice more with the round-headed mallet, then he dropped to one knee, the drum standing beside him. "O Bride of Eadro," he intoned. "I present to you the Candidates for Seyling, these arrthoïr, twenty in number, who will contest for the Seyling of the Bride and the Promiser."

Mirrialta rose to her feet, acknowledged the presentation with a shake of her rattle, then settled herself back on the bench as the line of arrthoïr bowed to her.

Her dreams and doubts both forgotten, she watched with pleasure muscles moving under oiled flesh as the Seyl fighters moved across the Pit in their appointed pairs and waited for the signal for the first elimination fights to begin. These were contests of the staff, no blood allowed, but broken arms, legs, ribs and heads were not unknown.

[7]

Radayam stood beside the oval table and smiled politely as the Achtaim ushered the group of Seers from the room. She'd had meetings all morning and she was tired of smiling, tired of talking, tired of playing the power games that were part of her role as Traiolyn. Though she'd got important Domain business done, those meetings had all been camouflage for the one that was about to begin.

She moved away from the table and went to stand looking out the tower window as the servants came in and began clearing away the debris left from the last meeting, the sheaves of paper, the pencils, the cups and the tea urn, bringing in fresh materials to set up for the next meeting. When the variable gusty wind blew toward her, she could hear muted sounds from the arena.

She hadn't expected to dislike her Wife quite so thoroughly. She had paid little attention to the character of the woman, relying on the suggestions of her Seers instead of her own observations. She needed to provide an Heir for Eadro, but she was profoundly uninterested in the details. Mirrialta was in good health, had reasonably strong Sight, was reported to be a capable administrator.

And she was born to one of the smaller, poorer Domains so one would not have to pay much attention to her kinfolk. She'd been fostered at Tiolan, but fosterage wasn't a compelling tie and Tiolan had been in tottery shape for the past several decades. They probably hoped for some aid and influence, but that would depend very much on the stand they took when the Purification began. Radayam drew her hand across her mouth. Best to call it what it was. War. An evil word, but out of evil would come goodness. I have to do what Right demands. In the end . . .

She heard the door open and turned to see the Achtaim ushering in four more women.

Radayam set her cup down and pushed the stack of notes aside. "That's well enough done but unimportant."

Teannal looked affronted, Cluayn amused, Shoneyn grave.

Mycill blinked nervously and lowered her eyes to the neat pile of papers in front of her. She was the oldest of the four, almost as old as Radayam, the one with the most raw power in her control, but in her behaviors she'd not grown beyond the girl Radayam had known so long ago. It made others overlook her ability and treat her as a nonentity; from this source came the pool of rage that simmered inside her—and this rage was one of the reasons that Radayam had selected her.

"I have a thought about the times and what we should do about them that I wish to share with you all and only with you. For the moment at least. If any of you consider that something you don't want to know, please leave now. There is no penalty for following the prompting of one's conscience."

Into the silence that followed this announcement the soft breeze brought muted cheers mingled with the sharp bite of the rattles and the boom of a drum along with the delicate scent of the flowering plums in the Lynhouse gardens. The bowl lamps flickered and added the fragrance of the scented oil to the other perfumes floating on the air. They also added to the warmth of the room.

Shoneyn tapped her fingernail against the porcelain of the teacup, a small musical *ting* that brought the silence to an end. There was a fine film of sweat on skin as delicately translucent as the cups and wisps of dark gold hair broke from her smooth braids to form a fine halo about her face. "We all know the signs. The Corruption marches toward us." Amber eyes only slightly darker than her hair glowed with a gentle fervor. "Not Corruption, but Cleansing—is that your dream, Radya? This touches my own dream, as you must know, else why am I here, now?"

Cluayn's long narrow eyes were half shut, her mouth compressed into a straight line. She nodded, but didn't speak.

Tenneal smoothed her hair, pleased to be included in what she obviously considered a circle of the elite. "Signs. Yes. I for one am deeply interested in what you have to say, Radya."

"I also." Mycill's syllables were clipped as if she bit off their tails.

Radayam smiled again, pleased that their responses corresponded so exactly with her expectations. "I thank you," she said. "There are four matters of consequence I wish you to consider. First, with the Corruption comes an increase of Power, a Gift of the All-Mother. It is my belief that this Power is given to us to wipe away the taint of this Corruption and those that have come before.

"Second, those who are stains on the purity of the land will not be easily removed. This will mean war with death and sad injury to the Pure as well as the impure, but once we have set our hand to the sword, we cannot lay it down until the task is completed.

"Third, there are those among the Lynborn who have fallen away from the Purity. They will oppose the raising of the army and must be led back into the true Way.

"Fourth, as the Corruption reaches its zenith, there will be much confusion and chaos in the land. The Purification must be completed before then and we must be ready to act as centers of calm and sanity for the Siofray until that other world has retreated from us and taken its taint with it."

There was a fifth thing on her list, but she said nothing of that to them now for she did not want to frighten them or wake ambitions too large for their gifts. She had no worries about Cluayn or Shoneyn. Cluayn was too intelligent and Shoneyn too devout, but Mycill was greedy and Teannal filled with the shadows cast by the thousand superstitions that inhabited the place in her where others would have prudence and with a petty spite that distracted her continually from important things.

Cluayn placed her hands flat on the table and smiled. "I have a tale to tell. May I, Radya?"

"The wand is yours."

"Last year about this time, one of the male Fuascala darocs ran; his eyes had turned and he knew what that meant."

Teannal leaned forward, taut with anger. "A Mage? Another Mage?"

"Hardly. This one was rather stupid, but he had an astonishing control of the Flow. It was his only gift as far as my sister Seers and I could tell. When we were closing on him, he sent out a call to that Mage we do know of."

Teannal pinched her mouth together. "You blame us for letting him escape. Everyone blames us."

"No, of course not, Tenna. The All-Mother has reasons for what She permits that we mortals cannot understand. As I said, the boy somehow thrust his voice into the Flow in a great cry for help. And it was a directed cry, aimed eastward at the Sanctuary Isles. We discovered later that no one but my sister Seers and I had heard it and it came to our senses only because we were so close to our quarry.

"This interested me and I have done some work with the discovery, finding it faster, less chancy and more private than scry-speak. I have managed to converse from the Fuascala Lynhouse with one of our bantars in the market at Valla Murloch. What is more, I spoke unheard by my sister Seers or anyone but this bantar. She is loyal and of our mind regarding the Riverines and the stain they put on the soil of Saffroa."

Radayam felt joy exploding through her body. It was a sign, a Blessing sent by the Prophet. When she could speak, she said, "Is this difficult to learn?"

"No. If I may . . ." At Radayam's nod, Cluayn stood and took a pouch from her belt. "I didn't know how many I would want to pass around, so I created a number of these." She dipped into the pouch, brought out a silver disk with a large moonstone set into the middle of it.

She set this on the worktable in front of Radayam, then moved over to Shoneyn. "Doing unmediated what that daroc did is tiring. You feel utterly drained after a session of more than a few words. So I worked out a . . . well, call it a shunt

. . . that will do most of the patterning for you."

She finished the round with Mycill, then went back to her chair. "The force knot is permanent. All you have to do is make the link with the Flow, then decide whether you want to speak mind to mind or through projected image. I find projected image more comfortable, but I suppose that is a matter of personal preference. I can show you how these work in less time than I've taken to explain what they are."

"Then let us meet in my meditation room after the entertainment tonight. The room is just below the tower roof and we won't be interrupted by servants or anyone else. This is a holy thing, Cluayn, and a sign that our alliance will prosper." Radayam got to her feet, lifted her hands and held them palm to palm above her head. "The All-Mother be blessed for her gift to our cause."

The four stood and echoed her words.

Radayam resumed her seat, then tapped her fingers on the tabletop to call the others to order. "Shoneyn, where does Domain Planda stand on the question of the Riverines?"

[8]

In the Fanai Circle at the edge of Ead Village, Alainn sat on the back steps of his van and touched the new guitar with a pleasure greater than any woman had ever brought him. The wood was silk under his fingertips, the delicate bone inlays gleaming in the firelight. Fonn must have been snooping. She was good at that, though not so good at keeping secret the things she heard. He smiled when he thought of her, stroked the guitar face again, his smile widening until he was grinning like a fool.

He hadn't expected a Commorta, especially last night when he came back to the camp, exhausted by demands of the Lynborn and the mind-numbing boredom of that dinner which he only saw and never got a taste of. He hadn't expected Master Bayn to be waiting for him with a plate of painted eggs or Master Cyddam to mark his progress with a new-made song played on his long black flute or Banria Marasc to come with cloths and warm water to bathe his face and hands.

"Journeyman Alainn," he said aloud, rolling the words on his tongue like sugarplums.

He heard a giggle with a hint of lisp that told him who it was. "Told ya," Fonn said. "Next Commorta, I said. Didn't say when, did I, hm hm, did I?"

"You should be in bed."

"Not my Mam, are you?"

He turned his head, saw she was in her shift and barefoot. "Fonn!"

"Tsah! Bemmi took my clothes away, but I fooled her." She tossed her head. "I'm gonna watch the dancing and no one's gonna stop me."

Alainn shook his head. "You're something, you."

She grinned. There was another tooth gone. "So you gonna sing my tooths into grass?"

"Didn't I say I would? When?"

"Tomorrow after sunhigh when the Vao Seyl's being fought. Won't want any fanai round then. So?"

"We eat and go. Why not." He made a face at her. "Fonn, your Mam will snatch you bald, she catches you out like that."

"Isn't going to catch me." She giggled, then faded back into the shadows that lay around the wattled walls of the daroc houses, moving so silently it was as if a ghost passed that way rather than a small wild girl.

A moment later the file of Masters came round the van. Master Bayn beckoned to Alainn and he joined the march to the dance ground.

A hand touched Alainn's shoulder; he looked around, saw Master Veidhal standing beside him.

"Break now. Short bit timer candle burning at the trestle table. You've got one band to rest and eat."

"Thanks." Alainn eased out of the group, slipped the guitar's strap over his head. Before he got two steps, he heard the fiddle slide into the mix and give Veidhal's special lilt to the music. Out among the dancers, sudden smiles touched

flushed and sweaty faces, feet kicked higher and faster. Someday, he thought. Someday that will happen for me too.

[9]

The last day of the Vao Seyl was hot and humid, the air heavy
with the threat of rain, so still that sweat lay in beads on the
skin and the smell of that sweat, of rancid oil and blood from
the fighters filled the arena, along with the stale perfumes and
other odors from the guests who filled the boscs and benches.

Radayam endured the boredom and distaste she felt for this
business because it was her duty. This was the right and proper
order of things. She glanced occasionally at Mirrialta, unhappy
with what she was seeing. The Bride was leaning forward,
hands on the rail at the front of the box, tongue flickering over
her full lips. Mirrialta's eyes glittered with a passion that Radayam had never felt for anything, not even her mission to
purify Saffroa—a passion Radayam found deeply disturbing.

I shouldn't have put the search into other hands than mine,
she thought. I wonder. Were they fooled, bribed or threatened?
No matter. Too late now to investigate the past. What's done
is done. I'll have to watch her, though, and watch my back,
especially after she has had the first daughter. She won't be
content with second place or with restraints on her actions.

Down in the Pit three pairs of arrthoïr circled in intense and
wary confrontations. Each flurry of blows within the pairs was
so quick the exchange was over and the men leaping apart
almost before it began, and the circling and feinting and
aborted strikes began once more. This was the blood level; to
lose at this point in the Vao Seyl was to lose everything. Of
the six men left in the games, five would be dead before the
sun set on this day.

Against her expectations, Radayam found her interest
caught—particularly by one of the fighters. He was quick and
unusually beautiful, not bulky like so many of the arrthoïr,
using intelligence as well as his reflexes and his strength. By
his darker skin and several other signs clear to her, he was
daroc-born and adopted into a Lyn when the rido fight-master

noted that his pupil's sparring partner was the better fighter. She approved of this as a way of importing new blood into the Lyns without changing the Prophet-blessed order of the Domains. A glance at Mirrialta told her that the Bride was furious at a daroc-born surviving the nonblood stages of the Vao Seyl. A little humiliation would be good for her soul, Radayam thought. When she turned back to the Pit, the daroc-born arrth had solved his opponent's defense and with an elegant, sure stroke dispatched him.

With the sound of the rattles applauding his victory, he stepped into the winner's bosc and waited for the other two contests to finish. Radayam disciplined the smile that twitched at her mouth and swung her rattle in subdued applause; Mirrialta hesitated, but gave a few shakes of hers also, then dropped it into her lap as if it were too hot to hold.

Radayam passed her hand across her mouth, hiding another smile that she couldn't suppress this time. This marriage will destroy my character. It's too enjoyable to thwart my Bride.

With considerable interest, Radayam watched the last contest, hoping the daroc-born arrth would be the Seyl. He would be an asset to Eadro, bringing intelligence and style to his role as Father of the Heir, and he'd be a help to her in the matter of controlling the Wife. She was annoyed when she saw the two Lynborn arrthoïr combining against him.

He survived longer than she had expected, but these men were nearly as good and two of them were too much for him.

The last contest, as the two Lynborn fought each other, was short, brutal and ugly. Both men were too tired for anything but hack and slash.

When one man lay dying on the crusted slates, the other stood panting and swaying, leaning on the hilt of the sword point down in a crack between the slates. The muscles in his arms jerking, his legs trembling, he waited for the formal acceptance from the Traiolyn, all emotion and character blanked out of his face, his eyes empty.

Radayam stood, walked to the front of the box and waited

for Mirrialta to join her. Around her the Traiolyns stood in their boscs, silent and waiting. Behind her the bantars and ridos of Eadro, the bantars and ridos of the guests, stood also and waited. The rido fight-master came to the front rail of the bosc and gave her a slip of paper with the winner's name written on it.

"I, Radayam ait é Eadro-Carlach, Traiolyn of Domain Eadro . . ." She touched Mirrialta's arm.

"And I, Mirrialta ait é Eadro-Mullach y Tiolan . . ."

"We call to you, O Bruyd y Dorseh, be our Seyl, the father of our children, the strong arm upon which we lean in times of trouble. Join to us in the name of the Prophet and All-Mother for whom she speaks."

The arrth's chest heaved, then he straightened his shoulders and with an effort lifted the sword high above his head. "My arm and my body are at your service, O Traiolyn and Wife of Eadro."

Radayam bowed her head. "So let it be heard, so let it be written, Bruyd y Dorseh is Seylmate to Radayam and Mirrialta of Eadro. Let it be written, Bruyd is of Dorseh no more, Eadro till in death he joins the All-Mother."

She set her hand on the front rail of the Host bosc, released the catch and stepped onto the slates, Mirrialta beside her. She gave Mirrialta's hand to the new Seylmate, then walked from the Pit one step ahead of them. She was disappointed in the outcome of the Vao Seyl and found the man's rank smell distasteful. Just as well that she had no intention of getting any closer to him than she was today. She permitted herself a small smile as she walked through the long tunnel that led from the Pit to the gardens beyond. It was the Wife's duty to bathe and tend the wounds of the Seylmate, to serve him a meal and feed him with her own hands. I will send servants with her, Radayam thought. She will know they are spies and she is wary of me still, so she will follow custom or face having contrition duty set upon her by the cantair. I think she knows what I will have ready for her is worse than anything custom demands. We begin as we will go on.

7

Breith at Sea

By the calendar of the Domains of Iomard, events dating from the 15th day of Trairin to the 1st day of Seyos, the sixth month in the Iomardi year 6535, the 722nd year since the last Corruption.

[1]

> . . . told me Ellar sent her away to Cyfareth to keep her from making trouble for herself and him. I've thought this over, Mam, Mum, Da, and I think I should do the same, go away, I mean. You won't have the Council and the Inquisition in your face if I'm not there and where I'm going they can't get at me either, so that's good for me too. By the time you read this, I'll be on a ship heading for Ascal. Don't worry about me. I will keep my head down and my shields up.
>
> Love to you all,
> Breith

Faobran crumpled the sheet of paper with its careful, cramped writing and flung it against the wall with a hoarse cry that broke past her usual control and contained within it all her anger at Breith and her fear for his safety.

The gasp from the housegirl who'd fetched her to Breith's

130 · *Jo Clayton* ·

room reminded her she wasn't alone. She shuddered, drew and
released several breaths and finally managed to retrieve the
disciplined face she showed to everyone but her closest. She
turned. "Ask Wife Yasayl and Seyl Malart to join me here,
please. And send a tray from the kitchen with tea and wafers."

When the girl was gone, Faobran walked across the room
and picked up the wad of paper. She opened it out, set it
against the wall and smoothed her hand over and over it, pressing out the creases, her eyes shut, her hands moving as if she
stroked a cat. This uncomplicated repetitive act brought calm
back to her blood. It also brought tears pricking behind her
eyelids.

After a moment, she took the paper and went to sit in
Breith's reading chair, the one near the bookcases. This was
no time for extravagance, no tears, no rages. "Silly boy," she
said aloud. "I'd be more impressed if I weren't sure that half
this nobility and sacrifice was fueled by your restlessness."

"What?"

She looked up and saw Malart standing in the doorway. She
lifted the letter. "Read this."

Yasayl tightened her hand on Faobran's shoulder. "For what
it's worth, Fori, I've had no warnsights about him."

"Would you?"

Yasayl patted the shoulder a last time, then tapped away to
sit on Breith's bed. "I don't know. Mostly I see broad lines
and how they diverge, but you know that. Unless Breith is key
to a change-node. . . ." She fell silent.

Faobran stiffened as she saw the sudden roil in the Pneuma
that always clung to Yasayl. "Yasa?"

Her sister/Wife sighed and relaxed. The whorls in the
Pneuma smoothed out. "That was odd," she said.

"What did you see?"

"Nothing. There was just a feeling of . . . well, of signifi-
cance, as if something I said had a meaning beyond what I
saw." She shook her head. "Don't bother asking. I don't
know what it was."

"Fori, I've found him. Come here."

Faobran hurried across the room to Malart. He was seated at the worktable, Breith's scrybowl in front of him. She put her hand on his shoulders, felt the knotted muscles. Without consciously willing it, she began kneading the knots away as she looked past his head at the image in the bowl.

Breith was curled up in a nest of blankets with a water jug by his head and his backpack leaning against a small crate. The image dipped and swayed, but that didn't disrupt the sense of comfort and ease.

"Stowaway?"

"Right. And he's made a good job of it. Set up near an air shaft, on top of some bales. Leather, I think. Wrapped in sacking. Nothing near to shift and fall on him if they hit a storm. . . ."

She slapped at his shoulder, the sound a sharp crack that broke through his words. "You sound like you approve."

"I was two years younger when I ran from Tiolan with nothing but a knife, a hunk of stale bread and my wits. And no training or discipline in the Sight. Breith is stronger right now than I'll ever be and he has a scholar's turn of mind so he'll work out what he has to know even without a teacher."

"He's a boy, Marl. Half the time he's got no sense at all. He'll do something idiotic and get himself killed."

Malart closed his hand over hers. "Fori, there are no schools or rules for what we are, Breith and I. You know that. Breith has to learn when to use his Sight and when to stand back and not interfere with what's happening. I've tried telling him what I learned, but that isn't . . . it doesn't really reach him. I'm afraid for him, of course I am, but he needs what he's going to learn about surviving and living with the results of his actions. He has a good heart, but this past year has been a hard one, more than you know."

"You're saying I don't know our son?"

"I'm saying the business took you away a lot. You had to go, but you've missed things I've seen."

Yasayl got to her feet, groped around for her staff. "Malart is right, Fori. There would have been trouble soon. Now Bré goes with love in his heart and excitement, not anger. If you bring him back here, the next time he leaves, he will be resenting, even hating us."

"Ascal ship captains are slavers. All of them. Given the opportunity. If Breith is found, what do you think the captain of that ship will do with him?"

"Keep him in good health so he'll bring a better price," Malart said dryly. "A Siofray boy of good family is a rare prize."

"They geld their male slaves."

"Not all of them. And not until they're sold. Why risk suppuration, which might kill the merchandise at worst and even in the best case cut his worth to a tenth of what it might have been?"

Malart flicked his fingers across the water in the scry bowl, dismissing the image. "Fori, I want Breith to be in a place where he doesn't need to use the Sight, just his natural cleverness. Pneuma is dangerous until his body settles down; he knows that, but as long as he was locked inside Urfa's walls he got so restless and wild he couldn't seem to resist using it. Twice he brought down on himself a Pneuma vortex that could have burned him to ash and Urfa House as well. There's no magic in Ascal. He's safer over there."

Angry to the point of tears, she moved away from him. Yasayl reached out and when Faobran took her hand, she tugged her older sister to her and, with her arm about Faobran, led her from the room.

Malart watched them go, his face stony.

Times like these his position as Seyl galled him. His mates shut him away, they paid no attention to his advice and wouldn't let him share in decisions. It was as if he were a ghost in the walls. Breith was his son too and a boy at that. But he was only a man, so what did he know.

He sighed, reactivated the scry bowl and began moving the point of view about the ship, locating her name, watching her captain, learning everything he could about her in case he needed to act quickly and pull Breith out of there.

[2]

Breith yawned and stretched. The air flowing through the vent had the cold dampness of night; after a minute he heard the voice of the watch cry the hour in the peculiar abbreviated seaslang they used on this ship. He hadn't thought about language, that he'd hardly understand a word the sailors would be speaking. It wasn't too bad. He'd picked up a few words from Tel when Tel was still his friend and some more from his sailing books, so he was beginning to puzzle things out.

Around him the ship was creaking and humming and he could sometimes hear the rush of the sea moving past the hull along with the scurry of rat feet and the slosh of the water in the bilge. The boxes and bales shifted against their anchoring ropes, adding their own rasps and thuds to the ambient noise. After a sennight at sea these sounds had become so familiar they were soothing and, with the motion of the ship, slipped him into sleep as gently as Mum's lullabies did when he was a child. And eased him as gently into wakefulness.

He yawned again, rubbed his nose, scratched at his chin. His bladder was telling him it was time to take care of matters and he felt grungy enough to dip up salt water and see what kind of bath he could make of it. That was another thing he hadn't thought about when he went running off after adventure. Staying grubby was no fun at all. He thought wistfully of the housegirls who used to carry in hot water for his evening bath and launder his things so he'd have fresh clothes to put on each day. Fresh from the skin out. If they got downwind of him now, they'd run off giggling and holding their noses.

He sat up, moving carefully. There was planking close overhead and he'd near knocked himself silly a couple of times. His belly growled and he frowned. Another thing he missed. Hot meals. Stealing biscuit and cheese from the galley and choking down strips of sundried meat hard enough to use as nails had gotten to be not-fun real fast.

With the same kind of caution, he pulled a thread from the Pneuma Flow, wrapped it about himself and used it to power a shunt spell that would turn eyes away from him as long as he didn't call attention to himself. It wasn't complete concealment like Mouse in Pocket, but it didn't involve the handling of much Pneuma so he didn't get the heat buildup. It was safer in another way. There was a Siofray weatherwitch on board. She hadn't much Sight, but it certainly would be enough to spot him if he started using the Flow the way he had before.

This annoyed him. She'd come on after him and spoiled all his plans. She wasn't supposed to be here. Ascalers didn't like the Sighted, that's what everyone said. He'd meant to open the Window and have long chats with Cymel to help pass the time away. Now that was impossible.

The wind was stronger than usual this night; clouds fled like runaway corachs across the moon and the deck was wet with spume.

Storm. Coming at them. He could feel the weatherwitch working to deflect the worst of it. He didn't like her being awake and alert while he was out of his hiding place, but she was probably too busy to notice a stray wisp of Pneuma moving about.

Bent low and holding as much as possible to shadows where the moon didn't shine, he darted to the rail and moved along it to his usual place near the davits that held the ship's boat. Sheltered from view, clinging with one hand to the posts of the nearest davit, he relieved himself into the heaving sea, pleased he didn't have to use the crew head. The place stank—he'd nearly lost the contents of his stomach when he went in there during his exploration of the ship—and it was far too close to the hold where the crew strung up their hammocks.

When he pulled his laces tight and knotted the ends, the wind was stronger than before and beating at him; staggering because the ship's movement was more violent, muttering because the storm was on them faster than he'd expected, he took a step away from the boat, then froze as he heard orders bellowed in the captain's voice rather than the mate's—orders that sent sailors boiling up from below to take storm stations.

Breith flung himself back under the boat, grabbing for the davits so the wash of the waves wouldn't drag him through the rails. He heard cursing and the slap of bare feet as several sailors ran past. The storm, he thought. It's going to be worse than I thought. Maybe one of those Chaos storms Corysiam was talking about.

The ship tilted under him then kicked up again. Scande! It already is worse.

He didn't dare move. The *Lalatikan* wasn't a big ship and she didn't carry deck cargo like one of the House Urfa riverboats so there wasn't all that much cover, especially when the crew was aloft. Even with the look-away shroud, someone was bound to spot him.

He shivered as more seawater crashed over him and the wind turned his fingers and his bare toes to chunks of ice. The storm was still building and could last all night. But *he* couldn't. He felt with his feet, found a stanchion and pushed against it, shoving himself closer to the davit so he could wrap his arms about it.

When he was as safe as he could make himself, he reached for the Flow. Gradually he made the pocket and sealed it around him.

The heat buildup was so swift this time that it frightened him, but it was heat he needed. He pushed the fear down and staggered across the deck until he reached the ladder into the cabin space. The door was shut, almost sealed by the pressure of the wind. He forced it open and pushed himself through the crack and pulled it shut behind him. As he let go, the ship lurched, caught him off balance and he tumbled down the steps.

The noise he made brought Jurmas the cook into the passageway. "Terk! Siapa djad? Apa jang?" Jurmas scowled at the ladder, stepped into his galley and came out again a breath later with a lantern which he raised and lowered so he could see along the passage. After a minute he shrugged and went back to his work. From the smells that drifted out of the galley, he was heating grog and making meat pies.

Though Breith didn't understand the words, the cook's actions were enough to tell him the pocket had held. With a half-swallowed sigh of relief, he got to his feet and hurried the few steps to the captain's cabin. In his poking about he'd discovered that the captain had a hidden trap under his bed that opened to the hold. He hadn't thought much about the reasons for this, but whatever they were, it was a handy way of getting back to his sanctuary without being discovered or swept overboard.

For three days wind and water battered the ship—and more than wind and water. The currents that drove the storm and whirled through it were saturated with Pneuma and great whorls of free Pneuma rode the air masses. He could feel the weatherwitch struggling to turn the winds aside, but the weight and might of the storm was too great for her to handle.

He was cold, hungry, thirsty and weary. There were moments of sheer terror when, lying in darkness, shut into the hold with nothing but sea around him, he felt as if the ship were sinking and taking him down with it. The rats ran about as if they'd gone crazy, filling the space with their squeals. The slamming-about that the ship took also stirred up the bilge and the smells kept getting worse. Worst of all was the growing sense that he was the reason that the storm wouldn't shift and blow itself out in the colder waters of the south.

Odd things happen as the Corruption blossoms, Corysiam had said. Those with the Sight grow more powerful, but they also make greater targets for the Chaos. When it finds them, it eats them out from the inside and they're dead before they die.

Eats them out from the inside. The phrase echoed in his head until he couldn't think, couldn't sleep.

They're dead before they die.

His water ran low, but he didn't dare leave the hold again.

He was down to the last swallow in the bottle when the waves at last smoothed out and the wind dropped.

That night, after he'd resupplied his stores and stowed them in the pack, he stretched out near the bow of the ship, on his back at first, luxuriating in the shimmer of the stars, the depth of the blue-black sky so high overhead and the yellow-white glow of the waxing moon. He'd shrugged off the nightmares the storm had brought him, telling himself it was just the dark and the wind working in him. Looking out and out and out and still not seeing the end of things seemed to wash all that away.

After a while he turned on his stomach and lay watching the fish the sailors call ikalum riding the bow wave, leaping high out of the water at times so they almost seemed to be flying, short-furred sleek creatures, long as a man, striped from nose to tail in dark green and gray, an oval white spot under each blunt snout. They danced on their tails and cried out to each other, then dropped back in the water and found the wave again, letting the sea lift them into another leap.

He could have watched them longer without worrying about discovery. Exhausted after the storm, the night crew were drowsing wherever they could find a comfortable place to curl up; only the steersman at the wheel was reasonably alert. But he was getting cold so he went below, curled up in his blankets and drifted into a dream-filled sleep.

[3]

Corysiam knocked on the doorpost, then stood waiting in the doorway.

Malart looked around, saw who it was and got to his feet. He touched his finger to his lips, pointed into the scroll room at one of the chairs by the long table. Before he closed the door, he took a long look at the corridor outside, his head turning quickly back and forth several times as if he couldn't quite believe that he really saw nothing but gloom and dust.

When he came back to her, Corysiam pointed at a small

waxed charm in the center of the table, careful not to touch
the wax even with the tip of her fingernail; it was one of the
most powerful wards she knew against oversight. "A cunador?
Have things got that bad? And why here instead of at Urfa
House?"

"Bad? Do I need to answer that, Cory?" He pulled out a
chair and sat facing her. "As to why here, it occurred to me
that it might be a good thing if you weren't too closely associated with us. As to why at all, Breith has stowed himself
on a ship heading for Ascal."

Corysiam raised her brows as he explained why Breith had
run away. When he finished, she said, "You want me to
Bridge him back?"

Malart rubbed his hand across his face. He looked exhausted, angry, frustrated. "No." The word a stone flung at
her. "Faobran will ask you, but I want you to refuse."

"Ascal is dangerous, especially for a sheltered Siofray
boy."

"You think I don't know that!" he shouted. Once again he
raised his hands to his face, pressed them over his eyes. Wearily he said, "I don't want to have this argument again, Scribe.
I've had it every day the past week while we waited for you
to get back to Murloch. She doesn't know another Bridge and
won't trust someone she doesn't know." He lowered his
hands. "I'm only a man, Scribe Corysiam. Only a Seyl. All I
can do is try to convince her that keeping Breith home and
protecting him will do more to harm him than . . . she won't
listen to me." He lowered his eyes to the table. "She never
has. Sometimes she indulges me and goes along with what I
want, but she doesn't listen." He straightened, fixed his eyes
on her face. "I would like you to look in on him now and
then, pull him out if he's in serious trouble, and by serious, I
mean facing death or maiming. Otherwise leave him alone."

"Of course." Corysiam leaned closer to the cunador.
"Have you considered that you're in danger also, Malart?"

His mouth curled into a wry smile. "I try not to think about
that, Cory. I have thought of running, but what's the point of

it? I'm not a young man any longer; I don't think I can handle living hard. And I don't see that my leaving would profit my family much. My taint's been rubbed on them for nearly twenty years now. I worry about Bauli, but she is female and the only Heir to Urfa House so I don't see how they can touch her.''

Corysiam shook her head. "I wouldn't be too complacent about that, Malart. There's lots of talk about giving the Council the right of last approval on the choice of an Heir, and too many traders and Councillors don't see the second edge on that weapon." She sat back, looked around. "From the amount of dust in here, this room hasn't been opened for generations."

"I doubt even Slionn knows it's here. Or that I'm here."

"Doesn't know and won't inquire?"

"Could be."

"The Councillors have been assigned personal inquisitors. Did you know that? Not just cantairs, inquisitors. Some ambitious people are very busy these days. Piety is a useful tool, a knife for the back and a paintbrush for the front. Yrahar of House Tualla was unseated by decree because she would not follow the guidance of her inquisitor. Wouldn't even let the woman into her workchamber and kept ranting in the Hall of Deliberations about the freedom of individual conscience. She went back to Soriseis mad enough to pound the first cantair she saw into the mud and use her as a wharf pile. Valla Murloch's pair haven't said anything; I don't know how they're going to jump. That visitation you got is not a hopeful sign, so keep a wary eye on events, Malart." She got to her feet, moved round the table and put her hand on his shoulder. "Or you might find yourself with a headache from the burnout of your Sight, looking at the world from behind the walls of a retreat that's more like a prison."

[4]

The days on the *Lalatikan* slid along, one much like the other except that each day was perceptibly warmer than the one before. Breith slept most of the day and spent the night wandering about the deck and watching the ikalum play in the bow waves. He had to force himself to keep up his precautions, wind himself into the look-away shunt and stay in shadow as much as he could. After the third week of the voyage he was so itchy to get off the ship he was almost ready to be captured just so there'd be something new to think about.

At the end of the third week the *Lalatikan* dropped anchor in the harbor of the largest of a spray of islands.

Breith woke from a sodden, nightmare-ridden sleep as the motion of the ship changed. At first he didn't understand what was happening, then the smells funneling down woke him from his dullness—a mix of spices and flowers, seaweed and dead fish. A moment later there were loud splashes and the forward plunge of the *Lalatikan* stopped.

Voices shouting.

Not the Ascal he'd picked up though there were similar-sounding words here and there in the gliding liquid flow of the speech.

Someone blowing on a flute or a horn, making a sound he'd never heard before.

Someone else playing a drum.

There was something odd about the mix of sound. It took a while for him to realize what it was. No women's voices. This puzzled him.

The captain and the crew of the *Lalatikan* were all men, but he'd thought of them as ridos or the male affiliates who did the digging and building and much of the smithing in Urfa House.

He gathered up his pack, the water jug and the blankets and hid them more securely, then retreated to a pile of crates beneath the hidden trap. If any of the crew came down into this hold to fetch trade goods, he wanted to have a bolt-hole close to hand in case they discovered him.

While he worked he could hear sounds in the stores hold, scrapings and curses as the smaller barrels were lifted out. Then the squeals and thuds as the ship's boat was lowered.

Laughter from the sailors. Shouted exchanges with the folk who lived here as the second boat was winched down. The sound of feet and the creak of ropes as the men went over the side and into that boat.

Water, Breith thought. This must be a supply stop.

The rest of the afternoon passed without anything happening except for the stifling heat—no air movement through the vents to make the hold bearable. Breith moved back to the leather bales, stretched out on them though the prickling of the burlap wasn't all that comfortable. The ship was as quiet as it had been when it was tied up in Valla Murloch. The witch was gone and the captain with her. The only one left onboard seemed to be a watchman. At long intervals he stumped by overhead, walking a circuit around the main deck, cursing his luck at being left out of the fun onshore.

Breith slept.

He woke to the sound of music and the smell of roasting meat sliding down through the air vent.

[5]

Wrapped in his spiderweb of don't-look-at-me, Breith lay in the shadow of a small house made of bricks with a roof made out of bundles of long narrow leaves from a kind of tree that he'd never seen before. The bricks were a pale yellow, thick and crumbly, and the thatch rustled more from the vermin living in it than the breeze that wandered through the village, though he heard these rustles only when the drummers and the shell-blower paused to catch a breath.

He felt Pneuma, rolled away from the house wall.

Lines of small creatures were crawling down the wall, like a chain of tiny squirrelmonks, clinging mouth to tail. No. Not squirrelmonks, but distorted little people, tailed people, some with fish heads, some like crabs, some he couldn't find descriptions for. Lumps of Pneuma given shape, not flesh.

They stared at him. He could feel consternation and fear flowing out from them—their fear wiping his away.

They vanished—as if they'd simply melted into the bricks of the wall.

He watched a moment longer, shrugged and went back to watching the islanders and their celebration.

The houses of the village were arranged in a wide oval about a flat ground where nothing grew, lit by torches on long poles and filled with dancers swaying and stamping their feet to the beat of the drums. As groups moved apart, Breith saw a fire pit in the center of the open area, several small carcasses on a spit dripping fat onto the bed of coals.

A little man, bone-thin, bald and wrinkled, glistening with a mix of oil and sweat, stood over the carcasses, painting them with a reddish fluid. Drops of this sauce sizzled loudly on the coals and added a pungent sweetness to the smells of the night.

These islanders were all little people, at least a head shorter than the sailors dancing with them, and they all wore wrap-around garments held in place by fish-bone pins. The women looked like pretty dolls with nothing above the waist but neck-laces of fresh flowers. The way their breasts bounced . . . Breith wriggled uncomfortably on the sand.

The heat, the drums, the way the firelight ran along the smooth bare skin, the perfumes drifting on soft eddies of the breeze that seemed to dance with the people swaying and stomping their feet, these crept under Breith's skin and he found himself on his knees, slapping at his chest in time with the drumbeats.

Appalled at how close he'd come to betraying himself, he dropped onto his heels and forced his hands down, but when they touched his thighs, he jerked them up again.

His hands shone with a red glow that was not a reflection of the torchlights. And they burned.

Terrified, he jumped to his feet and ran through the trees and into the harbor.

At first the water exploded away from him in clouds of steam, but as he waded farther out and started swimming toward the *Lalatikan* he could feel the sea draining the heat out of him. By the time he reached the ship he was shivering and sick.

In the hold he stripped down, used one of the cached blankets to rub himself dry, wrapped himself in the other and stretched out on the leather bales.

The throbbing of the drums crept into his body, muted by distance, soft and insistent, smoothing away his troubled thoughts.

He slept.

When he woke, the ship was at sea again and a fever had him by the throat.

[6]

Corysiam groaned and crawled from the bunk. She'd spent thousands of miles in the saddle without a twinge or a sore, but a trip like this on a riverboat made her feel like an ancient daroc worn out from work in the fields. Prophet be blessed, this was the last stop on the trip north. She sighed. All to do over again when she went back south, but that was at least a sennight off and she didn't have to think about it until then.

It was early summer but this was Soriseis, the northernmost of the Riverine Citystates, and the air that crept through the cracks in the translucent fused shell that the boatmakers used instead of glass was damp and cold and she could hear sporadic flurries of raindrops beating against the western wall of the cabin block.

An unpleasant day in many senses of that word. She had official business to take care of, delivering certified copies of the new laws and regulations from the Council to the City Managers. She wasn't happy about this, but it did give her an excuse to travel to all the Citystates along the Siamsa River and talk with people there about certain unofficial matters.

Soriseis was a city of wood, shell and slate, built on the shore of Lake Piorrog, much of it carved out of the vast forest that spread from the upper Siamsa north to the treeline and west to the Scaraym, the mountain range that separated the two lobes of Saffroa. To Corysiam, born to sunshine and heat in the flat grasslands farther south, the forest was an ominous monster, looming over the city in silent threat. Those trees and the black waters of the lake inhabited her nightmares when she slept here.

Since it was only a little after noon, the city was almost empty, the morning shopping over, the barrow sellers dozing in their niches, waiting for the midday long meal to be finished and the streets to fill again.

These streets were roofed with shell from the giant brellacs that the Soriseins fished from the lake, shellfish the size of rowboats that crawled along eating the weed that grew thick as fur in the bottom's black muck. The rain was dissolving the last patches of snow on those street roofs, though most of it had already melted and run off through the flumes that led to the lake.

Little sunlight reached the streets, but they were filled with brightness. Soriseis was called the city of lamps because of the crystal and silver lights that burned year round, day and night, to lighten the gloom in her streets and in the rooms of her houses with their thick walls and small windows. They didn't burn oil like ordinary lamps, but used Pneuma to create a steady white glow. It was a trick that only the lampwitches of Soriseis knew, and they kept the secret close.

Corysiam made her way to the Scribe Hall, signed for a way-room and left all of her packs there except for the leather case that held the law parchments. With that off her hands and her mind, she headed for the center of the city and the Manager's offices.

According to the time candles, it was almost night when she came out, the signed receipt tucked into the folder with the others she'd collected. The lamps that lit the streets were burning more brightly now and the walkways were filled with Soriseins who all seemed to be talking as loudly and rapidly as possible. In addition, there were fanai clansmen drumming and playing their fiddles in many of the niche-parks, and folk who passed by them spent some time dancing to the beat, snapping fingers and stomping feet. Their soprano yips cut like knives through the creak of wooden wheels as barrow sellers took their goods home and all the rest of the night-noise of Soriseis, a cacophony trapped beneath the street roofs that was like a blow in the face.

Corysiam winced. She hadn't expected to be here so late, but Manager Danadan had left her sitting on the hard benches of the reception chamber as long as she dared. She knew what the Scribe was carrying and that she'd be responsible for executing those laws and directives as soon as she'd signed for them, not a pleasant job even in the best of times, which these were not. Soriseis was a long way from Gabba Labhain and went its own way with a stubborn Northland pride. The Manager had to deal with this pride and with the reality that the Riverine Council controlled access to the southern markets. It was a difficult dance.

Corysiam started for the Scribe Hall then changed her mind. Though she was tired and feeling gloomy, this was as good a time as any for the first of her unofficial visits.

Yrahar sat at her worktable in a room gloomy with shadows, all the light from the lamps focused on the ledger open before her. She set her pen down when the housegirl showed Corysiam in but didn't speak till the girl was gone and the door shut behind her. "What does the Council want now? I thought we had nothing left to say to each other."

"This isn't Council business. I was in Soriseis and I thought I'd give you greetings."

"Why?"

"Admiration. You spoke the truth without fear or favor. Not many are willing to do that these days."

"And you see what it got me." She took up the pen, put her other hand on the book, her forefinger at the last of the entries. "Thank you for the courtesy, Scribe." It was dismissal.

Corysiam ignored her tone and remained seated. "There

was another reason," she said. "I want your help."

"Then you're a fool for coming here."

"Because you're watched?"

"What do you think?"

"I think there's no doubt of it. I also think this room is warded. Hm. Hard to know exactly where you put them." She looked slowly about the room, then smiled at Yrahar. "The lamps, probably. Masked by the Pneuma glow. Very well done, too. Not perceptible even this close. The watchers know they're blocked, of course, but they're not bold enough yet to challenge you."

"If you're right about the wards, Scribe, and I'm not saying you are, the wards wouldn't be set in place for me. This is the accounts office of Tualla House. Tualla keeps her business private."

"Interesting isn't it, that you meet me here. Rumors?"

"This is wasting time and I have work to do. What do you want, Scribe?"

"Many things. This in particular. I want to set up a History Runda. Scribes accept what the Domains give us and store it for later study, but there are great gaps in the data. Whatever the Domain Historians and Traiolyns think might embarrass them, they suppress. The Historians of Labba Gabhain write their own recountings of events from the view of the Scribes. Even here those records are tampered with. The Priom makes sure these contain nothing disturbing or unfavorable to her regime. The gaps betray whoever tries to use the past to plan for the future."

"Why now?"

"Do you ever look across to Glandair?"

"Occasionally. I find their antics sometimes amusing, sometimes a warning of flaws we on Iomard might do well to see in ourselves. I have not been in the mood for such entertainment in the recent past."

"Have you heard of the Watchers of Glandair?"

"No."

"They've done what I want to do. The Watchers watch and

record what they see and their Daybooks are collected, catalogued and stored. They don't see everything but they suppress nothing. They Watch Iomard too, especially during what they call the Settling. When Iomard and Glandair come together. We call it the Time of Corruption. According to a Watcher I know, that time is on us now and it means serious trouble.'' She went on to explain in detail what she had learned from Ellar.

When Corysiam finished, Yrahar sat quietly for several minutes, her eyes focused on nothing. Finally she said, "You're courting trouble when you speak like that to me. To anyone.''

"Spy and seducer?'' Corysiam shook her head. "Not now. The time's not ripe for that kind of folly. By the end of this year, perhaps. We will all be warier then because the level of hysteria will have reached a point where those who hold power will be seeing conspiracies everywhere. Besides, I need you. To get trust, you have to give it.''

Yrahar laughed suddenly, a web of small wrinkles dancing across her face. "Why do I think most of my erstwhile colleagues will never understand that?'' She raised an eyebrow. "And why do I think there's more you're after from me? No, don't answer. We'll take this a step at a time. Count me in on your scheme. How can I help?''

"We'll need repositories and message centers in the City-states along the Siamsa. Eventually in all the Confluence, East and West, but I'm not ready for that yet. Archivists. Collectors. Give me a name or two of those you think would be interested and silent.''

"I'll have to think about that, but I can give you one name. She'd be my choice for Archivist here in Soriseis. Lonra na Gustal. She's one of yours, oddly enough. Broke her back in a fall from her horse when she and her roadmate were attacked by a band of scurds and hasn't walked since. She worked as a Scribe Historian at Gabba Labhain and was good at it, but someone decided she didn't have sufficient purity of belief. She was removed from her position and sent back here. She's not young, but even if she can't walk, she goes where she wants in her wheeled chair, she's vigorous, her mind is sharp as ever and she's bored to tears."

"Sounds good to me. Hm. We'll need funding, property and a reason for existing. I'm looking for suggestions from everyone I speak to. I'm here for a sennight, then I have to head south again. Anything that occurs to you, let me know." She got to her feet. "Prophet bless and thanks."

Yrahar stood also. "Wards or no, they'll know you've visited me and I suspect the others you've talked to will be much like me, on a list of the suspicious and dangerous. You won't have much time before someone decides you're as dangerous as we are."

"I've kept that in mind, Yrahar. But I'm Walker and Bridge. I'll watch for poison, but there's not much else they can do to me."

[7]

Breith felt coolness on his face and opened his eyes to see a woman bending over him. She was bathing his face with a folded rag, so intent on what she was doing that she hadn't noticed he was awake.

Siofray. The weatherwitch.

"Wha . . ." His voice was a hoarse croak and even that small effort made him dizzy.

"Ah! You're back with us, are you?" She dropped the rag in a basin of water and straightened up. "What's your na—" She broke off, stood staring at him. "Green and brown, put him down." She grabbed hold of his hair, pulled his head up and reached for her belt knife.

A hand caught her wrist before she could slash the knife across Breith's throat.

A hand slapped the witch's face. Hard crack of flesh meeting flesh.

The grip on his hair went away. His head dropped onto a pillow. His eyes blurred and he felt himself sliding back into he darkness that had sucked him down and down. . . .

Fear goaded him into fighting that darkness.

When he was awake again, he tried to lift his head.

Weak. So weak.

He forced his arms up, managed to fold the pillow and prop
is head up so he could see what was happening.

The weatherwitch and the ship's captain were standing by
he foot of the bed, confronting each other. She'd brought up
er hand and pressed it to her face, but Breith could still see
ed marks from the slap. Her chest heaved and her eyes were
lled with a mix of fear and anger.

"T' siapa kau bik e kau pikiri?" The captain shook his fist
n the witch's face. "Budj' asok aku kipun iada!"

Like the slap, a man acting like this around a Siofray
oman made Breith feel deeply confused. He clung to the
ords the captain was shouting as if they were a lifeline. What
o you think you are doing, the captain said. The boy is my
roperty, the captain said.

Breith closed his hands into fists that held wads of the sheet
ulled over him and continued to puzzle out the verbal battle
onducted down by his feet.

The witch says:

He is dangerous. A sport that needs to be pruned. He will
kill us all unless we kill him first.

Odd, Breith thought. She isn't saying anything about me
aving the Sight. It's her best argument. I wonder why . . .

The captain repeats:

He is my property. Do you have any idea what kind of
price a young Siofray male will bring if I put him on the
block at Pelateras? By the time we reach port I want him
healthy, I want him fluent in Lateran. And if you so much
as touch a hair on his head, I will drop you overboard
and you can swim to shore. Do you hear me?

Breith expected her to protest and come out with the Sigh
thing, but she didn't. She lowered her head, stared sullenly a
the floor. After a tense moment she nodded.

Breith closed his eyes, the tension running out of him. I
minutes he was asleep.

Three weeks later the ship's carpenter fitted leg chains t
Breith's ankles. Before this the captain had given him the ru
of the ship, confident there was no place for him to go. Th
chains meant they were nearing Ascal.

He was excited. The fever had been no fun at all and mos
of the voyage had been simply boring. Now, he thought. No
the adventure really begins. I wonder what it's like, being
slave. If I'm so valuable . . . He grinned. Oh, I think I'm goin
to have me a time. I am. I am.

8

Trouble on Nyddys

By the secret calendar of the Watchers, events dating from the 2nd day of Pumamis, the fifth month in the 738th Glandairic year since the last Settling.

[1]

Cymel lay curled up on her bed, reading the last letter from her father. The hot bottle nestled against her middle sent warm waves through her body and helped ease the cramps that had kept her home from the Tyrn's Birthday celebrations.

Because he wanted to speak freely to her without fear of the Tyrn's spies, Ellar sent his letters by messenger and the seal of the letter packet was spelled. If someone other than Cymel had got it from Little Noll (unlikely) or any of the other messengers and tried opening it, the packet would crumble to ash.

> *Dear Mela,*
>
> *I miss you, but Scholar Henannt has sent me glowing reports from your tutors. He says that you're settling into the life of an underscholar at University as if you were born for it, but he is a little disturbed by rumors—and some complaints—that you're running about with people much older than you are, people some would consider raff and scaff. I'm not going to tell you to stop this. You*

*are enough like me that such a command would drive
you into excesses I do not like to think of. All I ask is
that you consider carefully the friends you choose and
use the good sense I know you have to keep yourself out
of danger.*

Cymel wriggled in the bed, brought her knees closer to her
chest and shifted the cooling hot bottle. The mooncloth chafed
her but she didn't want to get out of bed to change it. She
reread the opening of the letter and smiled as she heard her
father's annoyance in those words. He was trying to be rea-
sonable, but if he were here, he'd be yelling at her, she knew
it. He wouldn't understand about Mole at all or Mole's girls.

And he surely wouldn't understand what Mole was teaching
her. Perhaps it was because he was a poet and constrained to
work inside ancient rules. Mole was guiding her to contrive
her own rules, to walk beyond all that was known before now.

She smoothed the letter out and began reading again.

*You'll remember Gryf. Young Talgryf, Lyanz's friend.
The times that I have managed to get away from Carcalon, Gryf has been showing me about Tyst, the side of
the city that most people do not see. It has been an interesting experience. I like Gryf. He is a bright, engaging
boy. Why I mention this—Gryf took me to meet his father—Lider, his name is—the last time I was in Tyst. The
man is dying and he won't see a healer, too proud to
take charity, Gryf told me. He hoped I could either do
something to help his father or persuade him to get help.
Unfortunately I am not a healer.*

*I offered to pay the costs, but Lider told me the boy
was wrong about his reasons. He would take charity if
there were not certain dangers associated with it. What
he truly feared was drawing attention to himself and his
family. He said even the gentle care of the Healing Sisters
would be a danger to him and his. We are thieves and
pluckers of coin from fools, he said. We survive like mice*

living in the walls of the city. Even the most benign notice is deadly for us. He loves his son and knows that the boy's mixed blood puts him at greater risk. He is also an intelligent man. Tyrn Isel's rule will not be kind to men like him or to the women who serve as conveniences— the people of the street who in his eyes mock his right to rule.

When Lider dies and that will be soon, I am afraid, Gryf will not have anyone to protect him. Mixed blood like his is a burden to a child. If nothing is done for him, no matter how clever he is, he is doomed to the mutilation served out to thieves and an early death. I've spoken with his father and he has asked me to be the boy's guardian. I have given this serious thought, and I believe I will do it.

Cymel crumpled the letter in a rage of jealousy. She was his blood. His daughter. He shouldn't go out and get somebody else to take her place. She burst into tears.

When the crying fit was over, she was ashamed of herself. She smoothed out the wadded paper and read the rest of the letter.

Do you miss the farm, Mela? I do, more than I thought possible. Tyrn Isel is a man of few gifts and many resentments. He has a stern and narrow piety that has wiped away all pleasure inside these walls. He resents me and finds all poetry corrupting of morals, but he will not let me leave. I was his father's choice as Court Poet and what his father had, Isel holds to with relentless greed—as if these things can make him the equal of Tyrn Dengyn. I thought his distaste would loose the bonds that hold me here, but I was wrong. Mela, if you hear that I am ill, do not fuss yourself. It will be a counterfeit I put on to break this impasse and win my dismissal. Isel is terrified of fevers and fluxes. With any luck at all, I will

*be home before the first snow. I hope you will want to
join me there during the winter break.*

*I worry about you, Mela. Please, please, take care. I
do not want you hurt.*

Much love, daughter,

Ellar Ilyarson

Feeling weepy and ashamed of herself, Cymel shifted cautiously onto her other side, repositioned the hot bottle. It was only tepid now and needed to be refilled, but she didn't feel like moving, not until she had to. This business of being a woman had some pretty miserable aspects to it. Pa asked her if she wanted to go home to the farm. Sometimes, when she was lonely and the Broon daughters had been particularly nasty, she wanted to go back to being a child and leave all these new complications behind. Most days, though, she liked being who she was now. What she was studying here at University seized hold of her mind and imagination and this made life so much more interesting and fuller than it had been.

No. She didn't want to go back to the farm.

Her life was so busy, she seldom had a moment to draw breath and she was enjoying it deeply. Today she could have gone with the Broon daughters in the Tyrfahouse on the round of parties celebrating the Birthday; they didn't want to invite her, but her connections made her too important to insult. The friends she'd made among the students and the artists had invited her to celebrate with them, not so much the Birthday, but the day off they'd got from work. The bird handlers had passed an invitation from old Derdo to a Stomp dance. Scholar Henannt sent word she could come to the Watcher's party if she wanted, though he hadn't been unhappy when she politely refused.

Her period coming down and bringing on the cramps was a blessing. It gave her some time to slow down and think.

She hadn't heard from Lyanz for several months. It was as if he'd dropped into a hole and pulled it in after him. *I could* find out, I suppose. Scholar Henannt probably still gets reports from the Vale and he'd tell me if I just asked.

She wrinkled her nose. What would be the point? That part of her life was done with, the door closed. She had her friends here, Lyanz would have his up in the Vale. It's over. We probably won't ever see each other again.

Breith. Funny how he was more important to her than Lyanz though she'd never seen him in the flesh, only through his Window. He hadn't talked to her since he went off in a snit last month. It wasn't like him to be silent so long. Maybe he's in trouble again.

I was too busy. I forgot about him. She couldn't do anything about it now, not till her body settled again.

Rhada Henanntswyf had helped her with her first flow and with the turmoil inside her that had her alternately burning up and shivering with chills as the Pneuma interacted with her physical and emotional reactions. Rhada was a healwitch, a brisk, practical woman whose calm was like a mountain river, cooling Cymel's heat. She gave Cymel breathing exercises and mind games so she wouldn't surprise herself too disastrously when things got a bit jagged.

Mela, she said, once your body is settled into the monthly routine and your coping games become automatic, the danger from the Pneuma will pass away. But be sure you tell Mole when you're having trouble. You don't need to feel embarrassed; remember his eight older sisters. They taught him all about female things. Um, he isn't . . .

Mela blushed, surprising herself. No, he isn't, she said. I'm too young for him to be interested. His girls are always a year or two older than he is.

Well, if you ever feel worried about him, come see me. Don't worry about me interfering or tattling to your father, but you might like to talk over what you mean to do. And remember that there's plenty of time to find out that side of life. You don't need that kind of complication right now.

*　　*　　*

Cymel wrinkled her nose again. Everyone was stepping so carefully around her. Everyone but Mole and his friends. Going round with them was such a relief. She sighed. Five more days before she could go back to working with Mole. It was a pain and a half.

I'll go see Marga tomorrow. She wants me to sit for her and I might as well. Nothing else I can do.

She watched the shadows cast by the tree outside her window dance across the white plaster of the wall as the wind blew its limbs about. It was full summer now and there was more heat trapped in these mountains than she could remember back on the farm, especially on late afternoons like this when the long slant of the sunlight cut through the net curtains and threw lines of yellow light across the sheet she'd pulled over her.

She wondered what her father was doing now. The letter was over two weeks old. Maybe he'd already taken Gryf to live with him and was making himself look sick so he could go home. She didn't like to think of that. She'd never seen her father sick, not even a bad cold. Something about being a Watcher protected him. Or maybe it was working with the Pneuma. I've never had colds or fevers either.

She felt warmth creeping down her leg, swore and rolled out of bed. Time to change mooncloths. What a plague it is being a woman.

[2]

The Nyddys Mage Oerfel Hawlson looked into his scry mirror and scowled as he saw the Watcher Ellar Ilyarson walk through the main gate of Carcalon, heading down the road to Tyst. Every time he saw the man, in the flesh or in the mirror, he was reminded of how disastrously he'd failed in his plans to kill the Hero. And as long as Ellar remained so close by, the Mage found his ability to act reduced to watching events rather than directing them. Oerfel's need for secrecy had not diminished as his long-range plans for Nyddys began unfold-

ing and he didn't dare do any large magics as long as Ellar
was close enough to identify him.

He had expected Isel to let the man go once the funeral rites
were over, but Isel was so jealous of his father's charm and
reputation among the Nyd-Ifor that he held on to everything
that his father had touched. He loathed poetry, suspected that
the farmer poet despised him and considered him a boor of
little intellect, yet he would not dismiss the man.

Oerfel had whispered in Isel's dreams and set his advisors
muttering that he should send the cursed poet home, but
though the new Tyrn was a truly stupid man, he had a certain
animal cunning that warned him when he was being manip-
ulated. And a stubborn vindictiveness that made such maneuvers increasingly dangerous. I hope you have laid your plans
well, Watcher. I'll do what I can to support them. I want you
out of here as much as you want to leave.

Oerfel watched Ellar a few moments longer, then turned the
scry mirror on the Vale of Caeffordian—reading body language, listening to comments and responses, taking considerable satisfaction in the cracks he saw widening between
cliques of Watchers—the original Valemen and those who had
moved to Caeffordian to find shelter from attack and to take
part in the training of the Hero. The image in the mirror shivered uncertainly, then opened out into a restless, hostile crowd
of Watchers gathered in a grassy field about Taymlo and the
Scribe Corysiam.

The Mage pulled a handkerchief from his sleeve, dipped a
twisted corner into a saucer of sweetwater and dabbed it at his
aching temples. He closed his eyes a moment, then eased his
back into a comfortable curve.

Amhar watched Corysiam's walk quicken until she was almost
running. A last step—the older Scribe's body hovered an instant while its image hollowed out—then even the solarized
outline vanished. Amhar sighed. Her last supporter was gone
and she was left in the middle of an unwelcome as intense as
any she'd met up with till now, even at one the most reac-

tionary Domains back on Iomard. And her prospective student apparently had that hostility drilled into him. He reeked of it.

But she didn't have to enjoy teaching him. This was business and it was time she started earning her place here. She set her hands on her hips in unconscious imitation of Corysiam, who had been her Sponsor/ProphetMother for as long as she could remember, and she began her inspection of the youth who was going to be her sole student.

Lyanz was beautiful.

Beautiful in a purely male way.

Beautiful as a Prophet's Messenger, but without the asexuality that put a barrier between the worshiper and the vision.

And so empty of magic that he was more like a shadow than a man.

Like women she'd known who'd been born with extravagant helpings of charm and beauty, despite his fit body and sure movements, he had a softness about him that hinted he'd fold under pressure.

The Hero for sure, Amhar thought. Prophet's Teeth! He can't know what that means.

The Hero who achieved apotheosis during each Settling lost everything. He would survive the Ingathering of the Magic in a way no other being could, but even his body would be changed. Nothing about him would be human any longer. Immortal. No kin. No kind. No links. Not with those who were now his friends. Not with the gods who were nearest to being his equals. He would read them all as if they wore glass fronts and proclaimed their thoughts and beliefs without any possibility of concealment. He would watch them wither and die, be reborn and die again in the blink of his eye.

This state might be a Mage's dream, but even cruel Hudoleth of Chusinkayam would be destroyed by the reality.

Lyanz would be better off dead and she'd be responsible for his pain if she helped him survive. Yet what else could she do? Iomard and Glandair depended on him to contain and redistribute the Pneuma Rivers that flowed through and powered both worlds—that would destroy both worlds, explode them to dust, turn the suns nova, if they were not contained, if that power were not redirected.

Ignoring Lyanz's glare and the silent hostility of the gathering Watchers, Amhar walked slowly around her prospective student, studying him closely, beginning to feel a surge of hope. Despite the softness, passion slumbered in him; if she could wake that passion and bring it to the study of the Art . . .

She loved the Art. Teaching the deeper understanding was her joy, though opportunities to do so were rare. Corysiam's nephew Breith was an excellent student, but he applied only his intellect to the learning, having little passion to give to it. None of the young apprentice Scribes were even that good.

By the time she'd completed the circle of inspection, she was breathless with possibilities—and physically aroused by his powerful male beauty, in an infatuation as absurd as if she were a first-year student at Scribe School.

The feeling was definitely not reciprocated. Lyanz slouched sullenly, his eyes fixed on the grass, his lips set in a grim uncooperative line.

Taymlo turned back to Amhar as Corysiam's outline vanished. "There's a visitor's suite in the gymnasium. I've arranged for you to move in there so you'll have your privacy but will be close to Lyanz and can take up his training at your convenience."

For the first time he noticed the group of younger Watchers who were crowding closer and closer to them, almost to the point of jostling them. He put his hand on Amhar's shoulder and closed it tightly, holding her still as well as offering support.

"Kellar, you have business elsewhere. Get out of my face and go do it." He swung his head around, transferring his angry gaze to the rest of the bystanders. "And the rest of you. Take yourselves where you belong."

The skinny man with the acne-scarred face lost the mix of resentment and fury that had been propping him up. As he turned and stalked off, Taymlo's mouth went grim. Kellar was at the heart of most trouble stirred up in the Vale for the past several months. He had been an adequate Watcher when he lived a hermit's life two valleys north of here with no visitors to stir up his nastier instincts. Unfortunately the Watcher's Talent didn't guarantee compassion or ethical behavior; it was just a powerful need to know as much as possible of what was happening in the world.

Propelled by Taymlo's authority, the rest of the crowd gradually thinned and vanished among the buildings on the far side of the plum orchards. Lyanz started to slink off with them but stopped at a gesture from the older man, though his body shouted his rejection of anything the Master Watcher intended to say.

Taymlo sighed. He'd allowed himself to be blinded by his respect for his original companions at the Vale; until Corysiam's warning, he hadn't noticed—at least, not consciously— how the atmosphere had changed. He dropped his hand and started walking again. Without looking at Amhar, he said, "This is going to be difficult, Scribe. You'll have all the support I can give you, but . . ."

"The difficulty made itself immediately apparent." Amhar's laugh was strained at first, then more natural. "I've run into similar situations on Iomard. Not that I'm experienced in resolving knots like this. Mostly I just went somewhere else as soon as possible."

"That's not possible this time." Taymlo led Amhar and Lyanz around a log baffle and opened the door concealed behind it. Beyond was a long empty room with thick mats scattered about a polished oak floor. The two-story-high windows held glass set in lead canes shaped into the twists of elegant grapevines, light filled with dust motes pouring through. "The gymnasium. You'll be working in here."

"Some of the time. I'll be doing as much outdoor training as possible since that's where most of what I teach will be used."

"Makes sense." Taymlo stood aside, holding the door for her and prodding Lyanz through it after her with a push of his hand. "Scribe, your room—"

"Not yet. Something I want to do first." Amhar turned to
e Lyanz. "Your training so far, Hero. I don't need details.
brief summary will do."

He turned his shoulder to her, glanced along it, then stared
the wall.

Taymlo started to speak, but Amhar raised a hand and
pped him with a shake of her head. "When I ask a question,
xpect an answer, a matter of courtesy between a student
d a teacher." She kept her voice low and pleasant, as if
at she said were of minimal importance and her correction
rely a matter of imparting information. "To act otherwise
to prove oneself a lout and a dullard."

"You're not my teacher. You never will be."

Three seconds later he was on his face on a mat, his right
n and shoulder caught in a hold that set his body on fire
d drained most of the strength from his muscles. He was as
lpless as a baby in swaddling. And angrier.

Amhar dropped the hold and stepped back.

The arm fell to the floor and bounced, still partially para-
ed; Lyanz's body shuddered, went inert again as he gasped
air.

"Until you can throw and pin me as easily, you're a stu-
nt," she said. "And whether there is any personal connec-
n or not, any person with mind/body learning so much
eater than your own should be considered a teacher and
ven the appropriate courtesy."

Somewhat to her surprise, once he was able to move again,
disciplined himself to a brief immobility, then rolled up
to his feet. She could feel his mind churning as he sought
rds and the proper order to lay out what he wanted her to
ar.

"Good," she said. "An excellent illustration of emotional
scipline. Go on."

His lips twitched, then his face smoothed out again, became
nd and immobile.

Well, no one said he was stupid. She was pleased with her-
f, having almost drawn a smile from him. Besides, the re-

sponse was a useful clue as to how she should work with hi

"A simple listing of the styles and forms will be sufficien
she said, and listened to a minimalist recounting of his ph
ical self-defense studies—boxing, wrestling, archery, st
fighting, sling work and knife handling. A sketchy knowled
of basic Art throws, formal to the point that they might ha
been dances rather than attacks. He had reached the level
understanding where he was beginning to combine individ
forms into strings of responses, but these strings were as mu
rote learning as the earlier forms, showing no sense of fluid
or improvisation. This was a sad disappointment for it mea
her hopes for any real teaching of the Art were an illusion

Then he lifted the practice sword built from split will
and cord. When he began to dance those forms, everything
lacked in his other skills was triumphantly present. The p
sion she'd sensed in him was finally there. Now all she h
to do was transfer it to the Art.

His headache banished by satisfaction, Oerfel sat smiling
he surveyed the play of expression across the young Scrib
face. What he observed of her overall disappointment left h
contented with the way things were going in the Vale.

[3]

His horse cantering easily, Ellar headed along the Tyst Ro
he needed a touch of reality to wash from his mouth the ta
of the meretricious nonsense he'd written for the Birthday.
there were some way he could keep his name off that . . . t
. . . he couldn't even think of an appropriate term for that c
lection of words misnamed a poem.

He turned his head and spat at the road dust as he reme
bered the pompous Master of the Inner Chamber informi
him that the Tyrn was pleased with his effort and wished h
to read it at the Banquet.

The day was hot and still. The sounds from Tyst were mu
by the lack of wind, but he knew the Tysters would be
celebrating the holiday despite what they thought of Tyrn Is

ll clerks and ladesmen and general laborers were given a day
f rest, so the shops were shut and the wharves closed down.
here'd be street fairs everywhere and street dances when the
un set. He didn't particularly like a lot of noise and jostling,
ut it was certainly better than being trapped at an official
anquet where he would have to watch every word he said
nd smile until his face felt ready to crack apart and fall off.

He left the horse at a livery stable and walked into the city,
10ving cautiously through the surging, noisy crowds. Know-
1g that these were not holidays for pickpockets and cutpurses,
e'd shoved his purse inside his shirt, then buttoned his leather
est over the lump. When he stopped at the food barrows, it
/as difficult to get to, but Tyst thieves were too nimble-
ngered and knowing for anything less.

ider's door was cracked open to get a flow of air through the
>om and some relief from the heat. Ellar knocked on the door
ost. "Ellar," he called. "Come to spend some of the Birth-
ay with you."

He heard a hoarse chuckle, Lider's voice, the words punc-
iated with small gasps. "Run away, did you, El? Come on
1."

"You got it. Up to some fine and fancy eating?"

Lider was stretched out on a cot near the window; the light
oming through the unglazed opening was cruel to the gray
allor of his face. It had been ten days since Ellar had last
een him and Lider had walked a good way farther along the
>ad to death.

"I'll get my pleasure watching you eat, my friend. I thank
ou for coming and giving my wife some time to herself."

Ellar set his shoulder sack on a small unsteady table beside
1e bed. He took from it a stoneware jar and a small wrapped
acket of ice. "I was about ready to choke in that smokehouse
alled Carcalon. I'm glad of the excuse to escape, Lider my
riend. Though I'll have to leave around fifth watch. I'm sup-
osed to read that garbage I wrote for the Birthday." He
oured thick golden plum juice into a mug, added a chunk of

ice and handed it to the sick man, then took up an apple and
began peeling it. "Hmp. If Isel the Crabbed ever saw some
of the true poems I've been writing, I'd be short a head." He
cored the apple, cut it into thin slices, took a linen napkin
from the sack, folded the slices of apple in it along with some
wine grapes. He set the napkin on the bed beside Lider. "Eat
what you can. There's no hurry."

Ellar pulled a chair beside the table, took one of the skewers
with its chunks of meat and onion he'd bought off a barrow
man and began chewing the meat from the pine sliver. The
noises outside, the laughter and shouts, the drums and the
horns, made the quiet room seem even more a haven from
chaos.

"Never told you about my first wife, did I? Gryf's mother
Zynnet. She was Rhudyar. A tall slim woman with long legs
and a stride like a man. Most folks wouldn't say she was pretty
but, ahh, the glow of her! A smile wide as the sun and twice
as warm. You don't mind if I talk about her, do you, El? I
haven't been able to talk and call her to mind for years. I
wouldn't have been fair to Bregga. She's a good woman and
she's been a fine stepmother to Gryf and fine wife to me, but
she's a comfortable woman with no passion in her. I some
times wonder if I have been the wrong man for her, though
she has never complained or seemed to want more than I could
give her. That comforts me these days. When I'm gone, she
will find another man soon enough, someone to help raise our
daughter. Little Moaren is a lot like her, I think. A nest builder
who can weave comfort about herself with whatever she finds
to hand.

"Gryf is more like his mother. You've only seen him laugh
ing, El. There are times when he's so sad he curls himself into
a knot and won't talk for days. Zynnet was like that. When
she was happy, sun and moon went dim beside her, but when
she was sad there was no light in her at all. When there was
trouble, she was stronger than a sword, yet as soon as it was
over she flew apart, wailing and beating her chest and mine
cursing me, cursing those who injured me.

"I had bad luck the summer when Gryf was two, my hands were just starting to go on me and I was a little slow and clumsy when I lifted a purse. I managed to get rid of it before the city guards caught me, but there was enough suspicion to earn me a flogging. My back went rotten and I was closer to dying then than I am now. She nursed me and supported the three of us by doing whatever work came to hand. Ah, she was magnificent in those days. It killed her. She spent too much of herself saving me and had no strength left when the fever came on her. It was like blowing out a match. One strong breath and all that fire was gone."

Ellar sipped at the juice in his clay mug. "I know what you mean," he said after a while. "Doeta, my wife, she was generous, full of life, light and passion. And headstrong? Tanew's Teeth, she'd get an idea in her head and nothing you could do would change her mind. It killed her. I worry that Cymel is too much like her. She was a good child, but I'm getting reports from Cyfareth that trouble me. She's not a child anymore, but not a woman either. People are hurting her because she's not pure Ifordyar but mixed blood. And I can't be there to help her."

"That's why I was worried about Gryf. Moaren will be all right. Bregga's sister has taken her in. The family will help raise her when I'm gone. No one will take the boy. They only see the color of his skin and where his mother came from. Bless you for taking him, El. You know how to deal with that."

There was a sudden commotion outside, screams, hoarse yells, sounds of trampling feet, horseshoes ringing on stone, the crack of whips. Ellar stood, started for the end of the bed so he could lean over Lider's feet and look out the window.

Lider pushed himself up and gasped out, "No, El. Don't. Could draw eyes here."

Ellar settled himself again in the old chair, leaned forward, his elbows on his knees. "What's that about?"

"It's something you wouldn't know, my friend. You don't move in these circles much and this is something new.

Thought that on the Birthday they'd lay off." His hand closed about the blanket beneath him. "Told Gryf to stay on Syopoor, not to work the bothrin."

"That's where he is. I saw him on the way here."

Lider closed his eyes. "That's another one I owe you, El."

"What's going on out there?"

"Isel's Sweep. Men in the bothrin are picked up by the city guards. Anyone who doesn't have proof of work is taken away for six years in the Tyrn's mines; if they have families, young children, a small sum paid to these each month. Unless they die. Then the money stops. Isel has decided that the bothrin is a nest of criminals and needs to be cleaned out as a moral lesson for the rest of Nyddys. I said men are taken, but it isn't only men. Boys as young as twelve. If they caught Gryf, nothing could save him from the mines. He's bothrin scum like the rest of the taken. The Tystgrath won't do anything to stop this."

"I didn't know. Lider, what do you want me to do?"

"If he'd go, I'd ask you to take him, but he won't. Not while I'm alive. There's nothing you can do. Let's talk of something else. There's an old book I want you to see. Breith found it in the flea market and brought it home." Lider chuckled. "I don't suppose he bothered paying for it."

The poet and the dying thief talked the afternoon away, until Bregga got home, thanked Ellar, then scolded him for tiring her man and sent him on his way.

Ellar bowed to the enthusiastic applause, walked from the speaker's round to his table apart from the great banqueting table that ran down the center of the hall. He knew the worth of that applause and the knowledge took his appetite away. He looked at them. Second sons whose only job was flattery, here to play their games and win favor for their families.

He played with his food and regretted his promise to Lider. He was stuck here until the man died and he could take Gryf away with him to the farm. He smiled as he thought suddenly how scared Isel would be if a number of the people here at the Banquet woke up tomorrow with fevers and fluxes. With an interior sigh of regret, he let the opportunity pass and ate a little of the bland and tasteless food as he watched a trio of Myndyar dancers who were supposed to be court entertainers at Banyakor. He suspected that was exaggeration at best, more probably an outright lie, but they were slim and graceful in their heavy robes, their masks and headdresses with jewels hanging free so they caught the light and shimmered as they swung with the movement of the dancers' heads. He also admired the skill of Secretary Oerfel in selecting entertainment that would be pleasing and at the same time decorous enough to be acceptable in this pinchgut court.

[4]

Cymel stretched and yawned. She'd gone farther into the Flow than ever before, almost merging with it as if her body were changing to Pneuma itself. Just beyond her grasp, she felt a knowledge that she wanted passionately, but it was a patient passion; she felt no rush to possess it, rather was looking forward to teasing out its aspects in a long and glorious seduction. She stretched again, groaning with pleasure at the pull of her muscles, then sat up and rubbed at her eyes.

Mole chuckled. "If your guardian saw you now, he'd roast me over the nearest fire."

She blinked at him, then blushed. "Oh."

The crystal room was full of shadows and muted half-lights that slid around them as if they swam in a pool of mountain water. Mole shook his head then crossed to one of the lamps and touched the wick with the tip of his finger. When it flared up, he moved about the chamber, lighting the others. Then he came back to the cot where she was sitting, pulled up a chair and threw himself in it and held out a comb. "Neaten yourself up so anyone who sees you won't think you've been doing what you look like you've been doing."

"Ruin your reputation, Mole?" She grimaced as the comb hit a tangle. "I swear I'm going to cut it all off one of these days. Shave my head. Save a lot of trouble, that would."

"You're joking but you're closer than you think, Mela. Scholar Henannt summoned me this morning. There's good news and bad out of Carcalon. Nothing to do with your father," Mole added hastily. "At least not directly."

"What is it? The Broon daughters complaining to their pas about me? Am I going to have to move out of Tyrfahouse?"

"I hadn't thought of that." Mole wrinkled his nose. "Probably not. Well, let's get to it. Tyrn Isel has decreed that all classes dealing with Pneuma will have to be monitored by a Brother from the Temple to make sure we don't touch on forbidden areas or blasphemy, whatever that means. I suspect that covers just about everything I've been teaching you. My giving you private lessons on University time is out. It worries the Governors that you're so young and a girl besides."

Cymel let the comb drop into her lap and sat staring at him, a cold knot under her heart. "No more lessons?"

"Oh, I didn't say that. Henannt has arranged for us to meet at the Watcher's Compound and go on with our lessons." He shrugged. "I'll have to be more circumspect, Mela. What we're doing now, well, I don't think even Henannt would approve. For all that he's a man of considerable intellect, he's a traditionalist. Like your father. Like all the Watchers. We'll be working on practical applications, spells and summonings, that sort of thing."

"But I touched . . . I can't quit now. Mole," she wailed. "To give up what . . . I can't!"

"Nor can I, Mela." Mole got to his feet again, stood looking around the room, his mouth twisted into an angry smile. He walked to one of the lamps he had only a moment ago lighted and pinched out the wick. Over his shoulder, he said, "You're teaching me aspects of the Flow I couldn't touch before. I have wider and finer control than you right now, but you have a reach far greater than I realized when we began this exploration." He came back and stood looking down at her. "I need you. But we are going to have to be very careful. Use the next few weeks to stabilize yourself at this level. Do the exercises I've taught you. And don't try melding to the

Flow on your own. I know you're going to be tempted, but you're a levelheaded girl. We'll think of some way to get round this interference, because we have to.''

Cymel took up the comb again. Without looking at Mole, she said, "I remember what you told me when we first met. It's simpler, you said, not to roil folks up, just give them a sop so they can tell themselves they're in charge.''

The strain in his face eased as he smiled at her. "Yes. Softly softly go little mole feet and who knows where they take him.''

Scholar Henannt shook his head and looked properly rueful, but unless Cymel read him wrong, he was more pleased than not that the unsupervised lessons with Mole had been stopped. "We certainly will not stifle the growth of your gift, Cymel. But perhaps going more slowly for a while will broaden your understanding of the Flow and your responsibilities to it.''

Mole feet, Cymel reminded herself. Softly softly. "I was afraid I'd have to stop my studies," she said. "Because I'm younger than the other students here.''

Henannt scowled. "That was suggested by several of the Governors. It's nonsense. You were better schooled by your father than many of the students who come here from the Broonies and who've been tutored and groomed for this. And you've got more good sense in your little toe than any of them. Besides, you are Watcher sponsored and that means something even if they'd like to deny it, prissy old fools." He stroked the thick white beard that was his chief vanity and shifted his gaze away from her. "Still, a certain discretion is advisable. They have the ear of Tyrn Isel. I have looked over the list of your tutors and have added a few names. Best not to spend too much time with young Gylas.''

He shook his head when Cymel looked mutinous. "Believe, Mela, this is for your own good." He went back to staring out the window behind her, and when he spoke again, she had the feeling he was talking more to himself than to her. "Though he is without doubt one of the most gifted of our younger Scholars, questions have arisen about his methods that I don't quite know how to answer. He has many friends among the faculty and students here, but few among those who handle magic. He doesn't share his insights; indeed, many of our Scholars think he considers them too . . . mmm . . . inept and narrow to understand what he is attempting and there is some jealousy that is exacerbated because he ignores it. I find him irritating at times and must confess I don't understand the man but I do recognize his peculiar brilliance and will support him as much as I can.''

"Scholar Henannt, is this part of the effect of the Settling? The beginning of the Chaos?''

"What? Ah! Your father, eh?''

"And my aunt from Iomard.''

"Hm. Well, we won't talk about your aunt or Iomard. If you don't mind. About the Settling? I don't know. There are threads . . . but since we can't read the Will-Be and can only compare the Now with fragments rescued from past Settlings—''

"I'd like to study the Settling papers.''

"Why?''

"I don't exactly know. It's just a feeling.''

After a moment's intense thought, Scholar Henannt nodded. "I accept that. Knowledge is always useful, whatever the reason for acquiring it. I will arrange for a tutor and access to the archives. If that feeling of yours becomes more . . . um . . . localized, I'd appreciate your informing me.''

"You and my father. I'll do that.''

Cymel left the meeting reasonably pleased at how it had turned out. Things would go on much as they had before; it would just take more time and more work to make this happen. She sighed. Since she'd first heard/read about the time of Chaos, she'd thought it was like when her father had to go somewhere and left her to fool round by herself, when she could run all over the mountain without worrying about him getting mad at her. A time of freedom from rules. But now she was confused.

this was the beginning of the time of Chaos, why was everything getting tighter and tighter around her until she could
barely move? Hm, she thought, are everything-possible and
nothing-possible two sides of the same thing?

She shivered and began to understand why her father and
the other Watchers were so troubled by what was coming.

5]

Oerfel jerked awake from a heavy, exhausted sleep. He'd finally loosed himself from the headache that had plagued him
since the night of the Birthday, kept him half-blind and on the
verge of vomiting. He pushed up and sat with his skinny
shanks dangling over the edge of the bed, his hands braced on
his thighs, as he tried to puzzle out what had broken into his
slumber.

The intense knot of Pneuma that was Ellar Ilyarson was
massive, motionless. Nothing there.

The smaller hotspots of healwitches and minor magicians
were the same as always.

He touched the Flow. And jerked back, startled. A Mage.
There's another Mage on Nyddys.

That's what had awakened him, the wavefront as the Mage
set foot on the soil of Nyddys.

North of here, moving westward.

Warily, careful not to betray his presence, he stroked and
probed the vast powersurge, searching for the key signatures
of the Mover.

Not Mahara of Kale. Not Hudoleth of Chusinkayan.

There were no other Mages on Glandair, so this one had to
be of Iomard. What was he . . . ah, yes, certainly he . . . doing
here? The Settling was still too incomplete to let him just step
across and a male Mage wouldn't be a Walker. For that you
had to be born Siofray and female.

Oerfel edged away from the surge. When he was clear of
the Flow, he groaned onto his feet and shuffled across the
room to the chest where he kept the most sensitive of his scry
mirrors.

*   *   *

The image was faint and blurred, but Oerfel did not try t<
bring it in more clearly. The chances were small that a Mag<
would feel a mirror overlooking him if it were properly used
but Oerfel knew too little about Siofray Mages to feed mor<
power into the glass; it might even start the Mage searchin;
for the cause of the itch he felt.

Oerfel dipped a napkin in the bowl of distilled water by hi
elbow, bathed his temples, then pressed the damp cloth to hi
eyes until the burn in them went away. When he looked agair
into the mirror, the image was still dim, but the details wer<
clearer.

The Mage was a tall lean man in a torn shirt, ragged trou
sers, his feet bare, a crossbow on his back and a small stocl
of bolts in a leather roll dangling from his belt, his face painte<
with designs whose purpose Oerfel knew very well, though h<
didn't recognize them. Oddly enough he looked like an amal
gam of the three races of the Dyar, with the bony nose, lon;
head, long legs and arms of the Ifordyar, while his skin wa
a mix of Myndyar gold and Rhudyar red. His hair was blacl
and coarse, braided into a club that hung halfway down hi
back. He looked more like a mountain thief than a powerfu
Mage, and at the moment he was acting like one, creepin;
toward a paddock of a coastal Broony, his eyes fixed on th<
horses moving in the turnout.

Once again Oerfel wondered why he was here on Nyddys
but he had no time to waste on such futility as speculatior
without data.

Glancing repeatedly at the mirror, he sat at his worktable
wrote a note to his aide saying he was ill and didn't want t<
be disturbed at any time during the day. Then he dressed him
self in his most inconspicuous clothing, filled a basket witl
emergency stores and left his room in the Cyngrath Tower, .
dark cloak wrapped about him.

The night was warm and dry. And dark. The stars wer<
covered with clouds and the thin sliver of moon had set som<
time ago. A yawning guard let Oerfel out a side gate the>

went back to his chair and his doze, the incident wiped from his mind.

When he was safe inside his workroom below the Temple, Oerfel sat on the pallet he'd pulled from one of the closets, blankets wrapped around him, and watched in one of the large mirrors as the Iomardi Mage rode his stolen horse steadily westward, showing no interest in anything south or north of him. The only Pneuma the Iomardi used was for concealment; he wasn't searching for anyone or anything. He seemed to know where he was going and he was intent on getting there as soon as possible.

The fear which had sent Oerfel into this sanctuary faded after a few hours, but he stayed concealed until late the next night, taking short naps, feeding himself, voiding, thinking, and always watching the Mage ride westward.

[6]

Cymel swung down the tree outside her window and stood listening in the shadow of the wydra bushes, wrinkling her nose at the overripe sweetness of the flowers scattered over them. When she had finished probing the house and was satisfied no one had seen her, she pulled the Pocket round her and slipped through the silent streets until she reached the rough at the edge of the University grounds.

She dropped the shield and drew her sleeve across her face, wiping away the sweat that beaded there. She was very tired, but fiercely determined not to miss her lesson with Mole. She was going to have to make some changes in the schedule, fewer meetings out here, for one thing. She hated wasting time because of old men's stupidity, but there was nothing she could do about that unless she wanted to lose more than time.

As the solitude and the comfortably familiar wildness of the mountain closed round her, the tensions dropped away and her fatigue mellowed into a quiet weariness. Her breathing slowed, her mind floating, she walked up the deer path, heading for the deserted hermit's hut where she and Mole did the work the Governors had forbidden.

When she reached the hut, she settled herself on the stone sill and leaned against the doorpost. She was early by design. She liked Mole, but this pleasure she could not share with him since it came from being solitary, having no eyes on her, no ears listening critically to every word she spoke. The blend of small and ordinary noises in the forest around her made a silence that seeped into her blood and cleaned away the tensions of the day.

Though Mole's feet were as soundless as his namesake, she felt him coming and saw him as soon as he rounded the last bend of the deer path, the moonlight glinting off his glasses and playing in the velvet of his pale gray shirt. She smiled and lifted her arm to wave lazily at him, then sat with her hands clasped in her lap, too comfortable where she was to get to her feet.

He pulled a crystal from the pouch at his belt and began tossing it up and catching it as he got closer, the trapped moonlight lending the smooth sphere a gentle radiance.

Behind her Cymel heard a soft scrape, but before she could turn, a hard kick sent her tumbling.

Mole yelled and threw the crystal at the shadow standing over her, then he lifted his hands, a glow kindling between his palms.

As Cymel landed, her head cracking against a tree, the breath driven out of her, a jet of white fire passed over her body and caught Mole.

For a moment he was a writhing black silhouette in the heart of that fire, then he was gone.

She screamed with rage and rolled onto her feet, but before she could straighten, a foot slammed against her head.

When she woke, she was belly down over the shoulder of a running man, her wrists caught in his hands, her stomach hammered by the muscle and bone in his shoulder, her nose rubbed in the rank sweat of his filthy shirt. Her eyes weren't bound as far as she could tell, but he'd done something to them; she couldn't see anything but darkness.

At the same moment, the memory returned of Mole burning in the heart of that fire.

She gasped and reached for the Flow.

Nothing.

Her captor blocked her as easily as a mother pushing her child's hand away from the fire. He didn't even stop running.

She started struggling, trying to fling herself off his shoulder; she had no hope of escaping, but maybe she could buy some time.

He swung her around and let her drop to ground.

She splatted down into the mud of the mountain meadow hard enough to have the wind knocked out of her for the third time, but she wriggled around while she was still gasping and dazed and tried to run.

Her captor's foot in the small of her back pushed her flat again, face in the mud. He held her down until she stopped struggling and had to turn her head to one side to spit out the mud and gasp for air.

"You have a choice, little bitch." The man's voice was deep and hoarse and filled with a confidence that frightened her more than the foot in her back. "Keep fighting me and I'll kick you till you're a skin wrapped around porridge. I don't need your body, I need your mind. Or you can be sensible, cooperate, and I'll let you go with only the bruises you've picked up so far."

She wiped her mouth on the tough wiry grass, moved her tongue across her teeth. "What do you want me to do?"

"Bridge me to Iomard. And don't bother telling me you can't, I'll do the powering, I just need your capacity for Walking."

"I don't understand." She tried not to shiver as she realized who he was. The Siofray Mage.

What he was doing on Glandair and how he got here wasn't important. He'd killed Mole. Tears pricked her eyes, but she blinked them away. She couldn't think about Mole now.

Couldn't grieve. Couldn't even afford to be angry. She had to stay alive long enough to make him suffer for that. Long enough so he'd hurt as much as she did. "I'm only half—"

He moved his foot away. "Stand up. You start running again, I'll break your knees. You don't need them to Bridge me. Remember that."

She took her time pushing up from black mud that squeezed up through her fingers as she put weight on the root tangle of the grasses. Cautiously, she tested the muffling blanket that cut her off from the Flow only to discover that her isolation was complete. The only tools she had were her wits and the hope that he'd make a mistake if she looked docile enough.

She stood with her head down and shoulders rounded, waiting for his next move.

He came up behind her, wrapped his arms about her and held her pressed flat against him.

Pain.

Head tearing open.

Fire. Slow fire. Eating at her.

Pain.

She screamed. The scream went on and on, tearing her throat, emptying her.

Pain.

Knives gouging at her, tearing her flesh, shattering her bone.

The mountain melted.

Pain.

A Great Noise as of cloth ripping. A giant's curtain, tearing apart. . . .

Nothing.

[7]

Corysiam was about to go aboard the riverboat when she felt the screams as the augmented child ripped through the membrane between the worlds. "Cymel? Cymel!"

No response to her call.

She gripped her luggage and stepped to the tree beside Ellar's front door. She dropped the bags beside the tree, and looked back at Iomard, searching for Cymel.

She saw a man—a daroc runaway, Prophet! The Mage—hauling Cymel across a wharf—where? Doesn't matter where—

She stepped to Iomard, brought her fists hard against the Mage's back the instant she landed, then she grabbed his hair and kicked his feet from under him. Before he could attack her, she snatched Cymel from him and Bridged her to Glandair, back to the farmhouse.

Ellar had set no wards about the house when he left for Carcalon. Cymel and Lyanz were with him so there was nothing left in it to protect from magical intrusion. Trembling with fatigue from the double Walk and the Bridging, Corysiam carried Cymel to the girl's bedroom and laid her unconscious form on the bed. Without wasting time, she set up her strongest wards about the bed and went back downstairs to draw herself some water from the kitchen pump.

The Mage. He had threatened Cymel before and had somehow got to her this time. Somehow he'd made the child into a Bridge years before she was ready for it.

Corysiam grimaced. Like throwing oil on a fire, forcing it to burn too brightly and too fast, and, for her comfort too closely kin to what the Domain Seers did when they burned out the mind of a Sighted boy. She tried to push the thought away, but the fear wouldn't leave her. There was only one sliver of consolation she could find. The Mage hadn't discarded Cymel as soon as he reached Iomard, but had tossed her over his shoulder and was running for a fishing boat with the girl bobbing like a carcass on his back. He meant to get more out of her and that meant there was something left that he could use.

When the trembling in her limbs quieted and the throb in her head muted to a mild ache, she opened a Window into Ellar's rooms. This was not safe, not with the Nyddys Mage around to overhear and no way she could block him out, but she'd need a night's rest at least before she could Walk again and she didn't dare leave Cymel alone. And Ellar had to know about Cymel.

[8]

Ellar knocked softly at the door, then put his mouth to the latchhole. "Lider, Gryf, let me in. Bregga, this is important."

He heard the bar slide in the hooks then the door opened just wide enough to let him through. Bregga shoved the bar back as soon as he was inside. In the pale gray starlight coming through the single window, her face was drained of color. "What is it? What's wrong?"

"No problem for anyone here. Wake Gryf, will you? I've got to talk to him and Lider."

"Ryn, Lider he's just got to sleep. Can't you wait?"

"Bregga." Lider's voice came from the shadow in the corner; it was weary and so soft Ellar could barely hear him. "I'm awake."

"Me too." Gryf sat up on the pallet stretched out at the foot of the bed. His black hair was tousled and falling forward into his eyes. He shoved it back with an impatient hand and sat with his arms folded on his knees.

Ellar stepped past Bregga, stopped at the side of the bed. His voice kept low, he said, "I've just got word that my daughter was taken by an enemy and badly injured. Her aunt rescued her but needs my help. I'm leaving Carcalon right now, can't wait for permission from the Tyrn."

Gryf rose onto his knees, caught hold of the end of the bed. "Mela? Hurt?"

"Not in the body, Gryf. Not seriously. In the mind. I think it would help if you came with me, that's why I'm here. Lider, you know what leaving without permission means. I'll be a named Werelos and won't have a happy time if Isel's men catch me. But my friends will give me what protection they can, and I know a place where the Tyrn's word won't reach." He drew in a breath, expelled it in a rush. "I can give you a short while to make up your mind, but I have to be away before this watch ends. I'll wait outside. You talk it over. I'll knock when I'm leaving.''

Ellar knew Lider's desperation, so he wasn't surprised when the door opened again and Talgryf slipped through the crack. The boy's eyes had a glitter to them that he tried to hide and he was carrying a cloth bundle. Ellar touched the narrow shoulder, then went swiftly downstairs, Gryf following silent behind him.

[9]

Smiling with satisfaction, Oerfel watched as the Mage killed the Scholar, scooped up Cymel and ran with her. His smile broadened as he saw the Mage wrap his arms about the girl and vanish with her.

He was not sure exactly what had happened, but it looked as if the Mage force-fed the girl while keeping control of her even when the river of Pneuma raging through her increased enormously. Perhaps the narrowness of the power channel enabled him to do this. Which was very interesting. Not useful now, and it might only apply to Siofray or a halfblood Siofray like that girl, but it was something to think about. Something to experiment with. Carefully, though. And not here.

Hardly a breath later the Iomardi Bridge was back in Ellar's house, carrying the unconscious body of the girl. The swiftness of this turn startled him—then it pleased him. The girl was damaged. Even though he didn't dare examine her too closely, he could read the broken angry waves of Pneuma that stormed around her.

He watched the Bridge's call to Ellar, nodding and smiling more broadly as he saw his biggest problem solving itself. He didn't understand Ellar's jog into Tyst and his interchange with that family of thieves, but that didn't matter. It simply made it easier for him to discredit the man. Hm. Thieves as friends. Yes. His smile widened. And Isel will be so happy to go along with this. Posturing fool. Sad but not vindictive. Stolen bracelet found in the so-called Poet's chambers, other loot carried off as the man fled from the generosity of his Tyrn and showed how unworthy he was of the mantle laid over him.

Oh yes. Yes. Yes.

9

Slave

By the calendar of the Domains of Iomard, events dating from the 9th day of Sakhtos, the seventh month in the Iomardi year 6536, the 722nd year since the last Corruption.

[1]

"He nearly died and you didn't say a word to me?" Faobran slapped away the hand resting on the curve of her hip and slammed her fist into Malart's chest. "I don't believe you, Marl. How could you do that? How!"

"He was sick, Fori, but he wasn't anywhere near dying. And he was getting the care he needed."

"From slavers!"

"I told you. He's valuable. They want him healthy. There was no point in worrying you."

"After this, let me decide if I should be worried or not. You make me so angry when you do this kind of thing, Marl. Please . . ."

Malart sighed. "Well, do you want to see him sold? He should be on the block about now if I've judged the time correctly."

". . . here we have the prize of the day. A young male Siofray." The auctioneer's looped whip moved down along

Breith's front, from his shoulders to his thighs. "Uncut and able, as he makes so abundantly clear."

Laughter from the small crowd in the auction room.

Blushing and wretchedly embarrassed because he was naked and had no way of covering himself, Breith stood on a small platform like an upturned barrel, his cuffed hands pulled above his head, the chains attached to them laced through eyes on a horizontal iron loop welded to the pole that rose behind him and snaplocked to a third eye at the back of that pole.

These slave dealers were very good about not giving him a chance at escaping or injuring himself. They were a lot like the drovers that brought the herds of tribuf into Valla Murloch, casually competent, no cruelty to them, no malice. Somehow that seemed almost worse than deliberate torture. They didn't—or maybe couldn't—recognize him as a person with will and desire. He lifted his head and stared back at the buyers, daring them to find out any weakness in him. Daring them to see him as a person not an animal.

"He's so thin, Marl. Skin on bone."

"Look at his face, Fori. He's embarrassed but he's almost enjoying this. Look at the young rooster preen."

"And you sound proud of it." She shook her head. *"Men! I'll never understand you."*

The loop of the whip touched Breith's face, then tapped him on the belly. "Observe the fairness and tenderness of the lad's skin. A sweet young girl would be pleased to have it. He is himself all the testimony needed to evoke your belief, gentle sirs, when I tell you he is Lynborn and a scion of an exalted House. Ah! the treachery and high crimes that brought this youth to this low estate would make a statue weep, were I free to tell the tale. Alas, I am not."

A voice came from the audience, filled with laughter and irony. "Just as well, Peddusta, for we would not believe you anyway."

"Ah, you may mock me, Tuayn Onjak, but can you deny

your eyes? Have you ever seen such a youth on the block before? I challenge you to produce the day and year. To my certain knowledge, the last such to appear was in my father's time."

"That's as may be, Peddusta." Another voice with the same cynicism like stink on the words. "Skinny scrap. You can count every bone in his body."

"Tuayn Rubahhan, the boy stowed himself in a hold and sneaked halfway across the ocean before he was discovered and in that time succeeded in starving himself a trifle. His teeth are strong, his bones are straight. A little feeding up and who it is has the fortune to buy him will have a fine rare specimen on his hands. Now I'm not saying he's suitable for a House with juicy young daughters ripe for bedding, but it would be a shame against the Great God if he were clipped before he sired a few like him. Consider the gift his daughters would have."

"Breeding stock! They dare!"

"Hush, Fori. If it comes to that and Breith can't prevent it, we can take the children away from them. Corysiam will Bridge them to us if we ask."

"I suppose so."

"Might have." It was yet another voice; this time the mockery was gone and a thoughtful tone had replaced it.

The exchanges between the buyers on their chairs out front and the auctioneer went on, the pace of this sale much different than those others that Breith had witnessed. After a while, he lost his embarrassment and was just bored.

Without trying to tap into it, Breith cautiously felt about for the Flow over Ascal. Everything he'd been told about this continent said there was no magic here, no one born with the Sight, not even pitiful hedgewitches barely able to light a match. His encounter with the weird creatures on the wall back on that island made him suspect otherwise.

What he didn't expect to find was not a Flow but a sluggishly moving Pool. He strangled a gasp before he betrayed himself when he felt the depth and quality of the Pneuma in that Pool. It was thick as crystallized honey. He had spent his time so wrapped within his defenses ever since the watch had sighted land, he'd hardly noticed a thing going on around him. He had felt a certain *heaviness* but he'd just thought that was the remnants of his fever dragging at him.

As the bidding finally started, Breith ignored the sounds that were going to determine the direction of his life for the next several months at least, and considered the meaning of what he'd just seen.

Honey that sat undisturbed for a long time wouldn't pour at all unless you heated it in a pot of warm water. Could it be that the Pneuma on this side of the world was never stirred up because there was no one to use it? Would it be cranky and difficult? Or maybe even refuse to let him pull bits loose so he could handle them safely? Or would it be like punching a hole in an overfilled wineskin, exploding all over him when he poked it?

He scowled over the tops of the buyers. First thing he should do was sniff around, find out all he could without getting too friendly with that strange Pool.

No. First thing was remembering that this place he was in was a city called Pelateras in a country called Latera and they spoke a language called Lateran. That Ascal was like a piecework quilt with dozens, maybe even hundreds, of small patches of land that had their own languages and their own ruling councils or whatever they wanted to call it. That this place was not at all like Saffroa where speech was everywhere the same and where it was the twist of the rivers that kept the Confluence together and not borders and language.

It sounded as if all he had to do was get out of Latera and he wouldn't be a slave anymore. He wrinkled his nose. Had to be harder than that or nobody would bother keeping slaves. *Too much I don't know about this place.*

Second thing. He'd have to test how much of this oozy Pneuma he could handle and just what he could do with it.

There had to be some way to use it without roasting himself in his own skin. Once he knew that . . .

He blinked as the bidders rose to their feet. There was a brief patter of hand smacking against hand, then the door crashed open and the guard stepped aside as the buyers filed out.

The auctioneer bustled away from the block, vanishing behind the curtains.

One man remained seated, waiting till the room cleared. He was a rotund little man with patches of black hair above his ears and a shining bald dome the color of blood pudding, a thick orangish-pink. A boy a year or two younger than Breith stood beside him, a lead plug pulling one earlobe down so that it bumped into his neck whenever he moved his head. The boy wore a tunic of coarse, unbleached cloth with a number of pockets and a belt—or perhaps a leash—of black iron padlocked about his waist; the end of the chain was linked to the iron bracelet the seated man wore about his left wrist.

Slave, Breith thought. Like me now.

The boy was barefoot and bareheaded; he carried a locked iron box, with a horn inkbottle chained to it and a sheaf of paper bound into a notebook and shoved through a clip at the top of the box. His dark brown eyes were fixed on Breith with a mixture of resentment and a nasty sort of glee.

And that's a Buyer's Agent. He looks like a hired man, not someone buying for himself. I wonder whose property I am. He contemplated that for a moment. It made him feel odd. To be owned. Well. Not for long. Only till I know my way around this place.

He decided he wouldn't think of himself as a slave or anything like that. It's learning time. I'm going to school again, except I'm the only one who studies here and I'm the only teacher. This conceit pleased him and he smiled.

[2]

Breith walked along what looked like one of the more important commercial streets of Pelateras, harnessed to four hulking guards. Even on the wharves at Valla Murloch he'd never seen men this big. They looked like they had muscles in places where he didn't even have places and they were so tall his head barely reached above their belts.

A copper belt had been fastened around his own middle, its tongue pulled tight behind him. Steel chains were fitted to the belt and their ends looped around the waists of his four guards so there was no way he could run even if he wanted to. The Buyer's Agent moved ahead of them, his short legs scissoring busily, his whole body urgent and fearful. His slave boy pattered beside him, forced to keep up by the chain that linked them.

Breith's guards marched him along the footway at the edge of a broad street paved with square blocks of stone, blocks so long in place they were worn hollow by the wheels of the heavy drays with their teams of head-bobbing bullocks that moved past the small group.

It was late afternoon, the street was dark with the shadows of the heavy, secretive buildings. The footways were crowded with people and the street with handcarts and dogcarts, odd two-wheeled carts with canvas roofs that carried only passengers and were drawn by running men who had twisted, wizened torsos and enormous thighs. There were porters carrying enormous packs on their backs and crowds of anonymous men moving with the mindless determination of ants.

A confusing, constantly changing mix of strangeness.

A noise that hammered at him until his head was throbbing, his whole body shivering.

A stench as threatening as the noise.

There were dog turds and horse piles, human ordure and bullock pats, sluggish streams in the gutters that were part urine and part something else that smelled rather like fishwash, with lumps of rotting garbage floating in the liquid. Flies were everywhere, biting him, crawling on his arms and trying for his eyes; they kept him busy brushing them off his face.

This was an ugly city. There was no green anywhere and every wall was dun-colored and windowless. A mud city.

He was sick with disappointment. He'd got himself across a whole ocean and been nearly killed by fever and scared and bored and now he was a slave and this place was BORING! UGLY! AWFUL! It wasn't fair.

He hooked his thumb behind the copper belt and tugged at it cautiously, trying to bend it even a little. No bend. Must be plated over steel. Scande! He thrust his other thumb behind the belt and did his best to walk along as if he weren't a pet on a leash. It wasn't easy. He was already tired and his legs hurt. He could feel his knees starting to shake and was afraid he would stumble if they made him walk much farther.

By the time the Buyer's Agent turned into a wide archway leading into a court with a number of vehicles scattered haphazardly across dark gray flags, Breith was sweating rivers and exhausted.

The Agent stopped beside a coach of a kind Breith hadn't seen before with two large horses standing patiently in harness, heads in feedbags, moving their legs from time to time, their shod hooves scraping over the flags of the enclosure. There was a closed front box of lacquered wood with an intricate design inlaid in the door; it perched above two large front wheels rather like a square egg in a sling. Two men sat on the driver's bench, one a small wiry individual with a very tall hat and a long whip looped in one hand, the other a younger replica—his son, if looks meant anything. Behind this box, resting more directly on two axles, was a flatbed with a fence of narrow pipe raised waist-high around the three open sides. A carrier, Breith thought. The masters would ride in front and their slaves would be chained to the pipes or just loaded on and forgot about since they'd be out of sight and hearing.

While the Agent and his boy climbed into the front, the younger of the drivers crawled across the top of the box and dropped onto the flatbed. He unlatched the tailgate and lowered it so that it formed a kind of ladder, then waited while the four guards and Breith scrambled awkwardly up it.

When they were settled on a hard wooden bench pushed up

against the pipe fence, the young man jumped down, clipped the tailgate in place, ran round to the side of the front box and climbed up beside his father.

Compressed uncomfortably between his four huge warders, Breith leaned against the pipes and watched the awful city go sliding past him. And smelled it. If anything, the stink was worse up here than down on the street. The steamy heat was much like deep summer days in Valla Murloch; sweat collected on his skin and stayed there until he was sticky all over. But Valla never had such a stench in its streets. Even the slaughter ground that tainted the air some days wasn't so bad. He'd never thought much about it before, but Evaleem the Housewitch and Deewy her daughter who was Stablemaid made sure that Urfa House was kept clean and sweet-smelling, so maybe there was someone who did the same thing for the city.

These Lateramen didn't have witches to take care of that here. He wrinkled his nose. Another thing none of the adventure stories said anything about.

The rough lurching of the carrier and the noisome smells combined with his weariness to start his stomach rolling. He swallowed but that didn't help much. He clenched his teeth and told himself he was not going to be sick.

The carrier turned inland and began to climb as the street rose toward hills the walls had hidden before. Breith felt the tilt and cracked his eyes.

There was still nothing much to look at. A little color to comfort the eyes—the tops of trees inside the walls and a few weeds poking their heads through cracks and moss like dark green fur, here and there tendrils from a flowering vine. The occasional flash of birds more brightly colored than the flowers. Cleaner gutters. Fewer people on the footways. No children playing in the streets.

The road climbed through shallow double curves, bending first one way, then another, then back again. The air stirred, sluggishly at first, then grew fresher, and though it was no cooler, it brought the tang of greenness and water and flower scents with it. Breith's nausea gradually eased away and the ache in his head went with it.

A pair of sprites darted from one of the trees and hovered in front of him, the shrill whine of their speech coming so fast he hadn't a hope of understanding any of it. A tiny naked man transparent as glass with glass wings that blurred because they fluttered so fast. A tiny naked woman held his hand. Her hair was as long as she was and danced out from her head like water grass caught in a turbulent current.

The skin of his face felt as if it had been brushed by nettles. Pure Pneuma, shaped and come alive, that's what they were. Like those queer things on the island.

The pair flew away after a few moments, but after that he kept seeing eyes looking at him from tree trunks and tiny homunculi peering at him from the roofs of the buildings they passed.

Pneuma working itself because no one else would?

His curiosity about this place grew the farther they climbed. What were Latera houses like? Were there Pneuma creatures everywhere? Would he be able to talk to them? Where would he be put? What would his life be like?

He glanced at the nearest of his guards. The lead plug in the man's ear swung close enough to make the seal that was pressed into it easy to read. Some kind of bird with a hooked beak sitting on a three-leaved branch. Below the branch two undulating lines that might be water. The plug was a thick round lead wire, pushed through a hole in the man's earlobe, bent in a U-shape, then the ends put into a crimper of some kind that flattened them out and impressed the image into the metal.

For the first time it occurred to him that these men might be slaves and they'd know a lot of answers if they chose to give them out. He straightened, gave the man a grin and held out his hand. In his halting Lateran he said, "My name is Breith. How are you called?"

His face blank, his eyes stony, the man turned to him and

opened his mouth wide so Breith could see the gnarled stump of the tongue.

"Oh," he said. "Sorry."

Mouth shut into a grim line, the man looked at him a moment longer, then shrugged and turned to stare out the other side of the carrier.

Breith swallowed. Being a slave was suddenly no longer an adventure, but something he wanted to get away from as soon as he could. All four of them must be mute. No wonder they hadn't said a word all the time they'd been walking him on his leashes and sitting on this bench beside him. Even darocs weren't treated like that. Prophet's Teeth, I've wasted too much time. I've got to . . .

Cautiously he teased a thread from the sluggish Flow and began reeling it into himself. He worked very slowly, keeping fear and impatience squeezed down till he could barely feel them. Each time he felt heat start building inside him, he stopped the pull, though he didn't let go of the thread.

By the time the carrier reached its destination he'd tucked away a fair-sized store of Pneuma.

The youth jumped from the driver's seat and trotted to the massive gate. He held up a ring, muttered something that Breith couldn't hear, then trotted back to the carrier and climbed to his place.

The gates swung open and a moment later the carrier was trundling along a dirt lane hidden by shrubs and trees from the grounds and from the huge house that rambled over the hillside as if someone had flung down a collection of clay boxes. Or at least so it looked in the brief glimpse Breith got as the carrier turned sharply left and plunged into the shrubbery.

Where they were up next to the wall the air was still and steamy, but the shade from the trees gave at least the illusion of coolness. Breith scraped sweat from his face and leaned his head back against the pipes. Reluctantly, he released the Pneuma thread and sealed away the store of power inside him. It was there if he needed it, but he hoped he wouldn't. Though he'd managed to collect the Pneuma without any dangerous moments, he was still terrified of what would happen if he had to call on it to save himself.

The drive inside the walls seemed almost as long as that from the auction house, but the carrier finally stopped in a small, barren court somewhere round back of the house.

[3]

The Agent unlocked the chain from his wrist and with a snap of his fingers sent his slave to stand in the doorway, then he moved around in front of Breith. "I was told you have enough Lateran to understand me, boy." He held up his hand as Breith started to answer him. "First lesson. A slave is mute until given permission to speak. Even if he is asked a question, he will not speak until he is told to do so. Is that clear?"

Breith opened his mouth, closed it again and waited.

"Good. I was told that you are intelligent. You understand me? You understand what I told you? Speak."

"I understand, Sep."

"I was told you have been left mostly unschooled in the courtesy of the slave. I see you have learned one thing. Speak."

"I be unschooled, Sep. The Sellspeaker make me say Sep to him."

The Agent gestured, a sudden slash of his hand.

The guard on Breith's right slapped him, his hand cracking painfully against the side of his face.

"Your second lesson, Slave. Know yourself less than the dirt under a free man's heel. You might be highborn across the ocean. Here, you are nothing. This is not a conversation. Keep your eyes on the ground and your stance humble. Your words were appropriate enough, but your body shouted insolence. Conform your body to your words or that insolence will be beaten out of you." He waved at the guard who had slapped Breith. "Release him and return to your barracks."

The guards took the belt off him and went away.

Shoulders hunched, Breith followed the Agent into the house.

[4]

"The reports were right. A charming boy."

The room was shadowy, the air in it kept moving by two fans turning ponderously just below the high ceiling. Windows cut through walls almost as wide as Breith was tall looked out on vine-covered arcades to a fountain whose waters leaped high above a plant cast in bronze and cascaded back to pour from leaf to leaf and splash at last into the pond. What little sunlight there was in the garden dappled thick emerald grass with splotches of bright yellow.

The Nyon Merya Shamba, the woman who'd spoken, was a delicate pink, not the fleeting pink of Siofray blushes but an unchanging color the shade of the rarest of the many plum blossoms on Saffroa. The long silky hair that flowed in graceful waves about her body was a deep maroon with highlights of polished copper. She was dressed in a robe of some soft white material that Breith didn't recognize. It was wrapped loosely about her and held in place by a series of pearl and silver clasps. Her small, delicate feet were bare, the toenails painted silver, the soles so clean that she could not possibly have walked anywhere.

"Bitch in heat!"
"But a beauty even so, don't you think?"
"Don't you dare laugh at me!"
"Never, love. Never in a fist of centuries."

Breith couldn't help lifting his eyes again and again to stare at her more than was healthy for him. She was the most beautiful woman he'd ever seen. The most . . . he didn't have a word for the effect she was having on him. He blushed and glanced down. His tunic was loose enough so he wasn't going to embarrass himself if he hunched his shoulders a little. He kept his head down, but sneaked glances at her, his breath coming rough, sweat popping out on his face.

The mute guard who'd brought him here closed his hand on Breith's shoulder and squeezed. It was a warning.

Everything today was a warning, most times painful.

Back in the kitchen he'd been turned over to the chief slave mistress of the house. A wide strap hung doubled from her belt. She watched while two of the houseslaves stripped and scrubbed him. Anytime she saw him getting uppity, she applied that strap to his buttocks, then told him exactly why she did it—like old Crafan training one of the working dogs; patience, firmness, and a good eye for behavior. Crafan didn't use pain as a conditioner, but he did correct the dogs with voice and hand.

Breith hated being treated like a stupid beast who couldn't understand words, but he controlled himself and the training worked on him, striking a deeper level than the mind. He told himself it was a necessary camouflage but he was troubled by what a mere three hours of such discipline could do to him.

The Nyon Merya Shamba lay on a long low couch, propped up by piles of pillows. A young girl stood behind her, the lead slave plug in one of her ears. She wore a white tunic much like the one Breith was ordered to put on after he'd been scrubbed and powdered and primped for this meeting. The girl was waving a fan woven from some kind of ridged leaf, being very careful not to touch her mistress as she sent a gentle current of air lapping about the woman.

"Bring him closer, Teket." The voice lost its velvety purr; it was shriller now, more imperious.

The mute pushed Breith two steps forward, then gave him a tap on the back of the neck, hard enough to make sure he got the point—the same point that had reddened his buttocks earlier.

Breith kept his eyes on the polished red and white tiles of the floor. As she looked him over, he stopped thinking of the woman as beautiful and exotic and seductive; she'd turned into Cousin Berrint the Houseward who'd taken a switch to him more than once when he was still in the nursery, though his nurse Aosh Tirral didn't like interference from outside her domain. Careful, he told himself. You have to survive this. You have to learn the rules. Then you can tell them all to go suck the Prophet's toes and you can scoot out of here to better places.

He was so intent on his thoughts that he almost missed the Nyon's orders.

"Turn. Show me what you look like."

He shuffled in a small circle. When he started to go round again because she hadn't said stop, she spoke, irritation in her voice.

"Enough. Teket, remove the tunic. I want to see what I've bought."

Breith blushed and kept his eyes on the floor as the mute whipped the tunic off him and stood holding it.

"A pretty boy but skinny. You could play a tune on those ribs. About as much fire as a sick calf. So it's true what they say about Siofray men. Milky worms without any ideas that their women don't stuff in their heads. Tsah! He'll do as a pet on a leash. Take him away and put him to work. But don't mark that fine skin of his. If I'm to show him off to the Chale's friends, he'll need to be presentable. And we can pretend he's dangerous because he's uncut." The Nyon curled her lip, then closed her eyes. She reached out and tapped the tip of her fingernail against a small ceramic bell on the table beside the divan.

As the mute hurried Breith from the room, before the door was shut behind them he saw another young girl come running from the shadows, carrying a tray with a glass and a small pitcher of pink liquid.

In the hall outside, Breith took the tunic the mute held out to him and pulled it over his head. He smoothed his rumpled hair back, smiled up at the large man. "Is your name Teket, or is that just what she calls you?"

The mute touched his lips.

"So you say, but what's that for, if not answering quesions?'' Breith pointed to the wax tablet dangling on a metal chain from the wide copper belt around the man's waist, only one small item among the many accoutrements that made the man clatter when he moved.

Without stopping, the mute lifted the tablet, unclipped a stylus, wrote briefly, then turned the wax surface toward Breith. READ?

Breith edged closer so he could puzzle out the word; he wished he could stop walking, but that didn't seem a good idea. ''Man who put chains on me taught me. Speak and read.''

The mute waited until they'd turned a corner and were moving down a narrow, dingy passage without the cool white tiles on the walls and floor, then he smoothed out the wax with his thumb, wrote, NYON = ALL MUTES = TEKET = ME = BAALIS.

''Balus?''

Baalis shook his head. He touched his forefinger to his lips, mimed the first syllable, exaggerated the rounding of his mouth and pulled his hand away from his face. Then he mimed the second, cutting the nonsound short with a quick tap of his finger.

''Baah-liis?''

The mute put his hands together palm to palm, then turned them sideways so Breith could see the narrow space between them, then he dusted his palms together and smiled. It was as if he said ''close enough for use.''

''Baalis, what's to do now? I don't know anything about you all over here, just what I read in books and I expect that's mostly lies.''

Baalis touched his finger to his lips, shook his head. Once again he wiped the slate clean and let it drop to dangle beside his thigh.

''No talking?''

A nod. He mimed a whip snapping. Then he touched the lead plug in his ear.

Breith wrinkled his nose. It was interesting that the mutes were as friendly as they were to a newcomer. They were way taller than anyone on Saffroa, and where the sun hadn't touched them, like under their chin and on the inside of the elbow, their skin was paler than his. Baalis had hair the yellow of sun-dried grass and almost the same texture. He wore it in a long braid hanging down his back, the end tied off with silver wire. Shorter bits of new or broken hair made a halo round a long bony face. His eyes were a milky blue, so pale that when his mind was off somewhere like it was now, they didn't seem to have any color at all.

As Baalis led him into a maze of corridors, they moved past silent servants who glanced at him, but didn't bother to speak—if they could speak. Since some but not all of them wore the lead plug that marked them as slaves, it was quite possible that these were as mute as the man who strode along ahead of him. Breith swallowed. No one had said he was going to lose his tongue, but it might be something as common as breathing so nobody thought to mention it. He prodded gently at the cache of Pneuma sealed off inside him.

Wasn't much there. Maybe enough to scare this lot if I have to. Burn my way out. Go fast and hope to lose anyone chasing me.

He swallowed and his knees threatened to fold on him. Sweat popped out on his face and trickled into his eyes, burning. Prophet, he thought. Please. Let them leave my tongue alone. Please.

With a casual flick of one big hand Baalis tripped the latch on a door and stepped outside.

The damp heat hit Breith like a kick in the belly, and after threatening so long, his knees gave out. He crumpled to the ground with just enough strength left to keep down the meager meal he'd eaten around mid-morning.

He felt a toe lift his ribs, then with a grunt, Baalis scooped him up and carried him off, head down under one arm.

A hand lifted his head, he could feel coolness against his mouth as someone put the lip of a jug against his. "Drink this.'' It was a woman's voice, harsh and impatient, but not unkind.

He opened his eyes and looked up at her. She was a pinkish-brown, with the same thick skin as the Nyon, but hers was lined and rough with nothing like flower petals about it. Her black hair was coarse and cut short, sprinkled with enough gray to suggest she was somewhat older than she looked.

They were in a small chamber with airholes up near a tile roof, but no windows. He lay on a bed of poles and rope, a greasy blanket beneath him.

The liquid she poured into his mouth was warm, a broth of some kind. At first it tasted wonderful, then his stomach started knotting. He clenched his teeth and clutched at his middle.

The woman handed the mug to someone standing in the shadows behind her, dipped a rag in a bowl filled with water and began passing it across his face and along his arms, washing away the sweat, drawing out the heat that had overwhelmed him. When he started to shiver, she peeled off the loose white tunic and wrapped him in another blanket.

''Tundja, the jerui.''

There was a scuff of feet, then a girl came from the shadows with a bowl in one hand.

''Eat the jerui. Chew until there's no juice in the flesh, then swallow it.'' The woman broke sections off the small round fruits in the bowl and fed them to him, one by one. The juice was sweet and tart at the same time and cool on his tongue. And his stomach found it easy to take.

After a while the woman made him drink more of the broth. This time it gave strength rather than taking it away and there were no cramps.

By the time he'd got it all down, he was too hot again and what strength he could claim after the wasting of the fever had come flowing back into him. He pushed fretfully at the blanket. ''My thanks to your gentle hands and your kind nursing, jonta. Could I have my clothes back?''

''Your clothes? *Your* clothes? You don't own anything, not

even your pretty face.'' The woman pinched Breith's cheek and it wasn't a gentle tweak. ''What'd your mother call you, mana laki?''

''Breith.'' He rubbed at his cheek. ''And what's yours, O tender dove?''

''What a cozening tongue this boy has. Watch it, young Breith, or they'll have it out of your mouth before you can shut your teeth. I'm Daripada. Just Daripada. No jonta handle to it.''

Trying to think of her as his old nurse, Breith grinned at the woman. He'd gotten around Aosh Tirral easily enough when he was just a kid and had done something that Mam or Mum would have his hide for. Tirral had saved him more than once from a spanking he knew he deserved. ''Itu itu, Daripada,'' his voice an ingratiating wheedle. ''Then is there something around I could use to cover me? I really really would rather not run round like a little dog in nothing but my skin and I'm not so pretty folks would care all that much to look at me.''

''Now there's an idea I wouldn't want to touch, young Breith.'' Daripada slapped his shoulder. ''But it certainly is better not to tempt the weak with so much sweet flesh. Tundja, fetch me a guni for honey-tongue here. Bring a belt too. We're going to have to feed you up, bone boy.''

[5]

Daripada and the mutes spent a week training Breith to survive as a slave, then on a day slightly cooler than the rest, shortly after the noon meal, Daripada stuck her head into the court where Baalis was teaching Breith sign. ''Honeyboy, the Nyon wants you to play escort tonight. Get yourself to the bathhouse and tell Minji to scrub you and oil you down for presentation, then you come see me.''

He was fuming as he stalked across the barren court between the bathhouse and the servants' quarters. The old woman called Minji had scrubbed him, ignoring his protests that he was old enough to wash himself. Then she went over his body, pulling out every hair she saw except those on his head. Then she spread some kind of lotion over his body and spent a small eternity kneading it in. Then there were four more hours of pummeling him and scraping him raw and, the worst of all, rubbing crystals of perfume into his skin till he stank like a plum tree whose fruit was rotten. And she'd bleached his hair to a straw color like Baalis's braid, then slathered on so much oil he felt like a Vision Day porker. Perfumed oil.

It got into the wound in his earlobe, eating through the new skin that was just healing enough so he'd taken the bandages off and let the air get at it. Though the lead wire the slaveward had shoved in the hole was thinner than that in the ears of the older slaves and it hadn't given him much trouble, the hole started bleeding again.

Minji packed it with grease and went on with what she was doing.

Slave! Meat to be handled willy-nilly. Slave slave slave. I hate this.

He heard carillons of giggling and whirled, scowling.

No girls. Not real girls. Green glass nymphlets leaning out of tree trunks, weedy green hair whipping in a wind that touched nothing else. Small hands pressed over mouths. Eyes like shadow pools.

He turned his back on them and marched on into the house.

Breith leaned his forehead on the doorjamb for a moment before he knocked to let Daripada know he was there. He struggled to control the anger that was shaking him. Every step from the bathhouse, it had gotten stronger, he didn't know why. He was hot and sweating as if he were back in fever again. The Pneuma hoard sealed inside him was sloshing about; he was afraid he could feel it starting to boil. Forgetting where he was, he banged his forehead against the varnished wood, his breath sobbing through clenched teeth. Not again. I won't let it happen again. I won't—

"Ahi ahi, Honeyboy, what's got into you?"

Daripada's callused hands were gentle on his shoulders. She pulled him against her, patted his back, then led him stumbling into her roompair. Because she wasn't a slave, but a person of importance among the workers in the house, she had a sitting room, a tiny kitchen and a separate bedroom all for herself. As under-Housekeeper, she did all the work while the impoverished cousin of the Nyon who held the title of House-keeper gave elegant teas and passed on the orders of the high-born.

She pushed Breith down on a hassock, then fetched a glass of water from the kitchen pump and brought with it a clean rag moistened with cold water. As he gulped the water down, she dabbed the rag at his face and arms, wiping away the sweat that beaded there. "You're burning up, Bré. Are you sick again? You can't afford to be sick, I hope you know."

He lowered the glass, hiccuped twice, then sat staring at the floor until he felt enough in control to speak. "I'm not sick," he said, biting the tails off the words. "I'm not."

"Aaah." The word had a knowing lift and fall. "Just furious."

He nodded.

"You don't like the perfume.".

He shook his head.

"Or the depilation."

"Why!"

"Because that's what the Nyon wants. That's the only answer there is. You're a slave, Bré. There's lots worse waiting for you. Get used to it."

He shivered.

She took the glass away, went into the bedroom, came back with a crocheted throw. "Wrap that around you."

She stood over him while he did, then started pacing back and forth, talking as she walked. "Trouble is, you're freeborn and you don't understand what happened when you stood on that block and were sold to the household of the Chale Teripa Teral. I look at you and I see someone who's led a happy life. Why you ran away from that life I don't know. And I don't want to know so don't bother trying to explain. Just understand this. That boy you were is dead. You can't go back to being him. You can get yourself killed or you can learn how to survive here. First lesson. You're in favor now. Enjoy it while it lasts and don't do anything to cut it short. Because you won't have that favor long. By the end of this year you'll find out just how much you can endure and keep on living."

She came back, tapped the tips of her fingers sharply against his jaw. "And you listen good to this, Honeyboy. If you mess up, it's not just you who suffers for it. And it won't be just the masters who see you punished. We will make you wish you were three times dead."

Breith huddled on the chair, knowing that what she said was true. Even if they didn't touch him, they could make life so miserable he'd be forced to run before he was ready and that could get him in more trouble than he could handle, could maybe even get him killed. As the silence continued, he looked up and saw she was waiting for a response. "I hear you," he said.

"Ahi ahi, you're so young." She clicked her tongue. "Listen, Bré, tonight what you have to do is keep as close to the Nyon as you can. Make her think you adore her. Do everything you can to flatter her. You know what I'm talking about. Don't let anyone, woman or man, get you away from her. You have no right to your own body and it'll get used however any of the freeborn feel like using it unless you are clever enough to make the Nyon your shield. Don't react to people handling you, even if they hurt you. Don't react to anything you see happening; pretend you're blind and numb from the neck down. Don't eat anything, don't drink anything. If you're ordered to, pretend. Hold your water till you get back here, I don't care how long it takes. There's probably something else I should be telling you, but I can't think of it at the moment."

[6]

Trying to block out the confusion around him and keep all Daripada's strictures in mind, Breith trudged up what seemed

like endless stairs after the Nyon Merya Shamba. He was
loaded down with her cloak, her silver evening pouch and a
chased silver box that held a pomander which smelled heavily
of the spice mix inside, an eyeglass, a small silver flask filled
with a mysterious liquid, jeweled counters for gaming, half a
dozen ivory cards with images and scenes painted on them,
long silver hairpins, a comb and a brush, small phials of perfume and cosmetics, all of these settled in nests and pockets
of crushed pink velvet. From the moment he slid the chain of
flat silver links over his shoulder, he'd coveted the box, though
he'd do something a lot more interesting with the insides if it
were his.

He was happy to be carrying the cloak because with a little
maneuvering it covered up a lot. He loathed what he was wearing, at least everything above the knees. The black boots with
their silver inlay weren't bad. He wore voluminous trousers
gathered in just below his knees, the long cuffs pushed into
the boots. The trousers were black but they were made of some
kind of cloth that was just about transparent and everything
he had showed through except where the cloth was bunched
up. He wore a wide belt of stiff leather, dyed black, orna-
mented with silver studs and buckled behind him with three
small silver buckles. He wore a stiff leather vest, black like
the belt and held together by two silver clasps.

> *"That miserable lowlife scurd, dressing my boy like a*
> *whore. I could . . . I . . . Marl, get him out of there."*
> *"Nothing has changed, Fori. Let Breith learn to deal*
> *with this."*

The Nyon Merya Shamba drifted up the stairs as if she were
carried on clouds, layers of silver tissue whispering around
her, silver slippers soundless on the crimson carpet. The tall
narrow lamps that marched up the walls burned with a bright
white light and woke answering gleams from the diamond
ropes she twisted in her dark hair and wound round her arms,

loop upon loop swaying with each graceful gesture as she greeted the others on the stair with her.

Except for slave attendants like Breith, they were all women on this curved staircase. It swept in a graceful arc up the sides of a ground-floor room big enough to house a dozen families, a space that seemed to serve no purpose at all but conspicuous waste. The men in their velvets and dyed leathers climbed a stair at the other end of the hall, its arc the mirror image of the women's stair.

He found all of this confusing but interesting. If he just had sensible clothes and didn't get hot all over when he saw people looking at him, he'd be enjoying himself. He hunched his shoulders and edged up another stair. He didn't dare bump into the Nyon, but he also didn't like the way that the woman behind him kept edging closer to him. She was a big woman, not exactly fat, but soft all over and sagging off the bone— where her flesh was visible. Most of it was covered with heavily embroidered ribbons and swags of strung pearls. And she kept patting and pinching him. At first he'd thought it was an accident, but no one pinches inadvertently. He ground his teeth and wished fervently the crowd would move faster.

Ceiling fans turned and, from somewhere, cool if somewhat moist air blew down on the climbing crowds as they moved slowly up toward the wide landing above and the brightly lit arches beyond it, the soft *thwop thwop* of the fan blades audible above the muted murmur of the guests.

He watched those arches creep closer and wondered about the purpose of this whole business. It didn't seem to him that anyone was having fun, but what else were parties for?

Prophet's Days in Valla Murloch meant dancing in the streets and troupes of fanai playing and singing everywhere and food carts and races. The gates of the grand Houses were thrown open and the snake-lines of the pilgrim dancers went from one to the other, throwing paper flowers and gulping down the mulled wine in the gartha cups. Everyone wearing their best clothes. Everyone out to have a good time. He and his housekin from Urfa House thought up tricks to play, got themselves switched a bit, but as long as they weren't malicious and didn't hurt anyone, those switchings were mostly a matter of form.

Sometimes Mam and Mum gave dinner parties for other traders, but those weren't for fun but business really, even if no actual business got done and it was just a bunch of folks throwing talk back and forth.

This thing . . . they'd spent half a watch climbing these stairs. The women talked to each other, occasionally lifted a hand in a greeting to someone higher or lower in the parade. Mostly they looked at each other from the corners of their eyes, cool, measuring glances more like two fichil players assessing the board.

I'm going to have to ask Daripada what this is all about, he thought. Baalis probably wouldn't know. This . . . this thing . . . must be important. They're putting so much energy into it.

The stair standing came to an end finally and Breith hurried to keep up with the Nyon as she swept across the landing, then scrambled to keep from bumping into her as she slowed suddenly when she reached the nearest arch.

A tall man with skin brown and smooth as a nut swung out from his side an elaborately carved and beribboned staff as he made an equally elaborate bow.

The Nyon placed a small square of ivory in his free hand.

He glanced at it as he straightened, swung round to face the crowd milling about the immense room beyond. "THE NYON MERYA SHAMBA," he cried in a voice so loud that Breith winced then looked around to see if anyone had noticed.

There was tension in the slender back ahead of him. With a lift of her head the Nyon moved into the throng, nodding, smiling, occasionally speaking a word or two.

A smell-off, Breith thought. Like a pack of dogs.

He watched her relax, her silhouette soften, as she played him as a prize and saw it work to enhance her standing. He was a rarity, something unique that none of the other women could exhibit. The comments they made were often coarser and meaner than the Barnward's assessment at the stockyards, but the Nyon took them as compliments; the nastier they were, the greater the compliment to her. He gave up blushing before the Nyon had moved a quarter of the way round the room and fixed on his owner the most adoring looks he could contrive. Daripada was right. This was the way to go, the only way he could see to ignore the comments without getting himself in trouble. Besides, the Nyon was arching her elegant neck and giving him soft-eyed looks which invited such returns.

When the round was finished, the ugly old woman the Nyon had been careful to greet first beckoned to her, waved away one of the others clustering about her so that the Nyon could sit beside her.

"Give us a look at the boy, Merya."

"It is done, Radja Kilau." The Nyon snapped her fingers at Breith, gestured impatiently when he started to carry his impedimenta with him.

He bowed, touched his brow and piled his burdens neatly on the floor, then stepped into the small space and turned in a circle, trying to hit some mean between the demeanor of a slave and of a prize possession. He pasted an idiotic smile on his face, widened his eyes until he was sure he looked like a newborn tribuf wet about the nose and shaky in the knees. When the circle was completed, he stood with his hands held before him palm to palm, his head bowed, his eyes on the floor.

"The rumors were right. A lovely boy. Very docile, though. I thought you were leaving him whole, Merya."

"We are for the moment, Radja Kilau. We plan to breed him to several of our girls to see if the cross will produce useful talents."

"Hm. You'll want to watch his get closely. You don't want to create monsters."

"Yes, indeed, Radja Kilau. We plan to cull any of the cublets who have dangerous traits. The males, of course, will be no problem. It seems those Siofray Damas have managed to breed docility into their sons."

Breith caught hold of himself, forced down the sudden geyser of rage and clutched at the cache of Pneuma.

"How charmingly he blushes and what deliciously fair skin he has. I declare I am envious, Merya."

"A woman is blessed who has a generous man, Radja Kilau."

"True. A man with a generous heart makes a good friend. Ah!" The Radja lifted a hand. "The music begins. An old creature with only sons to light her days has no place on the floor, but you are young and a pleasure to watch when you sport your foot, so go and dance. I'll guard your boy and return him to you intact and as innocent as I got him."

Breith sat on the floor beside the Radja's backless chair, the silver box by his feet and the Nyon's cloak bunched across his lap. He watched the dancers gesture, point their feet and skip about like limping chickens, smiles painted on their faces, watching each other from the corners of their eyes as they'd done the whole time they'd been here, as if they wouldn't know they were enjoying themselves if they weren't seen to be delighted.

"Boy, tell me your name. Speak."

"Breith, Great One."

"Does that have any meaning in your homeland? Speak."

"No, Great One. It is just a name."

"Have you done jolo yet with your mistress? Speak."

"I do not know that word, Great One."

"The two-backed dance, boy. I'm sure you understand that. Speak."

"Oh no, Great One. The Nyon is so beautiful, so wonderful, so . . . so, oh, I no have the words. It is a bad thing in me to even think such a thing."

The old woman snorted. "Scruples in a slave. We do live and learn. But you're a very new slave, aren't you. Speak."

"Yes, Great One. It is two weeks past when I was sold."

"Tell me about the Siofray. What is it that these grand Siofray Damas do that makes them so powerful? Speak."

"I do not know what you want me to say, Great One." Breith hesitated, frowned at the floor. He wasn't about to tell them about Mam and Mum. Pelateras was a port city and the chances were good there'd be folk about who'd been to Valla Murloch and knew House Urfa, folk who might have thoughts of using him against them. "The Traiolyns of the Domains are women of great power. Yes. They can call fire and water and shape wonders. They can kill with a gesture of a hand. They can protect themselves from being killed. . . ." His eyes on the floor, he rambled on, scratching memory for everything he'd picked up about the Domains. It didn't matter if it wasn't quite true; this old woman wouldn't know that. He was glad she was curious. It kept him from thinking about . . . things he'd better not think about.

"Stop," the Radja said. "It is enough for the moment. Be silent and wait the return of your mistress."

[7]

Though he was exhausted and there was no hot water and only such soap as he could steal from the kitchen, Breith scrubbed himself until his skin was raw and even his hair hurt.

By the time the Nyon was willing to leave the party, the moon was long down and he could smell dawn on the rising wind. She was pleased with him but not interested in dalliance, so she let him crouch on the floor of the carosh and serve as a footstool as she dozed during the short journey back to the Chaletat.

He emptied the bucket he'd used as a basin into one of the flower beds. Before he could straighten something touched his face; it felt like the tickle of insect legs. He brushed at his face and jumped to his feet, then stared.

The apparition was like thickened mist, a slender naked woman with long thin fingers, eyes that were gleams sparking from black smudges, a mouth so dark the lips might have been bleeding. Her long long hair floated about her body, blowing apart and back together. She touched him again, her fingers moving along his bare arm. Lines of blood drops emerged from under her black nails and after a few breaths, he felt the cuts sting.

Then she melted away. Between one breath and the next she was gone.

Confused and uncertain, he wiped at the thin cuts with the still soapy scrub rag, dropped it in the bucket and went inside. He sneaked the diminished soap back to its place and went shivering to the small room that had been assigned to him and that had provoked some jealousy among the other slaves. Male and female, slaves slept on pallets in long bare dormitories. Even the servants—all but the most important—shared their rooms.

He'd wondered about his room, but after tonight, he knew why he had it. It wasn't a bedroom, it was a breeding chute. After his value as a one-month wonder was used up, he was supposed to add the Siofray strain to the Chale's slave stock. The idea appalled him.

Weary and miserable, he crawled onto the bed and pulled the quilts over him, burrowing deep enough that only his nose was out. I have to get away from here, he thought, I have to get . . .

10

Working Toward War on Iomard

By the calendar of the Domains of Iomard, events dating from the 21st day of Seyos, the sixth month in the Iomardi year 6535, the 722nd year since the last Corruption.

[1]

Startled by the unexpected blow, Dur sprawled on his face on the worn planks of the wharf. He pushed up and whirled, but Cymel was gone and shouts from the owners and crews of the boats tied up along the wharf warned him his time was short. These men and women were ocean seiners doing a little smuggling on the side and anything else that brought in coin. They were tough, dangerous and single-minded about their ships and anything else that belonged to them.

He glanced along the boats, chose the one he meant to take, then he whirled, lifted his arms straight out, closed his hands into fists, whispering the chant that summoned a blast of wind, holding it back, holding it back. . . .

He opened his hands, blew them off their feet with that wind. Before they could scramble up again—those without bones broken where they slammed against walls and crates piled on the wharves—he had cast off and was raising sail. He gave them another taste of the power of a Mage wind and was left to go as he pleased, though he could feel the hot musky anger swirling behind him.

The little boat was cranky and needed close watching so he couldn't relax a moment on the trip to the Sanctuary Isles, but she was faster than many and her sails were in suspiciously good condition. He was pleased with her. He didn't want to think right now and she gave him the excuse he wanted.

It had been mid-afternoon when he'd come to Iomard, riding his forced Bridge, and the sun was setting when he tacked into an inlet north of Gavachtag on Isle Tuays and shoved the boat up onto the scrap of sandy beach. He tied her to a small tough scrub tree, then climbed out onto the beach and eyed the rough rock slopes in front of him.

He was tired. His house was likely taken by someone else in the months he'd been gone. He didn't care about that, he could evict whoever it was easily enough, but it was just one more drain on his energy that he didn't want to face right now. He climbed back into the boat, found a spare sail in the sail locker, wrapped himself in it and dropped immediately into a deep sleep.

[2]

The assembly rang early, the harsh clangs of the iron triangle drawing the Ead Village darocs from their houses and away from their livestock. Didn't matter that the milking was half done, the chickens unfed, when that summons rang there was no choice about answering it.

Urs threw the last handful of coarse meal into the chicken pen and hurried round to the front of the house. Aron was stumbling out the door, shaky fingers fumbling at the ties on his shirt; he'd been down with a rheum for several days and the early morning air wasn't good for him. Urs hurried over, got Aron's old cloak from behind the door and flung it around the Rememberer's shoulders. With Aron leaning heavily on him, the two of them moved slowly along the lane to the Dance Ground.

The Eadro Wife stood on the music dais, her arms folded,

a ghost of a smile curling the corners of her mouth. Seer Amadan stood beside her, a sheaf of papers in her bony hand.

Aron's breath hissed through his teeth.

Urs looked up. "What?" he whispered.

"Names. That 'un has list of names. They looking for the gone."

Urs bit his lip, glancing hastily around. Ead Village had nearly five hundred families so the dance floor was packed with people and he couldn't see much more than the backs of a lot of heads, but even so he could name at least five who weren't here with their families. And there were probably lots more. Eaders didn't talk about this kind of thing, not even to each other.

Aron touched his shoulder. "You go be with your Mam," he whispered. "I'll do fine."

Urs twisted his face into a black scowl, but he knew Aron was right. Since his Mam was head Elder and Speaker for Ead, her family would be the first called. Breathing fast and agitated, he reached his family group as the Seer pronounced Mam's name.

When the calling was done, the sun was well up, the dance floor smelled of sweat and anger and nearly fifty women stood in a group aside from the rest—those heads of household who had daughters or sons or nieces or nephews or grandchildren among the missing. The Seer stepped back, stood reordering her lists. The Eadro Wife's smile was fierce and her eyes glittered.

Urs shuddered, remembering the gossip about this woman.

"You see before you," the Wife said in her deep, musical voice, "those who have broken faith with the Domain. Who have neglected their duty to that which sustains them." She broke off, frowning. Turned her head to look over her shoulder. Urs heard hoofbeats, a horse coming rapidly toward the village.

The Wife turned back and spoke more rapidly, not pausing to savor the words as she had before. "A punishment is prescribed for such neglect, a punishment that must be doubled for perilous times such as these.''

The bantar pulled up beside the dais, handed a folded sheet of paper to the Seer.

''All of you know what it is, five strokes of the whip, five more for the doubling. This—''

The Seer touched the Wife's arm, interrupting her. She gave the Wife the paper the bantar had brought.

The Wife held it a moment as if she wanted to drop it and stomp it into the planks of the dais, then she mastered her anger and read what was written there. She folded the message, tucked it into a pocket, took a long breath, then spoke again, her voice harsh from the anger she was denying. ''This time we will be merciful and only administer a warning. Your names are noted, Oath-breakers. Take care how you deal with Eadro henceforth.''

[3]

With a sense of enormous relief and a springlike efflorescence of the power that lay within him, Dur drew the last of the red signs on his body. Though he didn't know exactly how it had happened, his time on Glandair had increased the complexity and the number of those signs. He set the paint pot on the flat top of a broken stalagmite, looked down at himself, then flung his head back, his arms wide, and shouted his triumph into the domed ceiling of that immense chamber, the shout echoing into a web of sound as complex as the web of powersigns.

Wrapped in dying echoes, he washed the red from his fingertips then took his seat in the throne chair that overlooked the mirror pool. He spoke a word. The surface of the pool rippled. When it cleared, he was looking down at the river plain of Tilkos and two armies engaged in a chaotic battle. Those on foot fought with sword and pike, small clumps of men hacking at each other, drowning in the din around them, intent only on the ever-shifting enemy in front of them.

The war wizards on both sides rose like kites above the fighters' heads, fell again, rose again, casting their stinks, their winds of disruption, their earth splittings, at each other, and did their utmost to deflect the enemy's spells back on him.

The Mage Mahara stood in midair above the Kale army, his arms folded across his chest, his body enclosed in a sphere of crawling blue symbols that shunted away all danger, either from the bows or the Tilkose war wizards.

Mahara's fingers twitched. A dart of light sped from them to a group of men clustered apart from the battle, atop a low earthen mound that had been thrown up for them—the Third Prince, his aides and the Prince's Guard. Horns blared, three riders raced from the Prince to different parts of the army and moments later came racing back; they swung into the saddles of fresh mounts while the exhausted beasts were led off to be walked cool, stripped of tack, wiped down and sent to the herd of remounts.

Dur watched the Kale army shift, drawing back here, pushing forward there, according to the orders carried by the couriers and the horn blasts from the Mound. Despite their superb riding and their fighting skills which were individually greater than any of the Kalemen, the Tilkose didn't fight as an army but as a collection of singletons and small groups, and they were getting ground up as if between millstones. And the Kale army's maneuvers were slowly but surely encircling them. If the jaws of that trap closed, Tilkos was done and Mahara had won his war.

He hesitated a moment, thought of searching for his askerit but decided he didn't want to know what was happening with them. Just thinking about them gave him a pain in the gut. He looked a last time at Mahara standing high above the battle, turning slowly, flicking his messages from the tips of his fingers. I have to learn that, he thought, then he moved a hand and the mirror pool went dark again.

He sat for several moments, his head back against the stone of the great chair, his eyes closed. The easy part was done. He knew how he was going to organize and fight his army, he knew where the fighters were coming from, but he had to have land to house and feed them. The Isles were too vertical to train an army and too barren to feed it. He needed to claim land on Saffroa. He needed to protect that land against attacks and spying by Seers.

He knew how to do that; it was simple—just shift the location of the chaotic Pneuma that defended the Isles and pin it down so it fenced the land he wanted to protect. But it wasn't going to be easy. It might not even be possible.

Once he started moving the Pneuma chaos, stretching it out like a fence, he couldn't stop till the job was done, and if it outlasted his strength, it would kill him or burn out his Sight so he might as well be dead.

He called up the image of his mother; that image had walked beside him in the Comconair, had helped him survive weariness, thirst and hunger. Her strength was his, her will passed on to him. Her dreams were his dreams. She was square and strong, burnt dark by the sun from working in the fields beside his father. Faded brown eyes as if someone had taken them from her head and washed them in harsh soap, leaching away the color. Coarse black hair. Scarred, twisted hands, with fingers that wouldn't close into fists because of the chalk disease in her joints that grew worse every year. She never talked much, never sang as some of the women did, but when she smiled at him she found a fleeting beauty.

He could see her clear. Could see her set her hands on her hips and click her tongue at him. "Now you're on the road where you should be," she'd say to him.

"You told me to reach as high as I could."

"Don't forget again."

"I won't."

Careful not to smear the signs painted on his face, he drank from his water bottle, ate two of the bars the Hisay made of berries, nuts and honey, then a stick of meat jerky. To give the food time to settle, he looked a last time into the book that Fanach had found for him while she was still alive and not wholly fuddled by the muscar. He stood holding the crumbling cover for a long moment, then slapped the book shut, walked onto the narrow path that ringed the mirror pool and began his dance of power.

[4]

The door to Radayam's office crashed open and Mirrialta came striding in, her eyes glittering, her color high. She stopped in front of the worktable. "Why?"

Radayam lifted her head. "Order yourself, Wife. Shut the door, come back and seat yourself properly, then we'll speak."

The color drained from Mirrialta's face and her dark eyes went cold. Radayam did not mistake this for surrender. For a moment Mirrialta didn't move, then she turned, marched to the door, closed it with mechanical control, marched back and settled herself into a chair by the end of the deck. "Why did you make a fool of me like that? Ordering me back here and telling Seer Amadan to ignore my instructions. Telling my whole staff they are not to obey me."

"You exaggerate and are inaccurate. I simply told the Seers—who are not your staff but mine—that you will not be the one who sets punishment for the darocs. They are to bring names and circumstances to me and I will order what is necessary."

"Why?"

Radayam leaned back in her chair and contemplated the coldly beautiful face for several moments before she spoke. "Because I want you to understand that certain practices of yours will not be acceptable here. Because you do not know these darocs and have made no attempt to know them, so you cannot grasp the extent and duration of the ripples your decisions create. I can see the thought in you: These are only darocs, ours to do with as we please, theirs to endure what is done. No, Mirrialta. The Prophet says this: The greater the power in her hands, the heavier her responsibilities become. When I see you assuming those responsibilities, then I will draw back my hand."

"So I'm to understand that you will continue to humiliate me?"

"Don't challenge me, Mirrialta. Do you think I didn't know what you were doing when you ordered those floggings?"

"My duty as Wife to uphold the discipline of the Domain while you are busy with your dreams, Radayam." Her nostrils flared. "Turn your back on darocs and they melt away faster than butter on a burner."

"The Prophet says justice and mercy are twin sisters joined at the hip; cut one from the other and both die. Discipline is out of your hands and will remain so until I perceive a greater understanding in you of the Precepts of the All-Mother and the needs of Eadro. You have other duties. Return to them."

The door closed behind Mirrialta with a faint click. Eadro's Wife walked away lightly so that Radayam could no longer hear her by the time she'd taken half a dozen steps.

Radayam let her head fall back against the chair and rested with the heels of her hands pressed against her eyes as she felt a coldness pass through her; her guilt left her bereft of the serenity that had been with her through the past months. "My fault, O Prophet," she murmured. "I did not care enough to take the proper steps to find a Wife and that which was placed in my care will be punished for my fault. I will do penance, O Prophet, tonight and each night until the march begins. And I will do what I am given to do to keep faith with my children and my kin."

She sighed, lowered her hands to the table. "But that's for later." She took up the pen, dipped the point in the inkwell and began writing again, organizing her thoughts for the meeting later in the evening. Planda's Traiolyn was being difficult. Hiacaylin was in sympathy with the idea of the Purification, but she would not be ruled by anyone. Whatever anyone proposed, she refused to accept even though she had said that very thing a moment before.

There were two problems with letting Hiacaylin lead the cleansing of the Western Lobe, indolence and corrupt motivation. She would smash Fasalla, Mionach and Teyas Brota because those port cities were festering sores in the heart of her well-being; they paid her no tithes and charged her port fees. Once they were gone, though, she'd lose her drive, and while the other Riverine Cities would eventually fall to her, she'd not purify them as she should. Cleansing the land cried out for fire and blood, and Hiacaylin had no fire in her, only greed.

We are all imperfect tools, Radayam told herself. And there is always Shoneyn. Who can stand against the force of Shoneyn? She sighed. If we can get this settled tonight, I can start calling in bantars and ridos along with their darocs. The herd-girls are ready to bring the herds close and start the butchering for the supply train. We'll gather here at Eadro. Have to work out the order of march. O Prophet, you show me again my sins against you. If I'd found a proper Wife, I could trust her to share this load.

She closed her eyes. Everyone told me Mirrialta was a fine organizer. Perhaps her folly comes because she has had too little to do rather than too much. Hm. I'll set her to planning how to handle the army, where people will camp, how to get the wagons we'll need to transport supplies. What kind of supplies we'll need. Give her a day to get over her snit. I wish I understood her better. I wish . . . She shook her head. This wasn't something she could deal with now. Too many other problems claimed her attention.

[5]

Dur collapsed on stone, too tired to stand, sweat running off him like water off a mountain in thaw. The lights from the stone candles shimmered unsteadily, losing their outlines in fuzzy blurs, sharpening again to flames. For several breaths he was too tired to think. Too tired even to realize his triumph.

When his shaking stopped, he rolled over into the mirror pool, using the intense chill of the water to shock himself awake. He climbed out shuddering and padded over to the hot stream that circled round the edge of the chamber, where he washed the red paint off his face and body and the sweat from his hair. Squatting by the stream, letting the heat soak into his chilled, weary body, he ate two more of the Hisay trail bars, put a chunk of jerky in his mouth to soften, and drank from the water jug.

Time passed and strength rose through him, drawing on the warmth and the energy in the food. Drowsy, pleased with himself, he rose and crossed the rough floor of the cavern, carefully watching where he set his feet because he was still too tired to lift them as he should.

He settled himself in the stone chair and spoke the mirror to life, focusing it on the land he had just taken for himself.

"Yesssss!" Now he could scry a part of Saffroa. His vision ended at a wall of gray mist that followed the turns and twists of the south bank of the Uwine River all the way to the eastern boundary of Domain Fuascala then turned north till it touched the icy rim of the Polar Sea. As the image shifted across what he had decided to call Eilyman Tyr, the Claimed Land, he was startled to see dozens of small camps, tents and pole huts neatly set up, rope corrals for a horse or two, gardens with rows of plants greening the turned earth, hides on stretchers drying in the meager light of the northern sun. A few of the camps had even acquired a milker from somewhere.

They listened, he thought. They listened and came.

"I'll see you free. All of you. If it takes my life, you and your kin will be free."

[6]

Worried and frowning, Radayam sat on a cushion in a small, bare room at the top of the highest of the House Eadro towers, a room that had once been her place of meditation. Sitting in an arc before her, the images of Teannal, Shoneyn and Mycill shimmered, strengthening and fading with the pulses of the Pneuma Flow, their speaker talismans glimmering like downed stars in front of them. They were waiting for Cluayn to join them. This tardiness wasn't like her; ordinarily she was one of the first to appear, wanting to talk with Radayam alone and gain whatever advantage she could from that.

A growl in the Pneuma, a wild fluctuation that almost scattered the other three images beyond remerging—and Cluayn appeared, her image forming, breaking apart, reforming until she finally managed a stable presence.

Cluayn pressed her hands over her eyes, then straightened. "I ask your pardon, friends, but you will understand my agitation when you learn why I come late to the meeting. The Mage has moved, has come ashore, but there is nothing we can do about that. He has shifted the chaos reefs and taken almost the whole of the Shabba Peninsula."

11

Things Fall Apart

By the secret calendar of the Watchers, events dating from the 19th day of Pumamis, the fifth month in the 738th Glandairic year since the last Settling.

[1]

Talgryf stood slouched on the pier, watching Ellar examine the lock on the chain holding the slim pleasure boat nose-in to the mooring. He didn't want to be there. He didn't want to leave the bothrin. He knew he was going to hate living on some dumb farm out the back of behind with nothing to do but dig in dirt and fool with dumb cows. He hated the memory of his father lying there, crying weakly, begging him to go. He blamed Ellar for that and hated him.

Ellar slapped lightly at the lock and it sprang open. He pulled the chain from the metal loop, dropped it on the pier. Holding the boat against the tug of the current, he turned to Talgryf. "Get in. Settle yourself in front of the mast where you'll be out of the way. By that box there. Hurry, the night watch will be along soon."

Talgryf took a last look over his shoulder at the towers of the Temple, then he swallowed hard, grabbed the rail and swung himself into the boat. As it swayed under him, he scrambled in near panic for the box Ellar had pointed out and crouched in the bottom, eyes shut. He heard a thump. At the same time he felt the boat slip sideways and come alive under him in a way that frightened him even more.

More sounds. Thuds. Rattles. A crack like a dishtowel snapping. The boat curling round. The rushing hiss of the river water.

He straightened and looked cautiously around. The sail was up and belly taut with a following wind. One hand on the tiller, one hand on a rope that was tied to the—Talgryf scowled—to the boom, that's what they called that stick. Ellar sat in the stern; the spectacles hiding his pale blue eyes glittered like ice in the moonlight and his face was a mask to frighten younglings. Scares the spit out of me, Talgryf thought.

Funny. He couldn't feel the wind and it wasn't because the boat sides stopped it; they weren't that high. He knew from Cymel that her father could do magic stuff, but he'd never really thought about it. Seeing it was . . . well, he'd always thought of Ellar as a nice man but weak and ineffectual, letting himself be jerked around by everyone without even the fight a fish would give a hook. I'm poor, I'm a half-breed and a thief, but I play games with town guards and lift purses and wriggle my way into rich houses to take what I please and nobody but my father ever tells me what to do.

If Ellar could do things like this without even twitching, why did he just sit and take it when the Tyrn and the rest of those stupid courtiers mocked him and kept him tied in Carcalon when he wanted to go home? Me, I'd turn them into trash fish and feed them to dogs if I had that kind of power. It wasn't weakness, that was sure. It was something Talgryf couldn't understand and something that called a reluctant respect from him. He watched the magic wind blow the boat along the river fast enough to make the banks go blurry even though the moon was nearly full and the sky clear and the night almost as bright as day and changed his mind about the man driving that boat.

He was getting cold. He rummaged in his backpack for the sweater his stepma had knitted for him and pulled it over his head, working it down till he could stretch it over his knees.

Stepma would have catfits if she saw him, but it felt good and he began to warm up and relax for the first time since Ellar came for him.

The next four days they fled up the river without stopping to rest. Ellar drank a little water, ate handfuls of raisins and nuts he had Talgryf dig out for him, but except for the few times he stopped to take care of the needs of his body, he never uncurled from his crouch by the tiller.

Sometime after sunset on the fourth day, Talgryf stood on a landing and watched the river current carry the boat away. He gave a warbling yell, snapped his thumb on the tip of his nose in a now-friendly insult, then hurried after Ellar who was striding off as if he didn't know what tired meant.

He led them to a long crude shelter made of woven twigs and mud daub, the rough room incongruous with its neat precision. A warehouse of sorts. Beyond that was a cottage with a stable larger than it was, tucked behind it. Beyond that there was nothing but a white dirt road that disappeared into a thick clump of trees.

Ellar was walking so fast that Talgryf had to run to keep up with him. He turned between two bushes, pulled a chain hanging down. An iron bell clanked off-key.

As if standing still had drained away more of his strength than all he'd done to get here, Ellar swayed as he waited for an answer to the bell's noise. He reached out hastily to grab hold of the support pole, then stood with shoulders rounded, his whole body trembling.

Talgryf blinked as the top half of the front door swung outward; a short pudgy woman stood in the yellow lamplight, scowling at them. " 'Tis late. Can't you wait till morning?"

"My daughter is ill, I have to get to her. I'll pay three days for two. For the boy." He waved a hand at Talgryf. "And for me."

"Ah well, if that's the case . . ." She turned her head, called out, "Rudd, haul on your leathers and come out to stable." She turned back. "If you'll walk round to the corral, we'll

ave you mounted and ready to trot before the moon's a whis-
er higher.''

Ellar rode first, holding his mount to an easy lope, though the
ension in his shoulders and the anxiety that Talgryf could
lmost taste was evidence that he'd like to push the horse till
s heart burst.

Talgryf came next, most of his attention fixed on staying in
he saddle. All he knew about riding came from stolen mo-
nents on other men's horses, clinging with knees to the barrel,
ands twisted in the mane, trying to find a comfortable way
o sit the bony spine. He hoped that the farm wasn't too far
off; by morning he was going to be hurting worse than he
iked to think of.

Rudd was younger than Talgryf by at least two years, prob-
bly the woman's son. He rode third. He was there to keep
n eye on the horses and pony them home after they weren't
eeded anymore.

Though the sky was graying toward dawn when they
eached the farm, the windows of the house were warm with
ellow light. Ellar stopped his horse in the middle of the path
hat led to the front door and swung down. "Corysiam," he
alled. It wasn't a shout, but there was great urgency in that
vord.

Talgryf tried to swing his leg up so he could dismount, but
is joints wouldn't work.

Rudd heard him grunt with pain and rode closer. "Give us
' hand, huh?'' He reached out, slapped Talgryf's arm, re-
eated what he'd said.

With Rudd's help, Talgryf managed to get his feet on the
round. His thighs burned and his knees didn't want to hold
im up. He clung to the stirrup leather and hurt so much he
wore he was never getting on a horse again, and if he had to
o somewhere and it was too far to walk, he'd just forget the
vhole thing.

The door opened and a woman came out and down the
teps. Talgryf could only see her outline because the light was

in back of her, but she was taller than most women he kne
and her hair looked like a bush after a windstorm. She w
carrying something. After a minute he saw that it was eith
a blanket or a quilt. A few steps on the path, then she lift
one hand in a looping gesture, said something he couldn
make out. She came on to meet Ellar.

"Mela?" Ellar reached out to touch her arm, his hand tren
bling.

"No change," she said.

He said nothing more, just ran past her, up the stairs an
into the house.

Corysiam—if that was her name and not a calling—stopp
by Rudd. "The barn's round there." She pointed. "Hay f
bedding and a pump for water." She gave him the qui
"There's a ward around the house, so don't try coming clos
than I am now, either front or back, if you don't want a pain
burn."

Talgryf let go of the stirrup leather. He could stand, but
didn't dare take a step, not wanting to end with his face in tl
dust.

Corysiam held out her arm. "Hard ride, him? Grab hol
When you're inside with some hot food in you, you'll sta
believing you'll live." There was laughter in her deep, war
voice, but Talgryf didn't mind. It flattered him that she too
as given that he could see the funny side of all this.

He'd never been in a farmhouse before. It wasn't all th
big, but it had enough room to house half a dozen bothr
families. And just Cymel and Ellar were living here alone. F
years. It was an odd feeling. He'd never been away from tl
sounds of people, coughs and hacks, voices, screams, quarre
laughter, grief, bumps and thuds, crash of pottery, a thousa
and a thousand sounds, even just breathing, hundreds of pe
ple breathing. The stillness, the silence, the emptiness here-
they made him feel cold and lonely.

Corysiam took him into a big kitchen with a black ire
stove and a tiled floor. Two loaves of bread sat on coolir
racks; the smell made his belly rumble and his mouth fill. Eve

rough his aches and his weariness he was hungrier than he'd
en in a long time.

"That's for later. Ellar says your name is Talgryf. Gryf for
ort. That right?"

"Uh-huh."

"Well, Gryf, in a bit I'll have some tea, toast and melted
eese ready to fill that void in your middle, but first thing is
hot bath to help ease out those battered muscles of yours."
e chuckled as she urged him toward a door on the north
d of the kitchen. "And get rid of the stink of horse."

The room beyond the door was floored with stone with a
le in the middle for water to run out. What looked like half
large barrel was filled with gently steaming water. On the
r side of the room a bronze chain with a handle on the end
as hanging from the ceiling. A bronze and glass lamp beside
e door filled the room with more shadows than light. Be-
ath the lamp was a short bench with a pair of towels folded
one end.

Corysiam pointed at the bench. "Take your clothes off,
ave them there and climb into the barrel; there's soap in the
lder. When you're finished there, go over to the chain and
and under it. Give it a good pull and water will splash down
d rinse off the soap. I'll be in the kitchen making breakfast
r you, but you don't need to hurry. Enjoy your bath."

ryf eyed the tub warily, but the way he felt, he'd try any-
ing. When he eased himself into the warm water and felt the
orst of the aches melting away, he sighed with pleasure. He
und the wooden seat built onto the side of the barrel and
retched out, water to his neck. He moved his feet a little
hen it cooled on him, sighed again as currents of warmth
rled around him.

Water up his nose woke him and he sat up sputtering.

He looked around, found the soap and began washing him-
lf. "I could get to like this," he said aloud. His voice
unded good in that stone room with its polished walls.
Ha!" He laughed at the faint echo at the edge of the shout,

then started singing as he rubbed soap all over him, even i
his hair.

[2]

Light was pouring in the bedroom window when Talg
woke. He was stiff and sore, but when he stretched cautiou
he didn't hurt nearly so much as he had last night. He laugh
as his belly rumbled, then he rolled out of bed.

When he was dressed, he left the room and went stroll
down a narrow walkway lit by sunlight coming through a p
tern of translucent shell set into the roof above the squa
spiral of the staircase. He went past two closed doors then s
one that was half open.

Cymel lay in a bed like the one he'd slept in. Her hair v
a black tangle on the pillow sham, her hands were up by l
face, but the rest of her was covered by a linen sheet. As
watched, she gave a small snore and moved under the she
She didn't wake up, but her face was flushed. She didn't rea
look sick. Maybe Ellar had done something to help her l
night.

The poet lay on a pallet beside the bed, sleeping heavi
He was on his side, curled up, deep lines in his face t
Talgryf hadn't seen before. He'd pulled his boots off, but
hadn't bothered to undress. He's going to feel like the ba
end of nothing when he wakes up, Talgryf thought.

Corysiam was opening drawers, shutting them with more fo
than necessary, jerking cabinets open, banging them shut. S
looked temperish and unhappy.

Talgryf started to back out, trying to be quiet so he would
draw her attention, but she looked up and saw him. He sto
very still, eyeing her warily.

She set her hands on her hips. "Not a thing to eat in t
house, not even a spare tea leaf. Tsaah!"

"Um . . . I could go set some snares if you want. Should
a good time for it."

"Tyst boy. What do you know about snares?"

"Hunh! I couldn't set 'em, we'd have starved couple winters ago when the hard cold come down and things got real tight."

She pulled the back of her hand across her face. It was as if she'd wiped the ill-temper away and replaced it with a grin. "Wouldn't know, young Gryf. I was in another place on a whole other world. Hm. I couldn't Bridge without leaving Cynel alone and unwarded . . . how good is your memory?"

He shrugged. "Good enough."

"So let's give it a test. Come on."

Corysiam opened the front door, pulled a hand through that looping gesture Talgryf remembered from last night, muttering as she did so, words that sounded like *cold stew*, though he knew that couldn't be right. Then she set her back to the door and fixed her eyes on him. The intentness of that gaze made him feel itchy.

"Say *stua oscalte*."

"Huh?"

"We'll take it slower. Repeat *stua*."

"I hear. *Stua*."

"Good. *Os cal tay*." She nodded when he repeated the word. "Now put them together. *Stua oscalte*." She listened, then nodded again. "That's good. Come here. Stand beside me."

She smelled nice when he got close enough to touch her if he wanted to, a delicate perfume rather like apple blossoms. Her skin was the color of cava with lots of cream and maybe a touch of saffron, smooth and soft, her breasts were big, her waist small, her hair was all tiny curls that went almost gold in strong sunlight. She had big hands, bigger than Ellar's, bigger than his father's, but they were beautiful, so soft and smooth and shapely. Though she was a head and a half taller than him and probably older than his stepma, he blushed, scuffled his feet and stared out the door.

"Can you see that flicker across the path? The way it arches up then down again?"

For a moment he couldn't, then he saw very faint sparks so pale and transparent they were like reflections off a rippling pool. "Uh-huh."

"I'm going to go through that arch and close it behind me. I won't be able to open it again from outside. I want you to keep watch. I shouldn't be gone more than a short while. When you see me standing on the path, open the arch for me. What do you say?"

"Stua oscalte."

"Good."

"What about the thing with your hand?"

"Don't worry about that. I'll take care of it when I release the arch. It's important to keep strong wards up and closed as much as possible. The Mage who hurt Cymel might be looking for a way to get at her again. He's very dangerous."

"Oh."

She touched his shoulder lightly then went out.

He moved closer to the door and stood leaning on the jamb, watching her stride along the path, her long black skirt flicking around her ankles. On the far side of the arch she did something, said something, then took a quick step and was gone. He blinked, then settled himself on the top step to wait for her to come back.

Half asleep from the hot sun, he watched for a long time of nothing happening, then he heard footsteps on the stairs inside. After a minute Ellar came out to stand beside him on the steps. "You know where Corysiam is?"

"She said there wasn't a lick of food in the house so she went to get some. I'm supposed to open the arch for her when she comes back."

"Ah. I suppose the boy has left for home with the horses."

Talgryf shrugged. "I didn't wake up till a little bit ago and I haven't been outside."

"How long ago?"

"A while. Not long."

"Better bring in some wood and get the stove ready, I suppose." Ellar hesitated a moment longer, then he went inside.

"Any problems," he called back, "I'll be in the kitchen."

The sound of his feet had hardly faded when Corysiam stepped from midair onto the graveled path. She was loaded down with canvas sacks, her hair was plastered to her head with sweat and her eyes sunk in dark shadows.

Talgryf jumped to his feet. He called out, "Stua oscalte," then hurried as close as he dared so he could help her with the bags.

Once she was through the arch Corysiam let the sacks down on the gravel and drew her hand across her forehead, scraping away some of the sweat. "Thanks, Gryf. If you could cart a couple of those to the kitchen, I'd appreciate it."

He grabbed the leather strap of one of the sacks, grunted at the weight and decided he'd better do this one at a time. He got the strap over his shoulder and trudged toward the house; when he reached the steps, he wriggled to get the weight settled better, glanced back to see Corysiam working on the ward wall, slamming the arch shut so they were protected again. He wrinkled his nose. Something *baaad* out there.

[3]

". . . value added by the skill of the artisans and the transport . . ."

Oerfel sat at his desk in the Cyngrath Chamber, taking notes in his invented shorthand while the Broony representatives wrangled with those of the Merchants' guilds over the relative worth of made objects and rental property as opposed to meat, grain and timber, a subject he found profoundly uninteresting. His mind wandered as his hands dealt automatically with recording the arguments.

That was a fierce ward the Siofray Scribe had set over the house. Even his scry mirrors were blocked. When he looked, all he could see was a shimmering silver dome; even the exterior of the house was not visible. He had tried to work his way through the woven forces, but he couldn't read the pattern. The ward was closed to him so completely that it implied a vulnerability in him because his knowledge was incomplete.

He had assumed that, because the Siofray dipped into the same Pneuma Flow as he did, their magic would be fundamentally the same. This was now provably untrue.

Bridges, he thought. Walkers between the worlds. I knew about those. I knew even Mages of Glandair could do neither. Why didn't I think about that before?

". . . care for our tenants and dependencies while you find yourself concerned only with the work, pushing off your responsibilities to your workers onto the Temple and the Healing Sisters where care is given without expense to . . ."

His hands had gone still. He blinked, brought his mind back to his recording, glanced at his notes and decided that he had not missed more than a few moments because the Grath who had been speaking the last words he'd taken down was still blathering on.

Who took the Gift of the Hero would hold in himself all the power of Glandair and of Iomard. And that All was suddenly greater than he had dreamed.

He cursed Cyfareth and the Watchers. As long as those prynoses kept sniffing about, it was as if he wore leg irons and were cramped into a tiny cell where he could do little but continue to exist. I might have to reach out for Mahara and Hudoleth, he thought. It might not be a disaster if I can convince them I'm too weak to challenge them. Once I put myself forward, though, that will add another two pairs of eyes watching me. Hm. If the three of us can get to the Hero and kill him, that won't matter because the alliance will fall apart the moment that's done. Let Hudoleth and Mahara go back to snarling at each other while I sit disregarded. Spider in the corner, quietly spinning a web they won't see.

He glanced at the undersecretaries busy scribbling at their desks. Getting today's session fair-copied into the Cyngrath Daybook and the use ledgers was going to take hours of work once the Graths adjourned this meeting. He'd have to transcribe his notes himself since no one else could read his shorthand, then stand over the cadre of scribes to make sure there were no blots or misrenderings. Tyrn Isel had twice complimented him on his immaculate pages; despite Oerfel's opinion of the man, he could not help being pleased that his efforts were finally recognized.

As the afternoon wore slowly on, the heat and humidity in the Cyngrath Chamber began to rub tempers raw. The Broony Grath whose turn it was to Order the meeting was not the most brilliant of men, but even he saw that continuing longer would produce nothing but rancor. He hammered the session closed and went steaming out. Oerfel tapped the ivory bell on his desk to mark the end of the recording, packed his ink and pens, gathered his papers and left the Chamber, his undersecretaries trailing silently behind him.

[4]

The dawn wind flowed through the open window, cool and a little damp as it moved across Oerfel's face. He was deep in a cleansing trance meant to replace the sleep he wasn't getting. The tax sessions held in the summer were exhausting, long days and work so boring that errors crept in as effortlessly as fleas into a dirty fleece. As the gray light flushed red, Oerfel opened his eyes. He lay a long moment staring at the shadowy ceiling. Tentatively, he lifted his arms over his head, stretched until his joints popped, then he pushed up and began a series of exercises to loosen his body and energize his mind.

Pushing back his impatience to get to his real work, he washed off the sweat and seated himself at a table where he ate with careful precision one oatcake and one dried plum, washing them down with distilled water. When he was finished, he cleaned his teeth and wrapped himself in a coarse-weave linen robe. It was going to be another hot day. And another long and futile one. Nothing would get done in the Cyngrath, but he would have another bundle of pages to enter, pages recording nothing but the petty quarrels of little men and women whose sole justification for being there was that they were breathing and mobile—and had influential friends.

He shook off the sourness of his morning mood, took a scrying mirror from one of the table's drawers and set it before him. He breathed on it, woke the spell and set it for the Vale and the Hero.

It had become his habit to observe Lyanz and judge his progress before he looked in on Anrydd. One way or another, he had to polish the surface of his false Hero so that Anrydd had at least a superficial resemblance to the true one. The work the Scribe was doing with that boy was starting to trouble him.

Oerfel reached into the fruit basket and selected a pear. He was tired, but most of the tension that had built up during the past several weeks had eased out of him because he'd finally made up his mind about his future course of action.

Lyanz was standing with an easy, loose posture in a grassy pasture, watching a pair of yearling foals chase each other. He looked bored and more than a little annoyed.

The Mage snorted as he saw a second figure slip from the thick shadow under the plum trees of the orchard beside the pasture. It was the young Scribe, stalking the Hero, reading those "tells" that gave her advance knowledge of how and when he was going to move. She moved quickly and silently, keeping herself where the youth couldn't see her.

He contemplated the stalk for several breaths longer, deciding as he watched that he had seriously underestimated Amhar's ability to handle Pneuma. His own understanding was based on words; his rituals and chants were the essence of his power. Amhar spoke through flesh and muscle in a wordless magic that was wholly alien to him but whose power was dimly apparent nonetheless.

Lyanz moved uneasily. He still hadn't seen Amhar, nor was he aware of her in any real way, but the subliminal pressure of her approach was making him nervous. She threw herself into a scything leap that cut his legs from under him and laid his face in the grass.

His reaction was considerably faster than it had been the first time she took him down; he almost managed to twist away but her manipulation of nerve and muscle held him paralyzed until she tapped his arm to signify that she was breaking the hold; she leaped back to wait just out of his reach for his recovery and reaction to her ambush.

Oerfel peeled a section of the pear and sliced off a thin layer of the crisp, white meat. As he nibbled at it, he scowled at the youth. He knew how Anrydd would react, but Lyanz puzzled him.

Lyanz lay on his face, breathing deeply, clearing out tension and anger as if, like any good Wyf, he wielded a broom across his nerves and swept away the debris. He was still not aware of how the complex of muscles in his back and shoulders betrayed his intentions to someone who knew how to read them, so when he whipped his body around, moving with a snake's striking speed, he expected surprise to give him an edge and let him take Amhar to the grass.

Again Amhar jumped back, just far enough to guarantee that he missed his grip.

Lyanz ground his teeth together, got slowly to his feet and stood scowling at her. "What's the Tanew-cursed lesson this time?"

"Several lessons," she said, continuing to watch him, eyes sliding across the muscles of his arms and shoulders. "Blind spot, for one," she said. "Triangle across the spine. Did you see me at any time after I left the plum orchard?"

Lyanz looked down at his hands, opened and closed them, then folded his arms across his chest, a declaration that he too had shifted his attention from action to words. "No. Not that I know how long that was."

Oerfel sliced off another sliver of pear and nibbled at it. The taut and angry stance of the Hero's body formed a wordless contrast with the growing calm of his voice. At present, Anrydd was incapable of such a split in his attention. The Mage continued to eat and watch, unsure whether he really wanted his False Hero to have such a skill. Easier to control the youth if he continued to be transparent in his reactions.

"About twenty minutes. It's simple. I knew ahead of time how you were going to turn so I was able to stay within the bounds of the Blind Triangle. Your back and arm muscles betrayed you. I could stay behind you and stalk you in plain sight for hours. My shadow might expose me." She glanced at the sun, nodded at the dark finger that lay on the grass, shifting in concert with that nod. "Or too direct a gaze might make you nervous and itchy. Otherwise, no problem."

"I've got 'tells'?"

"Yes. Your reading lessons start today. I don't think you'll find this difficult, Laz. It's rather like point awareness when you're working with the sword."

"Second thing?"

"Timing. You gave me entirely too much time to get ready to counter your strike. Good strike, fast and vicious, but I knew exactly what you were going to do and when—so you didn't have a chance to succeed with it."

Abruptly, Lyanz's body tightened into hard focus. "One lesson," he said. "The reading is the key. Show me."

Oerfel cut away the rest of the peel, sucked juice from his fingers and watched the beginning of the lesson, then blew on the mirror again, setting it on Anrydd.

And swore as he saw the young fool come scrambling from a window at the back of a farmhouse and run for a clump of trees where his horse was tethered, his trousers wadded under one arm along with his sword and swordbelt. As he disappeared into the trees, the house seemed to vomit men. There were only five of them, but the noise they made and the intensity of their rage made them seem more. Two of the younger brothers took off after Anrydd on foot, the three older men ran for the corrals and the horses penned there.

Oerfel widened the area of focus and scanned the countryside. A few orchards, some fields planted to crops, but mostly the fields were grazing grounds with flocks of sheep, herds of cattle and the occasional hog run. Few fences, mostly thick, thorny hedgerows. Anrydd was a splendid rider and none of those farm boneracks had a chance of catching Sernry, but the light was strengthening rapidly and once they got a good look at the rider, they didn't need to catch him. Tyrn's justice would do the job for them and Tyrn's justice they would get. Isel would take considerable pleasure in punishing one of his father's bastards, especially one who wore his paternity on his face and form. The girl might know who he was, of course, but her word would carry little weight. Oerfel had to make sure those men couldn't support her claim.

At least there was no one with the talent to read Oerfel's sendings now that the Watcher had fled Carcalon. He made the avert sign to ward off ill fortune; too great a pleasure in the smiles of the Dame was a foolishness he wasn't about to indulge in.

Fog, he thought. Yes.

He began the preparation chants, whispering them so softly anyone a step away wouldn't hear the words. When the focus was tight and the charm wound up, he began to coax wisps and curls of fog from the damp earth, from the grass and the leaves. Thicker and thicker the mist grew until it was a dank fog where direction was confusion and sound came from everywhere and nowhere and there was nothing to see but white walls around each rider.

Oerfel kept the fog rising for another half hour, then let it burn off.

He tapped away the image and put the mirror back in the drawer, then sat staring out the window at the brightening sky.

Anrydd was restless and bored and more careless of his behavior with every day that passed. No one could touch him with sword or lance and few could match his scores with the crossbow. He had learned all the martial arts that Toc Ubanson gan Goolad, once Captain of the Palace Guard, had to teach him, though he had ignored the courtesies that gan Goolad also sought to teach because he thought them weaknesses rather than strengths. No one at Broony Brennin could come close to challenging him, no one was strong enough to make him do anything he didn't want to do.

He was an irritating mix of cunning and stupidity, very much like his father. He *knew* he had to keep his face clean, but he was acting on impulse again, as he had when he rode with those miserable rats he called friends and nearly burned down Whore's Row on the south side of the bothrin. He'd come close to getting himself hanged for that. The Tysters were in a rage at the death and destruction. Fear had kept him docile for a while, but the incident was more than two years old now and the effect had worn off.

If some of his games were discovered, the mystique that Oerfel was trying to build up round him would shatter like a blown eggshell dropped on a rock. I need a way to drain off that energy without ruining him. Hm. He has no experience in the practical use of those skills. Raids. Yes. He'd enjoy that. Not in the western Broonies. They have little influence here in Carcalon. Too far away with the mountains between.

The eastern foothill Broonies. Yes. The mines. Wealth from silver, gold, iron and copper feeding the arrogance of those Broons. Tyrn Dengyn kept them sweet and eased taxes out of them so deftly they never felt the wounds. Isel loathes the lot of them. He'll twist their tails when they yell for help. Good good, that's the way to go. Raids and assassinations will blood Anrydd's cadre and meld them into a tight unit. Hone his capacity to lead and fight, use his attacks to jar loose whatever loyalty the mining Broonies have to the Tyrn.

Oerfel smiled. It was earlier than he wanted to begin the campaign, but the chance for a double strike like that was not to be missed. With any luck, the experience with the Siofray Mage had burned out the brain of that miserable girl. He pictured her as a drooling idiot and laughed aloud. And her father would be busy caring for her.

He left the table and stretched out on the bed, his eyes closed. The raiding party will have a considerable distance to ride, will have to cross the mountains to reach their targets.

That means a string of supply and remount stations . . . hm . . . that will take time and a stack of coin . . . use gan Goolad to suggest the raids and work up Anrydd's enthusiasm . . . let the young fool think there's a secret cabal working to set him on the throne and toss Isel to the carrion birds . . . hm . . .

[5]

Early on the second day at the farm Gryf leaned against the doorjamb, watching Cymel's father work on her.

Ellar knelt beside the bed, touching Cymel's head with gentle, exploring fingers, turning it this way and that. His body was so filled with power, he outshone the sunlight streaming through the window and looking at him brought tears of strain to Talgryf's eyes.

A hand touched his shoulder. He turned his head.

Corysiam pointed to the stairs. "Nothing you can do here," she murmured. "Come help me in the kitchen."

Talgryf looked from the pile of gnarled yellow roots to the heap of dirty brown skin he'd peeled off them. He made a face at them.

Enough is enough, he told himself. I'm no kitchen slavey.

"I want to go outside," he said aloud.

Corysiam gave the stew a last stir, then turned to face him, standing with hands on hips, her head tilted to one side. "Hm," she said finally. "I suppose it would be safe enough. You know to keep away from the wards?"

He nodded.

"If you feel a prickliness on your skin, step away fast."

He pushed the chair back and stood beside it. "I know." He made a face when he heard how impatient and irritated the words sounded, but he didn't apologize.

She shrugged. "Whatever. Come on. I'll open a way through the kitchen garden gate. When you want back in, yell."

*   *   *

The forest started near the garden fence and climbed up the mountainside toward the distant peak. He walked over to the stream that came boiling from under the trees, circled the house and went rushing off toward the river. When it came time to set his snares, he could follow the stream and not get lost in that gloom under the trees. He didn't want anything to do with that forest. It looked to him like one big mouth set to eat him whole. He touched his back pocket with the coil of cord. Not now, he thought. There's hours of light yet.

He strolled back along the garden fence, poked his nose in the barn and from the smell decided that Rudd definitely hadn't cleaned up after himself.

The birdhouse was empty except for the dust that had settled on everything.

The henhouse was empty.

The creamery was padlocked and he couldn't get in there.

Behind the barn were a series of corrals, then a fenced field where a herd of fawn-colored cows were grazing; they were smaller and more agile than the cows he was used to and they had wicked-looking horns. The cows that lived in backyards in Tyst were all polled; in those small spaces horns would have been too dangerous.

He leaned on the top rail of the fence and stared thoughtfully at them. More than once, especially when things got hard in the deep winter, he'd slipped into one of those backyards before dawn and coaxed milk from a cow, a cup for him and a bottleful for his baby sister. That was easy enough. All he had to watch out for was a servant coming down early and finding him. This lot with their horns and their snorting gave him the idea that any stranger going out in that field would be dead meat before he'd got very far.

There were calves out there and several of the cows were still heavy with the calves they were carrying. They had dark eyes set in a kind of white mask so it was easy to see them watching him. "You can watch all you want," he said. "But I'm not silly enough to climb in with you."

The sun was getting too hot for comfort, so he went back

to the stream and began climbing up the mountain, following a faint path where someone, probably Cymel, had done a lot of walking. In the pools between the rapids, the water was very clear and more than once he saw fish swimming in it. If Ellar has a net, maybe I could catch some of those. Whoo! Look at that one. Long as my arm. That'd make a meal and a half.

But fish weren't what he wanted today. He began watching the stream bank to see where small game came to drink, hunting for a place to set his snares.

[6]

Sullen and resentful, expecting a scold for his recklessness, Anrydd walked into Toc gan Goolad's office and threw himself into a chair. He glanced at the man seated at his worktable, then stared out the window.

Toc folded his hands on a stack of papers. "Your manners are as execrable as your judgment is lacking. However, I didn't call you here to talk about that."

"So?"

"You are without doubt the greatest warrior on Nyddys. I would not be startled to find you also the greatest beyond Nyddys."

Anrydd sat up, surprised and pleased at something he himself knew but never thought he'd hear in the other man's mouth.

"Unfortunately, that is a useless distinction unless you learn the larger arts of war so you may get the value of your skills. Power, Anrydd. Against the Tyrn's power your muscles are puny. Isel could not stand against you for one minute, but he'll never have to." Toc flattened his hands on the papers stacked before him and looked grim. "We move to the next level of your training by the end of this month. You are going to get practical lessons in battle through a series of raids on certain targets. I'll explain later why these targets were chosen. You are going to learn the importance of supplying your troops, both as to food, arms and mounts; of learning the lay of the

land; of providing for a fast and efficient retreat when chance
turns against you; of training troops who follow orders rathe
than acting on the impulse of the moment. You won't be livin
off the countryside in these first forays; a string of suppl
depots is being arranged by interested parties. There's a reaso
for this. These are exercises to get you ready for the rea
thing."

Anrydd leaned forward. "Why not now? Why wait till th
end of the month?"

"Because, by Tanew's Hairy Ears, you've got work to do
Head work. Strategy and tactics. Logistics. And if I'm no
satisfied with your efforts, we go through the whole thing
again and again until you've got it. You're going nowher
until then." Toc slapped at the tabletop. "You've been actin
the fool these past weeks and I'm going to sweat that nonsens
out of you. Listen to me, Anrydd. I told you there is a grou
of important men backing you. The Circle. But they'll dro
you like spoiled meat if you don't control yourself. I've ha
a warning from them. Unless you shape up, this Broony wil
be closed to you, your funds will be cut off and you'll b
dumped over in Faiscar to make your way however you car
You will be killed if you try to return to Nyddys. I was tol
to make it clear to you that they have a broad choice amon
Dengyn Tyrn's bastards. There are a lot of those around."

[7]

A tenday after his decision to prepare for Anrydd's raids, Oer
fel leaned over the basin, his brow braced against the wall, hi
arms trembling. He was exhausted. Ten days of heat, of re
cording quarrels that went nowhere, of snarls and insults. O
entering those to his exacting requirements in the Daybook
Of fighting the headaches that blinded and nauseated hin
Nights given over to setting up waystations, to funneling coi
from the Tyrn's Treasury to pay the keepers and stock th
stations with remounts and trail food.

His head wasn't aching yet, but he could feel the aura tha
announced the worst of the attacks. Cleansing trances weren'

nough. He needed sleep. A full night's sleep. Several full
ights' sleep. Yet how could he take the time? He unwrapped
e leaf folded around a chunk of bindroot and began chewing
e root and swallowing the juice. It wouldn't stop the head-
che, but the numbing qualities in the bindroot would make it
earable. And it would stop the nausea that tied his gut into
nots.

The bitter juice dripping down his throat, he pushed clear
f the wall and stood rubbing at his temples, trying to convince
imself that the aura was fading. Then he splashed water over
is face. The water was tepid and gave no relief, but he set
rimly to washing face and hands, lathering with soft soap and
nsing it away. He spat out the fibrous remains of the bind-
oot, chewed the end of an eddi twig and cleaned his teeth
ith it, rinsed his mouth out.

By the time he was ready for bed, a lazy breeze was stirring
e air, bringing a faint touch of coolness into the room. He
retched out, laid a damp cloth across his eyes and folded his
rms across his ribs. Despite his utter weariness, his thoughts
ept marching in endless loops.

Have not looked at Mahara and Hudoleth for months now
. . wars . . . should watch . . . Anrydd . . . flawed tool . . . need
 keep stricter control of him . . . need to be here in Carcalon?
ave my savings . . . could move back to Tyst . . . hadn't re-
lized how much time this steals from me . . . don't want to
e tied too closely to Isel's reign . . . distance . . . yes . . . oth-
rwise when he goes, he could drag me with him . . . illness
. . yes . . . that won't be hard . . . resign because I can no
nger keep the product up to my standards . . . Hero . . . left
im alone long enough . . . complacent . . . but Watchers . . .
ey'll be on guard the moment they sniff out interest in them
. . as good a time as any for an attack . . . Ellar out of it,
cused on that girl of his . . . the Siofray Scribe . . . same
ing . . . University Watchers in a roar over the Siofray Mage
. . that teacher killed . . . if Mahara can break loose from his
rmy . . . time . . . Hudoleth . . . the three of us hit the Vale at
e same time . . . break through wards . . . get fighters in there

. . . slaughter those ungits . . . and the boy . . . and the boy .
and the boy. . . .

His musings dissolved into fractured images and even the
vanished as he finally dropped into a heavy sleep.

[8]

Talgryf knelt beside the set of snares and began loosening t
cord about the neck of a fat mountain coney. He put the con
in his game bag and leaned forward, reaching for the next.

A crossbow bolt clipped hair from the back of his head a
thunked home into the trunk of a tree on the far side of t
game trail. Talgryf flung himself to one side, scrambling f
cover in the trees.

"Poacher!"

"A Breed! You saw."

"Get 'im."

Three youths a few years older than Breith trotted out
shadow whooping and yelling. One of them was working t
claw on his bow, one was bent over, reading tracks as
moved and the third had his bow up and was moving it in
slow arc as he sought a target.

The tracker straightened. "That way. He's in there."

Talgryf ran.

After a couple of steps he felt a hard blow against his l
arm and several breaths later pain like fire. A bolt skewer
the outside of the muscle of his upper arm. At least it h
missed the bone, though he couldn't move the arm and eve
jolting stride brought new waves of pain.

Got to get away. Got to get home. Got to . . . downhill. G
back to the path. Downhill.

He began weaving through the trees, losing ground to
hunters, but keeping trunks between them and him so the ne
two bolts hit wood instead of his body.

All three of them were old and bigger. Faster. They'd
him for sure if he couldn't do something. As he ran, he us
his right hand to wriggle open the pouch at his belt. He pull

the sling out, gasped as he nearly dropped it, then got one of the thongs wrapped about his thumb.

He was afraid of losing the sling if he used his thumb to pinch up one of the stones bouncing at the bottom of the pouch, water-smoothed pebbles he'd collected from the stream, but it kept slipping away from the two fingers he was trying to lift it with. And he couldn't stop running. And he couldn't concentrate on getting the stone. He had to keep his eyes on the ground so he wouldn't trip over roots or rocks or run into trees.

As he finally got the pebble out, he heard crashing to his left where the path was. One of them was curving round to cut him off. Half crazy with pain and anger, Talgryf set the stone in the pocket and turned to run toward that crashing. When he caught a glimpse of the runner, he slowed until he was no longer running and started the sling whirring.

He lost the runner in the shadows, saw him again and loosened the stone at him.

The cheng fell with the looseness of a worn-out dust rag.

I killed him, Talgryf thought. Tanew's Teeth, I'm in trouble now.

"There he is. Get him!"

A spurt of fear cut through the dizziness from the continuing loss of blood and the hard run. Talgryf got round the nearest tree an instant before a bolt glanced off the trunk and went skittering through the thin brush. Driven by will and fear, he burst from the forest onto the path and kept on running.

Staggering and dripping sweat, his arm hot and hurting, he flung himself toward the fence of the kitchen garden, pulling up just before he hit the wards. With his last strength he screamed for Corysiam, then collapsed on the grass.

[9]

Talgryf came to himself with Corysiam bending over him tying off a bandage around his arm, Ellar standing behind her, frowning. He was in his room, stretched out on his bed; his

clothes were gone, he was wearing a clean nightshirt that was
roomy enough to have belonged to Ellar and a folded, damp
cloth was laid across his brow. The burn was gone from his
arm; the skin around his wound felt wonderfully cool and the
pain was pushed so far away it seemed only a ghost of itself.

"Well, I see you're back with us." Corysiam straightened.
"So what happened?"

As soon as he heard the tale, Ellar was out of the room. Talgryf could hear his feet thudding on the stairs though he was
surprised to note they were going up, not down.

Corysiam brought him a glass of water, lifted his shoulder
so he could drink. "Heading for the tower," she said. "He
has certain tools there to show him what's happening."

"I wasn't doing anything."

"I know, Gryf. Don't worry. We'll make sure nothing happens to you."

"I killed one of them. Tyrn's men, they'll hang me."

"That they will." She sighed. "The other two will lie themselves blue in the face and these are their people. But they
have to catch you first and I've got some ideas about that."
She set the glass on the bed table, fluffed the pillow and eased
Talgryf back down. "So you get some rest, young Gryf. You
lost a lot of blood and you have to make it back."

[10]

When he woke again, the window was dark. He tried to sit
up. The minute he put pressure on his wounded arm, he gasped
and fell back on the pillows. "T'teeth," he whispered. "That
hurts."

As if she'd been waiting for him to stir, Corysiam walked
into the room carrying a lamp which she put down on the bed
table. She turned to stand over him, her arms crossed, her eyes
glinting yellow in the lamplight. "How're you feeling, Gryf?"

"Like day-old dog vomit."

She snorted, grinned at him. "A little hot food and a sling
for that arm and you'll feel almost as good as fresh dog vomit."

Ellar will be here in a moment. He'll help you dress and get you downstairs.''

With the sling holding his arm still, the stew and fresh bread warming his middle, Talgryf blinked lazily and waited for the other two to start talking, though his interest in what they had to say was draining away as the heat of the fire made him sleepier by the moment. The couch in the back parlor had been pulled up close to the fire; he was sitting on it propped up by piles of pillows. Corysiam was cross-legged on the hearth, a blank book open in her lap, an inkpot beside her. She would put a few scribbles on a page, look off into the distance for several moments, then write some more. Ellar was standing at one of the windows, looking out into the darkness.

Ellar turned his head. "The one you killed was called Wesgit Goligson. The big one, the leader, is Orog Dyrysson. The third could have been any of several who run with Orog. Neither Golig nor Dyrys is rational when it comes to their sons. They'll believe nothing bad about them, even when it's the word of a neighbor whose family has been here for generations. As for outsiders . . ." He sighed. "This was my father's farm and I grew up here and I've lived in this house as an adult for over twenty years. That means nothing. I'm an outsider and always will be.''

"Which means they'll be coming for Gryf. How much time do we have?''

"They're not exactly afraid of me, but they won't come after me in the dark. So we should be safe as long as we're away by sunup." He passed a hand over his face. "They'll burn the house, you know. Not the barn or the rest. But I'll lose the house." He walked away from the window and stood beside the worktable, the fingertips of one hand resting lightly on the polished surface. "Memories. All gone.''

"We could leave the wards up.''

"Cory, Bridging me tied to a ward would be swimming upstream against a flood. A good way to get us both killed.'' He lifted his hand, gazed a moment at his fingertips, then wiped them on his shirt. "I go where Cymel goes. I won't stay behind just to protect a house. Have you decided where you'll put us?"

"Urfa House seems the safest as as temporary refuge. Can't be more than temporary, I'm afraid. These are difficult times in the Confluence." She got to her feet. "Explain to Gryf while I go lift the wards."

When she was gone, Ellar crossed to stand beside the couch looking down at Talgryf. "Did you understand any of that?"

"Some. She's going to take us to where she got the food that time."

"Not exactly, but close enough. A quick journey to a place no one can reach from here. No one on Glandair can Walk between Worlds or Bridge others across; only the Siofray of Iomard have that gift. Bridging—it's an odd thing. One step and you and what you carry have gone a distance that even I can't imagine. Lift a foot on Glandair, set it down on Iomard."

Talgryf straightened up, wincing as pain knifed briefly along his arm. "Are we ever coming back?"

"Oh yes.. We don't belong there. You're thinking about your father, aren't you."

Talgryf stared at the fire and wouldn't answer. He didn't want to talk about his father. Not now.

"I'm going to put some of my things in the root cellar and hope the fire won't get to them. You won't be able to take most of what you brought here, nothing you're not wearing or have in your pockets. You might want to stow the rest in the tower. Don't move yet. I'll be back in a moment."

Talgryf sat staring at the fire. Everything seemed to be happening so fast it made his head swim. His arm was throbbing again and he was so tired and sleepy he could barely keep his eyes open. He wanted to go home. He wanted to be stretched out on his pallet at the foot of his father's bed. He wanted the crooked busy streets of the bothrin, the neighbors who cursed him more often than not but were sometimes carelessly kind. He wanted familiar sights and smells, wanted walls that on the blackest of nights he only needed to touch to know where he was.

"Drink this down, Gryf. You'll feel better in a few breaths."

The glass was cool in his hand, the liquid in it a bright green with flecks of gold floating in it. Talgryf sniffed at it. Sweet and tart with a touch of mint. He took a sip, then gulped down the rest. As he held the glass out to Ellar, warmth and energy were flowing from his middle into his arms and legs. "What is that stuff?"

"Something I wouldn't be feeding you if circumstances were different. Give me your hand. Time you were on your feet. You don't have to go back upstairs. Corysiam brought your gear down. It's over there by the door. Sort through it and I'll be back in a bit to stow what you're leaving. Remember, what you're wearing and what you can stuff in your pockets, that's all you can take."

[11]

With Cymel's limp body draped over her shoulder and one hand closed firmly about Talgryf's belt, her knuckles poking him in the back, Corysiam stood on the path by the needle tree and took several deep breaths. Talgryf closed his eyes, then forced them open. Spooky or not, he wanted to see as much as he could. Wasn't likely he'd ever get the chance again.

He felt Corysiam's body shift, then he was in a howling windstorm, pummeled by a sound that was no sound, by swirling, shocking colors, streamers of light. He was beaten into a small, hard nubbin and at the same time was torn to shreds and the shreds driven to the ends of whatever this place was. This lasted forever, but forever was only a single beat of his heart, then his feet slammed into grass, Corysiam's knuckles pulled away from his back and he went crashing to his knees.

His eyes blurred with tears squeezed out as the pain from his arm jagged through his body.

When he could see again, Corysiam was kneeling beside

him. She eased Cymel onto the grass, folded the limp hands
on the chest. Then she was standing again. Her breathing
slowed, the trembling in her arms and hands stilled. She
smiled at Talgryf. "Be back in a little while," she said.
"Don't worry."

Talgryf cautiously resettled his arm in the sling, then wiped
the sweat from his face as the pain retreated. The night was
dark; either there was no moon in this place or it had already
set and a thick layer of clouds covered the stars. It wasn't
cold; he was wearing his stepma's sweater and was starting to
sweat. It wasn't all that strange either, even if it was a whole
other world like Corysiam said. He was sitting on grass and
he could hear the creak and rustle of trees moving in a warm
wind that stirred his hair but didn't touch his face. And there
were walls all around him, but no lights showing. Whoever
lived here must be still asleep.

He edged closer to Cymel, bent over to get a better look at
her and saw that her eyes were closed and her mouth sagged
open. He laid the back of his good hand against her face and
felt a proper warmth so she was still alive. "What happened
to you, Mela?" He caught hold of her hair and shook her head
lightly. "Wake up. Please . . ."

He stiffened as he heard a door open and saw yellow light
race across the grass. He set Cymel's head down gently and
got to his feet, swaying a little as the effect of that drink wore
off and fatigue and pain began creeping back.

A woman in a long narrow robe stood in a doorway, frowning at him, lamplight spilling around her. "Se ya tus?" The
phrase had a kind of music as if she half sang, half spoke
them. "Cad eya denan?" Her voice was deep as a man's. The
second question had the sound of a demand despite its lilt.

Talgryf managed a bow without falling on his face. "I don't
understand a word of that, O Rynnat."

She frowned. "Glandair? How come you here?" Her Nyd-
Ifor sounded odd because she gave the words the same inton-
ation as her own speech, but he relaxed when he heard them.
He trusted the nimbleness of his tongue almost as much as

that of his fingers. Not being able to say or understand anything here had frightened him more than he wanted to think about.

He started to answer then fell silent as Corysiam appeared with Ellar.

She sank to her knees, gasping, her eyes glazed, sweat rolling down her face. Ellar was pale and shaky, but he took in the situation immediately, crossed to stand beside Talgryf, his hand on Gryf's shoulder. "Cay Faobran. Our pardon for this intrusion, but our need was great and immediate."

"Your need, Watcher? What could come of this intrusion you make so lightly may be great harm to this House." The woman stepped from the doorway. Now that she was no longer blocking the light, it washed across Cymel, showing how limp and pale she was. "What is this?"

Corysiam rose wearily to her feet and came to stand beside Ellar. "My sister's child, Faobran. I ask for a three-day guesting while I find a place to take her."

"What happened to the child?" As she spoke, Faobran knelt and reached out to touch Cymel's brow. "Why is she . . . ?"

Cymel screamed.

Faobran drew her hand back, but the screaming went on and on. Cymel began writhing and twisting, striking out with arms and legs, banging her head on the grass.

12

Slave Life

By the calendar of the Domains of Iomard, events dating from the 24th day of Sakhtos, the seventh month in the Iomardi year 6535, the 722nd year since the last Corruption.

[1]

Two hours after his head touched the mattress cover, the Caller whipped Breith awake and sent him stumbling to the kitchen, bleary-eyed and incoherent from lack of sleep.

The head cook snorted. "And what use you'll be, I wish someone would tell me. Here." She pushed a sharkskin pad at him. "Tadja, take this walking dishrag over to the kangat pile and put him to work scrubbing."

Tadja was a weedy child with arms like broomsticks and huge green eyes that gave her a fey look as if she were somehow related to the tree sprites who giggled at him. When the cook called her, she was chopping vegetables, the knife hitting the board with the regularity of a heartbeat. Without a word, she set the knife down and marched over to Breith. He winced when she shook hold of his arm. Her fingers were hard as roots and they were pressing down on the scratches the apparition had left on his arm.

She looked at the arm, raised her brows. When he opened his mouth to explain, she shook her head vigorously. She shifted her grip to his wrist and took him to a low table at the gloomy end of the kitchen. A large pile of knobby, reddish, dirt-crusted roots sat at one end, two tubs of water beside it and a basin to hold the cleaned roots sitting on a bench between the table and the wall.

When he was seated beside the empty basin, she took the pad from him, reached across him and dipped one of the roots into the first tub, then began scrubbing off the skin and the dirt. She showed him the pale yellow meat of the cleaned spot and whispered, "It should look like that all over. Then you dip it in the clean water, toss it in the basin. Change the clean water every twenty kangats." She slapped at his arm. When she spoke again, her whisper had the malevolence of an angry snake. "This is what *we* eat, adjai. The skin tastes nasty. You don't get it all off, we make you sorry you breathing."

Breith enjoyed cleaning the kangats. It was restful work. Uncomplicated, just hard enough to engage his attention.

The morning passed in a blur. Rub and wash, rub and wash. Fetch clean water from the pump. Rub and wash. Sometimes his head felt strange, as if he were sitting in water that sloshed about his ears. Other times he had the notion he was sleeping with his eyes open. Most times he wasn't thinking at all, just looking at the kangat he was holding in one hand while he rubbed the skin off with the pad in the other. He was aware of the others bustling about the kitchen but that was only a background noise like the shrill hum of bloodsuckers on a warm summer night.

When he was near the bottom of the pile he noticed that the rinse water had pink threads curling through it. He frowned at these, then noted a drop falling from his hand. It unreeled into more pink threads the moment it hit the water. My fingers are bleeding, he thought. How strange.

"What's this?"

Breith blinked and lifted his head. That was hard. It was so heavy his neck hurt.

Daripada stood beside him, a look almost of fear on her worn face.

That startled him. He stared at her through the haze of weariness that thickened whenever he tried to put two thoughts together.

"Give me your hands."

When he stretched out his arms, they trembled with weariness and the four scratches looked inflamed. The tips of his left-hand fingers were bloody, as were the knuckles of his right hand.

Daripada caught hold of his wrists, lifted the hands higher. "Diatas, get over here. Look at this. 'His skin is not to be marred.' Those were the Nyon's orders. Look at what he has done to himself. If she sees this . . ." She set Breith's hands on the table. "I want hot water in the bathhouse and Risiko attending me with her creams and tonics. Herrel, fetch Baalis from the stables; I need him to carry the boy. Mighty Tuhan be thanked, the Nyon Merya Shamba will not be rising for another hour at least. We have time."

[2]

When Breith woke, the shadows of late afternoon were closing round the Chaletat slave quarters, the rows of shacks and dormitories hidden from the main house by dense thorn hedges twice as tall as a man. Despite a lingering heaviness, his fatigue was gone and his hands didn't hurt any longer. He closed them into fists, felt a few pulls from skin still not as flexible as it should be and a brush-burn or two.

And he was hungry. Daripada had fed him a bowl of some kind of slop after she and the other one had finished working over him, but that was only a distant memory.

He pushed himself up, waited out a momentary dizziness, then got to his feet. There was a fresh tunic hanging on a peg by the door. He put that on, found the pot of cream salve that Risiko had left behind. He sat on the edge of the bed and began working a dollop of the salve into his hands. The scratches on his arm were almost healed, just faint pink lines drawn on his skin. As he scooped up more of the salve and spread it along the lines, he frowned, wondering about the apparition. What was it? Besides shaped Pneuma, of course. What did it mean by drawing blood from him?

That wasn't a comforting thought.

There was a light knock on the door, Baalis came in, carrying a tray. He set it on the crate that served as a bed table, signed: *Daripada say you eat, don't need to work rest of day*.

Breith took the covers off the dishes. There was half a bird of some kind, a pile of white grains and some green stuff. A pot of tea. A small loaf of fresh-baked bread and a scoop of butter. "Come on, Bay. This is too good to eat alone." He tore off the bird's leg, held it out. "I won't tell if you don't."

Grinning, Baalis sat on the bed beside him and raised the leg in a salute.

Baalis stood, patted his stomach, bowed his thanks. He reached for the tray, hesitated, then turned to face Breith. He touched his lips, shook his head and pointed to Breith's hands. *Stable*, he signed. *After moonrise. If can, come sit with us. We talk. Home. Old things. Tell stories*.

Breith signed: *That is good. I try*.

He watched the door shut behind Baalis, then lay back on the bed, his hands laced behind his head. He thought about the quiet hour after supper when the sun was still up but low in the west and the bare paved courts by the barracks shimmered with heat. Baalis and four or five of the other mutes would settle in the only shade, the shadow cast by the end of the building, their reddened skin freckled with the sweat that was never absorbed, their long fair braids coiled and skewered atop their heads. They taught him their signs and talked now and then, not about much. Little things that happened during the day that could raise a smile.

He felt comfortable with them. And privileged. As if he were being brought into a sacred rite that most folk would never even know about, let alone share in.

[3]

They met in the haymow above the stables, sitting in a rough circle in the light from the full moon that flooded through the large square opening where the hayfork was hanging. At that end of the mow, the hay was cleared away from the rough planks of the floor, leaving an empty space that smelled of night-blooming flowers, the hay and now the acrid but rather pleasant odor of the men.

Breith was silent and filled with awe as he watched Ascal Pneuma flow in with the moonlight; it settled on the men, made masks of their faces and bright lamps of their hands, every gesture, every sign, as clear as if it were etched on the air. Though he hadn't willed it, hadn't known it was possible, the Pneuma was working on him too, teaching him. He'd only learned the most elementary signs and understood them only when the mutes slowed down as if they spoke to a baby; when their hands flowed in their ordinary speech, he found most of it incomprehensible.

Tonight was different.

Everything was clear, every nuance plain to him.

And he could see the mutes responding with a heightened well-being to the caress of Pneuma they didn't know was there. As if the Pneuma blessed them.

The oldest of the mutes was a wiry bent ancient with skin like molasses over charcoal and faded tattoos on his face and arms. His name was Fittar, though no one called him by it except the other mutes. He trained and cared for the Nyon Merya Shamba's horses and slept on a pallet in the tack room where he could hear his charges and deal with injuries and illnesses before they had a chance to become problems. Breith had fetched and carried for him for one afternoon, but was dismissed because Fittar saw he had neither knowledge of nor affinity for the horses. The old man stood, moved into the circle of mutes and began signing.

Fittar

We have a stranger among us.
Let the stranger be made welcome.
Let the stranger be reminded of our burden and his.

Let nothing that is said here be repeated in any other place.
Let nothing that is said here be hinted at in any way.
Let all that is said here be hidden in the heart.
Remembering is forbid us.
Speaking of home is forbid us.
What we do here is forbid us.
Yet what is a man if he will not look his sorrows in the face?
What is a man if he will not remember his kin and his kind, his fields and his beasts and his house?
What is a man if his heart is cut out of him?
They have taken our tongues and our seed, they have branded us like cattle and called us their meat, but they do not own our souls.
We are men.
We will speak.

He stepped back to the circle and sat, moonlight and phosphorescent Pneuma shining around him.

There was silence a while then a second man leaned forward, struck his palms together and began signing. He was tall and well muscled with a face like a gentle horse; he'd lost most of the hair on the top of his head, but the rest was plaited into a number of small braids, finished off with windings of red thread. And he was one of the guards who brought Breith from the auction house to the Chaletat. At first his eyes were fixed on Breith as if he told his story for the boy alone, then he forgot all but the memories. His eyes drifted upward until he was looking into the shadows beyond the moonlight and his hands flowed from sign to sign as if the finger dance were impelled by something outside him.

Davvul

I was born in a tsal raised beside a narrow sorm far north of here, a place where winter is one night long and

*in summer the sun never sets. I ran through meadow
grass on that endless summer day, hunting coneys with
a sling and herding the goats that were half the family
wealth. I had three older brothers and two older sisters
who were more beautiful than the sun and wiser than the
moon. My father was a man of worth who could give two
wives their due and house his unwed younger brothers in
a bachelor's eval.*

*The other half of our wealth were the two swift ships
that brought home great heaps of bryfish for the smokehouse and prizes taken in raids, bracelets and necklaces
and brooches, mirrors and needles and cloth, good things
to gift kin and king.*

*My twelfth winter was harder than most. The snow rose
higher than the ridgepole, the storms were more terrible
and in the month before the sun came back the food
stores were almost empty, for in the summer before, bryfish were thin in the fishing grounds and myrkweed grew
secretly in the grass. Before we knew it was there and
could pull and burn it, four of the goats ate of it and
died.*

*When thaw came, we crept from the tsal and dug for
roots and the moon-seeded mushrooms that grew in ice-
melt. Though the winds were too strong for safety, my
father, my brothers and my uncles took the oldest boat
to sea to bring food by raid or net, whichever seemed
most fit.*

*As if they knew our weakness, the slavers came three
days later. Do not look to sea or mountains to shelter
you from man's greed. Where man can go, the slavers
can follow, and once you are owned there is no walking
away. All who see you can seize you for their profit.*

When Davvul straightened his back and dropped his hands,
Baalis leaned forward to take his turn at memory.

Baalis

*My kin are timbermen and the guardians of trees. We are
called Denharysz.*

*If you climb these soft-shouldered shrunken mountains
and look across the lowlands, you will see giants with
silver hats scraping the sky from the horizon to the north
to the horizon in the south. Should you wish to go closer,
you can follow the river that circles this stinking city and
empties filth into the bay and in time you will come to
the foothills. When you climb these, you will see a great
wave of peaks, gray granite with threads of white in
cracks where the shadow never leaves the ground and
the snow never melts.*

*Even so you have not reached the greatest peaks of all,
the Jinoistars. The Denharysz live on the slopes of the
Jinoistars. We harvest trees, and every second year, we
take great rafts of them down the river we call the Va-
davann, though they who live here give it another name.
I rode the logs three times after I passed through the
Dream Walk that made me a man. The river in flood
could not drown me. The river thieves who sought to cut
loose outriding logs or steal the coin they brought could
not defeat me. The city Pelateras could not corrupt me.
I was strong and true to the Way of the Dènhar.*

*And Zahra daughter of Kabriss looked on me with fa-
vor. She walked with the grace and lightness of a deer
and her eyes were bluer than the sky of a summer's day.
When she spoke, the birds went silent for shame because
their song could not match the music of her voice.*

*To our shame we share fleas with the cities of the
coast, or should I say those two-legged wolves that prey
on men. There are bands of outcasts who steal what
they refuse to make and destroy what they cannot steal.
They sniff out villages gone careless with good living,
they come with fire and catapults, with poison and sleep*

*dust and other sly and honorless devices. They kill the
old and babies and sell the others. I rode the rafts to
Pelateras a free man with reputation and worth. I rode
to Pelateras in the belly of a longboat, with chains on
my arms and legs, no longer free.*

*Though you have strong neighbors, true kin and a
good wall, if you do not keep sharp watch, the greed of
man will find you out and steal all you have, even your
own body. How much sooner comes the fate of a man
alone. A man alone cannot watch his back. A man alone
is owned.*

Three more of the mutes signed their histories and their
thoughts, all of their tales ending with a warning about the
impossibility of escape, then they turned their eyes on Breith
and waited.

His soul expanded in the warmth of their regard. It would
be such a relief to relax and let his hands tell the story and
not worry about remembering old lies and fitting the new one
into place. He was part of the circle now and no one would
know what he said here. He could talk about Mam and Mum
and Da and little Bauli. Fittar was right. It was terribly important to remember and almost as important to speak your
memories.

Breith

*I have lied to the Lateramen about my people and who I
am. I did this to protect my family because my mothers
are heads of one of the great merchant houses and their
name might be known in Pelateras since they trade often
with ships from Ascal. I will not lie to you.*

*You may have heard that women rule on Saffroa. From
the time they move in the womb, they have magic. Some
have a small portion, others are born with power to make
and destroy beyond the dreams of the unSighted. This is*

*not a thing to be learned. Men do not have magic, thus
are born to be ruled.*

Except that in every generation there are a few boy
babies born with Sight. In the Domains when they are
discovered, they are cut so they will not pass this Sight
to their own boy children and the gift is burned out of
their heads. Families who protect these boys and refuse
to bow to the will of those who govern are punished. The
mothers are stripped of their property, turned out of their
homes to live on the charity of strangers. And the fathers
are killed. And there is no way to escape discovery because we are marked. When we cross from boy to man,
our eyes change color. A man with Sight has one brown
eye and one green.

In the River city where I lived, the rules are much
relaxed. No one bothers about the few Sighted men who
came for sanctuary and managed to make good lives for
themselves. My father was one who ran from the knife
and the burn. My mothers and he knew from the time I
moved in the womb that I had got the gift from him, but
they said nothing to anyone about it. I was cherished and
taught how to use the Sight and how to keep silence.

Times changed. The River Council began to tremble
with fear before the threat of the Domains and those
women came to rule who wished to make the River Cities
into the image of the Grand Domains, thinking they
would have the power of the Damas who ruled so sternly
out on the plains. And a delegation came to our House
and demanded that I be given over to them. Rumors that
I was Sighted had reached them and they meant to take
me and deal with me as the Domains would have done.

I watched them in the scrying mirror that was my father's gift. I watched my mothers refuse to bow down to
them and my father stand with hands in fists because he
wanted to strike them down. And I thought about my baby
sister who would be head of our house in her time. I
thought about the housekin who were blood of my blood,

*all the people who lived in our House who would lose
everything in the fight that must come. It seemed to me
there was only one thing to do. If I were gone, the danger
that hung over my family would be gone. So I stowed
away on a ship to Ascal because there is no magic on
Ascal and it was far enough away that our enemies would
not bother to search for me. And I thought it would be a
great adventure, like those in the books I read. I have
grown much older since then and perhaps a little wiser.*

*I remember so many things. My baby sister walking
three steps for the first time, waving her arms, losing her
balance and sitting down suddenly. Laughing when I
picked her up and danced round and round with her. Or
playing the slap game with my friends from school. Or
sailing on the river with my father. Or riding with Mam
on one of her riverboats. So many things.*

*I want to go home. I can't go home. I . . . CAN'T . . . GO
. . . HOME.*

[4]

For the next double dozen days Breith spent all the time he
could with the mutes, content to watch them talk. The work
the handlers gave him was easy, the slaves and servants treated
him as a pet, the Pneuma-born creatures followed him everywhere, teasing and playing with him so his fear of vortex and
fire eased and he began trying out small magics; he managed
to slip into the Chale's library so he could study maps of the
coast and snoop about for other things he might need if he
decided to run.

The nights that the Nyon Merya Shamba took him to the
galas and musicales were unpleasant and tedious, but he was
careful to follow Daripada's advice and he suffered nothing
but boredom. Occasionally the Nyon took him with her when
she was paying calls on her acquaintances in the city. They
were an idle lot and seemed to do nothing but trade gossip
and sweet-voiced poison about other women. There were more
of the sniffing games where each sought advantage over the

other. He called up memories of his Mam and his Mum and the Scribes he knew and marveled at the difference. Though Mirrialta would fit right in, he thought, then changed his mind. She'd wipe the floor with this feeble lot. He hid his grin behind his hand at the image this brought to mind.

The days slid by, folding one into the other and all the while he did nothing about his escape.

The moon waned and waxed again until it was nearly full once more. A morning came when Breith was in the kitchen washing vegetables for Tadja to chop.

Though the day was already hot and the kitchen so filled with steam that a steady succession of drops plopped into the rinse water from Breith's nose and chin, the room seemed unusually busy. After a while he looked round and saw three girls staring at him, whispering and giggling. Several other girls walked toward the outer door, glancing at him repeatedly before they vanished. He shrugged and went back to his job.

Daripada came for him when he was about to sit down with the other slaves for their midday meal of kangat porridge flavored with scraps from the master's food. As he left with her the silence behind him grew thick and portentous. It made him nervous, but he didn't dare ask Daripada what was happening. That lesson had been beaten into his behind with the wide soft straps that wouldn't mark his skin but hurt anyway.

A meal of red meat and peppers, a side dish of shellfish and a tall glass of pale green liquid waited on the crate he used for a table. "Eat that," Daripada said. "All of it. I'll be back shortly."

Breith scowled at the tray. It probably meant he was going somewhere with the Nyon Merya Shamba though she didn't usually order special meals for him. He didn't much like such overspiced food, but he ate it, then sat waiting for Daripada to come back.

* * *

Followed by a mute with a can of hot water, she came briskly into the shack. "Over there by the tray," she said. "Take the tray away with you and go back to what you were doing."

When the mute was gone, she stripped the straw mattress, slid a clean linen cover over it and tied the drawstring. "Wash," she told Breith. "Hands, face, private parts. Feet too. When you're finished, sit down on the bed and I'll explain what this is about."

Breith did what she told him, cold knots in his belly. He was afraid he already knew what was coming.

"I will tell you more than you need to know, young Breith. I want you to understand how important this is. The Lahtoan rules in Latera; he rules free men and slaves alike. All we are and all we own comes to us at his pleasure and can be taken away should he grow displeased. Agents of the Lahtoan have approached the Chale Teripa Teral, your master. They have hinted that the Lahtoan would be charmed and most generous in his turn if the Chale found it in his heart to present you as a gift to Him Who Is the Fount of All Good." She reached out, smoothed back a lock of hair that had fallen across his eyes. "You understand, though the words are mild and indirect, this is not a request."

Breith nodded.

"Arrangements will take time. Dealing with the Lahtoan is difficult. The most propitious day must be determined, the words to be spoken by the Chale must be approved along with his dress, the styling of his hair, even the way he is to hold his hands. This should take at least from full to new moon. During that time, the Chale intends to get what use from you he can. Each day until you leave, a girl will be sent to you and you will lie with her. You are young, but you are not ignorant. You know what I am talking about. If you refuse her or fail to perform your duty with her, you will not be touched, but you will be forced to watch the girl beaten bloody, not with straps but with the nine-tail whip."

Breith stared at the floor. Every word Daripada spoke made

him more determined to leave no child of his in this place.
She was a good woman, kind and easygoing, but she could
order without blinking things that were appalling. He tried to
think of some way to postpone this. If he just had a little more
time, he could get away. Maybe . . . He snatched at one of the
ideas that flitted through his head. "But Daripada, I can't do
that. I can't! The Prophet says who lies down in lust outside
the Seyl bond is not welcome at the Court of the Chosen where
there is neither man nor woman, only pure soul. I'll be cast
into the howling dark. It isn't right. You can't—"

Daripada slapped him hard. Then she stood back, her hands
on her hips. "You're a slave. You are nothing. You have
nothing, no god, no will, no soul. Nothing. Your body belongs
to your master and he has the right to use it any way he
chooses."

She walked to the door, turned her head to give him a last
warning. "I'll send the first girl to you in one hour. Think
about what I told you and prepare to take the consequences
of your actions. Or lack of action."

When she was gone, Breith swung his feet up and stretched
out on the bed. He was trembling with anger and a hatred for
the whole idea of slavery stronger than anything he'd ever felt
before, even the spasms of intense desire as he watched the
housegirls working and laughing at the same time. It was a
lie, what he'd said about the Prophet. And it hadn't even
worked. His head swam, his body began to burn and he could
feel a vortex forming round him, but he didn't care. Let it eat
him up, let it destroy this horrible place.

The Pneuma-born roof gnomes came scampering down the
walls. They leaped onto the bed and snuggled against him,
cooing at him in sounds that were no-sound, drawing off the
heat. Two tree nymphs came oozing through the walls; they
knelt beside the bed and wrapped their arms around him, singing to him in voices like the chime of crystal goblets, voices
he heard with the ears of the mind rather than those of the
body. They held him till his anger turned to grief and help-
lessness and he wept.

They kissed the tears from his face, gave him a last pat and went away, taking the roof gnomes with them.

Too weary to feel much, he was still dimly astonished at the protection he'd been given.

It was as if the Pool over Ascal had waked from its sluggish torpor and understood it needed him. To stir it up for its health, for its . . . he didn't know what to call it . . . nor did he really think that the Pool was self-aware or had anything like a mind to think and understand with—though it did have children— of a kind—the nymphs and the gnomes and the sprites— children who thought and acted on what they thought.

He closed his eyes and felt cradled in Pneuma. It eddied around the bed, it wrapped itself around him. For a moment he forgot everything but this improbable union. It was like what happened last full moon in the circle of mutes.

But it couldn't last. He tried not to think about the girl and what he was going to do with her, but he could feel a heat that had nothing to do with Pneuma, a tightness in the groin. He wanted to do it. His body was demanding that he do this. He couldn't do it. One time might not matter, but how could he take that chance? Maybe he'd father a girl . . . who'd be sent to someone like him and bred like a bitch in heat the moment she showed blood. Or a boy to be gelded, his tongue torn out. His child.

Oh Da, you must know how to stop . . . how to not . . . how to do this with a girl and be sure you didn't make a baby. Why didn't you tell me?

There was no answer. How could there be?

He rolled off the bed and started pacing about the small room, his thoughts going round and round like a mule on a treadmill in a flour mill. He couldn't run. Not yet. He didn't want to die. He'd seen the nine-tail whip and felt it too on his second day in the Chaletat, a light stroke to teach him to fear it.

He flung out his arms, cried, "Prophet. All-Mother. Help me. What can I do? How can I stop this?"

As before, there was no answer.

He let his arms drop and went to sit on the bed.

The shack had a single window covered with scraped and hardened gut and an ancient shutter on thick leather hinges that were cracking and half rotten. This being summer, the shutter was tied open and a dim gray light came through the brittle gut, enough to see by, but little more.

Between one breath and the next, the room grew brighter. When he lifted his head, he saw a stream of Pneuma flowing through the window as if the gut were not there at all. The flow reached him and splashed over him, then ebbed as rapidly as it had come. He looked at his hands. They shone like the mutes' hands had shone; instead of pale blurs, they were sharply defined. He could almost see the bones beneath skin and muscle.

This was and was not like the pocket he had several times pulled about him to shield him from discovery. There was no heat. Though the Pneuma shone like blue-white fire, it lay cool on his skin, a thin layer like an expensive glove that fitted every wrinkle and dip. He stripped off the slave tunic and looked down at himself. A full body glove it was.

He looked at the tunic dangling from one hand, he looked at the door that was going to open soon.

And understood what the Ascal Pool had done for him.

He wept a few tears of relief.

And felt them sliding between the Pneuma skin and his own skin till he tasted salt on his tongue.

He looked at the door again and grinned.

The grin widened till his face ached with it.

He went to the bed and sat on the edge, staring at the door, impatient for it to open.

[5]

Breith stirred as he felt fingers pinching him and pulling his hair. Mumbling a protest, he tried to hit the hands away from him, but he touched nothing and the small torments continued until he was awake.

He opened his eyes.

A roof gnome perched on his chest and others were on his legs. They'd stopped their pinching, but their eyes were fixed on him.

The gnome on his chest spoke. *Go. Now.* The not-words were a command from the greater thing looking out of its luminous eyes.

Breith sighed. "I hear," he said.

The gnomes nodded their rootlike heads, the hair of their top-knots bouncing comically, then they jumped for the wall and swarmed up it to their nests under the shingles.

The Pneuma glove was gone, pulled off him or absorbed into his skin. His thighs were sticky and made a faint tearing sound as he pulled them apart. He made a face at the discomfort, but the grimace melted into a fond smile as he walked bowlegged to the washstand.

An hour later he pushed through the trees that grew along the outer wall, a well-filled pack on his back with a blanket roll and water-skin strapped to it. He had coin from the Chaletat Bursar's office, maps from the Chale's library, clothes from the storehouse and food from the kitchen. It was a heavy load and he was tired and sleepy, but the Ascal Pneuma had spoken to him and he knew better than to ignore it.

The tree girls were leaning from the trunks, their bodies translucent in the light of the not-quite-full moon. They stroked him as he moved past, sang farewells and blessing to him. He wished they wouldn't. Too many good memories hung suspended in those bell tones. He'd miss Daripada and even waspish Tadja and especially Baalis and the mutes. And he felt guilty. He was leaving and he knew they could not.

At the wall he untwisted the slave wire from his ear and flung it aside while he listened for the scrape and thump of guards' feet. If the jokes the mutes told about the night wall-guards had any truth, most of them were in the watchtowers, snoring. Still, one of them might be restless.

When he'd heard nothing for several moments, he shaped the Pneuma into a solid rope with big knots in it and a grapple at one end. He hadn't learned how to do this, he just did it. He set the grapple, climbed the rope, reversed the hooks and climbed down the outside of the wall. Then he dissolved the rope and started walking along the road, heading for the city.

The Pneuma dropped continually around him, a soft feathery fall like down from a duck's breast, feathers brushing against his skin and melting into him. The night sky was brilliant with stars though the moon was low in the west, near setting. The air was heavy with the scents of flowers and mosses. The road up here in the hills was empty, not even a wandering dog to break the stillness with his trot.

As he drew near the city and the road flattened out, he began to see the dark shapes of beggars curled in doorways and niches, but none of them woke enough to notice him.

He moved effortlessly, as if he were floating, walked in an eerie silence where even the wind was soundless.

Though the moon dropped lower and lower and finally set, he felt as if time had slowed to a stop and the whole city lay under a Mage's enchantment where he alone was awake and aware.

When he came at last to the street where the guards had walked him from the auction house to the carrier, he was not at all surprised to find a horse waiting for him, a fine dun gelding with black mane and tail. It was all part of the dream.

He looked up into the Pneuma fall and murmured, "I can't ride bareback."

Pneuma clumped and flowed, vibrating faster and faster, shattering the languor that had insulated Breith from fatigue and fear. His shoulders ached from the pack's armstraps, he was hungry and tired enough to collapse in a puddle if he let himself relax for a single moment.

He blinked. The horse had blanket, saddle and bridle now, the reins of the bridle looped around a leather-covered cleat at the front of the saddle; the tack looked so real he couldn't believe the Pneuma had created them. He could smell the leather and the unbleached wool and when he touched the stirrup leather, it was solid, smooth. He sniffed at his fingers and smelled saddle soap.

The horse shifted impatiently, turned his head to look at Breith.

Hastily Breith caught hold of the stirrup, got his foot in it and pulled himself into the saddle. "I've had a little teaching, but I'm not much of a rider, horse. But I've got Pneuma." He grinned. "And you're going to have to put up with me."

By the time dawn grayed the eastern sky, Pelateras and its ring of farms were far behind and the road north had shrunk to a pair of ruts cut deep in the chalky soil. Both Breith and the horse were ready to quit. It was light enough to show him that he was in open country—rolling hills, piles of granite boulders from fist-sized to giants tall as a man, gray-green grass stiff as needles, scraggly brush with thick round leaves and curved spines on the branches, the occasional clump of trees with lacy foliage that spread out like opened umbrellas and tattered white bark on the stubby trunks.

As he rode past a tree clump close to the road, he saw a trickle of water that was quickly absorbed by the parched soil beyond the trees. "I wonder, horse. I've got water, but it would be helpful if we found a seep you could drink from. Not this close to the road, hm."

Abruptly the scene in front of him seemed to blink. Then it changed.

The dry scrublands were gone.

Tall cloud towers puffed high above a distant city whose painted roofs were gleaming in the light of a yellow sun, roofs of dust-red and muted purple, of a dozen different greens and blues. Beyond them, pointed tower roofs glittered silver in the harsh and brilliant light.

Another blink.

He was back on the sorry excuse for a road, riding a tired horse and suffering a thirst that turned his mouth to leather.

*　　*　　*

Half a watch later, he worked his way out of the saddle and stood hanging on to the saddle leathers as his knees threatened to go soft on him. A short distance off he saw a cluster of hummocks like pimples on the earth's skin. There were trees on the far side of those swellings, only their foliage visible. "Shall we go see, horse? If there's enough water, we can stop and rest a while."

The trees grew beside a heap of boulders and from beneath those boulders a tiny stream emerged and pooled between two knobby roots. The grass was lush and green and a kind of watercress grew on the banks. Breith sighed with pleasure. "Pneuma luck, horse. I haven't grain for you, but look at the good stuff for grazing."

He tethered the horse to a trunk, giving him enough rope so he had plenty of graze within reach. He stripped the tack off the horse, half afraid it would melt in his hands, and was pleased when it didn't. Then he found a place where he could stretch out upstream from the animal and suck up the cool clear water until his belly felt bloated and his mouth felt alive again.

While the horse grazed, he sat eating bread he'd torn from a small loaf and a hunk of cheese. "The simple pleasures, horse. Where would we be without them?"

When he finished, he splashed water over his face, used sand from the bottom of the stream to scrub his hands, then he rolled up in his blankets and went to sleep.

He woke at sunup, stripped naked and with an aching head.

The horse was gone.

The backpack was gone.

The blankets were gone.

Whoever had knocked him on the head had thrown a bunch of rags over him. He pushed them away and tried to sit up, but his head swam and he felt sick, so he lay back on the grass. The rags were filthy trousers and a tattered shirt. He could feel scuttling on his belly and thighs where they'd been.

"Pneuma luck," he said aloud to the lacy leaves blowing about overhead. "How come I don't feel lucky right now?"

13

Runaways

By the calendar of the Domains of Iomard, events dating from the 13th day of Sakhtos, the seventh month in the Iomardi year 6535, the 722nd year since the last Corruption.

[1]

Urs crouched at Aron's knee, watching as Cheaasa and her daughter/apprentice Beati moved their hands through an elaborate dance around the edge of the small clearing where the rest of the hidden council met, weaving daroc wards meant to turn aside a Seer's gaze so gently the Seer would not realize she was being maneuvered. Daroc magic. Slow and secret, but strong as water eating away stone. Since he'd apprenticed with Aron as Rememberer, he'd learned a lot more about that and what he'd learned pleased him. The Lynborn had no idea what darocs like his Mam and Cheaasa the Healwitch could do.

The night was warm and the moon was swollen to near full, flooding the glade with light, so they hadn't lit a fire between the logs drawn up as seats. As soon as Cheaasa and Beati were seated on the ends pointed toward the Eadro Lynhouse, their presence there an additional shelter against overlooking, Urs's Mam, head Elder Reyar, straightened her shoulders, folded her hands in her lap and spoke, her voice a murmur barely louder than the rustle of the night wind in the leaves overhead. "Three weeks ago the Wife overstepped herself and gave away what Radayam wanted kept secret. Do you agree?''

Cheaasa, Plesc and Aron nodded. Gara closed her hand in a fist. ''Yes,'' she whispered.

''The Seers will be pricking names for the army in a day or so. All the able-bodied between fifteen and thirty, if I guess right. We knew it had to come soon with folk pouring in from the other Domains like they are, but we've no more time at all. Any disputation?''

Plesc slapped her hand against her thigh. ''Not here, Reyar. One day, two, and it will be too late to run. There'll be dochta leashes riveted to all the pricked and we can't break those.''

After a murmur of agreement from the others, Reyar glanced up. ''Two more days and the moon's full. Those who choose to go will have a long night's run before they have to go to ground. Urs, I'll need you to whisper the word, come morning. Cheaasa, we'll want the strongest possible eye-turn charms for each of them.''

''I've been working at that, Reyar. Beati and me, we'll be ready when you have the count.''

''Gara, supplies?''

''With all the butchering and the smokehouses working full time it's easy enough to slip what we need out of there. Imm is baking extra loaves whenever she can and sealing them. She has a fair supply stowed up under the thatch. We have a supply of canvas for packs, thanks to Fiodor and Rothla. We can get that cut and out to folks tomorrow.''

''Reyar.''

''Aron?''

''A Rememberer has to go. Even if we're split, we're all Eaders and we shouldn't look away from that. The way my knee is these days, I'd just slow them down. We talked it over and Urs is willing if you are.''

Urs watched his mother start to object, then she pressed her lips together and closed her eyes and he knew she was going to agree.

''Can Urs do the job? It's only been a short while since he started with you.''

"He knows the basics and he'll take paper to write down what happens each day. Once he's past the Mage's Wall and settled, he can go back and memorize what he has written."

Reyar touched her brow, her hand hiding her eyes. When she dropped the hand into her lap, her face was composed. "Then that is how it will be. Is there anything else?"

"Beati and I will be pricked. There's no doubt of that." Cheaasa spoke quietly. "An army needs all the healers it can get hold of." She touched her daughter/apprentice's face with the back of her hand. "She has refused to leave me. Tell her to go. I'll be treated well enough."

"You're daroc, Mam. You know the Lynborn will use you and throw you away when you can't keep up. I don't care what anyone says to me. I'm going with you. I'm going to take care of you."

Reyar smiled at the girl. "And right you are, Beati. Cheaasa, I know what you're like. You'll spend yourself till there's only a thread left unless there's someone around to scold you into resting. And aren't the pricked and taken Eaders also? Besides, Beati will be safer with you than on the run across the Domains."

Plesc frowned. "When the pricking is done and the pricked are called, there will be more heads of household on the flogging line and this time Radayam won't stop the Wife. We need to be ready for that. Cheaasa, if you and Beati are taken, who will tend these wounds?"

"I have thought of that. Beati and I have been filling gourds with goil salve and herbs for poultices. Best send someone round in the morning to collect these and stow them where the Lynborn won't find them. I'll leave instructions about making the poultices. The goil is easy enough to use, though not so easy on the whipcuts."

Urs jumped to his feet. "Mam, if I go, are they going to beat you?"

"No, that's not something you have to worry about. Not me, not Aron. You're too young to prick for the army; so far as the Lynborn are concerned, you don't count." She smiled at him, the moon catching a twinkle in her eyes. Embarrassed, he sank down on his heels and moved closer to Aron so his master's long bony legs would keep the others from looking at him.

Gara smiled, then shook her head. "More than the whip to worry about. Ama got permission for a family visit tonight. After supper we went for a walk round Ead, she and me. She told me she was scrubbing the hall floor outside the offices this morning and she heard the Wife talking to one of the bantars. Everything in the storehouses except seed stock and half of this fall's harvest will go to the army. Of what's left, half will go to the House and we're left to live on the rest. Provisioning the runners is something we need to do, but we'd better start thinking about our own selves too."

"Hm. Whatever else she is, the Wife is no fool. She'll be watching for us to skim. Best to start thinking about this. Give Ama our thanks, Gara." Reyar stood. "Anything to add? No? Good. We'll meet again after the pricking is done, those of us who are left. The All-Mother bless and keep you all, wherever you go."

[2]

In the stone throne above the mirror pool, elbows on knees, hands dangling between his legs, Dur leaned forward, tracing the line of chaotic Pneuma, renewing the pins that kept it in place. It bulged and billowed constantly, ever on the verge of breaking loose and returning to its natural configuration. He hadn't realized it was going to take such continual effort to maintain that barrier. He grudged the energy and time it cost him, but it was a price that had to be paid if he was to have a chance to build the army that would sweep away the Domains and set his people free.

When the repinning was finished, Dur straightened, ran his fingers through his sweat-drenched hair, then spent a few moments rebraiding it, using the simple task to regain his calm. Then he returned the mirror to look at Darcport.

The town growing up around the end of the bay was crude

and haphazard, the buildings constructed from unseasoned timber, most of it already warping and splitting, but it was filled with energy and excitement. Darcport they called it. The darocs' own port city. Two ships from Ascal were anchored there this day as well as smugglers from all along the coast, as far south as Valla Murloch. On the farms that ringed the city, the houses might be sod huts, but crops were already in the ground and the furrows were green with new growth.

His city too. His creation. In the first days he'd been everywhere, greeting newcomers, assessing them, choosing those with authority, the intangible ability to lead, fitting them into the system of governance he'd set up, using his memory of how darocs managed their villages, his experience in the Kale army and his observations of the Graths of Nyddys. He'd used persuasion and power to get that system established and was pleased to see it working and his ideas spreading beyond the city into the burgeoning villages of the interior.

His soul expanded as he watched his people take hold of their lives, change old traditions into new ones. He lingered over the vision for a long time. More time than he could afford. But it warmed his soul and woke his passion in a way nothing else did.

He renewed his promise to the women and men who moved through the streets of Darcport and those on the farms and in the villages of his salvaged land. I will make this hold. I will make this nation of the redeemed last a thousand and a thousand years.

Eyes on the teeming, vigorous Darcport, he sighed. Soon he'd have to sail south along the islands to Isle Seord. That island was cut in half by the Turbulence; all he had to do was take a few steps, then he could scry the mainland and with a few quick dips find out what the Traiolyns were up to. He knew he was much stronger now and he'd learned skills they didn't have, but the Seers had a grip on him he still couldn't shake off.

Reluctantly, he wiped that image away and turned the mirror on Glandair so he could observe the Mages and learn more about the coming Corruption than meager reports in the old books stored here.

[3]

In the bare tower room Radayam set the talisman on the floor in front of her, touched it alive and waited.

A few breaths later, a soft glow bloomed in the shadows across from her, a glow that resolved itself into flickering images of Shoneyn the Seer and Hiacaylan ait é Planda-Andar, Traiolyn of Domain Planda. Shoneyn's talisman rested on a low table between the two women and both kept a finger on the silver disc though neither touched the stone in the center.

"In the name of the Prophet, be welcome, Hiacaylan my Sister."

"The All-Mother bless you and yours, Radayam my Sister."

"The work goes well here. The army grows quickly greater as each day brings more Seers and bantars, ridos and darocs with wagonloads of bolts, lances and other weapons, of grain and tubers. Herdgirls bring tribuf, the fires of our smokehouses burn day and night. We will be ready to march north by the next full moon if Planda agrees to this."

"Planda agrees. Our ridos say the training has gone well. Our Seers tell us that the Riverine filth expect us but have little they can do to stop the Cleansing. We too shall march north. Mionach will burn and the mixes will cease to poison the soil of Saffroa."

"Till the full moon, Hiacaylan my Sister."

"Till the full moon, Radayam my Sister."

The image vanished, but Radayam didn't move.

A few moments later the glow reappeared, but the only figure that emerged this time was Shoneyn.

Radayam smiled. "Well done, my friend."

"It wasn't all that difficult, Rada. All I need do is remind her of port fees and taxes and her enthusiasm blooms again. Planda's Wife is doing the work. She's a capable woman and her heart is in this."

"Then I take it the report is accurate enough."

"Indeed. We could march within the week if it were necessary."

"I think it best we begin in harmony no matter what the end of the summer brings us."

Shoneyn's lovely face was suffused with the glow of her fervor. "Yes. Yes. Let the misbegotten and the apostate see the pure act with one heart, one mind, one soul."

"Prophet Bless, Shonya my friend."

"Prophet Bless, Rada."

Exhausted by the long day, Radayam climbed to the roof and stood leaning on one of the merlons that circled the top of the tower. She took comfort in the campfires dotting the dark out to the horizon—the Army of Purification was in truth growing stronger every day. That was not just soothing syrup poured on Planda's Traiolyn. Beyond the fires the tribuf herds ate dried grass laid out for them since graze was long gone from the fields; the wind brought to her the acrid musky smell of those herds. Off to her right, the butchering floor was surrounded by dozens of smoking torches, the flickering uncertain light washing over the blood and entrails, the oozing heaps of black hides, glinting off the cleavers of the ridos as they cut the carcasses into sections, the knives of the smokehouse women as they took the meat off the bone and reduced the chunks to strips.

She pushed back and walked around so she could watch the butchering. Daroc boys pulled carts with squealing wheels back and forth along the meat tables, the women tossed the strips in them; when the carts were full, the boys hauled them to the smokehouses. Busy. Day and night. It's really going to happen. By the next full moon we march.

She rubbed at aching eyes, moved to the center of the tower and lowered herself to her knees. She bent forward in a deep bow, her brow touching the cold stone. "All-Mother bless this gathering. Prophet, in Your Name, not mine. I am nothing. I serve with heart and soul and all that I have. I serve."

She stayed as she was, waiting for the inflow of peace which she thought of as the gift of the Prophet.

It didn't come and didn't come. Cold crept into her bones and ache into her joints. Still she waited.

In the end she sighed and let go of her expectation. She got to her feet and took a step toward the trap and the ladder.

The Prophet's Peace came into her and geysered upward, filling her, wrapping her in glory.

Then it was gone.

Eyes pricking with tears of joy, mind suffused with a new understanding, she stepped onto the ladder, pulled the trap shut and went down the ladder to the landing at the top of the spiral stairs. With each step she whispered her new understanding. *I serve. I command nothing. Empty myself. A vessel only. Expect nothing. Desire nothing. I am nothing.*

[4]

Urs watched as Tuat, Peyn and their older sons slipped away in the darkness. He touched the turn-eye about his neck as he saw them blur and blend with the night the moment they got beyond the light from the nearest house.

His belly knotted and there was a burn in his throat. He wasn't exactly afraid, but he'd never been away from his family, never been even a day's walk from Ead Village. Maol stood a short distance off, still fighting with Gara. He wanted her to come with him, but she would not. She was one of Ead's Elders and might not be pricked because of that; and she was one of the Hidden Council. Urs had heard the arguments over and over. She was glad Maol was going, but she simply could not in conscience leave Ead. Siun stood apart, his arms tight around Beno; she was pregnant with their third child and he didn't know when he'd see her again. Laod was touching Morea's face over and over as if he were trying to memorize every curve and hollow. She had a crippled foot. Though she got around well enough in ordinary times, the runners' long journey was too much for her.

His mother came from shadow and stood beside him. She

didn't say anything but after a while she reached down and tugged on a hank of his hair. "Made you some honey chew," she murmured. "Catch." She dropped a small leather pouch stuffed tight with the leaf-wrapped candies.

He caught it, tied the pouch to his belt. "Thanks, Mam."

"You get yourself killed, I'll chase you with a tikka switch to the end of the seven levels of heaven."

"Laod's sneakier'n a dozen Lynborn. Remember the time he lifted Traiolyn's hens out under the nose of that sniffy bantar who thought she was hot stuff?"

"Don't know what I'm going to be doing with my time now that I won't be chasing after you." She pulled his hair again. "Prophet Bless, Urs. It's just about time you were going."

He looked back once, when they were turning the end of a hedgerow, and saw his mother standing at the edge of the moonlight. He lifted his arm in a wave, saw her wave back, then hurried after the others.

14

Strange Havens

By the secret calendar of the Watchers, events dating from the 29th day of Pumamis, the fifth month in the 738th Glandairic year since the last Settling.

[1]

"Bring her inside, Fori. Bré's room."

Talgryf swung round. Another woman stood in the doorway; she was very like the first, but with deep, old scars on the upper half of her face and her eyelids sewn shut. Out of courtesy, perhaps, she spoke Nyd-Ifor; her accent was purer, not nearly so much of the odd lilt to the phrasing.

"I'll carry her." Ellar started to kneel.

"No." The soft voice of the blind woman turned sharp. "Let Faobran do it. You and the boy come here. Corysiam, if you will join us?"

When Faobran touched Cymel, fire leaped from the girl's writhing body, curled about the woman apparently without touching her. Ignoring the flames, she slid her arms under Cymel and lifted her, holding her firmly enough to minimize her flailings. She strode swiftly into the house while the blind woman blocked the others with her staff.

Chewing his lip, worry putting more knots in his belly, Talgryf trailed behind the others. Weird, he thought. It's too weird to swallow. I wish . . . He saw a maid servant peeking round a door at them and scowled at her. Pull your nose in, cow, before somebody snips it off.

Just one room in the set of rooms where Faobran took Cymel was bigger than the place where his whole family lived. The bedroom had shelves and shelves of books, model boats, a bin of cured wood with a tool chest left open so he could see chisels and small saws and all sizes of carving knives.

Cymel was still burning but her shrieks and howls had muted to hoarse cries. Listening to her made his throat hurt.

The blind woman leaned her staff against the wall, laid her hand on Faobran's shoulder and began an odd humming, wordless song.

A man touched Talgryf's shoulder and moved him gently aside then stepped into the room. The newcomer nodded to Ellar as he crossed to the two women. He touched Faobran's shoulder and clasped the blind woman's free hand. Talgryf felt a kind of locking-in, as if the three had suddenly become one. The air shimmered about them.

Cymel went quiet.

The flames vanished.

She gave a long sigh and opened her eyes, stared up at the women, sighed again and went back to sleep.

Faobran laid Cymel on the bed. "She'll do now. Corysiam, I'd like an explanation, then you'd best get some sleep. Malart, take our other visitors and get them settled for the moment. We'll decide later how to deal with this."

[2]

Talgryf looked at the red-brown liquid in the delicate porcelain cup. He took a tentative sip, decided he liked it and settled back in the chair, letting the tea slide down his throat and warm the worry out of him.

Malart sipped at his tea, then set the cup down. "Truly you had not much choice, Watcher. I can't fault you for that." He smiled at Ellar. "You might not know this—I only discovered it by accident—but my son Breith and your daughter Cymel have been secret friends for several years now, talking together and fighting with each other as friends do. Breith has the Sight and you know your daughter's gifts."

"I . . ." Ellar scowled past his knees at the floor, though Talgryf decided that all the man was seeing was something inside his head. "Knew. Cymel keeps her secrets close, but not from me. At least, not until I sent her away."

"Ah. I raised this for a purpose, Watcher. To explain why your presence makes difficulties for us, though we don't grudge you the shelter here—for the moment. There is a faction in our Council which wants to brainburn boys with the Sight. They're spying on us constantly, bribing housekin or getting them drunk. They use these troubled times and play on fear to gain power and wealth. One of the ways they do this is by forcing Houses like ours to rebel against Council edicts. This gives them grounds to seize everything we own and declare us outcast and traitors. Breith ran because he understood that, because he knew we would never bow to edict and hand him over. He's about the age of our young friend here"—Malart nodded at Talgryf—"and he wanted to save us. However much sympathy we feel for your daughter's troubles, wasting our son's sacrifice is something we will not do."

"Soon as sun's up, they'll know you have visitors?"

"Yes. If anything is certain, that is."

"How soon before there's a demand that you produce us?"

"I can't say for sure. By sundown probably."

Talgryf blinked as the cup tilted and spilled its dregs on his leg. His eyelids felt like they had weights tied to them. He set the cup down. With the men's voices droning on behind him he moved about the room; sleep sloshed like warm water about his ears and walking felt more like floating. A long low couch with piles of bright pillows on it was pushed up against one wall.

He drifted over to the couch, stretched out on it. Sleep fell on him like a load of black ash and everything else went away.

[3]

"Mm mmmhh mmm . . ."

Cymel opened her eyes. She was lying on a bed in a darkened room. A woman sat beside the bed, humming a pleasant, soothing tune and knitting with such expert flicks of her long pale fingers that Cymel found a drowsy pleasure in watching her work.

After a moment, though, the woman laid the knitting down and turned toward the bed.

Cymel sucked in a breath as she saw her face. The upper half was deeply scarred, old scars that had gone soft with time, and her eyes were sealed shut.

"Ah, you're awake. Don't be afraid, child. You're safe here. My name is Yasayl and this is Urfa House."

"You're Bré's Mum." Cymel shifted in the bed as she got ready to sit up.

Yasayl heard the creaking. "Don't get up, Cymel. You've been hurt and you need to stay still a while longer. Your father is here too. Would you like me to call him?"

"Yes, please." She watched as Yasayl tucked her knitting into a bag and hung it by its handles from the back of the chair. The blind woman took her staff and walked from the room. She had a casual certainty about her movements that Cymel found oddly reassuring.

Hurt, she thought. What . . .

Memory came flooding back.

Mole. Walking toward her. Waving. Grinning.

Mole at the heart of a fire so hot he was dead instantly and cinder a breath later.

The Siofray Mage behind her, wrapping his filthy self around her, his hands on her breasts, his legs pinning hers.

The Siofray Mage bursting into her head, into the heart of who she was, a rape far more terrible than any violation of her body.

She could feel him moving in her head, crawling like a worm in her head.

Burning.

She burned as Mole had burned, but she didn't die, he wouldn't let her die.

She sobbed at the memory of a pain beyond anything she'd ever imagined.

She heard someone saying something to her, but couldn't understand the words, they were just noises until she heard her name. Mela Mela, someone said. Mela. It was like a mooring post. She caught hold of it and her dizzily swaying world steadied. She forced her eyes open and saw her father bending over her.

"Pa. Oh, Pa."

He sat on the bed, lifted her onto his lap. He held her and rocked back and forth, back and forth. "It's all right, baby, all right, Mela. You're safe now. I won't let anything hurt you."

Fear left her, but that made room for grief.

She wept for Mole and knew she'd loved him, as a friend but more than that. She wept for all the things between them that might have been, things that the Siofray Mage had stolen from her. Wept until she was exhausted with grieving. Then she lay against her father's chest, shuddering with weariness and the aftereffects of the crying.

"My head hurts," she said finally.

"Don't worry yourself, Mela. The burning will go away, but it will take a while. Just be patient and stay as quiet as you can manage."

"It was the Mage, you know. The Siofray Mage."

"I know. Corysiam took you from him. You owe her more than thanks, Mela."

"What did he do to me?" She could feel her father hesitating. "Tell me. I have to know."

"He made you Bridge him to Iomard. You weren't even ready to Walk, but he force-grew that part of your Sight and it's possible he burnt it out of you. How much more damage he did, well, we'll have to wait till you heal to learn that. Mela, I know it's going to be hard, but I don't want you using the Sight. Not for the smallest thing. Will you promise me?"

Cymel sighed, a shudder in her expelled breath left over from the crying spate. She was so tired and the burning in her head made it hard to think. But her father was waiting for her promise and there didn't seem to be any reason not to give it. "I promise, Pa."

He stood, lifting her as he rose. He held her a moment longer, then put her back on the bed. "Are you hungry?"

She thought about that a minute. "Not really. Thirsty. My throat hurts."

"I'll ask Yasayl to send you some tea. And some sandwiches. Try a bite or two, you might surprise yourself. Mela, I don't want to worry you, but you've been asleep for about two weeks. You need food to get your strength back."

"Two weeks? Mole!" She sat up, braced herself on her hands till the dizziness went away. "Pa, does University know about Mole?"

"Mole—that's Gylas Mardianson, isn't it? Last I heard from Henannt, he was your teacher. Henannt says he's the most brilliant Scholar he's seen in decades. What happened?"

"The Mage killed him. Burned him to cinders without a chance to defend himself." A sob lumped in her throat, then burst out of her and she was crying again. Gulping, her voice breaking, she told her father what had happened, why they were up on the mountain, the telling all jumbled about, the bits coming as she thought of them.

When she was finished, Ellar drew his hand gently along the side of her face, then used his thumbs to wipe away the tears beneath her eyes. "A sad waste of a splendid life. That's what a Mage is, Mela. A sower of waste, a reaper of destruction. He builds his structures with hollow bricks and they crumble to sand even before he dies. Young Gryf is with us. Would you like me to send him in? He can tell you about what happened while you slept."

"Gryf? What about Breith? This is his house, isn't it?"

"Breith is not here right now. We'll talk about that later, Mela. Don't worry, he's fine. His parents are keeping an eye on him." He put his hand on her shoulder. "Lie down. Rest."

"Oh, all right." She let herself slump back into the pillows. "Gryf will do. But you'll scry Breith for me, won't you, Pa?

Later? I want to see for myself how he's doing."

"We'll see. Do try to eat something when the tea comes, will you?"

"Yes, Pa."

[4]
Corysiam slept for three hours, then left Urfa House.

As she waited for old Neech to do his job, she saw the group of Enforcers on the far side of the cliff road pretending to be idlers, playing a desultory game of shakestone. Their trerai was a tall gaunt woman whom Corysiam had met before at sessions of the Riverine Council in Gabba Labhain, one Vitril na Shergam. She was a member of Councillor Granna's staff. Corysiam despised Granna and disliked the trerai Vitril at their first meeting, a feeling she was sure was reciprocated in full.

She smiled grimly as she heard Old Neech muttering curses as he pulled the chains to open the gate for her. From his mouth to the All-Mother's ears.

As she sidled through the narrow opening, she saw Vitril stand and stare at her. She set her hands on her hips and faced the trerai, her anger visible, daring the woman to say anything to her.

Vitril went pale and her mouth set into a thin line, but after a moment, she looked away. She dropped to her knees and reached for the stones. With a casual gesture, she flung them out on the board, shrugged and let the next in the circle take them.

Corysiam walked briskly along the road, pleased when its shallow curve put Housewalls between her and the watching Enforcers.

She pulled an avert-shield around her head and shoulders, then moved into the crooked, winding streets where the un-affiliates lived, streets that swarmed with children, barrow sellers, even a few of the smaller fanai clans playing lively dance music to lighten the feet and the purse of the walkers at the same time. She changed directions a number of times, stopped in the shadow of dusty trees to feel about her for signs of interest. When she was as sure as she could be that she was unobserved she changed direction a last time and hurried toward the back of a small, shabby house. The walled garden was given over to weeds and the rampant growth of herbs left to fend for themselves.

She lifted the latch and pushed the back gate open, then followed wobbly stepping stones to the house where a short dark woman waited for her, hands clasped beneath a washworn apron.

The woman said nothing till the back door was closed, then she smiled, a wide beaming smile that changed her face completely and gave her a fleeting beauty. "Cory, welcome. Good to see you." She raised her thick dark brows. "Or is it?"

"How's your mother, Gwynna?"

"Well enough to be embroidering a blouse for me. She so loves her needlework. I can't tell you how pleased I am to see her perk up like this. You want to see the depository?"

"Not today, I think. We'll talk here." Corysiam looked around and smiled. "I do like your kitchen, Gwynna." It was a pretty room with white walls and crisp white curtains, scrubbed clean and full of light. The smells of fresh-baked bread and a spicy stew underlined the sense of peace and comfort. "What I need to say is trouble so it needs goodness around it."

"Ah. Then sit and I'll bring you some tea."

Corysiam wrapped her hands around the warm mug and stared into the russet liquid. "The Mage is back on Iomard. He forced my niece to Bridge him here and meant to take her with him to the Sanctuary Isles. I got her away, but I want a warning passed. He has learned some new tricks that scare me to the marrow and the worst is how he can control women of power. I'm afraid he'll be looking for another horse to carry him. A Walker. Probably a Scribe. He amplifies the Sight in them and uses that power until his mount is burnt out. I'll tell you true, we don't have anyone strong enough to fight him alone.''

Gwynna shivered. "I'll certainly pass that on. What about the other Scribes, the ones who follow the Priom?''

"They have to be warned, but I'll do that myself. I don't want any of the Runda involved. It was my niece who was taken, so I've got that direct experience I can testify to.''

"The Sinne Council will want to question the girl.''

"I'm sure they will. And they're not getting the chance. She's half Ifordyar and you know how most of that lot from the Priom down feel about mixed blood.''

Gwynna grimaced. "So I do.''

"Ah! I'm sorry. I forgot.''

"Why I like you, Cory. Because you do forget.''

Corysiam gulped a mouthful of the tepid tea to cover her embarrassment. Gwynna was a particularly sensitive scryer, able to look longer and with sharper detail than any other Scribe, but she was the daughter of a barrow seller who'd listened too long to the sweetly cozening tongue of an Ascal sailor, an island man who vanished long before Gwynna was born. At the beginning of the year, she was purged from the Scribes at the request of one of the inquisitors assigned to oversee the activities of the Scribes in residence at Gabba Labhain.

She set the mug down, shook her head when Gwynna lifted the teapot. "That's my news. Anything of interest happening in the Domains?''

"Too much.'' Gwynna shook her head. "Eadro is gathering an army. Not ready to march yet, but from what you brought over from the Glandair Watchers, the Purge Wars will begin before the end of summer. I say wars, because over in the west lobe, Planda is also pulling in fighters and supplies. It looks as if Planda and Eadro are working together, but I haven't been able to see any messengers riding between them. They must be communicating some other way. Gryoth in Fasalla set herself to finding out, but I haven't heard from her in several sennights. I tried scrying for her, but got nothing. I'm afraid she was taken. Druaym and Chiaro got themselves up as traders and took passage for Fasalla on an Ascal merchanter yesterday. They're carrying messages to the West Runda, but mostly they're going to see what happened to Gry.''

Corysiam clicked her tongue, shook her head. "We haven't enough people to go chasing down ratholes."

"This rathole is important, Cory. If we can find out how the Domains are talking to each other, we can know their plans before they act on them."

"True. Well, I'd best get back. I have to Bridge my niece back to Glandair before she gets Urfa House into more trouble than they're already facing." Corysiam pushed her chair back and stood. "From day after tomorrow I'll be on Glandair for at least a sennight. The Vale of Caeffordian, if anyone wants to reach me."

[5]

Cymel walked around the room, touching Breith's model boats as if they could call him back from wherever he was. She missed him a lot and she was worried about him. Nobody would tell her why he was gone or where. She touched his silver scry bowl. No water in it and besides she'd promised her father she wouldn't fool with Pneuma. She moved away from the worktable and took a book from the shelves, an ancient book with leather covers that looked as if they'd been handled a lot.

When she opened it, she was disappointed. She'd learned Siofray speech, but they used something like small squashed images, not proper letters. She leafed through the book, looking at the illustrations, black and white line drawings that were quite nice. The inside of the book made it even clearer that this was a book that people used. That Breith had used. Pages were turned down, with stains on some of them, worn spots. It showed the insides and outsides of ships, how they went together, how the ropes went and other details like that. She glanced over at Breith's ship models and found several of them pictured on the pages.

She carried the book across the room and stood looking back and forth from the drawings to the models. The fine detail of paint and carving, the tiny knots and precision of the rigging amazed her. They showed her a side of Breith she'd never have guessed at, not with his temper and the arguments they got into every time they talked. She ran her finger along the silky smooth side of a ship and felt like crying though she didn't know why.

There was a quick knock at the door, then Gryf stuck his head in without waiting for an answer. "Mela, your pa said to come get you. My guess, we're moving again."

Ellar sat in a wooden armchair, looking harried and exhausted. Cymel hurried to him and stood with her arm across his shoulders, scowling at the Siofray women.

Corysiam smiled. "Don't worry about your father, Mela. It's because he's a Watcher. That ties him closer to Glandair than you or Gryf. He needs to get back to what gives him strength."

"We're going to the farm?"

"No. Not Cyfareth either. The Tyrn declared your father Werelos and put a price on his head. Seems he didn't bother to get permission to leave Carcalon when I got news to him about you. About the only safe place on Nyddys right now is the Vale. You wouldn't mind seeing Lyanz again, would you?"

Cymel glowered at her. Before she could tell her aunt not to treat her like a baby, her father caught hold of her hand. When she looked down to see what he wanted, he shook his head. The light glinting off his spectacles mostly hid his eyes, but she had the feeling they were twinkling at her. She sighed.

Corysiam raised her brows but said nothing about this exchange. "We'll step off from the patio in a little while. Ellar, you agree to what I proposed?"

He got to his feet, stood holding Cymel's hand. "Yes. I don't particularly like the idea, but I think it's necessary. Gryf, you're ready? Good. We'll wait in the patio, Cory."

[6]

Talgryf pushed his hands in his pockets and wandered about the patio, kicking at the grass and glancing at a reddish sun that wouldn't let him forget how far he was from home. Ellar was a short distance off, rubbing gently at the nape of Cymel's neck. Something about that bothered Talgryf. Maybe the look on Ellar's face.

Corysiam came through the door, nodded to Ellar. "They're ready," she said. "Anytime."

Ellar's mouth went thin. He brought his other hand around, cupped it over Cymel's brow—and caught her as she crumpled, unconscious. He carried her to Corysiam and got her settled over the woman's shoulder, then stepped back.

Corysiam stretched out a hand. "Come, Gryf. We work it as before. You know how it goes."

They landed on grass again, field grass with horses grazing a short distance away and rows of apple trees to the east of them. The familiar yellow sun was hanging just above the peaks over Talgryf's right shoulder and the shadows were long on the grass. The light breeze that ruffled his hair and slid up under his shirt had a nip in it that was colder than he was used to but everything else was *right*. It was like a weight rolling off his shoulders.

Corysiam let go of Talgryf's belt and laid Cymel on the grass. As she straightened up, a tall man came from the trees, long staff in one hand and a glass in the other; cider from the color. He smiled at her and handed her the cider. "Heavy work, Scribe."

"And not done yet. Thanks, Taym." She drained the glass and handed it back. "Gryf, this is Watcher Taymlo. Do what he tells you." Her eyes got a distant look in them, then she stepped into nothing.

"She said—"

"Scribe Corysiam."

Talgryf squinted up at him, then shrugged. "Scribe Corysiam said Laz, Lyanz I mean, he's here."

"Yes. He's at the Staffyl with the other boys training in the Vale. He wanted to be here to meet you, but too many people have tried to kill him and we didn't want to take chances."

"Oh. But—"

"We thought it best." Hearing the finality in the man's voice, Talgryf decided not to push things further. Taymlo went to his knees beside Cymel, flattened one hand and drew it slowly along her body, leaving a full span between his palm and her. The hand slowed, almost stopped, over her heart, then over her groin, but he didn't say anything.

"She . . . Mela, she's all right?"

"Hmm? Oh. She'll do." Taymlo stood, then bent to brush off his knees. "How long were you on Iomard?"

Taymlo's tone was casual and he seemed more intent on removing bits of dried grass from his brown robe, but Talgryf had been reading body-speak before he knew his letters and he knew the answer was more important than it seemed. He turned and twisted the question, trying to see how knowing that would matter. He couldn't and he was going to have to live here a while, so he couldn't just refuse to answer.

"Less than a day. Why?"

"There seems to be some sort of disturbance. The Scribe is having difficulty breaking free of it to bring Ellar across. Ah. She comes."

A moment later Corysiam was with them, sagging to her knees under Ellar's weight. Even after he moved away from her, she stayed where she was, shuddering and gasping. "That . . . was a . . . hard one," she managed after a moment. "Taym, I . . . have to get . . . back there. Lend . . . me . . . your . . . staff."

"You wouldn't be much use if you kill yourself."

"On the . . . contrary, Taym." She managed a grin as she used the staff to lever herself onto her feet. "Fori could use my corpse to embarrass the inquisitors till they expired from the heat of their blushes. Unfortunately, I think I'm going to survive. These back-to-back Bridges are a pain, but not really all that dangerous. I'll see you in about three days.''

She sucked in a long breath, let it trickle out again, repeated this, then, the long focus back in her eyes, she stepped and was gone.

Talgryf watched with envy and a nervous tickling on the back of his neck. When not even a tickle was left, he got slowly to his feet and looked around.

Ellar was helping Cymel to her feet. Her face was flushed and she was holding on to him as if she were dizzy, but she was mad enough to spit. He grinned. Now she knows what I felt like, my folks shoving me around like I was a sack of flour, without sense enough to know what I wanted.

He followed Taymlo and the others through trees heavy with green fruit, around the end of a thorn hedge and through a long arch that led into a paved courtyard with houses on two sides, a stable on the third side and a wall on the fourth.

Lyanz waited in the doorway of the largest house, grinning broadly as he waved to Talgryf.

Plots

By the secret calendar of the Watchers, events dating from the 26th of Pumamis, the fifth month in the 738th Glandairic Year since the last Settling.

[1]

When the Stentor called his name, Oerfel knelt before the throne where Tyrn Isel received all petitions. He bent forward, touched his brow to the floor, then lifted himself cautiously till he was sitting on his heels, blinking at the lined, sour face of the Tyrn.

If his head weren't throbbing, the pain blinding him when it peaked, Oerfel would have been enjoying this. The closer his acquaintance with the Tyrn, the more he despised the man and the more he enjoyed anything that pricked Isel's too tender skin. He'd chortled with glee when Ellar decamped.

Isel was ideal as the Tyrn everyone was learning to loathe. When the time came for Anrydd to strike for the Seat, his opposition was going to be tepid at best.

Though he personally found Ellar's poems deadly dull, Isel had taken his departure as a personal insult and sent guards out to fetch the truant poet back to face his anger. He was still picking at that scab. And now he had to contemplate losing the Secretary to the Cyngrath.

The Tyrn pinched his lower lip as he tilted his head and

listened to the murmured explanation of his Reader.

He nodded when the Reader finished, lifted his head and scowled at Oerfel. "You've done well enough at this post, why do you want to leave us?"

Oerfel cleared his throat, swallowed. His eyes fixed on the floor, his hands in the posture of petition that Isel preferred, he put a whine in his voice, not enough to call for comment but certainly enough to irritate the ears. "Sry Tyrn Isel, your kindness is boundless, but the truth of this matter is that my eyes are failing me and my body grows more feeble. The time comes all too swiftly when I can no longer produce work worthy of you, Sry Tyrn."

"And just who is going to take your place? We do not wish the recording of transactions to have any gaps."

Oerfel let his voice shake. His headache was turning his face green and the pain brought runnels of sweat coursing down his face; he could feel the drops gathering on his chin and falling to the floor. Isel was beginning to look queasy so this miserable interview should soon be finished. "There are competent men among the undersecretaries who could manage an interim appointment until the Sry Tyrn has found a candidate who suits him."

Isel listened a moment longer to the murmur at his ear, made an impatient movement with one hand, then spoke with pompous solemnity. "Let it be so. Oerfel Hawlson, your term of office will end at the fifth day of Foolsreign. Let it be said that We are satisfied with your work and saddened by the loss of so faithful a servant. May Dyf Tanew bring healing to your body and ease to your eyes."

Oerfel touched the floor again with his brow, then got heavily to his feet and shuffled out. He still had the last four days of Pumamis and of Foolsreign to get through, but at least he had an excuse for passing the greater part of the work to Undersecretary Pontidd and malingering happily while he tended to work far more important than the blatherings of the Cyngrath.

*   *   *

In his office, he set out the documents he had prepared, collected the scry mirrors, packed them carefully into a leather bag with his personal ink and pen set. Then he sent for Pontidd.

The undersecretary was a stout man with black hair that curled untidily about a large bald spot. He looked guileless and a little stupid, but that was quite misleading. The man seethed with ambition and energy, and the news Oerfel was about to give him would be red meat to a starving dog.

"For reasons of health I have resigned my position as Secretary to the Cyngrath. This will become official at the end of Foolsreign by the generosity of the Tyrn. I wish you to be my surrogate for those times when I am unable to appear." He separated one of the parchment sheets and pushed it across the worktable. "This gives you the authority to act in my name when my health prevents me from attending the Cyngrath sessions. This"—he laid a second sheet on the first—"gives you the authority to appoint and dismiss Scribes." He added the last sheet to the pile. "This gives you the authority to disburse the sums needed for expenses and salaries. You will have free access to this office and the scriptorium, and to all of the Cyngrath records. When I am not present in the office, the keys will be kept in the central drawer of the worktable. Do you have any questions?"

Pontidd's tongue flickered between his lips. He'd gone a bit pale and kept his eyes lowered in the hope that Oerfel couldn't read the hunger in them. "This is very generous, Ryn Oerfel. I don't know what to say."

Oerfel stood, slipped the strap of the leather bag over his shoulder. "The agenda for the next four days is here." He touched a sheet of paper. "I leave it in your hands with confidence you will see that things will be done properly. I will be in Tyst, but I am not leaving directions where I can be found. If anything unusual arises, you will have to handle it yourself."

*   *   *

His old set of rooms in the bothrin were dusty and shabby, with none of the elegance and comfort of his quarters in the Cyngrath tower, but after his first sneezes as he unlocked the door and walked in, he felt tension flowing out of him. His head still ached but the aura was gone and so was the queasy feeling in his stomach.

He yawned and went into the bedroom. He tore off the dusty coverlet, dropped it onto the floor, dropped his black Secretary's robe on top of it, then stretched out on the quilt and closed his eyes.

When he woke, the light coming through the dusty, cobwebbed window was the pale gray of early dusk. He was hungry. He hadn't been hungry for months. He hunted out the basket he'd used when he lived here before, dressed himself in his old clothes and went out to find barrow men who sold food he could eat—skewered lumps of beef and onions cooked in oil so hot it seared the surfaces so there was only the hard brown crust and a delicate interior free from grease; slices from sweet/tart fruit flans; pickled vegetables wrapped in corn shucks. So different from the rich foods at the Tyrn's table.

He came back half an hour later with the basket filled and his hunger rampant.

He ate, sitting by the window of his bookroom, looking down into the Temple's back court where the vergers lived with their families in semidetached houses with minute kitchen gardens and communal pens for their livestock. The court was filled with children playing noisy ball games and hop-and-jump in the last light of the day. On another day he would have been irritated by the distraction, but today he found them part of the music of the city, a music he'd missed more than he'd known in the tightly controlled precincts of Carcalon.

He finished his meal as the red of the sunset reflected off the silver tiles on the walls of the Temple towers. The noise in the court faded away as mothers called their children to supper and bed. A soft breeze wandered through the window, touched his face and stirred his thin hair, stirred the dust around him.

Leaving the neat pile of discards in the basket, he pushed back his chair and fetched his cleaning tools. Sweeping and dusting the rooms, he took pleasure in the humble job and was amused at himself for his sentimentality. Soon enough he would miss the serving maids of the Grath tower and grow annoyed at the intrusion of these daily tasks, but for the moment he might as well enjoy his necessities.

Moonlight splashed through the bookroom window, shimmered on the silver tiles of the towers, made the surface of his scry mirror gleam like still water. For years he'd avoided handling Pneuma in these rooms, but the time was coming soon enough when his anonymity would be broken and, in any case, scrying was difficult to smell out. He laid the mirror on the table where he'd eaten, whispered the charm, and saw Anrydd kneeling on a hillside, looking down at an iron smelter that was a confusion of impenetrable shadow, torch-lit fumes and pump lanterns whose wicks gave off a blindingly brilliant white light.

[2]

The leafy branches of the lightning-struck tree drooping around him, concealing him from anyone who happened to look his way, Anrydd scanned the settlement in the vale below him. He'd located the usual guards, standing watch in the usual places, but there was a fugitive movement among the smelter structures—a shadow that bulged for half a breath from the side of a shed or the edge of a girder and retreated before he could put a shape to it.

With the patience that three earlier raids had drilled into him, he continued to watch. If that was a guard, sooner or later he'd be careless for a moment, and a moment was all it would take. There was another trick he could try, something gan Goolad had taught him. He turned away from the structures below, focused his eyes on the mountainside beyond, then moved his head around very slowly so he was watching from the corner of his eye.

Near the center of the smelter area the shadow bulged again. A head. Satisfied, he started to draw back, then stilled—a second bulge appeared, just a flicker of shadow, but he knew there were two roving guards down there, not one. And he also knew where they met. That was information enough to neutralize them.

He dropped to his belly and wriggled away from the tree, moving as soundlessly as he could, careful to keep brush and other barriers between himself and the vale.

The fifteen men Anrydd had left of the score who'd ridden away with him from Broony Brennin were in a shallow valley higher on the mountainside, some hunkering about a small fire concealed by a pile of boulders, others dozing, heads on their saddles. Anrydd brought the sentries with him as he strode into the camp.

He stood by the fire, grinned at them. "Not expecting visitors tonight, they aren't. Wyst, that was one copping good idea, skipping north like this. Couple valleys down the way, I'd wager there's a small army getting ready to slaughter a bunch of shadows." He watched the firelight glint on teeth bared by fierce grins and was satisfied. Time to get serious now. "Wyst, you make like a shadow not so bad yourself. I want you with me. We've got a pair of rovers we're going to have to take out before we hit the guard posts. Corl, you and Geff, you'll start off first. Work your way to the west end of the valley. The stable's there, next to the tram rails, got a guard watching it. Plenty of cover and he's leaning against the corral fence; looks like he's just about half-asleep. Take him out, but wait till you hear the horn before you start killing the mules. That'll mean we've taken out the guards and we're ready to start burning. Taran, you and . . ."

[3]

Oerfel smiled as he watched this ceremony, for a ceremony it was, meant to bind his followers to Anrydd. He was satisfied with what he saw. Despite all too many flaws, the boy was a quick learner and good at putting on a hero's face. Unlike the young men in Anrydd's band, he could look behind that face and see the cool calculation that dictated every move and nearly every word. He approved of that also. A counterfeit passion was a better tool than a real fury that rushed bull-headed into trouble.

Though the figures in the mirror were tiny, barely larger than ants, their body-speak was eloquent. They'd been blooded and survived, knew what they were doing and did it with a quiet competence that Oerfel found impressive. If Anrydd could extend that sense of loyalty and enthusiasm to a larger army, Isel's forces would melt like snowflakes on a griddle.

Two men stayed to guard the horses while the rest of the band slipped into the vale to attack the smelter.

Roving guards taken out. No alarm.

Stable guard down. No alarm.

Other guards down. No alarm till the horn blew and the burning started.

Mules dead, sounds of screaming mules, sounds of trampling as the beasts tried to escape the crossbow bolts and saber cuts.

Stable fired.

Shouts, confusion, workers rushing from the smelter. Cut down. Fires set along the walls of the structures. Torches thrown onto the thatched roofs of the cottages where the workers lived. Screams of children. Women trying to get them out of the burning houses. Men roused from sleep trying to find someone to fight. No one to organize. More confusion.

Anrydd's band slipped away, unseen and unharmed. They reached the horse herd, mounted and rode for the stream Wyst had scouted for them; riding in water, then over granite, dragging brush behind them, they wiped away their backtrail—with more help than they realized. Oerfel breathed a narrow wind along behind them and erased those signs they left despite their care. Less than a watch later, they were far to the south, heading for one of the way stations gan Goolad had set up to provision them.

*   *   *

Oerfel yawned and tapped away the scene, calling up the Vale and the Hero to replace it. The last few times he'd accessed the Vale, he'd been both disappointed and bored by what he'd observed. If that happened again, it was probably time to move to the next stage of his plan.

"Stay!"

Lyanz froze, his body extended in the lunge that was meant to be the penultimate move of this freemix form string.

Amhar grinned at him. "Repeat that string, but this time, don't move your feet."

He groaned. "Not again."

Amhar danced close, ruffled his hair with the tips of her fingers and leaped back before he could react. "Smooth and exact, Li'l Laz. No feet all the way."

Late afternoon sunlight poured through the line of tall windows that marched along the side wall of the gym, pale light alive with gilded dust motes. Those golden motes clustered along the outlines of teacher and student, shimmering halos that gave the handsome young bodies a glory that lifted them above the merely mortal. Cymel rubbed at her eyes and looked briefly away; though the scene troubled her, she couldn't leave it. Worse than a sore tooth, watching was painful, not watching was impossible.

Since Corysiam had Bridged her across from Iomard, each day was more and more something to be endured. Her skin burned as if it were being brushed by nettles and the air she breathed tasted hot and lifeless. Silent and unseen, she huddled in a darkly shadowed corner of the huge bare room and watched the lesson proceed for several minutes longer, then rose to her feet and crept from the gym, more disturbed by the growing intimacy between Lyanz and Amhar than by her own physical discomfort.

She winced at a burst of laughter startled out of Lyanz; it followed her out the door, a warm joyous sound that only served to emphasize her own loneliness. Even her father was too busy with the other Watchers to have much time for her and no one else cared what she was doing.

Oerfel let the mirror follow Cymel a while longer, savoring the spectacle of her pain. It was payback for all the trouble she had caused him. Inadequate payback, but still satisfying.

When he reset the mirror to the inside of the gym, the lesson had turned to an increasingly intense flirtation, a circumstance no doubt interesting to the pair involved, but useless to Oerfel. Anrydd already had plenty of experience in the arts of seduction and far too little restraint when it came to acquiring more.

Oerfel grimaced. Enough, he thought. Yes, it's certainly time to move on. Go after the Hero and rid myself of these pestilential Watchers as a bit of gilding on the cake.

The Watchers were the only ones who could break through his protection and spot Anrydd as the instigator of these raids, but they wouldn't interfere. They had no liking for Isel and thus good reason for their silence.

The new Tyrn loathed Cyfareth University and was making tentative moves to shut it down. Now that was something that should be encouraged. Oerfel leaned back in the chair, enjoying the images that presented themselves.

Watchers dispersed, their power diminished by distance so he could pick them off one by one.

Watchers forced to earn food and shelter by the work of their hands. Or bowing their heads to the whims of Broons and merchants.

The great Repository in the hands of the Tyrn, which effectively put it in his hands.

Oh, it was a pleasant dream. And more than dream. It could happen. With careful planning and a bit of nudging here and there. And if it came to that, Anrydd could continue what Isel began.

Oerfel yawned and got to his feet. There was a great deal more to do, but none of it really urgent. A good night's sleep, a day spent wandering about Tyst, reacquainting himself with the feel of the place, then tomorrow night the most delicate work would begin. Tomorrow night he meant to plant messages with the Mages Mahara and Hudoleth, the first cautious step that would lead to a conference with them.

The Hero had to die and he knew with painful certainty that he couldn't manage that without some powerful help.

[4]

Oerfel clicked his tongue, his nose twitching with disgust as he swept rat droppings from the corners of his workroom in the crypts under the Temple. He'd sealed the place, but somehow rats got in past the tightest bindings he could weave. With a vigorous thrust of the broom, he sent the droppings flying out the door into the dusty passageway outside.

He closed the door, dropped the twin bars into their hooks and ran his thumb about the cracks between door and jamb to make sure no light seeped out. Prowlers were unlikely on the third level below the Temple, but he wasn't about to take any chances. What he meant to do before dawn was dangerous enough without attracting unwanted attention from snoops.

When he was ready, he washed his hands, arms and face carefully, patted them dry then pulled on a long narrow robe of unbleached twill. He settled himself on a backless chair in front of one of the larger mirrors he'd brought from Chusinkayan.

He contemplated his own reflection for a while. He was thin and pale, all his colors faded, his features undistinguished, a shadow man. This gave him considerable satisfaction. Hudoleth was a beautiful woman who'd cultivated that beauty for the power it gave her. Mahara had a powerful physical presence, sensual, charismatic, handsome. Both would consider Oerfel too feeble to be a threat. And Oerfel intended to compound that judgment by a recitation of his several failures to kill the Hero. The True Hero. It would be easy enough to convince them of that. They just had to look at the boy.

He sang softly to the mirror and watched as mist blew across the surface as Pneuma fed sparingly into the delicate indirect connection with the Hero that he'd laid out after much thought, one the Watchers who protected the boy would neither sense nor trace. It took a long time to establish itself, but he waited patiently for the image to clear.

And when it did, his hand jerked and he swore. That girl again. That miserable interfering little bitch.

Lyanz was talking and laughing with a smaller, dark boy, a vaguely familiar mix that Oerfel had seen on the streets of Tyst, part of the refuse from the depths of the bothrin. Ellar's daughter was sitting cross-legged on a couch, listening to them. She looked tired, but contented.

Lyanz was nearly eighteen, almost the same age as Anrydd. Both were handsome youths, golden lads to compel the eye, yet if you stood them together, Anrydd would be a coarser, paler imitation, fool's gold as set against pure gold.

The Hero's beauty had an oddly asexual quality to it as if he were more spirit than flesh—a mistaken impression, Oerfel knew. Since the arrival in the Vale of Ellar's daughter, miserable interfering child that she was, Lyanz's hostility had dissolved entirely; indeed, for the past several months he and Amhar had been involved in a circling dance of passion, working closer and closer to consummation.

He focused the mirror more tightly on the Hero. When he saw the image he wanted, he clicked his tongue and froze it. A short chant later and it was held in potentiality, waiting for him to recall it when the time was right. He composed a brief message to Hudoleth, attached it to the image. Then he banished the scene at the Vale.

He was even more cautious as he reset the mirror to search for Hudoleth. She was subtle and dangerous. Mahara thought he could stand against her and finally crush her, but Mahara was something of a fool, a man of impulse rather than thought.

The image gradually cleared.

The viewpoint was near the floor in Hudoleth's workroom. She seldom looked down, even when she was following about the Semmer girl who cleaned for her to make sure that the girl didn't touch things she wasn't supposed to. The room had no windows, only mirrors and birds in silver cages. In daylight, the mirrors caught light from the outside brought in by mirrored shafts and illuminated the room with a knife-edged brilliance that sent shudders through Oerfel's body. Now, a pair of glass and silver lamps were burning.

With the difference in time between Nyddys and Lake Mizukor amounting to more than two watches, it must be near dawn where Hudoleth was. She ordinarily arose about noon, but she was seated at her worktable with half a dozen small, neat packages of dead and discarded birds piled near her elbow. Her eyes were closed, her face slack, lines of strain on her ordinarily perfect skin making her look nearer her true age, a powerful testimony of how much power she was expending.

We're all working like oxen, Oerfel thought. He frowned. I need to mark that down. The one with the most strength in reserve will win this match. If I believed in gods the way the common folk do, I'd think they were making a joke out of us. All our learning, and it's the body in the end.

He let a thread of Pneuma flow along the scrypath and coil like an earthworm on the wall. Then he waited, watching Hudoleth intently.

A muscle twitched beside her mouth, but her eyes remained closed and the tense concentration in her body did not change.

Moving with delicate deliberation, keeping Hudoleth in the corner of his eye, he sent the Pneuma worm crawling up the wall toward one of the mirrors.

When the tip of the worm touched the edge of the mirror, he waited again.

Again, no reaction.

Hudoleth was extended to her limits. He could guess what that was—feeding commands into the dream states of the Emperor and her commanders in the field, drawing data from her web of spies, most of whom had no idea what was happening to them, stowing information from them for later consideration, watching Mahara to gauge his progress toward the thing they both wanted. In other words tugging and tuning the immense web of her overt and covert war against Mahara.

He sent the worm onto the mirror and watched it spread

over and melt into the glass, then he chanted softly, brought the image of the Hero and his message to Hudoleth from the nonbeing of potential into actuality and laid that actuality into the mirror.

The instant Hudoleth's mirror filled, he blanked his own. Shaking with exhaustion, his chest heaving as he panted, he took a handkerchief from his sleeve, patted at his streaming face.

When he had his breath back, he got to his feet and circled the room, testing the wards, making sure there were no weak spots in the weaving of his spells. He poured water in a basin, splashed it onto his face. The coolness washed away some of his fatigue. He moved along the bench to the plate with its pile of small sandwiches made with meat paste and diced pickles. He poured a glass of water from the ewer, then took both to his seat in front of the mirror. He ate slowly, methodically, sipping water from the glass to wash the paste down. His stomach tolerated food better if he kept it well moistened.

When he was finished, he carried the plate to the workbench, washed and dried his face and hands with the same methodical care, then went back to contemplating the mirror. He repeated the steps he'd taken for Hudoleth's message, attached the message for Mahara to the new image of the Hero and placed it into the being-nonbeing potentiality. Then he turned the mirror to an overview of the Kale army.

Tilkos was still in the clutches of night, being much closer to Nyddys than Chusinkayan.

The army encircled the walled city Kar Markaz, the administrative center of Tilkos and, except for a few raider bands that worried at the supply routes, the last fragment still resisting the Third Prince's march across the land. That march had been interesting to watch, but Oerfel hadn't seen much that he found useful. Nyddys and the Ifordyar who lived here were simply too different.

When he eased the point of view into Mahara's tent, he was startled to see the Mage awake, bending over one of his scry bowls, speaking into the thin layer of water.

". . . would not listen to me, and rightly so. Nor are they willing to move without your explicit approval. Is there any chance you could return soon?"

Cautiously Oerfel slid the point of view up the wall of the tent and into the deep shadow gathered under the peak. When he looked down he saw the shadowed face of the Third Prince floating on the surface of the water. He formed a receptor and picked up the Prince's words, spoken in a voice like a gnat whining.

"Not for another month at least. The Mourning Month for my father closes with the Ceremony of the Burial three days from now, but after that there's the Elevation of the First Prince to the Year of First Trial, which means another round of Ritual. To say truth, Mahara, I don't dare be absent. You speak of the army beginning to fall apart. Rueth's hot Breath, my base here has turned spongy as sodden paperplant. I've spent every spare moment cutting out deadwood and planting backbone in the rest."

Oerfel raised his brows. The march with the army must have brought a bond between these two—or Mahara was a more subtle operator than he looked. This candid a speech from a Prince raised in the swirl of conspiracy at Aile Kuvvet was at the least unexpected.

"Hm. Write your orders for the attack and give them to a courier you trust, put him on board a windcutter. I'll blast open the Parma Bight so he can land at the burned fort and come inland from there. He'll save at least two weeks' travel time that way. Hm. A hard breath against those walls will topple them. The military governor should be in place by the time you return."

"Good. And I will return. I don't relish a whole year of watching everything I eat and drink, even the air I breathe. Be making plans to march into Nikawaid." There was a chuckle from the water, a high, harsh grating like a corpse beetle's nightcall. "I can count on my brothers' continued support. They have not forgot their hope that a lance or a crossbow bolt will take care of their problem for them."

"Rueth spread his wings for you, My Prince. I will watch and wait."

"As will we all, my friend."

The moment the water cleared of the Prince's image, Oerfel brought into being the Hero's image/message, dropped it into the bowl and got out of there fast.

He stiffened the wards about his workroom, made sure the mirrors were insulated from the outside, then pulled the damp handkerchief from his sleeve and once again patted the sweat streaming down his face. His work for this night was done; he'd planned and protected himself against every contingency he could imagine. That didn't make him safe. Things not thought of always happened and always threatened to trip up the most careful of planners. Nonetheless, he was satisfied for the moment.

He cleaned up the workroom, sealed it behind him and went home to a long contented sleep.

[5]

Two mirrors were angled so that each could reflect the other. A single candle on a black iron stand burned beside the backless chair where Oerfel sat at the fourth point of the diamond, his bare feet in the thick dust that covered the stone floor, his mouth curled in a thin blue smile as he watched Mahara and Hudoleth contemplate each other.

Rash, impatient Mahara was the first to speak. "Why this boy and none of the others? They survived, didn't they?"

Oerfel set his hands on his knees and leaned forward slightly to put more force behind his words. "Why did they survive? Luck? Getting past you when you were occupied with others? This boy not only sailed in and out of Kale right under your nose, Mahara, he survived five separate direct attacks. Though I may not have the fullness of power that flows through your hands, O Mage, and though I am hampered by the presence of so many Watchers on this island, I am not an impotent fool. You know of the Companions of the Hero?"

"You did not mention the Companions." Hudoleth's

creamy voice was cold water on the growing heat. "Elaborate, please."

Oerfel sat blinking as he pushed aside the anger Mahara had wakened in him. After a moment, he said, "According to the fragments I have assembled, the Hero draws to himself a band of five or six Companions who protect him while he is in training and again while he searches for the Empty Place. This Myndyar boy Lyanz has acquired at least four such people. First, Cymel, a Watcher's daughter, a mix of Siofray and Ifordyar blood, a young girl with a great deal of raw power and almost no training. Second, the Siofray Amhar, an apprentice Scribe from Iomard, a Walker but not a Bridge. Third, the Siofray Corysiam, the oldest of the lot, a Scribe and a Bridge. Fourth, Talgryf, a mix from the streets of Tyst, part Ifordyar, part Rhudyar, a thief of some skill, but un-Sighted as far as I can determine. The Hero will probably acquire one more Companion, perhaps one of the Watchers, perhaps someone new." Oerfel cleared his throat. "I should add two things. First, three other boys are in training at the Vale of Caeffordian. These have no followers nor can I sense anything unusual about them. I ask you, Hudoleth, has there been any ingathering of such Companions at the Kunhatakin? Have any of the boys who survived your sweeps shown any such draw toward outsiders? Second, two years ago, in the course of my day life here in Tyst, I met that boy. He's empty, a vessel waiting to be filled. I knew what he was the moment I saw him."

Hudoleth nodded slowly. "Those are good points. I believe you are not mistaken. This Myndyar Lyanz is the Hero. I have a question, though. He is essentially in your hands. Why call on us? You must understand, to do that is to lose him. I will not share."

Mahara grunted. "I agree. He's it. Why did you call on us?"

"Because there are nine Scholar/Watchers in that Vale, more than a dozen transplanted Watchers with their own agendas and two Siofray Scribes, plus that witch girl with her unpredictable gift. I can't reach him without help." He shrugged. "If I could, would I be talking to you now?"

Hudoleth smiled. "You've let him be for two years. Why now?"

Mahara moved impatiently. "Why not just wait till he comes out and hit him then?"

Oerfel sighed. "Haven't I just told you how I tried to get him before? Five times? Failed every time? Why now is this. The Settling will be complete by next summer at the latest so the Hero will be leaving the Vale soon. Coming into a world of increasing chaos where it will be very difficult to trace him. Remember what I said about his emptiness. Once I knew about him, I could scry him, but he's close to invisible to my Sight if I'm not standing right in front of him. And I don't know what other protections he will have if he leaves according to his schedule. What I want to do, need to do, is get to him before he comes into his full being. While he's standing still, in one specific place."

Mahara's image hooked a stool across to where he was standing and settled onto it, the petulance and impatience gone from him. "How do you figure to get us working together, since I surely don't trust either of you and am not about to lower my defenses for any kind of Watcher meld."

"I have considered that, O Mahara. I have worked out a method of attack wherein none has to trust the other." Oerfel took a sheaf of papers from his sleeve, spread them open across his thighs. "Hudoleth, you and Mahara can guard yourselves yet work together to break through the shield the Watchers will close about the Vale the moment they have the first intimations of the coming action. Strike at the shield as individuals, but work out the timing so that each blow comes just slightly after the last one, giving the Watchers no chance to rest. The vibration you induce in the Pneuma wall will shatter it even faster than a single assault of equal force. I will provide fifty men for the strike force and will shield them from attack. They will be mountain reivers of disgusting habits but an admirable capacity for slaughter. Once the reivers are through the shield, you can let them kill the boy or protect him as you choose. I will not interfere with that." He gave them a sour smile. "Principally because I desire to remain alive. And I want the Watchers dead. All of them."

Hudoleth returned his smile. "And because you can't do that yourself, you're using us as your weapon."

"Of course. It's logical, is it not? It's a good bargain that gives us all what we want."

"Clever man." Mahara grinned at him. It was like looking into the face of a hungry wolf. "When shall we do this thing?"

"The next night of the Dark Moon. I need the time to assemble the band of reivers. You perhaps need the time to arrange your own affairs. Let us make this a formal pact before we go our ways. Is it a bargain, then?"

Hudoleth nodded. "I agree to attack the shield of the Watchers and take the Hero from the Vale alive, for we need him to discover the exact location of the Empty Place. I make no concession as to which of us will have possession of the boy."

Mahara got to his feet. "And so do I agree—thus far: I will attack the shield of the Watchers and take the Hero from the Vale alive. I make no concession as to which of us will have possession of the boy."

Oerfel rose also. "I will do as I have said, provide the butchers and shield them from attack. I will not contest possession of the Hero nor will I interfere with you while you are nonmaterially present on Nyddys. I will do what I can to prevent you from returning." He dropped the papers on the floor and bowed. When he straightened, he said, "Thus let it be."

The images in the mirrors blinked out. He yawned, moved his shoulders to work out the small ache that sat between his shoulder blades. Then he got busy purging the mirrors of all connection with the outside. Finally he moved over to the door, winced at the creak of the ancient hinges as he shoved it open.

He carried the mirrors up a flight of stairs and down the

corridor to his workroom, wiped them down, covered them with clean twill and put them away in one of the cupboards that lined the walls. He changed his clothes, buckled on his sandals, poured himself a glass of distilled water and stood beside his workbench sipping at it till the dust was cleared from his throat and his nervous thirst was gone.

He was a cautious man, always seeking a way of throwing confusion about who and where he was. There was a chance that either Hudoleth or Mahara could trace the location of his mirrors. Not much of a chance, but he'd done what he could to avoid even that thread of danger.

Later, when he lay down to sleep in his room set, he was smiling. No more indirection, no more slips. This time **it** had to work.

16

Breith's Leap

By the calendar of the Domains of Iomard, events dating from the 5th day of Ekhtos, the eighth month in the Iomardi year 6535, the 722nd year since the last Corruption.

[1]

As Breith got to his knees, he swayed and grabbed at the nearest tree. A moment later he was bent over, clutching at that tree's roots, emptying his stomach on the grass. When there was nothing left to come up, he crawled to the stream and put his face in the cold water until the world steadied around him.

Once again he balanced on the balls of his feet and braced himself against the trunk; he was disturbed by how shaky his arms felt and how tired this small effort made him, but his head needed attention so he sucked in a breath and held it as he probed for a wound.

He found the lump in less than a heartbeat. The hair over it was matted and tangled in a thick blood clot and even the brush of his fingertips drew a grunt of pain, but he kept working at it until he was fairly sure the bone beneath the skin wasn't broken. He dropped his hands into his lap and sat hunched over and shivering.

"Scurds," he muttered. "Not slavers. They took my stuff."

He thought about the discarded clothing. "Scurd. Just one. One miserable stinking scurd . . . no . . . not a scurd, a scrash . . . roadman . . . not good enough to be a scurd . . . clothes held together with scum and fleas . . . sneaked up on me and I just kept sleeping like baby in its crib . . . took my stuff!"

He groaned, then stretched out again on the bank of the tiny stream and began cleaning the wound of blood and the dirt and leaf fragments matted into it.

As the sun climbed higher and the day warmed up, Breith began to feel better. Once he'd got the wound clean, with a Pneuma patch to keep it that way, the pain settled to a dull throbbing that he could ignore if he worked at it.

"Time I got busy," he told himself. "Scande, I'm hungry, but I better see what I can do about clothes first. Either I grow fur, or I clean up the luffa the scrash left behind."

Holding the filthy, tattered shirt with the tips of his fingers, he shook it and tossed it on the grass. He gathered a great blob of Pneuma and dropped it on the shirt, saturating the cloth, then he rolled the Pneuma forward, picking up the stains and body soil, driving the fleas ahead of the roll. When he was finished, he kneaded the Pneuma into a lumpy ball, tossed it in the air and set it on fire.

The shirt was little more than a collection of threads, but at least they were clean threads.

He repeated the process with the trousers, then got dressed, breathing a sigh of relief as he did so. When he was running around naked, he didn't feel like a proper Siofray.

Watercress from the stream and a double handful of the tiny fish that swam there cooked over a fire of twigs until they were crisp took away the worst of his hunger pains. He thought about moving on, but he was so tired and shaky that he discarded that idea almost as soon as it occurred to him. He managed to walk a circle round the clump of thorn trees and the pile of boulders, setting up warn wards, then he curled up on the grass and went to sleep.

[2]

Radayam spread Pneuma wings and spiraled upward, feeling the damp, cold northern air trying to close around her and drag her down. The great pinions flexed and drove her up and up till she reached an eddying air current slow enough to let her circle above her army.

The Army of Purification crawled across the land, ridos and bantars in their fighting bands, Seers in an amorphous mass, the darocs marching by Village. In the rear, the supply wagons rumbled along, the support cadres walking beside them—healwitches, smiths, carpenters, fletchers, cooks, horsehandlers, all the myriad skills that kept an army healthy and moving. Radayam had to fight to keep down the pride she felt in what she saw. It had taken three years, intensive planning, picking up and reworking thousands of broken threads, and endless persuasion; the whole enterprise fell apart in her hands over and over again, yet she'd kept on, sustained by her vision and the Prophet's Peace that renewed her faith and her strength each time she was so drained she couldn't even contemplate going on.

"Not mine but thine, O All-Mother," she chanted under her breath. "Thy glory, Thy will, Thy promise."

The ground was broken and difficult so the progress of the Army of Purification was slow, and the dark, secret Forest of the North with its hidden evils pressed in on the left side, forcing the army to lengthen and narrow itself so it could pass between the Forest and the River Siamsa. It was almost time to cross the river, merge with the straggling forces from Tiolan and join those of Fuascala marching south.

From this height she could see the Ward Dome the Riverine Seers had raised above Soriseis; it festered in the sunlight like a boil on a buttock. Despite this and despite the warnings they must have heard from their leaders, on Lake Piorrog dozens of the shell divers were out, their red sails like leaves scudding across the dark water. In their greed and their drive for profit, the Soriseins were ignoring the threat that advanced on them.

Cooperating in their own downfall. Radayam smiled with satisfaction.

But she had better reason than gloating to lift herself so high, so she left the glide and climbed into a faster current, then powered herself toward the river.

The Siamsa ran between deep earthen walls and made few bends as it marked the boundary between the broken ground claimed by Eadro to the west and by Tiolan to the east. Radayam flew over scattered patches of tilled ground farmed by runaways who gave their allegiance to Citystate Soriseis—more evidence of how treacherously and slyly the Riverines were stealing from the Domains, not only people but land. This was Eadro land. Whether Eadro had used it or left it fallow did not matter.

She quelled her anger. The theft would be punished in good time; now she had to find the proper place for the Army of Purification to cross into Domain Tiolan.

[3]

A low, growling rumble and a shift in the earth beneath him roused Breith from his uneasy sleep. He groaned and sat up.

A group of scraggly nymphs who looked more like dried weeds than minor Pneuma-bred demigods crouched beside the trickle of water left in the stream bed, clutching at each other and moaning with fear. When they saw him looking at them, they shrieked and fled back to their trees.

His head was throbbing and hot. Cautiously, he dissolved the Pneuma patch and probed at the scab. It was soft and gave under his fingertips. He crawled to the streambank, lay down on the grass and spent an uncomfortable few moments pressing the pus from the wound.

By the time his fingers showed blood rather than yellow discharge, the trickle from the spring under the pile of boulders had returned to its usual strength and there was a pool of clearing water at his elbow. He scooped up a palmful, heated and clarified it, then began washing the wound. It was a slow and exhausting process, but when he finished, the infection-

heat was gone and his head felt better. He slapped on a new
Pneuma patch, then folded his arms, rested his head on them
and dozed a while longer.

His stomach growling from another inadequate meal of burned
fish and wilted watercress, he was back on the road again as
soon as he'd eaten, trying to catch the last light of the day
and get more distance between himself and Pelateras. Though
he'd lost nearly a full day of his escape time, he couldn't see
how the Lateramen could trace him. He hadn't put foot to
ground for hours and even now that he was walking, he'd
sealed his feet in Pneuma boots so he wasn't leaving scent
behind, not on the ground, anyway.

The mutes had told him over and over again how fero-
ciously the owners went after the ones who tried to escape—
chilling stories about the hidung bai, the hounds who tracked
down slaves and tore them apart while their handlers watched,
rescuing only the slave's hands and head to testify to the iden-
tity of the scraps of blood and bone.

His maps were gone, but he'd studied them carefully on the
ride; it had helped pass the time, for one thing, and kept him
awake so he didn't fall off the horse. His memory told him
that he had at least three more days' walking to reach Latera's
northern border and the next realm, a place called Hahaitsibal.
There were a few herders' crofts where he could steal food,
so he wouldn't starve, but even if he managed to sneak across
the border without being caught by the Lateramen, according
to the mutes this Hahaitsibal had a pleasing habit of hanging
escaped slaves in metal cages until they rotted and fell apart.
And Hahaitsibal's closest port city Yashta was a good two
days away from the border. And maybe there wouldn't be any
ships at Yashta heading for Saffroa. There should be, this was
the heart of the trading season, but with earthquakes and
chancy weather maybe the trader captains wouldn't want to
risk their ships on an ocean crossing.

He kept plodding along the road because he couldn't think
of anything else to do. The clout on the head and the starvation

neals had drained way most of his vigor and left behind only he stubbornness that kept his feet moving.

The earth rumbled and shifted under him several times, once strongly enough to force him to stop walking and work to keep his balance. Twice he felt a change in the light and looked ound to see jagged, snow-covered peaks rising against a western sky that was the wrong color, as the wind carried the wrong smells to him. Glandair, he thought. This must be what Corysiam was talking about. Earthquakes and floods and the membrane between the worlds wearing so thin that you can step from one world to the next without even knowing what happened.

He'd hoped to come on one of the crofts so he could steal something to fill the hole in the middle of his body, but the sea in the west was empty, the beach he caught glimpses of deserted except for birds and mudcrawlers and the wasteland that stretched to a flat horizon in the east was empty of everything but grass, brush, stone piles and tree clumps.

A while later he couldn't seem to get enough air through his nose and gulped it in through his mouth. His throat turned dry and leathery and his lips cracked. He began looking about for the tree clumps with their promise of water even if it was only a seep.

Breith plunged his whole head into the tiny rock pool, the coolness of the water sweeter than anything he could remember, then he began drinking, forcing himself to take small sips and let the water trickle down his burning throat. He stopped drinking before he wanted to, rolled onto his back and stared at the patches of blue sky visible through the tattered lace of the thorn tree leaves.

After a while, he touched the bump. It hadn't changed much, still felt like a small mountain under his fingertips, but there was no heat so no infection. And though there was some discomfort around the lump, it was a dull and distant ache. The stabbing pangs were gone.

He didn't feel hungry, but his hands shook whenever he

lifted them from the grass. And his back teeth kept clenching as if he were using them as braces to help support his spine. "I don't think I can go anymore."

As he heard the whine in his voice, revulsion brought Breith to his knees. His father had spent months in the wild country and survived it, not a puny two days. And Malart didn't have anyone he could call on to help him. Breith stared at the pool and knew that he could use it to scry his father and send a call for help. That Corysiam could lift him out of here and have him home in almost no time. "No," he whispered. " won't give up until there's no hope at all."

He got to his feet, shuffled shakily about the tree clump collecting as much dry wood as he could find. He tossed the wood down, spent the next moments bringing in small stone and setting them in a circle to keep the fire away from the grass. He broke and arranged the wood as his father had taught him and set up two forked sticks to serve as support for a spit. "All right," he said. "Now I need to get something to cook. The only tool I have is Pneuma. There'll be gorras and iora and other small lives out in that grass. No time for snares. Besides I don't need snares, I can whip a Pneuma noose about a gorra's neck, strangle it and drag it in. I'll need a knife. Maybe the Ascal Pool will help again, maybe not, but as long as I can get a point and an edge, I don't need anything fancy."

The coals of the fire were a crawling red patch in the comfortable darkness, the smell of dripping rising with their heat as good as any perfume. Breith ate slowly and chewed the gorra meat until all the juice was gone from it. The carcass was burnt in places and too raw in others but by the time he had half of it in his stomach, his trembling had stopped and his dark mood was gone.

He set down the bone he'd been chewing on and licked his fingers. "Dumb, Bré. You should have done this before. Those curst fish weren't worth the trouble to cook them. What it is I was thinking about escaping and not about surviving." He poked through the bits and pieces of gorra left, picked up rib section and began stripping the tender meat from between the bones. "I keep taking this long"—he swallowed, gnawed at the next rib—"to figure out what to do next"—he broke a bone free and sucked the marrow from it—"I'm going to get myself killed. Or worse."

Comfortably replete for the first time since he left Pelateras, Breith wrapped the offal and the bones into the skin of the gorra, carried the bundle to the edge of the tree clump and flung it into the darkness for the local scavengers to fight over. Then he went back to the fire, doused the coals with water from the pool and dug out the roots that had been roasting there while he cooked and ate the gorra.

He broke them open, left them to cool enough to handle while he washed away the grease from the meat.

As he dabbled his fingers in the trickle that led from the pool and wiped them on the grass, he heard an odd sound—a deep throbbing, soft and distant, but with a musical quality that was almost like singing, bass notes climbing to alto, dropping again.

"Hidung bai!"

All his plans and his new sense of competence vanished in the panic that sent him running blindly through the night. All he could think of was get away get away get away. . . .

His feet splatted on the grass; he kept from tripping and falling but that was only luck, not any intent on his part.

Away. Get away.

He stumbled into the road and fled along it because it was the best footing.

The sound was louder, closer. He could hear the individual voices of the hounds.

Away. Get away.

Breath burned in his throat, his heart pounded so loudly he could hear it over the belling of the hounds.

Away.

The night changed. The air changed. The ground dropped under him and he went rolling until he crashed into the trunk of a tree.

Breith scrambled to his feet, using the trunk to pull himself up.

The hounds were silent.

He was standing on a mountainside beside a stream, close enough to feel the drops as the water crashed into boulders in its bed. He rubbed his hand against the trunk. It was rough and fibrous, not the smooth bark of the thorn trees. He looked up. There was a moon but it was only a thin crescent, not the full moon he'd seen only a moment before.

Glandair.

Somehow he'd crossed to Glandair.

And he knew that stream. It was Cymel's stream. If he followed it down, he'd find the farmhouse. Maybe even Cymel home for a visit.

"Pneuma Luck," he breathed. "I'll never doubt you again."

[4]

With her Seers around her and two ridos standing at her side, Radayam seated herself in her armchair and waited for the two Scribes who were walking from Soriseis under a white truce flag.

They came to a halt the required six paces from her, but when one of them prepared to speak, Radayam stopped her with a lifted hand. "I speak only to the Pure," she said. "Seer Shoneyn, if you will?"

Whispering the test spell, Shoneyn moved gracefully toward the leftward of the Scribes, her beauty warm and golden in the thin northern sunlight. "If you will permit . . ." she said and laid her hand on the Scribe's arm. "O Prophet Blessed, this one is daroc without mix."

She moved round behind them, laid her hand on the other's arm, but said nothing this time until she was back beside Radayam. "The second is tainted with foreign blood. She is not Pure."

Radayam smiled, a tight quick lift of her lips. She spoke to the daroc who took the name of Scribe. "I have neither need nor wish to hear what you have to say, daroc. What I do is blessed by the Prophet and that is all I require. Carry this message to the woman in charge whatever it is you call her. Soriseis will cease to exist before the rise of the half-moon. The city will be burned and those who live within her walls will be sifted, the daroc born returned to their proper roles in the Domains, the tainted destroyed. This will happen and nothing you can do will stop it. If you care to save lives and suffering you will surrender to the Army of Purification. If you refuse and resist us, we will overcome that resistance."

Radayam folded her hands and ignored the Scribe's protest. To the ridos beside her, she said, "Do what you must."

One of the ridos caught hold of the daroc Scribe by the arms and simply held her. The second rido approached the tainted Scribe and with a smooth, powerful lunge, drove his sword through her heart.

He retrieved the sword and walked back to stand beside Radayam, polishing away the blood with a bit of sueded leather.

"You broke truce." The daroc's voice was filled with indignation and fear.

"I honor only the Pure," Radayam said. "You don't make truce with beasts of the field. I release you now because you have a message to carry into Soriseis. When we take the city, you will be sent to your proper place in one of the daroc Villages of the Domains. Go now. If you linger, you will be whipped first then sent back."

Radayam watched the Scribe vanish through the gate. Then she rose to her feet. "I see no purpose in waiting," she said. "The Riverines have always been recalcitrant and there is no reason to expect them to change. We will sing the Be-Mindfuls and when all is prepared we will strike their dome."

Soaring on her great Pneuma pinions, Radayam amplified her voice and chanted:

> Be mindful that you are Mother to the children of the Oath.

Below her she could hear the thousandfold echo of her words, a great crying-out that lifted and sustained her.

Be mindful of daroc and Lynborn.
Be mindful of the herdgirls and the beasts they serve.
Be mindful of the words of the Prophet and the duty
*   you owe to her teachings.*
Be mindful of the state of your soul, for a clean soul
*   means a healthy and contented Domain.*
Be mindful to avoid sin and the occasions of sin.
Be mindful that justice is yours to give, that you in all
*   things submit yourself to the will of the Prophet.*

As the last echo died, Radayam came round to face Soriseis. "NOW!" she cried and stretched out her arms to receive from the Seers what she would shunt onto the recreant dome.

Below her the Seers lifted their arms.

Streams of raw Pneuma poured into her, merged into a coherent beam as great around as she was; guided by her hands the beam struck the dome and ate at it, a foam of Pneuma hissing up and dissipating into the darkening air of late afternoon.

The dome fell.

Radayam cried out a wordless triumph as she felt the deaths of the Riverine Seers who powered it. She held the beam a moment longer, swinging it across the wall first, blowing stone from stone, then across the suddenly visible structures behind the wall.

Some dissolved, some burst into fire. Soriseins in the streets watched the shell roofs explode and screamed with pain as the fragments fell on them—but those touched by the beam made no sound, simply vanished.

When the beam began to falter, Radayam opened her arms and let the Pneuma soar free. "Enough."

The Seers gave a collective sigh like the last wind after a storm and collapsed onto their knees or fell on their faces in the sudden relaxation that gave permission for them to feel their exhaustion.

She spiraled lower. "Bantar-char Osloïr," she cried. "This part is yours. Attack!"

[5]
Tired and his belly growling with hunger, Breith followed the path downward, glad he was going downhill rather than up, though part of the strangeness of Glandair was that he felt lighter here. Though the faint trace was hard to see in the dim light, the sound of the stream close by kept him from losing it and he found himself moving faster and faster, excitement rising in him. He was going to see Cymel. He could touch her, hold her hand. . . .

Hastily he pushed that line of thought away, his face hot with an uncomfortable mix of shame and pleasure.

As he burst from the trees, he saw Ellar's Watchtower, then the fence of the kitchen garden where the little gods of this world gave Cymel such a hard time.

And beyond the fence a blackened shell of a burnt-out house.

The barn and the other buildings were as they'd always been; two teams of horses stood in the stalls and the milking area showed signs that cows had been here recently. Plows had fresh dirt on them and a reaper had been left near the double doors. Someone was working this farm but he had a feeling it wasn't Ellar. He started worrying harder about Cymel and feeling guilty because he hadn't tried to talk to her once he was settled in Pelateras. Forgot old friends for new ones, he thought.

"Da!" He slapped his forehead. "I've got to let him know what happened. If he tries looking for me . . ."

He circled the house, picked his way through piles of charred brick and burnt boards to the door of the Watchtower. The east had a pink line along the hilltops. Dawn was coming and whoever was doing the work here was bound to show up anytime now. He touched the door, pulled back his hand as something bit him. More cautiously he touched the door a second time, trying to read what was protecting it.

Not any kind of ward. Wrong feel. No. A skin of Pneuma clinging to the stones and wood; if a would-be intruder didn't have the right key it would stiffen hard as steel and keep him out. If he could get it to accept him, he'd be as safe as everything else inside. The farmhands obviously left this tower strictly alone. Probably scared of it.

Ignoring the prickly burning on his palms, he flattened both hands against the door, closed his eyes and thought about Cymel and Ellar, projecting warmth and friendliness and need.

The burning grew worse, but he didn't move.

Abruptly the door swung open. He caught himself before he fell and he stumbled hastily inside. "If you'll just close up again, we'll both be happy as a squirrelmonk with a full belly."

Sense of lightness, almost laughter. There was a flavor of Ellar in the response, though nothing of Cymel.

Breith listened a moment, but the sounds coming into the tower were just general night noise. Deciding he could chance a quick exploration of the tower, he made a light sphere and sent it floating ahead of him; the few windows were barred with black iron and half lost behind the dead leaves of fire-killed vines.

In an alcove separated by a single wall from the rest of the ground floor, he found something that was not quite a kitchen, with a pump and a sink, a hearth and two cupboards. Inside one he found loaves of bread, small round cheeses, apples, chunks of dried meat, each sealed within a thin layer of Pneuma. When he unsealed the loaf, the aroma of fresh-baked bread still warm from the oven filled the alcove and flooded his mouth with saliva. Hastily unsealing a cheese, several apples and a strip of dried meat, filling a glass from the pump, he put his gleanings on a platter he found in the second cupboard, then followed the glowsphere up the stairs and through the rest of the tower.

When he returned to the bedroom that took up half the floor beneath Ellar's workroom at the top of the tower, a cool gray light was coming through the windows in the outer wall. He let the glowsphere dissolve, set the platter on the bed table and settled onto the edge of the bed. For a moment such a fatigue swept over him, exacerbated by sore muscles, hunger and disappointment, that all he wanted to do was stretch out on the rustling straw mattress and sleep. But a draft of dusty air brought with it the seductive smell of the bread, his stomach knotted and rumbled and he laughed and gave in.

His hunger ran out before he expected it to and sleep came heavily down on him. Dirty feet forgotten, hands and face sticky with apple juice, he stretched out on the bed and was almost immediately asleep.

It was near dawn again when Breith woke.

He touched the Pneuma patch over his wound. The soreness was almost gone so he decided he'd leave the patch in place for another day. He'd slept so heavily and so long he felt thick and clumsy as he rolled off the bed. A tall wardrobe shoved in one corner provided a shirt and trousers. They were way too big for him, but he could use one of the kitchen knives to cut off sleeves and pants legs and a rope in the belt loops would cinch the trousers in enough so they wouldn't fall off him. He draped the clothing over one arm and started for the door, then came back for the tray. There was half a loaf left, most of the cheese and several apples. No point in wasting food. Who knew how long he was going to have to stay here?

Because the moon was down and the stars were covered by a layer of clouds, the darkness on the stairs was dangerous; he crept downward, holding firmly to the banister and trying to keep the tray level. After his days in the Chaletat, being alone felt odd and the sense of well-being he'd had yesterday was gone.

He was probably safe for the moment, but somebody had burned the house down so there were enemies out there in the dark. They might be Ellar's enemies, but anyone who'd burn a house wouldn't hesitate to include Ellar's friends and acquaintances in their vengeance.

Working the pump handle also worked out a lot of the fog

in his head and splashing cold water on his face took care of the rest. He stripped, kicked his inherited rags away and scrubbed the sweat, dirt and other muck from his body. The second cupboard provided clean towels and in minutes he was sitting down to eat, dressed in Ellar's work clothes and feeling energy pour back into him.

"Have to figure a way to get some wood for a fire. I could make a stew with those root things and the meat, some hot tea. Ahhhh. That sounds good. Hm. When I get finished here, I should open the Window to Iomard ... wonder if I can do that from this side? Have to let Da know where I am and that I'm all right. He can tell Mam and Mum. Then I can try finding Cymel."

He quartered one of the apples, cut out the core and leaned back in the chair and savored the juice, the crisp texture of the apple. Outside, he could hear men's voices; the Pneuma that sealed the walls of the tower muted sounds so he couldn't hear the words, but the tones were familiar enough. They sounded very much like the housekin who worked with the House stock and the gardeners who tended the ornamental plants and the more practical kitchen gardens that fed everyone at Urfa House. Farmhands come to work Ellar's land.

Though his uneasiness had diminished, he didn't want to go out and face them. If he'd learned nothing else on this adventure of his, he'd had one thing scrubbed into his soul; perfectly nice people, kind and loving to their own, can be demons to outsiders. Especially if they saw reason to fear the stranger.

Having tucked the last apple into a pocket, he wrapped what was left of the bread and cheese in a film of Pneuma, left them sitting on the crumb-dusted platter. A glance out the window showed him a man taking the reaper past the tower, the pair of hefty blacks Breith had seen in the barn harnessed to the gangling collection of blades and iron straps. The huge iron wheels squealed, the blades and straps rattled, almost drowning the raucous song from the three hands who followed, three-tined forks on their shoulders.

Breith wrinkled his nose, put the cup on the ledge beside the pump and went out of the alcove, heading for Ellar's workroom. Depending on what part of the year they were in, Iomárd and Glandair were within a watch or two of the same time so his father should be waking soon, if he wasn't already up. Malart was a man who liked to work in the clean freshness of the morning hours; that was the time he chose to teach Breith about the Pneuma and things he could do with it.

Yesterday before dawn, his only light the glowsphere, he'd been too tired to more than glance at the room, so he'd got an impression of emptiness and severity. The light of the morning sun pouring in through the eastern windows showed him how wrong he'd been. It wasn't a fussy room. There were no curtains on the windows, no decorations except two watercolor portraits hanging where someone lying on the couch in the middle of the room could see them when he opened his eyes.

He crossed to the portraits. Though he knew little of such things, he could tell they were fine work. The liveliness and character in the faces gave him the feeling that the images could step out from their frames and start talking to him. He recognized one of them instantly. Cymel, much younger than she'd been when he first opened the Window and greeted her. Her long black hair fell over her shoulders and mingled with the black fur of the cat curled up on her lap, its yellow eyes both feral and amused at whoever stood out there looking at it.

The second portrait was of a woman. Though she didn't especially look like Cymel, something about her face and the blue-black shimmer of her hair told him she was Cymel's mother and Corysiam's sister, Doeta. The set of her bones, skin like day-old cream and other details underlined what he knew from Corysiam. Siofray. A Walker with a stubbornness she'd passed on to her daughter. Her face revealed recklessness too, a sense that sitting still wasn't something she did very well. A woman of many passions and little humor. "If Mirrialta came after you, Doeta, you'd eat her raw and spit out her bones.'' He thought about what he knew of Ellar and shook his head over the complicated lives that adults made for themselves.

The couch was a leather-covered seat without a back to it, about as wide as a big man's shoulders, with one end raised at an angle so that the Watcher's head would be higher than his hips. Breith lay down on it. The aroma of the leather and the cream Ellar used to keep it soft rose round him, a pleasant smell, homey and relaxing. He glanced at the portraits, then lifted his eyes to the roof, a complex of beams carved with interlocking spirals and beast forms. He found himself tracing out the spirals and watching the play of the mice and other small lives that scampered through the carved lines; his mind quieted and his body slowed.

When he finally pushed himself up, the sun was high enough to shine directly into the eastern windows. He'd lost almost a full watch tracing those spirals. Amazing.

He went round the room, exploring the shelves that rose shoulder high up the walls. He found bound books, some full of neat tiny handwriting, some blank and waiting for the Watcher, silver mirrors and bowls for scrying, ewers for scry water, lamps, boxes of candles, sticks of black ink, pen points, pen holders—everything Ellar would need to Watch and record.

The worktable was meticulously neat; the only object on it was a stone ink bottle washed out, the lid placed upside down next to it. He frowned at the polished wood, realizing that all this fiddling about was because he was nervous about talking to his father. He scratched at his nose. ''Fool,'' he said aloud. ''You know you have to do this.''

He fetched the largest silver scry mirror and set it down near the right edge of the table, then he pulled out the chair and sat down. For a moment he stared down at the smooth surface of the wood, seeing his shadow stare back at him, then he went through the familiar steps of setting his target and opening the Window between Worlds.

The Pneuma Flow bellied out at him, opened a great and

terrifying mouth that threatened to swallow him. Screamed rage and hunger as it flared.

Psuedofire burning him, he hastily shut down the spell and sat leaning on his hands as he caught his breath.

A trap, and not Ellar's.

The Nyddys Mage. The one who was after Cymel.

Hmp. Can't work from here. No doubt all the tools are corrupt in one way or another. No major problem. I can always go outside. I do need to let Da know where I am but there's no rush about it.

A glance at the scry mirror brought another shake of his head. "Nothing from in here. Kitchenware might be safe, but I don't really want to try it."

He stood. For the first time he felt lonely and under threat, but he quickly shook that off and went back to his cautious exploring.

[6]

The Army of Purification marched south, a great plume of gray white smoke rising behind them.

Soriseis burned. And the tainted burned with her, saturated with fish oil, tied to beams with broken furniture about their feet.

The darocs and their descendants who'd thrown aside the roles the All-Mother created for them and fled the Domains were on their way in chains to Tiolan, along with the sick and injured of the Army—and the dead, their bodies preserved against the day of triumph when they could be buried with the honor they had earned.

The Corruption was on Iomard, but Radayam intended to drive it away before it meant more evil poured on the land. Drive it away and forever prevent it from returning.

17

The Vale of Caeffordian

By the secret calendar of the Watchers, events dating from the 1st day of Seimis, the seventh month in the 738th year since the last Settling.

[1]

Cymel ran through the orchard and flung herself onto the grass. The wind that ruffled her hair was cold and damp and it made her ears ache, but she hardly noticed that. Her brain was on fire. Every time she moved, every breath she took, the pain flared. Trying to think was like drawing fingernails across a nettle rash.

In the orchard the trees were heavy with ripe fruit, apples and plums and a scatter of nut trees. Wind plucked at their leaves, set them rustling and creaking, and blew the scent of the fruit over her. In the fenced pastures to the west of the grass where she lay, geldings and yearling colts grazed and played, chased each other in games of tag, squealing and teasing.

Stretched out on her stomach, her head on her crossed arms, Cymel lay for a long time, trying not to think, sinking herself into the sounds and smells around her. She lay like that until the itch to move building up under her skin and around her knees and elbows became too insistent to ignore.

Wincing as each movement brought more spikes of pain,

she rolled onto her back and began bending and straightening her legs and working her arms until a thin film of pain sweat covered her body and the nebulous but irritating itch was gone. Then she lay staring up at the clouds floating past, not really noticing the sky itself until the ground seemed to shudder under her and the wind carried hot dry smells alien to the Vale, smells punctuated by the sounds of distant howling.

The intrusion vanished almost as soon as it began but the clouds exploded away and the Flow was no longer a smooth current like a deep running river, nor did it have that curdled texture she'd seen when she first became aware of the secrets hidden in the sky. A tormented cataract roared across above her. Its speed was frightening and the great silent sound of it hammered at her.

And yet the very violence of the Flow was somehow easing.

Mole's gift, she thought suddenly and ached for him. She'd already cried all the tears she had, so she stared dry-eyed at the chaotic currents overhead and was sick at the waste of his life and of his peculiar genius. What he'd taught her was only a fragment of what he knew, a first step on the track he was forcing into the realities of the Flow, a track that led far beyond the rote manipulations of the Watchers and even the Mages. Tricks, he'd called them. Learned by rote with no understanding of the forces that worked to produce the results they demanded.

She rubbed at her eyes. Her father and Pneuma were wrong to isolate her from the Flow. She needed to soak in it, to let it repair the damage the Siofray Mage had done to her head. But that wasn't going to be easy. Her father was keeping an anxious eye on her as well as a dozen other Watchers here. And Amhar, who didn't like her much.

Again, Mole had the answer. Those last days he'd been teaching her how to touch the Flow without anyone else knowing that she was present. It was rather like taking three steps on an oblique line, two forward and one back, circling round obstructions, avoiding traps and slipping into the Flow without triggering any alarms.

As she had done before, she glided through the turbulence, riding the white-water slides, adapting to the immense and dangerous current, crossing to a countercurrent to bring herself back until she established a circuit she didn't have to think about. Then she rested, sliding round and round, accepting passively all the Flow was willing to give her. Round and round, the pain washed away, her brain cool and quiet. Round and round.

The Glandair wind strengthened and grew cold as it brushed over her—the ordinary wind, moving air blowing down the mountain slopes. Cymel stirred, sighed and opened her eyes.

The burn was gone.

That was good. But she could feel scars and a stiffness when she thought or moved, mindscars like the scars she used to get on her legs and knees, scars that itched and pulled and sometimes hurt until the cream her father gave her softened them and eventually eased them away.

She had to keep coming back until her flexibility was fully restored.

The sun was near setting. As she got to her feet, she heard the clang of the first-call bell. Almost time for supper.

Her stomach growled. For the first time in days she was really hungry.

She started running and found herself enjoying that too. It was so good just to run as fast as she could, to let her body act without the need to will each movement against the constant negative of the pain.

She slowed to a walk as she reached the School area, pushed her hair into a semblance of order and wiped the sweat from her face. These Watchers were like the ones at University, not comfortable with those who moved outside their rules and their expectations. Except the man coming from the door to the Infirmary, Elizeth Bourne of Lawheade, the Infirmarian.

Elizeth grinned at her. "You've been up to something, my girl," he said. Hastily he lifted his hand. "No. Don't you dare tell me one word about it. But if I can help, let me know."

She returned his grin and kept the silence he wanted. If

others were like him and Mole, the world would be a better place.

Lyanz, Amhar and the other boys came from one of the buildings; talking, laughing, punching each other. Too busy talking to notice her, they moved toward the dining hall under the indulgent eyes of their teacher. For a moment she was homesick for Cyfareth and the dramas and the friends she'd made, then she sighed and shook her head. It wouldn't be the same without Mole.

[2]

"The Ethics of Amethair, from the Introduction." The youth at the lectern cleared his throat and began reading in a steady monotone. "I, Amethair, son of Maturos who was a freeholder south of the troubled port of Dadeny, returned home one summer in time for the sowing of the winter wheat. . . ."

The dining hall was small and warmly inviting, made so by several small hearths with fires crackling behind woven bronze screens and by the shell and bronze lamps bracketed along the walls and sitting on each of the three tables. The Watchers sat at a table on a dais at the far end of the room, a table long enough for all of the dozen chairs to have their backs to the wall. The reader's lectern was on a small outthrust at one end of the dais.

The students and Amhar sat at a second table which was parallel to the first, though lower—down on the floor with the students in a row, facing their teachers and guides.

Cymel and Talgryf sat as far from the others as the room would allow, their small, round table tucked into a corner where they'd be out of the way, but still in sight.

"I held a seed grain in my hand and I saw that all of man's being could be comprehended within the smooth curves of its outline. . . ."

Gryf snorted. He skewered a chunk of tuber with his fork and pushed it around in a pool of melted butter. "Why do they always read such stuff?" he muttered, just loud enough for Cymel to hear. "Even your pa's poems aren't that boring."

Cymel pressed her lips together. She was still irritated that he was welcome in Lyanz's classes and she wasn't. "So, don't listen," she hissed at him. Her head was starting to hurt again as the scarred places stiffened. She wanted to get out of here and go float in the Flow again. She knew she needed to wait till tomorrow, but being sensible was very annoying.

Talgryf ignored her, pretending all he thought about was chewing on the tuber and deciding what bit of meat he wanted to cut loose from the overcooked steak.

Cymel shrugged. She cut a piece off her own steak, started to lift it to her mouth, then dropped the fork as an enormous FORCE struck at her, a fistblow to her head from the hand of a Giant. Seconds later, there was another. Then another.

She shoved herself back, the legs of her chair squealing across the floor tile, then jumped to her feet and ran to the middle of the room.

Talgryf followed, stopped beside her, his head turning quickly side to side. "Mela, what?"

"I don't know. Be quiet."

The reader at the lectern abandoned his book and jumped to the floor, running to join the other students who were closing in around Lyanz.

Amhar leaped away from the table and went racing out one of the many doors. She returned almost immediately, staff in hand, elbowed the other students aside and placed herself half a step ahead of Lyanz.

The Watchers were on their feet, Ellar among them. They stood very still, almost touching, a sheen of sweat and lines of strain in their faces.

Taymlo broke the silence. "Mages," he said. "Mages working together!"

Cymel stopped, shuddered. Mages. Now that the word was spoken she could feel them out there, a man and a woman. Both of them were Hunger, both of them were Rage and Need. The half-healed wounds in her head broke open and fire laced along the fault lines. She whimpered.

Talgryf put his arm round her shoulders. "Don't, Mela! Your pa won't let them hurt you."

Ellar broke away from the others, went to the edge of the dais. "Mela, come here." His voice was sharp and frightened.

Taymlo frowned. "Belloc, Held, Orl, Landlyn, you're our strongest meld. Out to the court and hold them off long as you can. Buy us time. Shandin, collect the servants, stockmen and field hands, get them armed and on the walls. Rhontar, get the gates shut and barred, then open the Armory. Ellar, take your daughter and the boy to Sanctuary, then meet me on the wall. It won't be only the Mages we face. Lyanz, you get to Sanctuary now; don't wait for the rest of us. Amhar, get your sword, your bow and as many arrows as you have in your store, then you join him. You're in charge of the defense of Sanctuary." His finger flicked to the two students seated at the table with Lyanz. "Trafel, Camparo, off to the Armory, get weapons for yourselves and our two visitors, then you do whatever Amhar tells you. Rest of you, follow me."

[3]

Cymel crouched in one of the corners of the room at the top of the tower called Sanctuary; she was numb with pain and rage, for the moment able only to endure. The brief joy of the afternoon seemed like a dream, its colors fading, the healing undone by the presence of the Mages. Not by the attack, but by the emanations that eddied around each of the massive blows at the Vale wards. She shuddered and without being aware of it scratched at her arms.

Time passed.

She was dimly aware of Amhar's crisp voice ordering the shutters closed and barred, the arrow slits in them uncovered. Of the thuds on the floor from the weapons that the two students Trafel and Camparo brought from the Armory and dropped into small piles scattered about the room. Of the muttering and anger with overlays of fear and excitement. Of Gryf's pleasure when he was counted as one of the defenders. Of Lyanz's frustration when he was forbidden to join them.

Of Amhar's chants as she fired up the Sanctuary's own wards. Of the sounds that penetrated from outside, shouts from the walls, the deep-throated chant of the Watcher Meld, the howl of an unnatural wind, the silent thuds of the attack, thuds that went beyond sound and muted all the rest.

When she shifted position to ease the tingling beneath her skin, she looked down and saw big red blotches on her arms, blotches like those she got when she was a child and ate some odd-looking fruits one of the messengers from Cyfareth brought to Ellar. She never found out what they were because her father had thrown them out while she was sick. Allergic, she thought. I'm allergic to Mages. He did that to me, that Siofray monster. And the wards here won't keep them out.

Why didn't I see this before? If I'd known . . .

Fighting to think around the burn, she smoothed a hand along her arm, feeling the itch roll along with the touch of her palm.

Hm. First time I was unconscious. Maybe didn't scratch myself and bring out the rash, maybe it was gone by the time I woke on Siofray. Second time I came through the Veil I was out again. Pa did that. He thought he was protecting me. Maybe I'm allergic to the between-Flow too, but not so strongly. And I got to the Flow here before I started scratching. Got to it the right way. Mole's way.

It's one explanation, anyway. Or maybe the rash came out because the Mages are so close . . . so strong . . . she focused a moment on the Sound that was tormenting her.

T'Teeth! Not only won't keep them out, the wards are like drumheads making them louder and stronger.

Though the itching worsened by the moment and the fire in her head spread and grew hotter, the discovery of this possible source of her pain and what propagated it brought relief. She didn't have to endure and suffer anymore. She could do something.

Careful not to interfere with the Vale defenses, she danced Mole's dance with the Pneuma and set a shield of her own weaving between her and the emanations from the Mages.

Then she folded her arms on her knees and watched the blotches that were like brushburns on her skin fade as quickly as they'd come.

Coolness washed through her head and her body.

She drew in a long breath and lifted her head.

Lyanz sat cross-legged inside a hexagram incised in the floor, the gouged lines filled with silver and polished till they gleamed. He had a sword laid across his knees. Since she was behind him and to one side, she couldn't see much of his face and the shield muted her sense of how he was feeling, but the knot of muscle by the end of his mouth gave her a fair idea of how unhappy he was about being treated like the prize in a game of slap-tag.

Amhar stood beside him, but outside the lines of the hexagram. Her staff was slung across her back beside a quiverful of arrows the length of her arms, her longbow strung and ready. She looked as taut and ready to coil and explode as that bow.

The three students and Talgryf were positioned round the room with cocked crossbows, watching the events outside through arrow slits.

Cymel pulled the shield into a cylinder around her, sealed the edges, then got to her feet. At one of the unguarded windows, she locked open an arrow slit and looked outside, careful not to let her own shield touch the ward wall.

In the center of the court the Watcher Meld knelt in a circle, their arms weaving a higher circle, each hand on another Watcher's shoulder. Their heads were bowed, their bodies straining as they fought to hold off the attack of the Mages. A second circle of Watchers ringed the Meld and fed them power.

On the walls and roofs of the buildings, there were more men she hadn't seen before, presumably the servants, field hands and stockmen that Taymlo had mentioned—and outliers from the hermitages that were carved into the stone walls that ringed the Vale.

Her father stood beside Taymlo on the wall facing the entrance to the Vale, both looking intently at the mouth of the gorge. Other Watchers were scattered about the walls, centers of command for the men around them.

Without warning someone in the Meld screamed, then all of them were burning, ash and cinders in a single beat of the heart. The fire and the illusion of fire were gone an instant later as the power ring force-fed Pneuma into the Meld. The four Watchers were whole again though they shivered uncontrollably under the impact of the strike. Cymel froze, then gathered herself, getting ready to act if the Mages struck next at Sanctuary.

Even through the muting of her shield, she felt a great cry of triumph from the Mages as the Entrance wards shattered and she saw huge faces hovering above the valley—a beautiful Myndyar woman in a lacy silver mask, a handsome Rhudyar man with a shaved head and blue lines tattooed over every visible bit of his skin. They hung in midair with fierce, exultant grins and greed like a halo about their heads.

A group of riders came galloping through the gorge, heading for the buildings, spreading wide as they came, half a hundred men howling promises of death and pain, confident in the protection of a third Mage, a sly, sneaking Mage who hid behind a shroud of mist. He stayed so far distant that even the most minuscule hint of his aura escaped her, though Cymel knew him despite that. By his caution and his cold and convoluted plotting, she knew him. He'd tried so many times, so many ways to kill Lyanz—and her. The Nyddys Mage.

That's what they all came for, she thought. Lyanz. To kill him or capture him. Yes! I know you now. I won't be surprised again. I'm going to get you. I'm going to get you for Mole who was everything you'll never be for all your power and scheming.

She leaned more heavily against the wide sill, glancing from Lyanz to her father, worrying about them—at same time deeply angry at and obsessed by the Mages as they struck again and again at the shields of the Vale, shields that the Meld was holding in place with the support of the other

Watchers. Her father was out there, vulnerable, his bow busy with the outcasts going after the wall while he sought a way to attack the Mages and spent his psychic strength defending the School against them. Elizeth Bourne stood beside him, killing with grim-faced efficiency.

Elizeth loathed killing and was a vegetarian by choice, but if he had to do it, he would be careful to make death come quickly and with as little pain as possible. He could have stayed in the Infirmary and concentrated on healing, but in his eyes, though probably only his, that would have been a hypocrite's choice, thus not one he would embrace. Selfishly she was glad to see him with her father since it meant Ellar would get the best treatment possible if ever he were struck down.

Once again Cymel cast herself into that Pneuma mount that Mole had devised, the off-angle dive and quick step that she called Mole's dance taking her around and beyond the ordinary uses of the Pneuma Flow. She plunged into the raging current, soaking up Pneuma and storing it inside herself, readying herself for the attack that would hurl Lyanz and his protectors away from the Vale and damage them so badly they'd have to creep into a hole to survive the wounds.

Moving easily, sneakily, slyly, she fit herself into the Flow, swimming faster and faster until she was dizzy with the speed with which she moved, until she began to sense the current she wanted, a current that would carry her around behind the Mages where she could hit them before they were aware of her presence. . . .

Suddenly, frightening her with how fast he could move, the third Mage—the Nyddys Mage—was inside the Vale.

He was aware of her in a way that shocked her, a way outside her experience—the Nyddys Mage—least known—least understood—most dangerous.

And he was coming after her. . . .

No. Mistake. Not after her. He too had discovered the oblique way. He was going after her father!

He circled around her, avoiding her as if she were fire, and struck at Ellar.

He lifted her father's body high into the air, hurling it up and up until it was a whirling blotch riding high above the roofs of the School. . . .

But not alone. . . .

The moment the attack began Elizeth flung himself at Ellar, meaning to protect him with the Infirmarian's own body. He wrapped his arms about Ellar, interposing himself between Ellar and the Pneuma hurled by the Mage—but the attempt was futile. Elizeth was torn apart, his throat was ripped open, blood geysering out over Ellar and himself. Elizeth Bourne of Lawheade, a man whose first thoughts were to give comfort of body and mind to his patients, a source of generosity and intelligence destroyed by Mage NEED and Mage GREED. Cymel yearned for revenge for him. She knew he would have scolded her for the thought, but she struck anyway. She killed no one, just brushed futilely at their virtual forms, an attack so feeble that the Mages didn't even know they were in a fight.

"You tried, my friend," she said aloud, "Tanew bless you and yours." That was her last coherent thought before she surrendered wholly to the Flow and to the molten anger that surged through her.

Using her as a point of stability, the Pneuma acted against the attackers with enormous and essentially mindless power. The two visible Mages tumbled into whirling flight, rolling top over toe away from the Vale, blown by a wind greater than any they could produce. Blown away from Lyanz and Cymel, the double target of their desire.

And the still nameless Nyddys Mage fled for shelter deep into the earth he claimed as his territory, shaken but not hurt.

At the same time Cymel CHANGED.

The PNEUMA ruling her forced that change and also the gathering of others into the Field that wrapped around the White Bird that was her new body. Lyanz, the dead bodies of her father and Elizeth, Amhar, Talgryf—they whirled around her like planets orbiting a sun.

Something else called her HOME, to that place where she'd spent her childhood, to the farm. Though she knew the house was ash and cinders, that nothing was waiting for her there, she was driven to return.

The great White Bird flew from the Vale of Caeffordian. Hours later, she dropped the burden she carried into the ashes of the farmhouse.

She was still not thinking, only reacting, a creature rather than an intelligent woman. As a wary bird would do, one accustomed to being prey rather than predator, she landed on a rocky upthrust and sat poised for flight.

She was startled and delighted to see Breith come running from Ellar's Tower, but when Breith called her name and she tried to change back to Cymel so she could greet him, she could not do it.

Filled with a sudden terror, she ran from him and powered herself into the air.

He leaped, caught hold of her somehow, but that hold was precarious. Almost immediately he was ripped away from her and fell away, crashing back to earth.

She plunged into the Flow and let it take her to a place where she might hide and heal—if healing were possible after this last terrible wound. As she rode the turbulent Flow, she wept for her father, wept for Mole, wept for Elizeth, wept for all those who had died to keep her alive for reasons she couldn't have explained if she were still capable of speech.

[4]
Breith watched the White Bird vanish into the heavy clouds that cloaked the mountain peaks, then turned to drag the bodies of the living and the dead into the Tower.

SCHOOL DAZE 2
OVER 150 MORE
OF YOUR FAVORITE
SCHOOL JOKES

BY
TERI JAMES-BRUMLEY
Pictures by Jerry Zimmerman

P9-DFU-42

DEDICATION
To Sandy. Thanks for being my silly songwriter!

THANKS
To Sarah and Luke Piotrowski and Jennifer and Jeff James for their contributions.

CONTENTS

THE STUDENT'S ANTHEM

Now I lay me down to rest.
I pray I pass tomorrow's test.
If I die before I wake,
That's one less test I'll have to take.

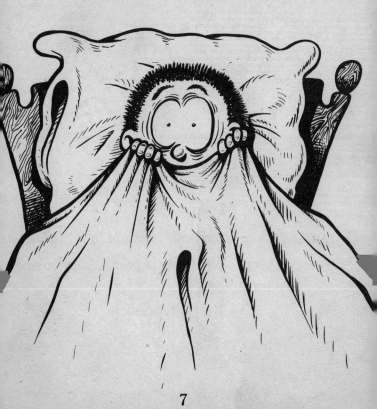

MEET YOUR TEACHERS

IMA N. SANE
English–First Period

NICKNAME: Looney Tune

FAVORITE BOOK: *You're OK, I'm Not* by R.U. Crazy

FAVORITE JOKE: What kind of people do squirrels like?

The nutty ones!

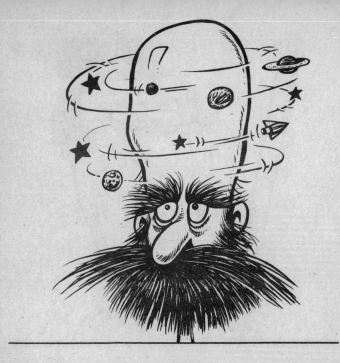

A.R. HEAD
Science–Second Period

NICKNAME: Space Cadet

FAVORITE BOOK: *The Milky Way* by Out N. Space

FAVORITE JOKE: What kind of show do they put on at the planetarium?

An all-star performance!

SARA PUSS
Math–Third Period

NICKNAME: Mean Machine

FAVORITE BOOK: *Math Made Easy* by Al G. Brah

FAVORITE JOKE: None. (Doesn't really have a sense of humor.)

BERTHA PLUMP
Lunchroom Supervisor–Fourth Period

NICKNAME: Big Bertha

FAVORITE BOOK: *1001 Recipes* by I.M. Starving

FAVORITE JOKE: What do you get when you add 3 hamburgers to 3 orders of fries?

Lunch!

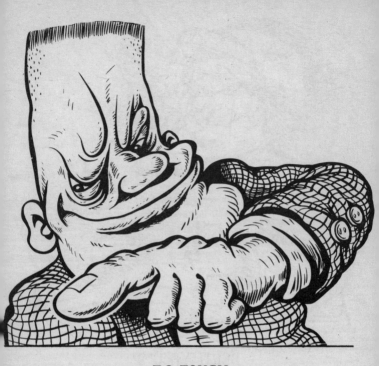

T.O. TOUGH
History—Fifth Period

NICKNAME: Yes, Sir!

FAVORITE BOOK: *I'm Watching You* by Dunt B. Bad

FAVORITE JOKE: How do most parents punish their kids for poor grades?

They start at the bottom!

12

BEA LOUD
Music–Sixth Period

NICKNAME: The Queen of Rap

FAVORITE BOOK: *Heavy Metal* by I. Scream

FAVORITE JOKE: What can you carry but can't put down?

A tune.

MR. D. TENTION
Principal

NICKNAME: None. (No one is brave enough to call him anything else!)

FAVORITE BOOK: *How to Relate to Teenagers* by R.U. Kidding

FAVORITE JOKE: What is the definition of a teenager?

A person who is afraid of nothing except cleaning his or her room!

B. TIDY
Janitor

NICKNAME: The Clean Machine

FAVORITE BOOK: *1001 Ways to Wash a Floor* by Mop N. Glow

FAVORITE JOKE: Why did the school secretary marry the janitor?

Because he swept her off her feet.

HOMEROOM HUMMERS

HAROLD: Is it better to do homework on an empty or a full stomach?

PAULA: It's best to do it on paper!

HAROLD: Do your parents help you with your homework?

PAULA: No, I get it all wrong by myself.

HAROLD: What are the three most used words at school?
PAULA: I don't know.
HAROLD: That's right.
PAULA: Huh?

HAROLD: What are the three most used words at home?
PAULA: Leave me alone!
HAROLD: Right again!

HAROLD: What is yellow, has four wheels, and always makes your mom smile when it comes to your house in the morning?
PAULA: The school bus.

HAROLD: I learned to write in school today.
PAULA: What did you write?
HAROLD: I don't know. I haven't learned how to read yet!

HAROLD:	My teacher told me that I have to learn to write more neatly.
PAULA:	That's good.
HAROLD:	But I don't want to.
PAULA:	Why?
HAROLD:	Because then she'll know I don't know how to spell.

| HAROLD: | I heard you missed school yesterday. |
| PAULA: | Not a bit! |

HAROLD:	I don't like school.
PAULA:	Why not?
HAROLD:	Well, I can't read or write, and they won't let me do the one thing I do best.
PAULA:	What's that?
HAROLD:	Talk.

HAROLD:	My folks decided to send me away to school.
PAULA:	Why?
HAROLD:	So they won't have to help me with my homework anymore.

HAROLD: My teacher gave all the sixth-graders an aptitude test today.

PAULA: Oh, what did you find out?

HAROLD: That my entire class should be in fifth grade.

HAROLD: I got my report card today.

PAULA: Was it good?

HAROLD: It was OK. English was poor, math needs improvement, but my health was excellent.

HAROLD: I'll never learn how to spell.

PAULA: Why?

HAROLD: The teacher keeps changing the words on me.

HAROLD: Why don't you take the bus home from school?

PAULA: Because my mom always makes me take it back!

FIRST PERIOD: AWESOME ENGLISH

Dig These Definitions

What do you call a yellow-bellied cow?
A coward.

What do you call a cool daddy?
A Popsicle.

What do you call an animal that likes to
ride in automobiles?
A carpet.

Why is a sleeping bag like a backpack?
Because it's a nap sack.

What do you call an alligator's assistant?
Gator aide.

What do you call a package for boys only?
A male box.

What do you call everyone's favorite tree?
A poplar tree.

What do you call cows with a sense of humor?
Laughingstock.

What do you call holes that are filled up?
Not holes.

What do you call a dead author?
A ghostwriter.

Bodacious Books to Read

How to Make Money the Easy Way
by Mary A. Millionaire

Cupid's Arrow
by Sheila B. Mine

Jail Can Be Fun
by Ike N. Fess

I Did It My Way
by Dun Good

How to Feel Your Best
by N.R. Gee

Do It Your Way
by O.K. Fine

Jealousy
by N.V. Ewe

How to Win the Lottery
by E.Z. Money

How to Lift 1000 Pounds
by Bette U. Kant

Dieting Made Easy
by X.S. Waite

SECOND PERIOD: FAR-OUT ASTRONOMY

What's a baby called in outer space?
UCO. Unidentified Crying Object.

What cartoon character is out of this world?
Pluto.

How many ladders would it take to reach
the sun?
One, if it were 93,000,000 miles long.

Why don't people stand on lines in space?
Because there's no weight to anything.

What works only after it is fired?
A rocket.

What planet can take your temperature?
Mercury.

What do Martians say when they are
interviewed?
No comet.

What is the center of gravity?
The letter V.

What planet can we see best without a
telescope?
The planet Earth.

Why did the cow jump over the moon?
To find the Milky Way.

What do you use to hold the moon up?
Moonbeams.

What kind of fish could you find in the
Milky Way?
The starfish.

What kind of fish is always beaming?
The sunfish.

When can't astronauts land on the moon?
When it's full.

THIRD PERIOD: GNARLY NUMBERS

When do 2 and 2 equal more than 4?
When they become 22.

What number is larger when you turn it
upside down?
6, which becomes 9.

If A to C is 60 miles and A to B is 20 miles,
how long would it take to travel from B to
C driving 100 miles per hour?

That can't be done.

Why not?

The speed limit is only 55 miles per hour.

It takes 12 pennies to make a dozen,
so how many nickels does it take to
make a dozen?
12.

What's always correct in geometry class?
A right angle.

Besides 0, what number can you take half
of and end up with nothing?
**Take the top half of 8 and you end up
with 0.**

Little Bo Peep had 10 sheep. All but 9 died.
How many sheep did she have left?
9.

How many months in the year have
28 days?
All of them.

If you had $100 and gave away a quarter and
then another quarter, how much would
you have left?
$99.50.

What's the best way to divide 9 apples
among 12 boys?
Make applesauce.

What has a foot on each side and one in
the middle?
A yardstick.

What's the best way to pass a
geometry test?
Know all the angles.

What's the prettiest figure in math class?
Acute angle.

RECESS RAP

What kind of dog does the science teacher have?
A laboratory retriever!

What happens when the biology teacher argues with the chemistry teacher?
You get science friction!

What do history teachers talk about at parties?
Old times, of course!

Why is the music teacher so good?
Because she's a sound instructor.

What's the difference between a locomotive engineer and a teacher?
One minds the train, the other trains the mind!

Why was the school so lonely?
Because it was in a class by itself!

What kind of garden do you find at school?
Kindergarten.

What is a ticklish subject?
The study of feathers.

What subject is the hardest?
Geology, the study of rocks!

What insect would you find in a library?
A bookworm.

What animal would you find in a library?
A catalogue.

Why are good students always on the run?
They're always pursuing their studies.

I just finished reading *20,000 Leagues
Under the Sea.*
Boy, you sure are deep.

FOURTH PERIOD:
LAME LUNCH

What does your cafeteria serve?
Everything from A to Z.
Oh, you have to eat alphabet soup every day too!

What food is never cold?
A hot pepper!

What do you call someone who steals cows?
A hamburglar.

Why doesn't Susan ever eat breakfast?
Because she doesn't like to eat on an empty stomach.

What kind of beans don't grow in a garden?
Jellybeans!

Slow down. You're eating too fast!
Why? Are you afraid I'll exceed the feed limit?

What's the best thing to put in an ice-cream soda?
A straw!

What happened to the boy who drank
8 Cokes?
He burped 7-Up.

What fruit is a real tease?
Ba-nana-nana-na-na.

What peels and chips but never cracks?
A potato.

What would you get if you stacked
hundreds of pizzas on top of one another?
The leaning tower of pizza!

What do you call a pie in the sky?
An unidentified flying pizza.

What's your favorite seafood?
Saltwater taffy.

What happens when two strawberries meet
on the street?
You get a strawberry shake.

What should you eat if you want to
get rich?
Fortune cookies.

Why did the cookie cry?
**Because his mother had been a wafer
so long.**

Why should you avoid the letter C when
you are trying to lose weight?
Because it makes fat a fact!

FIFTH PERIOD:
HISTORIC HYSTERICS
AND GOOFY GOVERNMENT

Historic Hysterics

What did Paul Revere say when he finished his ride?
Whoa, boy.

What was Ben Franklin's kite made of?
Flypaper.

Why does history keep repeating itself?
Because no one ever listens!

When was Columbus born?
On Columbus Day.

What happens when you send a telegram to Washington?
Nothing. He's dead.

If April showers bring May flowers, what do May flowers bring?
Pilgrims.

Which president did horses like the least?
**Teddy Roosevelt, because he was a
Rough Rider.**

Which American president had the largest
family?
**George Washington, because he's the
father of his country.**

What's the Gettysburg Address?
Where Abe Lincoln lived.

What kind of music did the Pilgrims like?
Plymouth Rock and roll!

Goofy Government

What hobby do all presidents practice?
Cabinetmaking.

Why did the dog go to court?
Because he got a barking ticket.

What happens if you illegally park a frog?
You get toad away.

What happened to the kid who stole the calendar?
He got 12 months.

What do you get when you cross a policeman and a skunk?
Law and odor.

What rises in the morning and waves all day?
A flag.

Why was the belt arrested?
For holding up the pants.

I Can't Get This
to the rhythm of "U Can't Touch This"
originally "rapped" and performed by
M.C. Hammer

Chorus:
Can't get this,
Can't get this,
Can't get this,
Can't get this.

My my my math book hits me so hard,
Makes me think, Oh my lord!
Thank you for blessing me.
Why am I so blind I just can't see?
Feel down when you don't get it,
But the answer to the problem, forget it!
And I know I'm smart,
But this is a class where I'm known as Bart.

41

Chorus:
I told you smart boy,
Can't get this.
Yeah that's what I've been given and you know,
Can't get this.
Look at the equation, man,
Can't get this.
Yo, let me bust out of this class.

Chapter 5, homework.
You started into it and you feel like a jerk.
You move around in your seat,
Hopin' for a way to cheat.
But you know if you hold on
You'll find a way to know what's going on.
Don't let 'em know that you're all set
And that math is the only class that you can't get.

Chorus:
Yo, I told you,
Can't get this.
Why am I sitting here, man?
Can't get this.
Yo, sound the bell, it's test time brother.
Can't get this.

Give me a poem or history,
But this math is a real mystery.
Now you know,
When you shakin' 'bout a math test I just say no!
There's slopes and angles,
But how to find the area gets all mangled.
I'll take a break
Before my brain begins to bake.
I'll quit.
I been workin' so hard I'm gonna throw a fit.

Chorus:
That's because you know,
Can't get this.
Can't get this.
Break me down.
Do.
Do.
Do.
Do.
Stop math time.

You should know it's said,
If you can't learn math you're better off dead.
How you gonna go to college
If you can't get the knowledge?
There's no time for dinner,
Without the numbers how you gonna be a winner?
Just move your butt.
Get the answer to the problem and you gonna
    make the cut.
Cut, cut.

Chorus:
Can't get this.
Can't get this.
Can't get this.
Break me down.

Please No Homework
to the tune of "Please Don't Go Girl"
music by Maurice Starr
originally performed by New Kids on the Block

We've had homework almost every night, teacher.
Do we have to now?

Please no homework,
I just can't take another night.
Please no homework,
Please no homework,
You will ruin my whole night.

Chorus:
Tell me no way
That there's no homework today.
I loathe it, I loathe it.
I guess I always will.
Girl, it's my worst dream.
It will make me scream.
I just want you to know
That I will always hate it.

Oooh girl

Chorus:
Tell me no way
That there's no homework today.
I loathe it, I loathe it.
I guess I always will.
Girl, it's my worst dream.
It will make me scream.
I just want you to know.
That I will always hate it.

Oooh girl

Please no homework.
I can't take it no more, girl.
I'm gonna hate it, girl,
Until the end of time.
You hound me, teach.
You always give it to me.
Please no homework,
You will ruin my whole night.

Chorus:
Tell me no way
That there's no homework today.
I loathe it, I loathe it.
I guess I always will.
Girl, it's my worst dream.
It will make me scream.
I just want you to know
That I will always hate it.

Oooh girl

Please no homework.
Please no homework.
Please no homework.

Rice Rice Baby
to the tune of "Ice Ice Baby"
music by Vanilla Ice, Earthquake, M. Smooth
originally performed by Vanilla Ice

Yo, students, let's kick it!

Rice rice baby. Rice rice baby.
We all stop, we're in mass hysteria,
As we make our way into the cafeteria.
The students ain't feelin' none too rightly.
The cause of their grief is none too lightly.
There's a smell that grabs hold of my nose.
What it is? Yo, it ain't no rose!

This odor it makes my taste buds quake.
How can it be? They're serving Salisbury
    steak!
Yuck. The sentiment fills the room.

48

They cover that stuff with poisonous
  mushrooms.
Deadly, it's cooked so long it's just my luck.
He's turned it into a hockey puck.
Eat it or starve, there ain't no other way.
It's all you get to eat for the whole darn day!
This food is a problem. Yo, I'll solve it.
I'll check out the food where the cook don't
  evolve it!

Chorus:
Rice rice baby, I'll eat it. Rice rice baby, I'll eat it.
Rice rice baby, I'll eat it. Rice rice baby, I'll eat it.

Now that the lunchroom is jumpin',
With my tray in hand my heart is pumpin'.
Straight to my seat no sense in fakin'.
Don't want this steak, I'd rather eat bacon.
He's burned them—this is one more bumble.
I go crazy when I eat his fumbles.
Is anybody eating? Yo, I don't know.
I grab my roll and decide to go solo.
The girls next door are eating their Jell-o.
The Salisbury steak, they're letting
  it mellow.
So I cruised on over to the jocks' table.
Even those guys ain't eating their steaks!
This food is dead!

49

Yo, so I continued to the goodie-goodie table.
The chicks were prepped out to do their
    mamas proud,
The dudes so clean they're as white as
    a cloud.
Even these kids who always do their homework
Say "to eat this stuff you got to be a real jerk."
So I wander straight back to my tray,
From my brain comes a thought to save
    the day.
The stuff on my plate it looks like
    ammunition,
And I bring my plan to its immediate
    fruition.
Flyin', the steaks start sailin',
Messed up, the girls start wailin'.
The jocks start gettin' into the food fight,
Winging those steaks with all of their might.
Why should you eat it when you'd rather
    throw it?
This stuff tastes bad, and the staff they ought to
    know it.
This food is a problem. Yo, I'll solve it.
I'll eat the stuff where the cook don't
    evolve it!

Chorus:
Rice rice baby, I'll eat it. Rice rice baby, I'll eat it.
Rice rice baby, I'll eat it. Rice rice baby, I'll eat it.

BLIND AMBITIONS
(or What Do You Want to Be When You Grow Up?)

JERRY: I want to be a marksman.

DEB: Why?

JERRY: Because I aim to please.

JERRY: I want to be a printer.

DEB: Why?

JERRY: Because I'm the right type.

JERRY: I want to work in a glue factory.

DEB: Why?

JERRY: Because it's an easy job to stick with!

JERRY: I want to be a football player.

DEB: Why?

JERRY: So I can get a kick out of work!

JERRY: I want to be a swimming instructor.

DEB: Why?

JERRY: So I can immerse myself in my job.

JERRY: I want to be a knife sharpener.

DEB: Why?

JERRY: Because I find everything dull.

JERRY: I want to be an electrician.
DEB: Why, so you can keep up with current events?
JERRY: No, so I can make good connections.

JERRY: I want to be a baker.
DEB: Why?
JERRY: So I'm always rolling in dough.

JERRY: I want to work in a blanket factory.
DEB: Whatever for?
JERRY: So I can be an undercover agent.

JERRY: I want to be a banker.
DEB: Why, so you can make a lot of money?
JERRY: No, because I've lost interest in everything.

JERRY: I want to work in an ice-cream parlor when I grow up.
DEB: Why?
JERRY: Because I like going to Sundae school!

JERRY: I want to work in a watch factory.

DEB: Why, because you like ticks?

JERRY: No, so I can sit around and make faces all day.

JERRY: I want to work in a mattress factory.

DEB: Why?

JERRY: So I can lie down on the job.

54

JERRY: I want to be a barber.

DEB: Why?

JERRY: Then everyone will have to take their hats off to me.

JERRY: What did the bunny rabbit want to be when he grew up?

DEB: What?

JERRY: A hare force pilot!

JERRY: I want to sit out in the sun all day long.

DEB: Why?

JERRY: Because I want to be a tanner when I grow up.

AFTER-SCHOOL ANTICS

What do you call a book about bicycles?
A bicyclopedia!

What happened when one bicycle met
another bicycle?
They spoke to each other.

What's the hardest thing about learning
how to ride a bike?
The pavement.

Why was the chicken thrown out of the baseball game?
Because all he could hit were fowl balls.

Why is tennis such a noisy game?
Because each player raises a racket.

Why was Cinderella such a poor baseball player?
Because she had a pumpkin for a coach.

Why do chefs make good baseball pitchers?
Because they know their batters.

57

What is a pitcher's favorite candy bar?
Mounds!

Why won't your mom let you join the
bowling team?
**Because she doesn't like it when I play
in alleys.**

In what sport can you hear a pin drop?
Bowling.

Why do you always swim on your back?
**Because my mom told me never to swim
on a full stomach.**

What's a boxer's favorite drink?
Punch.

ARNOLD
THE UNDERACHIEVER

Why doesn't Arnold go to history class anymore?
Because he says they make it faster than he can learn it.

Why did Arnold take a parachute to school?
In case he had to drop out.

Why didn't Arnold show up at your party?
Because the invitation said "between 6 and 9," and Arnold's 10!

Why did Arnold take a baseball bat with him when he went to the principal's office?
Because he heard he was going to be bawled out.

Why did Arnold throw a bucket of water out the classroom window?
Because he wanted to make a big splash!

Why did Arnold take a pitchfork to bed with him?
So he could hit the hay.

Why did Arnold send his mom a note of congratulations?
Because it was his birthday.

Why did Arnold keep putting his hands in the alphabet soup?
Because he was groping for words.

Why was Arnold afraid to walk on the marble floor?
Because he thought it would roll away!

THE 10 BEST
REPORT-CARD EXCUSES

1. "My grades were better than the class bully's so he took it home."

2. "The principal decided that grades are meaningless."

3. "It blew up with my chemistry experiment."

4. "I was just taking it out of my pocket when a blast of Arctic wind took it away. It's probably at the North Pole by now."

5. "The dog ate it" (also one of the top 10 home-work excuses).

6. "It was so-o-o good my teacher is having it framed."

7. "Frog guts got on it in biology class."

8. "Really Dad and Mom, F stands for 'Fabulous.'"

9. "Would you believe the baby ate it?"

10. And if all else fails, try this: "Oh, didn't I tell you? We don't get those until next week" (the hope is that this excuse will give you enough time to get out of the country before your parents find out the truth).